Praise for Victoria

"Smartly written and successf[...]ew
cozy series ... exudes authentic[...]

—*Library Journal*

"Victoria Hamilton's charming series is a delightful find!"

—Sheila Connolly, *New York Times* bestselling author

"A wonderful cozy mystery series."

—Paige Shelton, *New York Times* bestselling author

A
GENTLEWOMAN'S
GUIDE *to*
MURDER

VICTORIA HAMILTON

A
GENTLEWOMAN'S
GUIDE *to*
MURDER

MIDNIGHT INK
WOODBURY, MINNESOTA

FIRST EDITION
First Printing, 2019

Book design by Bob Gaul
Cover design by Shira Atakpu
Cover illustration by Kimberley M. Guillaumier / Kim G Design

Midnight Ink, an imprint of Llewellyn Worldwide Ltd.

Library of Congress Cataloging-in-Publication Data
Names: Hamilton, Victoria, author.
Title: A gentlewoman's guide to murder / Victoria Hamilton.
Description: First edition. | Woodbury, Minnesota : Midnight Ink, [2019]
Identifiers: LCCN 2018043246 (print) | LCCN 2018044322 (ebook) | ISBN
   9780738759340 (ebook) | ISBN 9780738758046 (alk. paper)
Subjects: | GSAFD: Mystery fiction.
Classification: LCC PR9199.3.S529 (ebook) | LCC PR9199.3.S529 G46 2019 (print)
   | DDC 813/.54—dc23
LC record available at https://lccn.loc.gov/2018043246

Midnight Ink
Llewellyn Worldwide Ltd.
2143 Wooddale Drive
Woodbury, MN 55125-2989
www.midnightinkbooks.com

Printed in the United States of America

Acknowledgments

There are *many* people who made this book better with their sharp eyes and intelligent criticsm.

First, I'd like to thank Jessica Faust and James McGowan for giving me valuable insight and direction in my first efforts to form the storyline of *A Gentlewoman's Guide to Murder*. It would not have been the same book without them.

I'd also like to thank Joshua Ian for his spectacularly insightful comments after his read-through of chapters 1 and 2. It helped more than I can express!

And finally, I'd like to thank Sandy Sullivan, production editor, for saving me from innumerable errors, and for sharpening and focusing the story with dedication and precision. Good editors are the making of a book.

Thank you all!

October 22nd, 1810, Edition of *The Prattler*
By: The Rogue
The Knight and the Vengeful Hobgoblin

Your Roguish Correspondent has been informed that there is a troublesome Sprite afoot. This Masked Avengeress has rescued little girls in perilous circumstances from the Gentlemen who use them for their Pleasure with no thought to their Innocence. This Woman of Mystery and Malice has, we are told, visited upon many men of Doubtful Character a Warning. We at *The Prattler* are offering a reward to anyone who can name this Implacable Hobgoblin.

Who will be her next Victim?

Perhaps we know already!

Your Wayward Rogue has lately learned that there are some men who cannot keep from attempting Congress with any Female, even should the Female be a Child. So it is with a certain Knight of the Ale, who, the Rogue has learned, will inflict his French Pox on the merest Maid. So Particular is his taste that he prefers those not yet troubled by the Menses. We hesitate to name him, but should such Wickedness persist, we see it as our Duty to the Scullery Maids of our Nation and will tell all the Certain Sir's predilections.

But it is possible that he will receive a visit from the Masked Avengeress, who will more forcefully echo our counsel.

....

ONE

October 24th, 1810
Clerkenwell, London, England

NIGHT HAD WRAPPED ITS arms around the city, and though folks were still about, even their most innocent dealings were cloaked in mystery and shadow. The moon was just a sliver, the waning quarter, at eight in the evening. The clopping of the horses' hooves and rumble of carriage wheels was muffled by fog that had rolled up the Thames and into the heart of London.

In the dark confines of a closed carriage, Miss Emmeline St. Germaine adjusted her mask of elegant black lace, retrieved from lost items left behind after a masquerade ball. Her gown was from the last century and over it she wore a crimson velvet cloak from a Shakespeare drama, theater castoffs too disreputable even for a period piece. She carried a slim dagger in a sheath on her belt.

From the open air of Chelsea they had traveled through the city to the open streets of Clerkenwell, taking longer than anticipated; her nerves were as taut as stretched catgut, every beat of her heart carrying the word "hurry" thrumming through her veins. The carriage, drawn by a sleek team of matched dun mares, finally creaked to a halt. She swung open the door and descended without aid. Josephs, her coachman, knew better than to offer his hand on a night like this. His task was to help the girl into the carriage and move swiftly once they were done. They must not be caught.

This was her seventh such outing, and her fame was increasing with every one; five girls and one boy had so far been saved, but this rescue may well be more dramatic, if what she had been told was true. She pulled the velvet cloak about her and shrank back into the shadows as a lamplighter trudged past along Chandler Lane, carrying his ladder and trailed by his apprentice. Once they passed, Emmeline looked to Josephs. Her driver, a shadowy figure in a many-caped greatcoat concealing his livery, pointed down the narrow alleyway.

He had sketched a map for her before their departure: a row of townhomes faced Blithestone Street, and business buildings faced the parallel thoroughfare to the west, Samuel Street, dwellings above each shop and office. Chandler Lane, bordered on one side by an open green, joined the two streets, and an alley ran from Chandler between the rear courtyards of each row of conjoined buildings. The structures were recent, constructed ten years or so before. At the back, each Blithestone residence had a brick convenience and a low brick wall around its tiny courtyard, with a gate that remained unlocked so the nightmen could empty the cesspits, removing human waste regularly to sell to farmers outside of the city.

There was a brick archway, open to the alley. Emmeline ducked through it; carrying a lanthorn and staying out of the light spilling from some windows, she crept down the alley, counting down the back courtyards of the connected townhouses that faced Blithestone, holding her breath against the odor of offal from the middens and human waste from the conveniences. She held the light high; there ... *that* was the residence, marked by Josephs on his scouting trip with a barely visible chalked blaze on the low brick wall that contained the townhome's back courtyard. She crept through the gate, the scuffle of her soft shoes echoing upwards, and approached the back door; it swung open at a push, as promised, silent on oiled hinge-pins. She set the lanthorn down by the door, then softly stepped on slipper-shod feet along the whitewashed wall, down the stone steps, and into the kitchen, pausing for a moment to let her eyes become accustomed to the light within. A woman, heavyset and sweating from the steamy heat, stared at her in alarm.

"I was sent to rescue the child," Emmeline muttered to the cook, her heart hammering against her rib cage. The woman glanced quickly about the kitchen—the potboy was to have been kept occupied elsewhere—and then nodded, swiping at her beaded forehead with one sleeved arm. The dim chamber was sweltering from a bubbling pot over the fire, steaming a pudding for the next day.

"Hurry, miss," the cook said, in a strangled tone and with a worried expression. "'E's got 'er." She pointed to a doorway, then returned to her task, punching down and kneading the dough she prepared to set near the hearth to rise for the next day's bread.

Quivering with a thread of anxiety mingled with excitement, Emmeline tiptoed through the kitchen. Every time she performed a rescue it was the same: the abject fear, the trembling in the pit of her stomach, the sense that she was about to cast up her accounts. And yet never had she been about to catch a villain in the act of abuse; a pure stream of apprehension pounded through her veins.

She took a deep breath, swallowed hard, pulled her cloak more tightly around her, and slipped into the passage the cook had indicated, down a whitewashed hall lit by flickering sconces toward the

4

housekeeper's office, supposedly deserted this time of night. The hallway was quiet but for the sound of her own breathing, which was surprisingly loud, echoing off the stone foundation of the townhouse. As she advanced, she heard grunting, muttering, and then the keening cry of a young girl.

Fury swept her nerves away. Urgent lashings of anger sped her pace. Had she miscalculated her timing? She hastened down the narrow hall swiftly and silently as a cat after a rat, pushed the housekeeper's office door open with one toe, and heard these words grunted: "Shut up, Molly! Be a good lass and stop yer wriggling."

With an intermingling of revulsion and burning fury, Emmeline pulled the dagger from her belt and stepped into the room. A young scullery maid moaned in fear and discomfort at the heavy weight upon her on a narrow divan. A man, grunting and heaving, thick hands scrabbling at her skirts, humped ineffectively. Hellfire! Emmeline had meant to arrive earlier and stop the vile animal *before* the girl suffered such brutishness.

"C'mon, girl, first time's the hardest, then it'll get easy." He grunted and groaned, fumbling with her skirts. "Come, my little temptress!" he growled. "I'll give you sweetmeats, ribbons, ha'pennies. Be a good girl and stop squirming so damned much!"

Be a good girl. Emmeline's fury chilled to resolve. She crept up to him and thrust the tip of her cunning little dagger into the saggy white-skinned rump that gleamed palely in the yellow glow of one tallow candle, a serving girl's faint light. A jewel-like droplet of ruby red blood oozed; he howled in pain, then stilled, the wail dying down to a whimper of fear.

"If you do not stop your persecution of the child this instant," Emmeline said, lowering her voice to a threatening snarl, "I shall insert this dagger where it will leave you so sore you'll be standing to eat your supper."

The scullery maid's employer, Sir Henry Claybourne, clambered off the shivering child and whirled, holding his injured bottom. His male member waved a salutation, then deflated like a pig's bladder, shrinking and softening as Emmeline waved the dagger menacingly. She was relieved to see that the girl, no more than thirteen years of age, had not yet had her skirts pushed up to her waist. At least Emmeline had prevented the worst of his assault, though the child was clearly terrified, her pale face tear-stained.

Swallowing back repulsed shock at the sight of his scrofulous, canker-marred prick, Emmeline lifted her gaze and noted that his bulbous nose was now red and his expression filled with both rage and apprehension. Unease squeezed her stomach. She must handle these next few moments carefully. She could not afford one second of carelessness. Every rescue was different, and each required intense concentration, but never had one been performed at such a pivotal point as this. "Child, go to the back alley," she muttered. "Pick up the lanthorn by the door and find the carriage at Chandler Lane. Safety awaits, I swear it."

The girl, moaning in fear, skittered away. Red-faced, Sir Henry incoherently babbled as he started to tug at his fawn breeches. One hand bloody from holding his rump, he fumbled, trying to pull up the fall. Emmeline pointed her dagger at his shrunken male member. This was no time to become queasy; she *must* persevere. "Did I *say* you were to do that?" She lunged and slashed, a ribbon of red oozing on his saggy thigh. "Leave that fall *down*, if you please, Sir Henry." Emmeline deduced that the thorny conversation would progress more easily if the knight felt vulnerable, and no man felt more defenseless than with his male appendage exposed. "You have raped your last scullery maid."

"Rape? It is not *rape*," he blustered, his neck waddles waggling in indignation. His thin gray hair was standing straight up, his pate gleamed in the faint light, and his chin was shiny from saliva. His waistcoat was disarranged, his breeches sagging down over his stockings. "They have a place to lay their head at night. I buy the girls sugarplums and trinkets aplenty, and any bastard born is sent away to a decent home."

"You speak of by-blows like they are unwanted kittens. How fortunate for them you do not drown them in the stew pond." Her mask, both actual and figurative, was starting to slip; t'was time to leave. Every second she spent with an execrable male like his lordship his confidence would increase, and thus her safety decrease.

"Bitch! Who are you?" he bellowed. He had decided Emmeline wasn't going to use her dagger to wound him mortally and was tugging at his breeches, his paunch drooping and concealing his penis like a coverlet over a bedpost.

She must make haste and leave, but she had a message to deliver first. "Listen to me, you poxy cit," she commanded, swirling her cloak like a jaunty highwayman. He stared up at her, his eyes protruding from his pouchy face. "If you defile one more maid—just *one* more—I swear there are a legion of women like me, and one of them may slip a knife between your shoulder blades while you sleep." He was about to bluster but she waved the dagger menacingly, and finished with, "Or she may decide the offending member must come off. Remember *that* when next your prick stiffens at the sight of a child!"

Emmeline turned and slipped swiftly back through the hallway and thence to the kitchen, witnessed only by the cook and another woman—probably the housekeeper—who huddled in the shadows together. The second female was a big, raw-boned woman, red of face right down to the cleft tip of her hooked nose. Both were silent witnesses to their master's depredations on young scullery maids, and one had summoned the courage to get a message to Emmeline's group, who were becoming known in certain circles for helping the downtrodden, especially females. Sir Henry's behavior was predictable, and her intervention had been perfectly timed to catch him in the act but before real harm had been done the child, so as to make the warning more effective.

Or was that true; *real* harm? Emmeline muttered a prayer that the girl would recover from her fright. She put one finger to her lips, then skipped up the steps and out the back door into the alley, and thence to her waiting carriage. She climbed in and banged on the roof with the hilt of her dagger. She heard the knight bellowing as he erupted from the townhouse before her carriage swiftly rattled away, turning a corner and—with any luck—disappearing into the night fog.

The child cowered in the corner. "Molly, fear not," Emmeline said, gently. "You're safe now. I *promise* you, on my word of honor, that you are going to work in a home where your employer will never abuse you."

TWO

MISS EMMELINE ST. GERMAINE, elegantly clothed in a new fall gown of russet net over cream muslin, and her companion, her mother's cousin Comtesse Fidelity Bernadotte, shrugged out of their cloaks in the hall of their hostess's home, a gracious townhouse in a newly fashionable square in London. All was perfection, from the gold silk-hung walls to the red and gold Turkey rugs, Oriental pottery, and family portraits. Lady Sherringdon's home was lovely, perfumed with the dueling scents of sandalwood and old dog.

An elderly maid, her tightly curled gray hair confined by a modest white cap, looked burdened too heavily by the cloaks necessary to ward off the late October chill. Emmeline watched her totter away, hoping the weight would not topple her. From experience, she knew it would be some time before the maid would return to announce them to the others. Her companion fidgeted with her reticule and smoothed her hair, adjusting her bonnet in the mirror over the Sheraton dressing table that Lady Sherringdon had placed there to hold the calling card tray and oddments. Emmeline bent down to pat Hugo, the friendliest pug dog of the house, as it snuffled and waggled on the marble floor at her feet, his asthmatic snorts and wuffles of welcome making her smile. Two more cautious pugs, rescued from unsuitable owners, watched from the dim reaches of the hall beyond the stairs.

Lady Sherringdon was a charitable soul; no human or animal in need escaped her goodness, and so her home was filled with servants barely able to work and pets no one else wanted. A one-eyed black cat glowered down from the landing above, its missing eye and abbreviated tail the sad victims of destructive street boys. In the years since her release from penury and abuse her ladyship had rescued more animals and humans than anyone could enumerate. Emmeline loved Adelaide Sherringdon for her generous heart and optimistic nature.

Adelaide was older than Emmeline's companion, Fidelity—who was fifty-three—by a dozen or so years. Addy, as her closest friends called her, had suffered deeply, first at the hands of her father, who sent her north to wed a man she'd never met. Her husband, Viscount Sherringdon, was cruel, breaking her spirit as casually as one does a horse's and with some of the same techniques: punishment, fear, and pain. When he died after twenty years of wedded misery, her relief was exquisite. She was wooed and won by a younger man (whom she married, though retaining her title as a courtesy), who swore to cherish her but instead wasted all her money at the gambling tables, then contracted a disease and died, leaving her penniless and ill.

One may have expected that her son by her first marriage, who had inherited his father's title and estate, would have invited his mother into his home. Offended by her second marriage, he did not; even shame would not move him. For a time, Adelaide lived with a cousin as poor relation, until she was left a legacy and this London townhome by a family friend, a kindly gentleman who was more father to her than her own had ever been. She now lived in comfort and shared her good fortune.

Fidelity sighed, and Emmeline smiled. The maid would come back at some point to announce them; it was a matter of patience. She returned to reflecting on the past: how Lady Sherringdon, because of her many kindnesses, was the first woman she had thought of when the idea for their group came to her. Their meeting was ostensibly a late-afternoon gathering of ladies to discuss their program of good works. If society chose to assume their "good works" involved providing Bibles to heathens and relief for the poor list, that was their error. In truth, their cause was a mission that Emmeline had begun out of a frustrated sense of the iniquity of some men who were supposed to, with their greater wisdom and strength, protect the females under their governance. She had suffered from injustice in her own life; the laws of the land favored the male sex over the female in almost every way. That could not fail to irritate her, since she believed herself to be much more level-headed than the men she knew, if she was sometimes more impulsive. She had used lessons learned from Lady Sherringdon to wrest control of her life from her older brother, but it was not a formal arrangement and could be rescinded at any time.

To combat injustice, she and Addy had recently formed a society of women dedicated to righting the wrongs inflicted on girls and women of all stations, from the lowliest scullery maid to a royal princess, if such should be in need of rescue. In the last year, she and Adelaide had gathered like-minded ladies to her cause, women who had suffered injustice at the hands of men: fathers, sons, and, in Emmeline's case, a father and brother. Though they conferred and observed, agreeing on suitable candidates for their group, Lady Sherringdon in general took the lead in making the approach. As a widow, she was freer and less vulnerable to criticism should anyone discover their secret mission.

Most, though not all, of their rescues were of young servants in abusive situations. They had so far relocated six mistreated scullery maids and one climbing boy, who had been beaten daily by his execrable master. The girls had been given new jobs in safe homes. As for the boy, Tommy Jones, his apprenticeship had been paid off, his freedom, in effect, purchased, and his master threatened that he would be turned over to the magistrate should the maltreatment of his apprentices continue.

Last night's mission, saving Molly from the loathsome Sir Henry Claybourne, had been a turning point, an indication of how important their work could become, given the situation in which Emmeline had found her. However, recently murmurings of alarm had evolved into a chorus among society's leaders, bleating about how dangerous it was that a woman, the so-called Avengeress, should be stealing children, regardless of those children's situations. Emmeline frankly reveled in it; never had she, as a woman, so affected people's emotions. She had oft wondered what there was to life beyond afternoon visits, opera in the evening, and balls in the Season, and now she knew. What did it say about her that the finest aspects of her life were hidden from friends and family?

Lady Adelaide Sherringdon bustled out of the sitting room. "You're here! Why didn't Tillie announce you?" She clasped Emmeline's hand and sought her eyes; the younger woman nodded, and her ladyship sighed, her hands trembling. "Thank goodness! Come in, join us!" she said, waving toward the sitting room.

Emmeline would enjoy relating the tale of how she had caught Sir Henry in the act and made him bleed. She had transported Molly to the agreed-upon location, from whence she would be sent to her new employer, the home of a gentle spinster in need of a companion and maid. Then, the rapid change in the dark interior of her coach as she jostled through city streets and home to Chelsea, from a "Bible reading," as she told her butler.

"You will find only friends inside," Lady Sherringdon said. "All eager to hear—"

She was interrupted by the door; someone employed the knocker with vigor. Tillie, who had finally returned from disposing of the cloaks, trotted toward it and Adelaide stayed behind to welcome her next guest as Fidelity and Emmeline entered the parlor and greeted the others. Emmeline could hear, in the hall behind them, echoing chatter, several voices competing for attention.

She glanced around at the ladies in the sitting room. Miss Dorcas Harvey sat by a window eating plums; she was alone, for once, without her bosom friend Mrs. Martha Adair. Miss Juliette Espanson leaned forward in deep conversation with Lady Clara Langdon, who glanced up as the most recent arrivals entered.

Emmeline hugged her companion's arm to her and whispered, "I'm so anxious to tell them all! If I don't unburden myself soon, I'll jump out of my skin."

Fidelity squeezed back. "Calm, Emmeline. You would think at your age you would have learned composure."

A lady was composed and gracious at all times, even when in a state of high excitation or expectation. A lady did not reveal her enthusiasm, did not walk too swiftly, neither did she lag behind. Emmeline conformed as best she could, the better to revel in her secret life, and so composed her expression as she greeted the others with a nod and pleasant word.

The voices from the entry hall were getting louder, accompanied by a shrill titter of youthful laughter. Adelaide glided into the sitting room followed by three ladies, only one of whom belonged. Mrs. Martha Adair, a plump, elegant lady in her forties, entered, flanked by two younger women, both fashionably gowned.

This was beyond annoying. There should be no strangers in attendance at this meeting. With them present, Emmeline could not tell the thrilling story of the previous night's rescue. Her attention was caught by the sly looks the two young women exchanged, and she felt a tingle of apprehension. In their group, Martha was the weak link, an inveterate gossip. Emmeline was not easy with her knowing all she knew, but there was no way to keep it from her.

Martha took her seat by Fidelity, folding her hands over her embroidered reticule. She glanced over at Dorcas, who looked annoyed, her thick brows drawn together, then glanced around at the rest. "Ladies, this is Misses Pamela and Honoria Schaeffer, my nieces," she said. "I was about to leave the house when they arrived *unexpectedly* from school. They attend Miss Woodhew's Academy in Richmond. I could not leave them behind, and so brought them."

Both young ladies were pert and pretty, no more than a year apart and looking very much the same, with dark hair and dark eyes and in modest pale gowns suiting their age. Martha and her nieces sat and the ladies chatted while Emmeline devised a scheme to meet the next day. During a brief lull in the general chatter, Emmeline looked around at her friends. "I hear that Gunter's has a new flavor of Italian ice. Would some of you care to partake with me tomorrow?" she asked.

"Gunter's?" one of the young girls said, brow arched in derision. "*So* exploded."

"Not fashionable," the other said with a nod. "No one of style goes to Gunter's anymore."

"Honoria," Martha said sharply. "That was impolite."

14

Miss Honoria Schaeffer ignored her. She leaned forward and scanned the other ladies. "You must have heard the *vastly* important news, did you not?"

Dorcas, her cheeks red with tamped-down frustration—she was protective of both their group's privacy and Martha's company—mumbled, "What, new fashion in hats? Puff sleeves still in?"

Miss Pamela Schaeffer cast the older woman a look of disgust. "As if you would be able to wear puff sleeves anyway," she said, obliquely referencing Dorcas's heavy, bosomy figure and ignoring the hiss of indrawn breaths at her rudeness. "No, something *truly* shocking! Our uncle owns a newspaper, so we hear everything in advance of others."

Emmeline's attention sharpened. "What newspaper, pray tell?"

Honoria eyed her and apparently found her fashionable gown and slim figure worthy of approval, for she spoke politely enough. "Our uncle is Sir James Schaeffer. He owns *The London Guardian Standard*," she replied.

"*The Standard*? They've been very harsh in their reporting on Sir Francis Burdett's attempt to reform the House." Emmeline's tone was sharper than she intended.

"And so they should be! That man would have everything dear about England change in an instant," Miss Honoria Schaeffer, apparently the elder of the sisters, retorted.

"Everything dear? Like children starving in Seven Dials, or corruption and bribery in our houses of parliament, or—"

Fidelity put a hand on Emmeline's and squeezed. Reminded that these two young ladies were strangers, and that she must not reveal her radical politics, Emmeline forced a smile, took a deep breath, and nodded. The Misses Schaeffer stared at her, wide-eyed.

In a milder tone, she said, "I must agree with you, though, Miss Schaeffer. Our nation has so *much* to be proud of. Did we not abolish the slave trade? Not completely, of course … slaves are still necessary in the colonies. We must not move *too* swiftly. Child labor, for example; we cannot afford to abolish *that*! Seven years of age is *more* than old enough to stop school and haul coal in the mines."

Miss Schaeffer eyed her with suspicion, but then nodded. "Too true, Miss St. Germaine. What good is an education if the child will end up working in the mines anyway?"

Emmeline bit the inside of her cheek and tasted blood as Fidelity squeezed her hand more tightly. The younger Miss Schaeffer impatiently said, "Honoria, that is not the news, that our uncle owns a paper." Miss Pamela sent Emmeline an unfriendly look and one of censure at her older sister. "The *news* is that a horrible crime has taken place!"

Her ghoulish enjoyment, dark eyes wide, mouth pulled in a grin, was interesting; as a genteel young lady, she should be recoiling if the crime was as ghastly as she said. "What has happened?" Emmeline asked her.

Martha sent Emmeline an agonized look of uneasiness. She stared back at her friend with incomprehension, not able to decipher what the expression meant.

Miss Pamela was about to reply, but Honoria leaned forward, eyes wide, and hurriedly said, "The brewer Sir Henry Claybourne was murdered last night, slit from throat to bowel, slaughtered like a *hog*."

There was a collective gasp, both at the dreadful vulgarity of her words and the news they relayed. Dizziness washed over Emmeline as she tried to comprehend.

Miss Pamela added, "There was a masked intruder earlier, a *woman* of all things, that Avengeress we've all been hearing about! Also, a scullery maid, just one month hired, absconded the same night, stealing all the jewels and silver! It is thought they were working together to slaughter Sir Henry and steal the household goods."

Ringing in her ears almost deafened Emmeline as the other women chattered, asking questions and demanding answers of the two sisters, who appeared slightly taken aback at the questioning and didn't answer right away. Fidelity's hand clamped tightly on Emmeline's arm, her fingernails digging into the tender flesh. The pain brought Emmeline back to herself, and the dizziness ebbed, horror flowing in to take its place. How was this possible? Was it even true?

"Such an awful tale," Fidelity finally said, her voice quavering, releasing her grip on Emmeline's arm. "But nobody relies on newspapers for the truth, do they?" Her tone was deliberately light as air.

She was giving Emmeline time to recover, as were Lady Clara, Lady Adelaide, and Miss Espanson, who drew the young Misses Schaeffers' attention by amplifying Fidelity's voiced skepticism, asking multiple questions all at once. They all knew of Emmeline's incursion into Sir Henry Claybourne's residence the evening before, but only Martha and Dorcas stared at her with dual expressions of unease. Neither had the social grace the others exhibited in ignoring Emmeline's discomfiture. At any moment, the Misses Schaeffer could notice the two ladies' focus on Emmeline, and she *must* present a calm face. She took a deep, shuddering breath, clasped her trembling hands together in her lap, and focused on the conversation.

"Our uncle's paper is *most* particular about printing only the truth!" Miss Schaeffer protested against the wave of disbelief.

Lady Clara Langdon, daughter of the Earl of Langdon, glanced over at Miss Juliette Espanson and then back to Honoria. "Your loyalty does you credit, Miss Schaeffer, but newspapers are terribly unreliable." She tilted her head in a haughty manner and gazed serenely at the two younger ladies. "Just last month *The Prattler* printed a *monstrous* lie about Princess Amelia, you know."

"*The Prattler* is a rag," the elder sister protested vehemently. "Our uncle's paper is a *serious* newspaper." Both young ladies were becoming agitated, but the conflict had served to sweep the murder and the masked intruder from the conversation and give Emmeline time to recover her equilibrium. It was kindly done. Emmeline mouthed "thank you" to Lady Clara, who nodded.

The young Schaeffer ladies had nothing more of substance to add to their tale, but neither did they seem inclined to leave Lady Sherringdon's. There was no possibility of speaking openly to the others about what had happened. Fidelity pleaded a terrible headache and they rose to leave. Lady Sherringdon, ever the good hostess, followed them to the entry hall and summoned her maid to fetch their wraps.

"I don't understand," Emmeline whispered, turning to their hostess and clutching her arm. "When I departed the house with Molly, Sir Henry was red-faced but quite alive, I assure you."

Adelaide tugged them toward the door. "Of course, my dear. This is shocking! But of *course* you are not involved. Go. I'll try to find out what I can from those two little idiots."

"I'll send you word if I learn anything," Emmeline muttered as the maid brought their wraps. "Perhaps we can meet tomorrow. I'll send a note."

They departed the house. Emmeline climbed into the St. Germaine coach. "Josephs, take the Comtesse home." Employing Josephs as the family coachman might seem a luxury in a city household, but it was a necessity to have a driver given their home was in Chelsea, out of the city proper. "After that, let me out at Carpenter's Coffee House."

Josephs inhaled sharply, but then nodded and shut the door, latching it securely. They felt his weight as he jumped up and the carriage lurched into movement.

"Emmeline, you will *not* go there," Fidelity said, her voice low and trembling. She reached over and grasped her charge's gloved hand. "What are you thinking? Please consider your reputation!"

"Fiddy, I *must* see Simeon." Simeon Kauffman was publisher of *The Prattler*, a radical newspaper. "He takes his coffee every evening at this time at Carpenter's. He'll know about this awful thing, if it's true, and what people are saying. I *need* to know. He's the only one I can trust to tell me the truth of what's going on."

"I understand, my dear, but you cannot go into that place. I beseech you, think!"

Fidelity was right, of course, and Emmeline nodded. Carpenter's Coffee House was a notorious meeting place in Covent Garden, where actors, writers, theater folk, and prostitutes mingled freely. Beyond that, it was said to be infested with vermin, both human and animal. Though Simeon frequented a more staid coffeehouse most of the day, in the late afternoon and early evening he had his usual booth at Carpenter's. There he saw what happened to society, he said, when hope was lost.

"I'll accompany you," Fidelity said. "We'll send Josephs in to find Simeon, and he can speak with us in the carriage."

It was a risk, even so. If they were recognized ... Emmeline took a deep breath, glancing over at her companion's worried face in the dimness. "You're right, of course, Fiddy. Thank goodness for your sense. My feelings run away with me."

She knocked on the roof of the carriage, gave her new instructions to the coachman, and then closed the door again. As the carriage lurched back into movement, she stared down at the twisted gloves in her hands; in her agitation, she had pulled them off. "It must be true, Fiddy, that Sir Henry is dead. But what of that nonsense, that Molly absconded with silver and jewels? Who would tell such monstrous lies?"

Fidelity shivered. "I don't know, Emmie. But it has a whiff of devious plots and stratagems!"

At their destination, Emmeline waited with Fidelity while Josephs retrieved Simeon from inside the coffee shop. She peeked out the curtain, watching as a lamplighter whistled a merry tune as he raised his ladder to the post and lit the wick, then moved on to the next. A shadowy figure slipped out of the coffeehouse, so Emmeline let the curtain fall. There was a murmured word, one sharp rap on the carriage, and Simeon flung the door open, glanced over his shoulder, and clambered inside. He bowed over Fidelity's hand and bumped his head on the roof when he tried to straighten. That bump disarranged his kippah, the skull cap that denoted his race and religious observance. Josephs, apparently on Simeon's instructions, set into motion, pulling away from the infamous purveyor of coffee and scandalous behavior.

"What are you doing here?" the publisher asked. "This is *most* improvident, to arrive so and have your coachman ask for me so openly. What if someone were to recognize his livery? You know as well as anyone that there are prying eyes everywhere, and information is money to these poor folk. Madame Comtesse," he said, turning to Fidelity, "Miss St. Germaine is reckless, but I would expect *you*, at least, to have better sense."

"Mr. Kauffman, I tried to tell her, but you know our dear Emmeline."

"Simeon, don't chide me. Something horrible has happened and I need your help." Pleading was not Emmeline's natural manner, but she was badly shaken by what she had learned and what it meant.

"Calm yourself, my friend," he said, his tone softer, his thick brows drawing down over his dark, deep-set eyes. He was a handsome man, but careless of his appearance most of the time, preferring to spend his time with his writing and study of humanity. "This is unlike you, so naturally self-possessed and calm most of the time. I apologize for my irritation, but your reputation is inviolate. If anyone should learn your secrets..." He shook his head. "I apologize to you as well, Madame Comtesse, for my discourtesy," he said as he turned to Fidelity once more. "How are you this evening, madam? You appear well." The carriage drew to a halt; they had apparently just gone around the corner.

"I *am* well, Mr. Kauffman," Fidelity replied. "How are Miriam and the children?"

"All very well, my good lady." Civilities done, kindness paid, Simeon turned back to Emmeline, his fine dark eyes flashing with a bit of lamplight that streamed through a crack in the window shade. "Now tell me, my young friend, what brings you here?"

She told him of her visit to Sir Henry Claybourne, not sparing the anatomical details she had unfortunately witnessed.

He was rigid with disapproval, and his cheeks flooded with color. "Emmeline, that is *mishegas*! You should not have done it."

Faced with her friend's agitation, Emmeline smiled. "*Mishegas*... Simeon, you say that often about my behavior, but I don't understand Yiddish unless you translate it for me, you know."

Simeon Kauffman was Ashkenazic Jew; his parents had arrived in England from Germany forty years before, just before he was born. "*Mishegas*, Emmeline, is foolish. To witness such things, an unmarried young lady... it's unthinkable."

"I'm not a sheltered hothouse flower, Simeon. You know that better than most. I *had* to do what I did. There was a child involved, a little girl a year or two older than your daughter. When I was that age, I was playing with dolls and running in the garden, not being abused by some filthy old lecher." Her rage had overtaken her and she was shaking. Taking a deep breath, she calmed herself. "You've often told me *Et hanaaseh ein lehashiv*," she said. "What's done cannot be returned. I can't undo it now. What I have to say is—"

"Of course I understand, Emmeline. I suspected your hand in this the moment I heard about it. *You* were the masked assailant who conspired with the scullery maid to rob him ... or so the people are saying as they jest about this crime."

He knew of her identity as the Avengeress, and disliked it, but he had not rebuked her. She once asked him why he didn't openly criticize; he replied that while disapproval was his right, doing what she wanted was *her* right. His was a unique position for a man, in her experience. Still ..."How can you make light of this, Simeon?" she cried, her voice cracking.

"I am simply reporting what the people are saying. I have a man investigating the murder—for I don't expect you are guilty of that— and we'll be putting out a broadsheet tonight. He has likely returned to the coffeehouse now, so I must get back." Simeon squinted, twisted his mouth in a grimace, and then sighed "I must tell you something unpleasant. The magistrate's men were at the newspaper office today. They wanted to know, who is the Rogue? And how did he know about Sir Henry and the girl he was abusing?" He gazed at her with a worried look. "And also they wish to know ... how did the Rogue know the Avengeress would visit Sir Henry, or was it a message to that lady?" He shook his head, his expression filled with worry. "What would they say if I *did* tell them who the Rogue is?"

What *would* they say if it was discovered that Miss Emmeline St. Germaine, genteel spinster, was also the renowned and scandalous gossip columnist the Rogue?

THREE

"You didn't tell them—"

"Of course not, Miss St. Germaine!"

"I did not expect the fellow to die when I rescued the child from his clutches."

"That was a truly unfortunate turn of events," Simeon said. "And a dangerous one, for you."

"For all of us," she replied.

In her alter ego as the Rogue, Emmeline was gossip columnist, radical critic, and, it was rumored, man-about-town, a roguish roué. She used the assumption she was male to say things as the Rogue that would be unacceptable from a woman. Perhaps she had been too blunt in her column, but when she wrote it, she had not foreseen Sir Henry's brutal murder the very night she raided his home. Asking for the public's help in unmasking the Avengeress had been a ploy to establish distance between her two personas, and maybe that would work to her benefit.

"I worry they will discover your identity, though it will not be from me," Simeon said.

"*I* worry that you will be jailed for refusing to tell."

"That is not your concern," he assured her. "As a radical newspaperman, I run that risk every day I publish. The truth is not appreciated by men in power, and so a free press is their enemy."

Emmeline was deeply shaken by the knowledge that the magistrate was already questioning the connection between the Rogue's column on Sir Henry's despicable sexual proclivities and his murder. It was of the utmost importance that she never be named as the Rogue *and* as the Avengeress. One or the other accusation would cause her to be the object of scandal, and could banish her from polite society. It would change her life forever, but she *might* weather the storm with haughty denial and grim determination. Both revelations together would be disastrous, and her family would likely cast her out.

If she were named a murderess, though, it would send her to the gibbet.

"I could not leave little Molly with that beast, Simeon." He nodded. "Now ... it is vital I am never exposed as the Rogue."

"No hint will come from my lips."

Simeon was a devoted father and a good man; the welfare of the children of London, Jew or gentile, concerned him deeply. So he encouraged her social commentary. Besides retailing society gossip and scandal, she also used her column to rail against the hypocrites of their city who piously prayed in church and then returned home to prey on their maidservants. He was as sickened as she by the women who knew about it—as Sir Henry's wife must have known—and did nothing to stop it, though women trod a precarious path, reliant on their husbands for almost everything.

"What do you know about the murder?" she asked, pushing away the fear that chilled her.

He shrugged and exhaled gustily. "Little, so far. The housekeeper and cook had set the latch for the evening, they say, and thought the master had gone upstairs for the night after the masked marauder invaded the house. They were frightened, but their master told them he would summon the magistrate in the morning. He was too upset to do so that evening."

"That is odd behavior," Fidelity said.

"I find it so," Emmeline agreed.

"Then, early this morning, he was found dead in the alleyway behind the townhouse."

Had she been used, Emmeline wondered? By summoning help for the scullery maid, it was possible that the housekeeper or cook had intended for the Avengeress's visit to serve as cover for a confederate robbing the house. Perhaps Sir Henry had caught them at it and been murdered. That seemed a tortured plot, though; there were simpler ways to rob the household. It was common enough for a maid to leave the latch undone after inviting one of her followers to make away with the silver.

What puzzled her more was Sir Henry's delay in calling in the magistrate. Why did he need time, unless he had planned to do something else first? Or perhaps, to *tell* someone else first. Did it indicate a guilty conscience? Sir Henry had not seemed the sort to have scruples of any sort.

"Look at her," Simeon said to Fidelity. "When she gets that look, I know she's thinking." He tapped the side of his head. "The wheels and cogs, they are turning. Go home, Miss Emmeline St. Germaine. This has been a shock; get some rest."

"You will send me the broadsheet when it's ready?"

"That and whatever else I learn."

He opened the door, looked both ways, and clambered down, slamming the door and rapping on the side of the vehicle. The carriage lurched into movement. Emmeline told her companion what she was thinking: that either the cook or housekeeper was involved. "Was I duped? Lured there to make me a suspect in his murder?"

Fidelity pondered that, but shook her head. "Surely the intent was honest, to catch him in the despicable act, rescue the child, and warn him to cease. If it wasn't his nature and his habit to abuse the little girl, he could not be tricked into doing it."

"True." She must ponder the possibilities.

Emmeline and Fidelity returned to Chelsea and had a late dinner. Her stomach was in knots, but her rigid social training supported her through the meal as Birk, the butler, stood by, ordering the removes. She sipped her soup—excellent as always; Mrs. Riddle, the townhome cook, was a sorceress of the soup pot—then broke up her food and made it look like she had eaten while talking inconsequential nonsense with Fidelity as servants brought food, then took it away, moving silent and efficient in their duties.

After dinner, they retreated upstairs to the sitting room. The ground floor of the spacious townhome, which had been in the St. Germaine family for at least two generations, was devoted to the reception room and dining room; the first floor to the sitting and music room, and a small library; and the second floor to bedrooms. Birk carried up a parcel that had arrived by messenger and offered it to her on a tray. His tiny, porcine-like eyes sparked with curiosity that was doomed to disappointment. Emmeline had a grave suspicion that Birk, in the employ of her eldest brother, Leopold, whose house this was, reported to Leopold any irregularities in her life: where she went, who she saw, and likely from whom letters were received. Simeon knew this. The messenger would have been a boy earning a few pennies, and the package held no return address to reveal its origin—Simeon Kauffman of *The Prattler*—nor did the messenger wait for a reply.

She and Fidelity retreated up the narrow stairs to their bedchambers. Emmeline's room, elegant and serene, papered in pale green and cream and with moss-green furnishings, was spacious, taking up the whole front of the second floor of the townhome, overlooking the Thames through a large bow window. Fidelity's smaller room was one of two that overlooked the back courtyard. Emmeline was greeted by her lady's maid, Delia Gillies, who helped her mistress into her night attire and braided her long hair. Then Emmeline sat down on a low chair by the marble fireplace, her hands trembling as she untied the string that bound the pages. Gillies was tidying her dressing table when there was a light tapping at her chamber door; Emmeline nodded.

The maid crossed the room and peeked out. "The Comtesse, miss," she said over her shoulder.

"Come, Fiddy, read with me. Gillies, come … I have no secrets from you two." The three women drew together, Fidelity on a low stool and Gillies hanging over her shoulder as Emmeline took out the *Prattler* broadsheet announcing the awful event. It was illustrated with a woodcut of a stylized thief in a long cloak, the miscreant slyly glancing back over his shoulder. Emmeline appreciated Simeon's deft use of the imagery to deflect public reaction; many would see it and think the masked intruder was male, even if the story correctly relayed that the interloper was female.

Emmeline read the story aloud:

"Most Horrible Murder!

An atrocious act of savagery—gruesome murder!—striking at the very heart of our great city of London, has been committed. The Prattler has learned details.

Last evening, October 24th, this year of our Lord 1810, at the home of Sir Henry Claybourne, newly knighted manufacturer, two crimes were committed. It is alleged that a masked intruder crept into the home some time after the dinner hour when the lady of the house had retired to her chamber. The purpose of this visit has not been established, though other newspapers will no doubt speculate with base rumors and conjecture. Also that evening it is said that the scullery maid, a newly hired child by the name of Molly, escaped the house; why, it is not clear, and neither is it sure that she took anything, though the silver cutlery is said to be missing.

The housekeeper—one Mrs. Young—and cook, a Mrs. Partridge, both assert that the latch was on that night after the intrusion and the escape of the scullery maid. In the morning the latch was found undone and the door to the courtyard open. A fish delivery boy found the slaughtered body of Sir Henry in the alley beyond the courtyard of his townhome, his throat slit. The boy claims that the gentleman was disemboweled, but there is no other information asserting that terrible image. Blood did flow freely; the pavement was awash in it."

Emmeline looked up at a noise from Fidelity. "Oh, Fiddy, I'm so sorry!" Her friend and companion was shuddering, her lined face drawn and bleached, her mouth trembling. "Gillies, do help her."

Her maid was sturdy and phlegmatic; no amount of talk of blood could shake a woman who had seen her own child dragged dead from a coal mine after suffocating to death in poisoned air. Gillies dampened a cloth in the wash basin and held it to Fidelity's forehead as the Comtesse took in a deep and shaky breath.

"For a moment, I remembered Jean Marc," she said faintly. Eighteen years before, as mobs ruled Paris during the Revolution, Fidelity's husband had attempted to help some priests who were attacked while being transported to prison in a tumbrel. Comte Jean Marc Bernadotte tried to take some of the men of God into his carriage—he and Fiddy were fleeing the city—when the angry horde attacked them, too.

"It was the talk of blood," Fidelity explained. "I saw my darling Jean Marc pulled from our carriage and slaughtered in front of my eyes on the Rue St. Martin. His throat was cut, and it was like a river of blood flowed down, drenching his snowy cravat. I'll never forget it."

It was a ritual, her repetition of the salient points of her husband's death; it appeared to soothe her, somehow, to reiterate the horror. She had fled France alone, having lost every sou of the Bernadotte family wealth in the Revolution, returning to England as a poor relation. She took a deep breath and nodded. "Go on, Emmeline. Thank you, Gillies."

Although Gillies was Emmeline's lady's maid, she served them both. As hardy and self-sufficient as the Scotswoman was, she adored the fragile and sensitive Fidelity, who had nursed the maid through a ghastly illness two years before. Gillies patted the Comtesse's hand, then tidied the washing stand while listening to Emmeline as she continued to read the broadsheet.

Emmeline found her place. As she'd suspected would be true, Simeon had managed to make light of the masked intruder and leave aside any suggestion of the sex of the interloper. "Let's see ... uh ...

"The watch was called, a constable summoned, and the local magistrate was also sent for. Lady Claybourne, upon being

informed of her husband's murder, fell down insensible on her bed
and could not be roused. It is reported that a neighbor witnessed
two villainous men approaching the house by way of the back alley
in the middle of the night; the watch accosted them, whereupon the
villains beat him senseless, then fled. The same neighbor has stated
that Sir Henry often had dealings with unsavory types, such as the
evil-appearing man who brought the young scullery maid to work
at the Claybourne residence a month ago."

This was interesting. Someone had witnessed the man who brought Molly to work at the Claybourne residence? And the neighbor saw two men in the neighborhood the night of Sir Henry's murder, as did the watchman who was beaten for his troubles. Had that inquisitive neighbor seen her arrive? Emmeline resolved to ask Simeon the neighbor's name.

Gillies paused in her tidying. "That Sir Henry, miss … you saw him doin' his worst. Ain't it likely there are others who'd want him dead?"

"Others could have wished him ill, certainly." If he made a habit of assaulting little girls, what else had he done, and to whom? "But murder?"

"I'd tear out the black heart of any man who harmed one of my bairns." Gillies's eyes gleamed with a savage light. She had assaulted the mine owner after her child's death. A sympathetic local magistrate had saved her from transportation or worse, on the promise that she keep the peace and never return to Scotland. Widowed and with the rest of her children grown and able to fend for themselves, she had departed for England.

"It's none of your concern, Emmeline, who killed him." Fidelity's voice was taut. Though she appeared outwardly calm, she plucked and frayed one edge of her shawl.

30

Gillies said, "Miss, if it comes out that you're the masked intruder, there'll be trouble."

"There's no reason to worry about that yet. Let's see what else Simeon has sent." Emmeline laid out the other sheets, along with a letter. "These are broadsheets from other publishers," she said. The headline of the top one foretold worse to come. It read, *Masked Strumpet and Killer Maid Slaughter Knight*. She pushed it aside, under one of the others. "I'll read Mr. Kauffman's letter first." Her voice cracked. She cleared her throat, then turned away and composed herself.

"Dearest, is everything all right?" Fidelity asked.

"I'm contemplating what Simeon has said." Emmeline swiftly read the letter. In it, he warned her that the broadsheets were terrible and worse would likely come. He recommended that she not read them, but acknowledged that in sending them, he knew she would. He recommended she retreat from the city to her brother's estate, though he knew she would not regard his guidance. In short, he said, while he had all manner of good wishes and advice to offer her, he was certain his counsel would end like most did, unheeded.

He was correct in one thing; she would not retreat.

Simeon gave her what information his writer had so far gleaned. The magistrate's men had questioned neighbors about what they heard or saw, but there was little to be learned. A neighboring potboy heard men arguing. Another neighbor saw two men in Sir Henry's courtyard quarreling with him but thought they left him alive and well, though he could not be certain. This all happened at least two hours after the masked woman stole away with the scullery maid. Though they had spoken with the servants in the Claybourne home, no one had yet spoken to Lady Claybourne, who was reportedly still distraught, so *The Standard*, even with as solid a reputation as it had, was lying when the writer implied they had. The area was on high alert, everyone fearful that the killer would strike again.

Simeon concluded, *I will certainly look forward to any information my usual correspondent might see fit to include for the newspaper.*

She was welcome, in other words, to write a Rogue piece for *The Prattler.* Emmeline turned back to her companion and her maid, who watched her, tension evident in every line of their faces. "This will not come back to me, and I pray it won't come back to Molly. Her name has been changed, and even we don't know exactly where she is. Only Addy does."

"But the housekeeper and cook saw you, did they not?" Fidelity asked.

"Yes, the housekeeper was there in the shadows in the kitchen with the cook when I departed. But it was dark and I wore a mask." The cook and housekeeper had known to expect her, though. They did not know her name, or at least she hoped that was so.

As shocking as it was to think it possible that an employee would murder her master, Emmeline supposed she must consider it, though every bit of her being revolted against the notion that a woman would deliver such a violent end on anyone, even one so deserving as Sir Henry Claybourne. It was far more likely that the murderer or murderers were the two men the neighbor saw in the night. Unless … perhaps it was the neighbor himself, reporting strange men abroad while in truth it was he who had killed Sir Henry for reasons known only to himself. However, the watchman had confirmed the existence of the two strange men who beat him, so they had been there.

Even as she had slipped away into the night, was there someone watching, waiting, using her masked visit as an opportunity to slaughter Sir Henry? The notion chilled her to the bone.

"Emmeline, I don't like the look of your brow," Fidelity said.

"What is wrong with my brow?" Emmeline felt her forehead, and encountered only some stray curls from her independent hair.

"It is furrowed, and that means you are thinking deep thoughts." Fidelity's tone was edged in hysteria. "I *forbid* you to think deep thoughts."

After years together, Emmeline knew how to calm her companion. "Dear Fidelity, my thoughts are never so very deep," she said, smiling and keeping her tone light as she took her cousin's hand and squeezed.

FOUR

She dismissed Gillies, who helped Fidelity to her room. Emmeline then slipped off her night-rail and took the broadsheets to bed to read by candlelight, hoping to acquire some tidbit of information among the conjecture and scandal. There was a time when she would have believed every word in the broadsheet, but she had learned, since starting to write for *The Prattler*, that not every writer or publisher was as careful as Simeon. Some paid for information—she had given money herself for tips—or made up scandal to order.

It was the way of the world. Scandal sold papers.

Among the articles one was useless; she knew it immediately. It was a page of doggerel verse, scribbled by an anonymous hack.

Murder in Clerkenwell
Or, The Ballad of Sir Henry Claybourne

T'was midnight dark when the female masked,
With bold intent, came stealing fast.

To the house of Sir Henry Claybourne, knight,
That she somehow knew was not locked tight.
Her courage high, her morals ill,
She stole the child, tho' no blood did she spill.

And all was done in the space of a breath.
... all in the space of a breath!

Then to further her scourge she did revisit for silver,
With the sole intent his home to pilfer.
Against the remorseless she-devil, a haggard crone,
The doughty brewer did protect his home.
But his courageous stance was all for naught,
Though for wife and household, the battle he fought,

Too bad for the [k]night, his ended in a brutal death.
And all in the space of a breath ... all in the space of a breath!
Alas, a lass.

Ridiculous nonsense and terrible even as verse. As the Rogue she must discourage these mistakes and assumptions, in her column, while still keeping her Avengeress self separate. It was a fine-edged balancing act, the continuous battle in her mind for supremacy; was she most the Rogue offering a varied diet of gossip, bald truth, titillation, scandal, and radical politics, or most the Avengeress, rescuing women and children? Which would gain ascendancy, or could she keep them in balance?

Still, she had a unique advantage. No other writer, nor magistrate, could know with certainty that the masked female who took Molly did not kill the knight. While it may indeed have been chance that Sir Henry's life was taken that night, it seemed all too possible that his killer had known of the incident earlier in the evening.

Though they had much wrong, even the doggerel got a few facts correct. Emmeline *had* entered by a door that was not locked tight, and she had taken the little scullery maid away with her. Who knew about the raid before and immediately after? The cook and housekeeper knew ahead of time, but a household of that quality would have other maids, a potboy, and perhaps a footman. Other servants in the home *could* have known as it happened, as would anyone watching the house. Sir Henry may have told his wife.

And ... Emmeline's heart thudded. Her group knew of her plans. In fact, one of them had relayed the message from the Claybourne house that Molly needed rescuing, and received the message that suggested the date and time. She wasn't sure who, since she had missed the meeting where Molly's rescue was first discussed.

She went back to the doggerel verse; something had bothered her about it, sticking in her mind and irritating. She read through it again, and *there* was the offending word. She was labeled a haggard *crone*? How offensive!

"Miss Emmeline," Gillies murmured outside her door, scratching on it. Her voice was muted by the solid wood between them. "May I speak wi' you?"

"Come," Emmeline said.

Her maid entered and began to tidy even as she spoke. "I'm troubled, miss, sorely. I canna put out of my mind the danger you're in." She gathered Emmeline's shawl, which was draped over the dressing table chair, and folded it neatly, putting it back on the chair.

"I'll be wary, Gillies. I have no wish to be blamed for this murder."

Gillies took the stack of broadsheets off the bed and piled them together. But she paused and read the first few stanzas of the doggerel, mouthing the occasional word as she came to it. "What a lot of havering! Why do writers blather on so with such nonsense?" She glanced at her mistress and added, "Begging you pardon, miss."

"Anything to sell a broadsheet for a penny. As long as the public likes verse, scribblers will keep producing it." Emmeline shrugged. "I *am* sorely offended to be called a crone, though."

"Why?" The maid straightened and set the stack of sheets down.

Emmeline eyed her lined and weary face. "How could I not be offended? A crone is a *witch*!"

Gillies shook her head. "Miss Emmeline, no! A crone is a wise woman, a defender, the woman people go to when they have troubles. Where I come from, every village has a crone. While the kirk dislikes it, it's nonetheless true. If you have troubles with your husband, or are worried for the future, you visit the crone. For a penny, she'll soothe your worries and give you a potion to make you right. 'Tis only in silly fairy tales that such an honored lady be a fearful hag."

Emmeline pushed the blankets down and sat up, hugging her knees. "I suppose I picture them like the witches in *Macbeth*, stirring a cauldron and chuckling hideously."

"*Macbeth*, miss? I've haird of it, but know nothing more."

"One of Shakespeare's tragedies, set in Scotland. You'd enjoy it, as it's very dramatic and hideously spooky."

Her maid was not much of a reader, but she did enjoy plays and so accompanied the ladies every theater evening, whenever there was room in the box. Gillies was an invaluable aid to Fidelity's comfort and useful to Emmeline, too, as she could fetch, carry, and most importantly listen in on conversations. Most theater patrons did not notice a servant, and the Rogue needed constant sources of information.

"We will attend the next time it is being put on," Emmeline continued. "It features three weird, or 'weyward,' sisters."

"Aye, but miss, those *are* witches, not crones," Gillies said, trimming the candlewick. "Witches are evil; crones help folk."

Crones help folk. As Gillies exited and softly closed the door, Emmeline turned on her side and closed her eyes. Maybe she was a crone after all. Maybe all her friends were crones. And in any case, who was it who said witches were evil? Men, of course, who held the law in their closed fists, wielding it like an iron rod to keep women and children quiescent. Not all men, of course; only the wealthy and titled. Poor men suffered as much as their women. One had only to look in the gaols and prison hulks, workhouses and sponging houses to see that.

But still ... every man, even the poorest, had rule over his women and children. Men could take up the law or the church, study to become surgeons, enter the military. Women were limited in what they could do to whatever their menfolk would allow. While men studied the healing arts with the approval of the church, women had been stoned for a millennia for brewing healing potions and doing their best to soothe the ill and troubled.

Her thoughts were full of questions, unfortunately none with answers, and all seemed a way to avoid the troubled vision she had in her mind of Sir Henry, slaughtered like a hog.

All the long night, Emmeline was haunted by her last view of Sir Henry, scrabbling at the buttons, trying to do up the fall of his trousers, his vast belly dangling, concealing his shrunken penis, his face twisted and mottled with red. As she'd backed away, then turned and fled, she'd heard him roaring that he would find out who she was and retaliate. He knew people, he said. She would pay.

When she did sleep, it was to be tormented by dreams. She was creeping from Sir Henry's house, but this time she knew there was someone in the shadows watching with evil intent, and yet she had no way of stopping him. A dark shadow loomed. A menacing presence crept close to her, so close she could hear him breathe. Then she would awaken shaking, and with her heart pounding.

The whole night was like that: tossing, turning, wound in her bedsheets until she could not breathe, then an abrupt awakening. She'd spent a few hours reading over the broadsheets; the awful crime was vivid in her imagination. While her writing as the Rogue was most often upon scandal and gossip, salacious rumor, and the pomposity of the peers and gentry who ruled their nation, she could not summon the wit to write such a piece. Simeon had invited her to write on the murder, so she penned something different from her usual Rogue-ish column, hoping Simeon would see fit to print it. It was of vital importance to establish the Rogue as a gentleman shocked by the knight's behavior, but also shocked that someone would take the law into his or her own hands. It would serve, too, to perhaps emphasize the separation between the Rogue and the Avengeress.

Emmeline then returned to bed and fell into another restless hour of slumber. She awoke to brittle autumn sunshine streaming in the window, and Gillies bringing in her tray with tea and toast. Two newspapers, *The Prattler* and *The Standard*, were pressed and folded neatly on the tray. *The Prattler*'s headline demanded, *Is NO Householder Safe?* and took the tack that Sir Henry must have gone out to the convenience or to smoke a cigar and was attacked by riffraff looking for an easy mark, perhaps the two assailants who had beaten the watch. Bless Simeon's heart for trying to protect her, but it seemed terribly naïve to publish such a story, ignoring what was already out there about a masked female and absconding scullery maid. He must publish what he normally would.

The Standard was direct. Beyond a shocking headline, the story had more information, but could she trust it? It would seem, from the quotes included, that the cook, housekeeper, and Sir Henry's wife had all been interviewed. But it was unlikely that a writer would have been allowed access to them, and that they would have answered so many questions. The household could be in tumult, with the master slain so viciously, but would Lady Claybourne not be shielded from such rabble as a writer for a newspaper, no matter how much an arm of the ruling class the journal was? The more likely source was the writers' imagination or secondhand information.

It struck Emmeline how little she knew about Sir Henry aside from his horrible partiality for girl children. She knew nothing of his family except that he had a wife. Would this loss doom the lady to a life of penury, or was it a sweet release? While he was nominally the head of the household, Sir Henry's wife would have had the day-to-day duty of running it, and so *must* have known her husband's horrible inclinations for abusing girls. Perhaps she hadn't cared, as long as the servants did their job.

Emmeline longed to investigate, knock on doors, ask questions, but the danger to her was terrifyingly real. Both as the Rogue and the Avengeress she was going to be suspected of the horrible crime, damned by her own crusading self.

She arose, donned her ivory lace-trimmed night-rail, and went directly to the small writing desk near the bow window in her room. She scribbled notes to the ladies of her group asking that they meet. She had questions that must be answered.

After she'd sanded, dried and folded them, Emmeline stacked them neatly to be hand-delivered by Josephs, along with her Rogue column, which was addressed to Miss S. Kinsman—the name she used to send Simeon her pieces—in a refined part of the city. The address was that of a gentile friend of Simeon's, the fictitious young lady "S. Kinsman," supposedly an invalid in the household; any mail addressed so would be passed on to him. Given Birk's spying, every step she took even in her own home must be covert and carefully considered. It was exhausting.

She sighed wearily and stretched her body, readying it for the womanly confines of the day, the stays that would give her a rectitude of figure if not of behavior. She must discover the truth of the matter and report what she could to her readers. Once more, the knife's edge ballet she performed commenced, as she kept up a semblance of upright feminine morality while her mind and heart delved into the evil that men—and women—did.

Gillies helped her into a sprigged burgundy day dress. Emmeline then sat at her dressing table. Gillies undid her nighttime braid and started taming her hair, brushing it back into a knot and coiling curls to frame her oval face.

"I must speak to the others," Emmeline murmured. "I was not at the meeting where rescuing the child was first discussed and so am uncertain which one brought her to our attention." At the time it hadn't seemed important. All that had mattered to her was the information, the plan, the rescue. She trusted them all; perhaps that was her mistake.

"Does it matter, miss?"

"I *must* find out how they heard about Molly, and who, in the household, was their contact." One thing was certain, Emmeline thought as she let Gillies perform her magic; she must impress upon them all the need for absolute secrecy. "Gillies, do you perchance know anyone in service near Sir Henry Claybourne's Clerkenwell home?"

Her maid ducked her head around to look her employer in the eyes, a worried expression on her lined face. "Why d'you ask?"

"There is so much I want to know and I don't know how to find out. The housekeeper or cook: which one of them summoned help for Molly? How long have they been employed at the Claybourne home? Did the *Standard* journalist actually speak with Lady Clay-bourne, or is there someone else in the household giving, or more likely selling, information to the newspapers? We well know the value of paid belowstairs informants."

Gillies squinted, pursed her lips, and then went back to her task. "You're not going to try to find out who murdered that filthy beast, are you?" she said, jabbing a pin in to keep a curl in place. "I'd say the good Lord had a hand in it. Sir Henry straight desairved what he got, miss, and I'd let well alone."

Emmeline sympathized with Gillies's viewpoint. However..."It disturbs me how brutal the murder was. I fear that whomever killed him may kill again. It would help if I knew *why* he was killed, what else in his life may have led to his death. Or was it a crime of opportunity, as Simeon has suggested in *The Prattler* this morning?" She paused. "I need to know if any of our friends are in danger."

"Miss?"

She brooded for a long moment, then glanced up at her maid's reflection. "It almost feels like the killer knew I was going there that night to rescue Molly, and that the murder was planned with that in mind."

Gillies, her pouchy face drawn and haggard as if she, too, had had a restless night, her hands on Emmeline's shoulders, nodded. "T'would take a brutal hand to do such a deed, even to one such as he. It couldnae be chance, surely, that meted out his airthly punishment on the same day you entered that house."

Emmeline met Gillies's gaze in the mirror. "It's a dangerous game I've played, speaking of Sir Henry in my article written as the Rogue, and then going after him for Molly's sake." She hoped she had not left a trail that would lead from the Rogue to her ladies' group, and thence to her.

"P'raps I do know someone nearby."

"Who?"

"A chandler, miss, on Samuel Street; that backs on the same alleyway."

Emmeline took a deep breath as Gillies settled a bonnet on her head and fastened it. She eyed herself in the mirror, chestnut brown hair beautifully curled and in clusters on each side of her head, chip straw bonnet trimmed in gold silk ribbon perched jauntily, framing a face neither beautiful nor ugly but somewhere in between, with a long straight nose and intelligent gray eyes. She nodded at her reflection. "Do naught right now until we know more. I don't wish you to endanger yourself."

"I would do anything to help you, miss." Gillies finished the outfit with a small dab of precious Houbigant perfume on Emmeline's neck. "I owe you more than I can ever repay."

Emmeline turned away from the mirror and took her maid's hand, staring up into her pale blue eyes, the faded freckles beneath them spattered across a creased and wise face, that of a fellow crone. "Gillies, whatever you may have owed me, if you indeed ever did, you repaid long ago. You are one of the very few people I trust *completely*," she said, squeezing her hand. "And you know I do not say that idly, given what I have experienced."

"You're a rare person, miss. Rare and fine." The maid, tears in her eyes, turned away and busied herself with gathering what Emmeline would need for the day.

Emmeline shook her head. If only she was half as good as her maid thought her.

October 26th, 1810, Evening Edition of *The Prattler*
By: The Rogue
Who Killed the Knight?

And so the Notorious Abuser of female children your Rogue spoke of four days ago is dead, Slaughtered, the Fishmonger's lad states, like an overfed Hog. Does that give your Wayward Rogue pleasure? Aye, for the Loathsome Knight will never force sexual congress on another serving Lass again, as Whispers and Rumors (the Offspring of Mother Gossip) said he had for many a year. He has paid in Blood for his crime, though Hangman's Noose would never have been secured around his neck, such is the terrible lack of value our Nation has for its poor children of either sex.

Should the Knight not have paid on this earth for his Crimes? Your Rogue challenges ye Britons of good conscience; how can we call ourselves a Civilized Nation when such as that dark-hearted Knight are allowed to exist unchallenged?

However, there *is* a Law to take such as him to task, but who will prosecute the laws of our nation when it concerns an Impoverished Waif? It leaves your Roguish Correspondent to wonder, did one of us decide to take the Law into his own hands and fulfill a Deadly Sentence? Someone in his circle must have known his habits. Perhaps that is the natural End to our collective Failure that one of us executed the man our Royal Sovereign saw fit to elevate to Knighthood.

Your Roving Rogue vows to find the truth.

....

FIVE

FIDELITY WAS UNWELL AND so stayed abed while Emmeline consulted with Mrs. Bramage, the St. Germaine housekeeper, concerning meals for the next couple of days, then visited their local stationer to complain about the quality of the quills. They frequently split, which was dreadfully inconvenient to someone who wrote as many "letters" (Rogue articles) as she.

The stationer, a Chelsea shop tucked in between a baker and a tailor, was small and crowded, smelling deliciously of ink and paper. Three customers departed, and Emmeline waited to be served behind two ladies making purchases. They were discussing the scandal in all the papers, Sir Henry Claybourne's brutal murder.

"I have heard that Sir Henry was nobly protecting the little girl in his employ," one said. She was a lady in her middle twenties, Emmeline estimated, fashionably but not frivolously dressed in a mustard-yellow pelisse trimmed in fox. She wore a chip straw bonnet with yellow silk ribbon trim over her rich auburn hair.

"*Protecting* her?" the other, an older woman gowned in a drab style of five years before and likely either a poor relation or companion, murmured deferentially, yet with doubt in her tone. "Perhaps not protecting her, but—"

"*I* believe that the dreadful female who invaded the house threatened to cut him and stole the child away for whatever nefarious unnatural purposes of her own!" Then the young woman leaned toward her companion and hissed, "Brothel!" Her abundant curls swung free from her bonnet in indignation and utter bliss, the opiate of gossip coursing through her veins.

Emmeline drew her breath in swiftly and held it. So *that's* what people thought? It was worse than she had even suspected if the Avengeress was reported to be in league with panderers. And yet she knew how gossip worked; it built, like steam in a kettle, until it poured forth in a hot stream of nothingness that evaporated once it hit the cold air. It did on occasion leave a scald, though, damage that took time to heal.

The older woman hesitated, watching the other, and then said, "Do you believe the cloaked lady came back and slaughtered Sir Henry?"

"I think it likely, indeed!" As the clerk disappeared into the back room to wrap her order, the younger woman glanced around and met Emmeline's eyes, but let her gaze slip away. "Perhaps he recognized her and she feared being revealed. I find it highly suspicious that the Rogue, that titillating columnist for *The Prattler*, knew so much about what the woman invader would do as retribution for some imagined slight on the serving girl. I wonder what their relationship is? Could they be lovers, do you suppose?" She tittered behind her gloved hand and the older woman dutifully joined her in mirth. "A bawd and her bully?"

The clerk came back with the package of quills and a sheaf of paper. The older of the two took the package into her market basket

46

and they departed. Emmeline, still reeling from what she heard, was attended by the clerk, a tall fellow she had dealt with in the past. She made her complaint about the quills splitting.

"Perhaps you place too much pressure on the quill, Miss St. Germaine," he said, looking down his long thin nose, collars stiffly framing his narrow face, his skinny neck wrapped in a voluminous cravat tucked into a frilled shirt and canary waistcoat. "Not to criticize, of *course!*"

"Of *course*," she said, anger building. He was the essence of politeness in manner but there was a faint sneer, an underlying implication that she must be unladylike to exert so much pressure. Where once she would have meekly agreed and gone away, she would no longer put up with inferior treatment. "I think 'tis not the writer who is in the wrong, but the quills," she rejoined tartly. "Your supplier is cheating you, and you are cheating me. They have not been dutched properly," she added, referring to the repeated heat-treating required to produce sturdy quills. He was reluctant, but she knew more about quills than he did, and in the end she came away with a package of replacements that she hoped would be better quality, or she would need to change stationers.

More significantly, she came away with a sense of how the public viewed the murder of the knight. It was a dangerous turn of events, the gossip bandied about by the young lady. It was perilous for the Rogue and the Avengeress to be coupled in the common view. The Rogue had stirred the gentle world with anger, it seemed, by presuming to care about the safety and treatment of scullery maids.

Josephs had returned with replies from her group; all agreed to attend Lady Sherringdon's that afternoon. She knew nothing of how the crime happened, or why, or by whom the slaying was committed. But she deeply feared someone who knew of her mission that night had whispered it to the murderer, making her a handy scapegoat. It was a matter of self-preservation to discover the truth, if that was even possible.

What she feared most was that one of them knew more than she was revealing. Her group was a unique assembly of ladies who all had one thing in common; the male half of creation had been unkind—in some cases criminally so—to them. Had one of them planned Sir Henry's execution? It should have been unthinkable, but it wasn't. She knew from experience that murder could seem a rational alternative when life became unthinkably heartbreaking.

She had considered the possibility that one of their group was involved somehow. Emmeline didn't truly know them well enough to decide if she could discount the idea completely. She had been close to Lady Adelaide Sherringdon for years, and Miss Juliette Espanson was the daughter of family friends, but some of the others were new acquaintances, women who had, in some cases, lost every bit of safety and privacy they had ever known. A year before, Emmeline had had a conversation with Lady Sherringdon concerning young Lady Clara Langdon.

"I'm worried for her ... *deeply* worried," Lady Sherringdon had said. Clara was Adelaide's niece by marriage, the daughter of her late husband's sister.

"I know she has been through difficult times, but she appears, the two times I have met her, to be self-possessed, cool, calm, and intelligent," Emmeline had replied. "I was thinking how admirably she holds herself, unlike most young ladies her age."

Lady Clara Langdon had returned to England from her family's plantation in Jamaica. Though Emmeline was not in possession of all the details, she knew that the young lady had suffered a crime against her person at the hands of a man, another plantation owner.

"She is *very* self-possessed, and—to my mind, at least—overly calm. Perhaps that is my worry," Adelaide said. "I would not expect someone who has been abused as she was to be so composed. She *should* be falling to pieces." Her breath caught in her throat on a sob. "But instead she is as cheerful as a ewe lamb."

"So you are concerned because she is handling too well the abuse that was meted out to her?" Emmeline asked. "Lady Adelaide, are you not judging her based on your own reactions? Perhaps she doesn't feel things as deeply as you."

The woman appeared troubled, the wrinkles around her eyes deepening to seams. "Or perhaps she feels them even deeper. She is as brittle as plate glass. *And* afraid of men to this moment; I have seen her flinch when a gentleman so much as smiles her way."

That gave Emmeline pause. When had women learned to be wary of men, to fear the stranger, yes, but even more to fear the familiar? And would it always be thus? Emmeline had agreed to issue the invitation for Clara to join their group and had never broached the subject with Lady Sherringdon again, nor had she attempted to push into Clara's private affairs. The lady had lost enough without losing the privacy of her mind and heart. Emmeline knew from bitter experience that there was no safe space but one's own thoughts, and even they failed one far too often.

But now she was hampered by not knowing enough of her acquaintances' intimate feelings. Had one of the ladies, either through an inability to restrain her gossipy instincts—Martha Adair came to mind—or through active malice betrayed the group?

That afternoon, Emmeline climbed alone into the St. Germaine carriage to go to Lady Adelaide Sherringdon's home. Fidelity was still too shattered by the events of the previous day to accompany her. As they traveled, Emmeline pondered; Lady Clara was the best example of how little she knew about some of her new acquaintances. That she could wonder if one was capable of murder should give her pause. Perhaps, in truth, she had kept them at arm's length because she had her own secrets to keep.

SIX

GILLIES RUSHED THROUGH HER duties—spot-cleaning a dress for stains and mending a tear in a shawl—and then informed Birk that her mistress wished her to do some errands in the city, among them to fetch thread to repair her favorite dress. If she left that moment, she might catch the post stage as it passed. She could have joined her mistress for the journey into town, but Miss Emmeline might forbid her plan, and Gillies was determined to help. The butler gave her a few more small tasks to perform while out, and then watched with squinted eyes as she donned her cloak and bustled out the door. She must do all her errands, for Birk would be sure to enquire when she came back. He was a gossipy old fart, that one.

It was a long ways to Clerkenwell, but Gillies was fortunate to take the post stage for a good part of the way. Once she was in the city, though, it was shanks' nag. She was used to walking miles; it gave her time to think. The knight's neighborhood in the daylight was no fearsome place. There were shops and tradespeople abundant. Lock-making and clock-making, printing and book-binding: all were represented along the main thoroughfares. And then there were the new townhouses, rows of them, each with their back alleys and squares. Gillies knew from a past evening of entertainment, when she had accompanied the Comtesse and Miss Emmeline, that they were quite close to Sadler's Wells Theatre, too.

But while the shop windows were enticing, none of this interested her today. Her mistress ofttimes made use of Gillies's connections to other servants and tradespeople to gather information for her writing. It was vital that she keep such information-gathering secret, so she had become creative in her quests for knowledge. It gave her a bit of a thrill knowing how much she helped Miss Emmeline gather gossip and secrets for the Rogue, but it was her mistress's work helping folk while disguised in a mask and cloak that she was more interested in.

The Brackenthorpes' chandler shop was on Samuel Street around the corner from Sir Henry's address on Blithestone, midway down a row of connected shops constructed of cheap brick, some with wood fronts and glazed bow windows. She made her way along the narrow walk, jostled by women carrying trays and lads pushing barrows. There were others, servants like herself, on errands too, and it was with another such as she that she entered the chandlery. She waited her turn until the other woman departed with her parcel of candles in her market basket. When the clerk finally turned to her, she said, "Is Tommy Jones working in the back? I have a message for him from a friend."

The clerk glared at her, eyeing her plain but serviceable cloak and maid's attire. He was new, not someone Gillies had seen at this establishment, a family-run business, before.

"That little street rat is gone," the fellow drawled, tugging at his cheaply made but smart-looking coat. "Lazy as the day is long. Wouldn't get up in the morn even when I kicked him."

Kicked him. That was his way of getting a child up from a too-brief sleep? Her heart ached for the lad, but she must not give voice to her ire. "Where did he go?" she asked. It was Gillies who had procured the boy this job after her mistress had rescued him from a brutal position as climbing boy, apprentice to a chimney sweep.

"Do you think I 'ave nothing better to do than foller a dirty little street arab to see where he went? He was turned away from here, that's all I care."

With his superior and offensive attitude, he was unlikely to tell her anything if she asked about the murder; a wasted trip, most likely. Gillies returned to the street outside, dodging a man carrying a barrel on his shoulder. Where was Tommy? Originally, she had wished to speak with him to discover if he knew what was going on in the late Sir Henry's household, but now she just hoped the boy was alive. Life on the streets was vicious and short for the young, the old, and the weak.

Next to the chandler's was a haberdasher, a narrow shop with a bow window in which hung a tempting display of lace and ribbons. *Hargreaves Haberdashery* was lettered in script on a sign that stuck out from the doorjamb. It was a newer shop on the street. She decided quickly; now was as good a time as any to find the thread to mend Miss Emmeline's favorite "at home" gown. Miss was hard on gowns, especially the elbows, as she planted them firmly on her desk when she was writing articles and letters. Gillies prided herself on making mends that didn't show.

She entered, a silvery chime of bells above her head announcing to the haberdasher her arrival. He looked up from his accounting ledger and rose, peering down his long hooked nose from his towering height. His gaze was assessing, but Gillies had no fear of what he would see. She was a respectable lady's maid, which surprised even her, given her previous life as a miner's wife in Scotland. Miss Emmeline had both saved her from destitution and given her a purpose. "Mr. Hargreaves, is it?"

"I am," he said, his tone haughty.

She saw through the superior act; he was just a Clerkenwell haberdasher who would provide second-rate buttons and ribbons to ladies trying desperately to ape their betters. "Do you happen to know a lad by the name of Tommy Jones? Wee scrap of a fellow, used to work for the Brackenthorpes?"

His lips curled. "I don't associate with *them*," he said, his tone becoming even haughtier. "Not since they've employed that … that *gentleman*. And I don't recognize the lad's name." His gaze strayed back to his ledger.

Gillies surveyed the shelves laden with cardboard boxes of buttons, a sample attached to the front of each, and skeins of ribbon and new machined lace, a cheap reproduction of Lille. "I would generally buy my mistress's threads at Wilding & Kent," she said, naming the superior London draper and haberdasher. "But as I'm here, I may save myself a trip."

He nodded regally, his attention sharpening with her expressed intent to buy. "Mr. Benjamin Hargreaves at your service. What thread are you looking for, Miss …?"

"Gillies," she said. "Just Gillies. Do you have green silk?"

"Of course!"

She found the exact shade of green she was looking for as they chatted about the neighborhood, which Hargreaves bent enough to admit was not as up-and-coming as he had hoped when he rented the shop and first floor apartment for himself and his sister, Miss Aloisia Hargreaves, several months before.

"Terrible business, that murder in the alley behind," Gillies said, eying him as she perused a tempting display of ribbons not of a high enough quality for Miss Emmeline but better than she could afford for herself.

"Shocking, but that fellow got what he deserved," Hargreaves said, his tone dark.

Gillies placed her hand over her heart, but then leaned across the oaken counter. "Why d'you say that, Mr. Hargreaves? The man was a respectable brewer, weren't he? Heard he was knighted?"

"Knighted! Sword should've 'it 'im a little harder, you ask me," the haberdasher said, his diction slipping as he got to the juicier gossip. "You want any of the peach ribbon? Would suit your coloring."

Perhaps ribbon was the price of gossip. "I'll have a yard o' the peach grosgrain. What was wrong wi' Sir Henry, as the broadsheets name him?"

The haberdasher took down the skein and picked up his long sheers, measuring the ribbon against the edge of the counter, where notches indicated length. "He was a foul fellow ... crude, grubby. *Not* a gentleman."

She was silent, watching him as he wound the ribbon and tied the length with string.

"As I said, Aloisia and I share the apartment above," he continued. "She takes in students to teach them French and sewing. That man gravely insulted her not two weeks ago as she was coming from the privy." Then his eyes widened and he put one long-fingered, well-kept hand over his mouth. Hastily he added, "Our, er ... *conveniences* are close enough to hail your neighbor across the alley, you see." His face pinked, the tip of his cleft nose turning red.

"What kind of gentleman would *do* such a thing, insult a lady?" Gillies leaned forward in the habitual stance of the born gossip and stared up into his eyes. "Did you see anything the night he were kilt right down in your own courtyard, almost? I haird he was set upon by a gang of robbers, *slaughtered* like a pig at the butcher!"

Mr. Hargreaves, a look of revulsion on his face, said, "Oh, no, that is not so at *all*! He was killed there, yes, but I'm sure there was no bloody slaughter." He bundled the thread and ribbon into a paper package and tied it with scrap of thin ribbon, making a bow with a flourish. "My sister's room overlooks the alley, but she saw *nothing* that night," he said firmly. "And as I told the magistrate's constable, I never did see the shocking woman thief who stole away the serving girl, but I *did* see men there later that evening, and witnessed Sir Henry quarreling with them."

Gillies trembled with excitement; this was information her mistress could use! Hargreaves must be the informant the magistrate found. "Quarreling? What was going on?"

He gave a moue of distaste and fluttered his hand. "There was one feller, but he went on his way right quick. There was two more, though. I couldn't hear much, but Sir Henry was proper in a turmoil about something, jawing with one while the other hung back." He paused as he handed the package to her. "He yelled an obscenity I won't repeat in front of a lady."

She had likely heard much worse, being raised by a father who thought nothing of letting loose a volley of obscenities and then backhanding his children when they dared talk back to him. "Perhaps they came back later and killed him?"

"P'raps," he said as he wrote out a receipt in a neat hand.

"Must've been so exciting to have all the broadsheet writers."

He looked up from his writing, ink dripping from the quill. "I wouldn't speak to such as them."

Something in the man's gaze suggested otherwise. "Maybe not you, then, but others must have. Didya not read the broadsheets?" With her eyes wide, Gillies added in a hushed tone, "Some of them writers said they spoke to Lady Claybourne, the poor lady. Did they no speak to you?"

"I chased them away."

"But you told the magistrate's men what you saw."

He nodded, his lips in a tight line.

She examined his face. "I'd be terrified to live here, with such a beast roamin' an' killin' folk." She gave a theatrical, exaggerated shiver. "Are you not frightened?"

"I'd wager whoever killed Sir Henry came *only* for him. He was a *dreadful* man and deserved what he got." There was a finality to the haberdasher's words.

He would not be drawn, after that, simply shaking his head. Gillies was, however, not convinced that his sister, whose room, he said, overlooked the back courtyard, had seen and heard nothing. She carefully counted out and then handed the haberdasher the money. "Your sister gives lessons in sewing, you said. Could I see her work? I may know someone who could lairn a thing or two about fancy stitching."

He brightened and reached under the counter. "Of course! She does up the clocks on gentlemen's stockings for certain customers as likes a bit of fancy handwork. See how neat her sewing is!"

Gillies gazed at the embroidery on the man's gray silk knitted stocking, a flourish of neat, flat satin stitches in a stylized fleur-de-lis at the top of a cream gusset. "What might be her direction, Mr. Hargreaves?"

"A note will find her here. She takes girls every day but Sunday. You will see a blue door to the left of my shop; her name and mine indicate our rooms upstairs."

"I'll see if the mother I know will have Miss Hargreaves teach her girls. Now, about Sir Henry," she said, trying to elicit more information. "Maybe someone in the household killed him if he is as nasty as you say?"

The haberdasher hid a quick smile, plastering a pious look on his face instead, hand over his heart. "God rest his soul. I may have thought him foul, but I have heard his wife is *dev*astated by his death."

"Oh?"

"After all, who will run the brewery now?"

He had nothing more to say. Gillies left the shop and headed around the corner onto Chandler Lane. As she strolled past the alley, glancing down it, she saw the haberdasher come out his back door and stare at the townhome courtyard behind his shop. She stepped back, concealing herself along the brick entrance to the alley, not wanting to be seen, then took a chance and peeped again. Hargreaves stared a moment longer, with what appeared to be an uncertain expression, looked up at his own building, then returned to his shop through the back door.

Gillies, perturbed by the curiousness of Hargreaves staring at the back of what she assumed must be the Claybourne residence in so distracted a manner, walked on and turned down Blithestone, basket over her arm, just another servant on a street busy with them. In front of the Claybourne residence she paused and dug in her basket while covertly examining the townhouse.

It was one of a row of newer modest townhomes, narrow and constructed of yellow brick above whitewashed stone, leased by the up-and-coming tradespeople of London. Opposite it was a small green park bounded by a black wrought iron fence and a locked gate, likely for the use of the Blithestone residents. Sir Henry's house would not have suited him for much longer if his brewery was doing as well as might be expected. Gillies didn't understand what the man had done to be knighted, but it ofttimes didn't take much beyond saying something kindly about the king. Poor dotty ducky; with the state of the old king's head—and whatever one could say about him, he was better, even mad, than his spendthrift son—it may not have taken much beyond a speech of support for the royal family.

On the pavement opposite the townhome was a fellow lingering near a lamppost. He was sulky-looking, his dark gaze now settling on Gillies. His eyes, even at a distance, glittered with inquisitiveness. He was about to start across the street but stopped suddenly.

A woman came out the front door of number seventy-three and glared at Gillies as she set a girl to work scrubbing the front doorstep. Housekeeper by the looks of her, Gillies thought, with a leap in her bosom. She was hard-featured, bitter-mouthed, her face deeply lined and her hair iron gray under her starched white cap.

"Pardon me, madam, but do you know th'time?" Gillies asked, holding her basket close to her body.

The woman consulted a pocket watch on her silver chatelaine, then snapped it shut. "A quarter of two."

"Thank you," Gillies said, curtseying. "I couldn't bother you for a sip of something to drink, could I?"

"No. Now get on wiv you." She kicked the child lightly and said to her, shaking her finger, "Mind, you get all them stains if you're to stay on 'ere." She glared at Gillies, then across the street at the skulking man—who suddenly started off, whistling a tune that carried all the way to them—then down at the child again. "And no talkin' while you're to be workin', or you'll get a beatin'."

Gillies walked back the way she had come, knowing there would be no prying information from the child. As far as what the housekeeper had said about a beating, she'd heard worse. Even in the St. Germaine home, Cook ofttimes threatened the potboy with having his ears boxed, though she had never yet carried out the threat. It was a fact of life for working children. At least they had food and a warm place to sleep, and in the Claybourne house the new scullery maid would not now be raped by the master.

She turned and headed back along Chandler, pausing to look down the alley once more; her mistress had slunk down it just a few nights ago. Through the brick arch she could see that there were privy houses lining the bottom of the back gardens of the townhouses on one side. The merchant establishments along Samuel did not have enclosed brick courtyards, but they did have brick privies—small, cramped, and dark no doubt—attached to each shop with two doors along the back of each unit, one from the shop and one from the upstairs rooms. That was where Sir Henry had insulted Benjamin Hargreaves's sister, near the privy. But was that even possible? It seemed an unlikely tale to her.

And in any case, it was surely not a grave enough offence to inspire Mr. Hargreaves with murderous rage. Depended on what the insult was, she supposed, and the temperament of the man. With a sigh, Gillies turned into the stiffening breeze and headed back to Samuel Street, where she could hope to find a post carriage or cart to carry her toward Chelsea. All she had done was find one more suspect in Sir Henry's murder, and she had not spied Tommy Jones even once.

SEVEN

THE LADIES WERE GATHERED in Lady Adelaide's parlor and this time there were no strangers to strangle their talk. They were uncommonly silent, these five good ladies, and looked to Emmeline with an array of expressions. Their hostess was tense, her favorite cat, the one-eyed black tom, on her lap. She petted him ceaselessly, her pale gray dress becoming littered with dark hairs until he growled, lashed out at her, and leaped down. She looked startled but otherwise didn't remark, holding her handkerchief to her scraped hand as blood oozed, staining the purity of the linen. "Emmeline, why don't you tell us why you have summoned us here today?"

Emmeline gathered her thoughts as she glanced at each woman, their expressions as individual as they were. Martha Adair looked frightened, her friend Dorcas Harvey wary. Juliette Espanson was wide-eyed, Lady Clara bemused. Emmeline took a deep breath and said, "We were all together when first we learned of Sir Henry Claybourne's murder. As we all had agreed, I visited him to rescue his scullery maid, poor little Molly. But I also delivered to him a pointed warning that if he ever behaved thusly again, he would not be dealt with so kindly."

"Demmed right, too," Dorcas said, her cheeks red. Dorcas was in that most difficult of positions, a poor relation tethered as companion to a sickly and irritable aunt whom she seemed to never please. Both women tormented each other with badly fitting personalities. Dorcas had once been a schoolteacher, but for some reason she would not discuss had been let go. "Should have had his ballywoggles cut off!"

Martha Adair shot her friend an alarmed look. "Dorcas, *please*. Such vulgarity!"

An outcry against vulgarity in a meeting to discuss a man's murder seemed ridiculous to Emmeline, but Martha was sensitive to crudeness. The absurdity of Dorcas's made-up word almost made her want to giggle. If she were not speaking of murder, she would have. Instead, Emmeline maintained her stern look, and even Dorcas calmed.

"As much as I condemn murder," Emmeline continued, folding her hands together and clutching tightly, "I cannot say I'm sorry Sir Henry is dead."

"How can we be sure *you* had no hand in it?" Lady Clara asked, one elegant brow arched. She was gowned in gray-green silk the color of sage leaves, snow white silk gloves to the elbow and gleaming pearls woven through her elegant dark hair. "I would have at least considered exterminating the rodent, given your opportunity. You did have a knife ... *and* used it, you tell us."

"*Of course* I did not slaughter Sir Henry!" Emmeline exclaimed.

There was a collective whoosh of expelled breath, several relieved sighs all at once. Was it possible that these, her Crone compatriots as she had come to consider them, thought her capable of such a vile crime, even in the defense of a helpless child?

"It was just a thought," Lady Clara said, her tone and mien coolly amused. "I commend you on keeping your temper."

"Who was it who brought the girl's predicament to the group?" Emmeline asked.

Miss Juliette Espanson raised her hand. Red-haired, freckled, and uncommonly pretty, with sparkling blue eyes, the young lady appeared subdued. Her high spirits—not *too* high for fashion, of course, as giddiness was frowned upon—usually buoyed them all, but this day she was downcast. "I couldn't bear the thought of that poor child being abused by such a loathsome man. And trapped! With *no* recourse, no escape. It haunted me."

Juliette was engaged to wed a wealthy but much older man. She was desperately unhappy about it and the law was on her side; if she wished, she could say no. But to say no to the match would be to incur her father's wrath. As her guardian, he could send her to her grandparents in the extreme north of Ireland, where she claimed she would have no more companionship of any kind but for the villagers and sheep until she was middle-aged or acquiesced. She believed in providence and would be saved, she said, from her fate at the eleventh hour.

"We all agreed that Molly needed to be rescued," she concluded.

"How did *you* know about her?" Emmeline asked. "And how did you know about Sir Henry's despicable habits with his servants?"

Juliette turned, frowning, to her closest friend among them. "Clara, you told me, I think?"

Lady Clara nodded. "I was appalled when I heard about the poor child," she said, her cool, calm voice warmed slightly by anger and husky with subdued feeling. "And about Sir Henry's execrable behavior in the past. An open secret, apparently, among a certain circle of servants."

"And who told *you*?"

"Dorcas said something," Lady Clara said, turning to the companion. "Isn't that so?"

Emmeline turned to gaze at Dorcas, who appeared confused. "Where did *you* hear of Molly's plight?"

Dorcas, her full face still suffused with red, frowned. "Martha, you mentioned something, did you not? And I said to Lady Clara that we ought to do something?"

"Did I?" Martha asked.

"*Think*, Martha," Emmeline urged, watching her become flustered. "Where did you hear about Molly?"

Martha's eyes welled. "It wasn't Molly I heard of first, it was Sally, of course, poor little Sally!"

"Who is Sally?" Emmeline asked patiently. Martha was one of those women who would become forgetful if pressed too hard. She needed to be led slowly to revelation.

"Sally was the last scullery maid."

"In Sir Henry's household? Sally was the previous scullery maid in the Claybourne home," Emmeline said, trying to be clear.

Martha nodded. "I heard through my housekeeper's sister's daughter's employer—or was it my housekeeper's daughter's sister's employer? I can't recall which—that being a scullery maid in Sir Henry Claybourne's household was a terrible fate for any child. She said … she said the last girl—the one *before* Sally—ended up in one of those horrible bawdy houses. One run by … oh, what was her name?" Martha furrowed her brow. "Maud something-or-other. I remember because Maud rhymed with bawd." She pinkened and nodded.

"Your housekeeper's sister's daughter's employer."

Martha nodded. "Or my housekeeper's daughter's sister's employer."

Emmeline shook her head; that was too twisted a trail to follow right at that moment. "So what happened to Sally?"

"Oh, didn't I say?" Martha blinked. "I helped her."

"*You* helped her?"

Martha nodded. "I hired her away from there. Picked her up myself in our carriage."

Emmeline bit her lip to keep from crying out, took a deep breath, and then slowly said, "You mean that you have employed Sally all this time? That I could have asked her for information on Sir Henry?"

The woman appeared baffled, and then understanding filled her eyes. "I never thought … that is …" Martha's voice faded and tears welled.

Lady Sherringdon moved to a chair next to her and took her hand, patting it. "There, there, Martha, you did nothing wrong." Adelaide gave Emmeline a look.

Emmeline nodded and straightened. "Martha, it wouldn't have changed a thing. However, perhaps *now* Sally could tell me more about the household."

Lady Clara eyed her, still calm and cool though her restless hands moved, tugging at the fingers of her elegant silk gloves. "Why?"

Emmeline paused, trying to find the right words. Should she tell them it was, in some measure, because she was afraid? She had been there; it was possible the cook or housekeeper could identify her as the masked marauder, and thus a suspect in Sir Henry's murder. "Both the newspapers and the magistrate are looking to blame the Avengeress, as they have named me. It is a dangerous position to be in."

Emmeline eyed Lady Clara, who waited for her to say more, though the others whispered together. She in particular—so icy, so unhappy, so desperately alone in her life—was, by her own admission, capable of such an act. It rather staggered Emmeline to try to imagine a perfect lady like Clara slitting the knight throat to belly with a knife. However … it was possible.

"I want to know the truth," she finally said. Information was the only antidote she could think of to this poisonous suspicion, this distrust of women she cared about and who were important to her. She met each one's glance as she surveyed her group. They *were* crones; each one, in her own way, a woman who had achieved wisdom through pain and tribulation and now trying to use that wisdom to aid others. But had one betrayed the group? Emmeline's gaze returned to Lady Clara and fell to her gloved hands in her lap. One of the pristine white gloves was marred now by a spot of red near the wrist, bleeding through from some wound on the lady's hand.

Emmeline's breathing quickened. But no, surely her worst suspicions could not be true. Lady Clara, so cool, so elegant, so refined? There must be many who wanted so loathsome a human as Sir Henry dead, and perhaps it was her task to find out who did before that killer became judge and jury and murdered again.

EIGHT

"**THAT STILL DOES NOT** explain why you need to know about Sir Henry's household," Lady Clara said.

"Sir Henry was murdered mere hours after I threatened him. Is that a coincidence, or something more sinister? The focus of the magistrate and his men so far is on me, and also on the men Henry was seen arguing with, but given his behavior, the killer could be someone within his household."

Lady Sherringdon nodded. "Martha, if you don't mind, Miss St. Germaine can visit and ask Sally some questions. I'll see what I can find out from Molly, but it appears she was at Sir Henry's only briefly, as was Sally, from what you say. When can Miss St. Germaine visit you, Martha, to speak with Sally?"

"Tomorrow?"

"Fidelity and I will call on you, Mrs. Adair." Emmeline rose. "I shall be on my way. Lady Sherringdon, if I may speak with you before I take my leave?" She nodded to the others and swept out to the entry.

As her friend joined her, Emmeline put her gloved hand on the woman's arm. "What is wrong with Lady Clara? She appears to oppose my wish to investigate further who may have harmed Sir Henry."

Lady Sherringdon glanced back toward the drawing room. She motioned to her maid, who closed the door and toddled away. Turning to her younger friend, she said, "I can only think that the stress Clara is under is causing her great inner turmoil. The man who abused her is returning to London from the West Indies."

"Surely she won't be expected to socialize with him?"

"Few know what she suffered, which is how she wishes it to remain, else the stain of the abuse will be on her head despite what society says to the contrary. Once a woman loses her reputation or virtue, no matter how, it is gone forever," Adelaide said. "There *are* those who would sympathize, but Clara would *violently* eschew such pity. I don't believe she has told me everything, and I doubt she ever will. Without revealing all she has suffered, she knows there will be no avoiding him. I suspect he understands her all too well, her pride and resolution, and will use their past to taunt her. I don't know him, 'tis true, but I know something of his type."

"We must help her!" Emmeline felt a thread of sick worry in her stomach. To have to face your abuser but never know ... it was unthinkable.

"We'll do all we can."

"I must go. Josephs will be waiting the carriage."

"Emmeline ..."

She gazed back at her friend and waited. "What is it, Addy?" she finally asked, using the pet name she seldom allowed to slip.

"Be careful," Adelaide said, laying one hand on her arm. "Don't ask too many questions."

"I don't understand."

"Just...be careful." Lady Sherringdon gave her a brief, trembling hug, then returned to her other guests.

———

Gillies was silent as she pinned her mistress's hair into a more formal style for that evening's dinner party at the home of Sir Jacob Pauling, Emmeline's late mother's brother. She then wove a string of creamy pearls through the dark braids, which had been wound together, and finished with an ormolu and seed pearl comb to fix it all in place. With a final pat, she stepped back and eyed the result.

Emmeline examined herself in the mirror. The deep rose velvet of her gown was adorned with a lovely trim of gold thread that glinted in the candlelight. It flattered her coloring, giving her cheeks the pink of youth. It was a gown from last winter, but Gillies had altered it slightly. "Very good, Gillies. I'll have the fur-trimmed cape tonight. I anticipate a freezing fog."

"Miss, may I speak wi' you?"

"Of course, Gillies. What is it?" Emmeline turned from picking up her reticule.

Gillies stood, fiddling with a tortoise comb. She appeared to be marshaling her thoughts. "Miss, I took a bit of an excursion, ye ken, down to Clerkenwell. Thought I'd check up on Tommy."

"Yes?" The mention of Clerkenwell set Emmeline's nerves jangling. She suspected there was more to the jaunt than Gillies's desire to check on Tommy.

"Happen I wandered into the next shop to the chandler where Tommy last was, though he's no longer there an' that's another story. I stepped in to the haberdashery to get some thread to mend your green daydress and I talked to Mr. Benjamin Hargreaves, the haberdasher. The shop backs on the same alley, you ken."

"Yes, and…?"

"He and his sister, a Miss Aloisia Hargreaves, live above the shop in rooms. Sir Henry insulted the young lady once, by the privy, and Mr. Hargreaves was sore angry. He's the one who told the magistrate he saw the men arguing with Sir Henry. Says his sister didn't see a thing, yet it's her room that overlooks the courtyard. I think he's protecting his sister from comment. Thought that information might help, miss."

Emmeline stared down at her fan, smoothing the feathers. She couldn't deny that the information was valuable. She looked up. "Was he angry enough, do you think, to kill Sir Henry?"

Gillies shook her head. "I dinna think so, miss. But you never can tell."

Since the young lady took in students for embroidery and French, the maid suggested, perhaps that was a way to approach her covertly and speak to her about it. The brother and sister may not be telling all they saw.

"Mrs. Martha has two gairls about the right age for teaching, don't she?"

Emmeline smiled up at her maid. "True. You're a clever woman, my friend. I'm going to Martha's tomorrow and maybe I can speak to her. I could stand as the girls' honorary aunt and take them myself to see if Miss Hargreaves would suit as a French or embroidery tutor."

"Aye, *you* must do it, miss. You can't send Mrs. Adair," Gillies said. She had no high opinion of Martha's intelligence. "P'raps the missus don't need to know the real reason for your interest in her gairls' education?"

Emmeline considered. Martha would undoubtedly be puzzled by Emmeline's sudden concern for her children, since she had never shown any before, but the woman was an accepting soul and could easily be persuaded. Not telling Martha the truth was simply a wise and logical choice, given her friend's inability to restrain her tendency to chatter.

"I'll send a note to this Miss Hargreaves tomorrow and ask Martha to let me take the girls to inquire about tutoring. Will you accompany me to Mrs. Adair's? I wish to ask her maid, Sally, about her life in Sir Henry's household, but she may speak to you more freely than to me."

That decided, Gillies gave a rare half-smile. "Aye. Nouw...on wi' you, miss. Enjoy dinner at Sir Jacob's."

"Check on Fidelity if you would, Gillies, before I descend."

"She's ready to set oot, miss."

Emmeline was looking forward to dinner with her uncle at his St. James townhome on a quiet street off of Jermyn. With inherited wealth beyond that of many in his position as a judge, Sir Jacob could afford such an exclusive address, one of several townhomes that enclosed a private courtyard. He enjoyed the district because it was close to the theaters, and he dearly loved theatricals, music, and every kind of entertainment. It was also close to his gentleman's club and all of the amenities it offered.

He was one of Fidelity's favorite people as well, since with him she could reminisce about her childhood, a golden time of joy in a life marked by suffering. Sir Jacob was one of the few living family members old enough to remember the blissful and innocent days of their youth, Fidelity often said, when he was a dashing Oxford student studying law and she the carefree little cousin whom he teased and petted, plying her with sugarplums and snatching all the best treats for her while playing Snapdragon. He had continued his affectionate treatment of her when she'd returned from France after being widowed, and Emmeline was grateful to him. Her companion had few joys in life; Sir Jacob was principal among them.

It was a small dinner party, twelve altogether. Sir Jacob had invited a few of his colleagues, three judges from the courts: Lord Quisenberry, Mr. Yarbrough, and their wives, as well as Mr. Fulmer and his betrothed, a Miss Purley. There were also Emmeline; Fidelity; Dr. Giles Woodforde, a family friend who had gone to college with Emmeline's second-oldest brother, Samuel; and a Mr. William Wilkins, Solicitor—Sir Jacob's man of business—with his betrothed, the lovely blonde daughter of a wealthy German brewer, Miss Gottschalk.

They gathered in the drawing room. It was spacious, with moss-green walls above white paneling and tall windows draped in gold velvet, and furnished with settees and chairs upholstered in a soft green brocade that complemented the décor. A portrait of Sir Jacob's parents—Emmeline's maternal grandparents, who had passed years before—adorned the space over the marble mantel, but the other paintings were landscapes by William Marlow, whom Sir Jacob considered vastly underrated. As her uncle was not married, Emmeline acted as his hostess, greeting guests once he had introduced her to his colleagues and their wives, and following the procession to the dining table last, on the arm of her uncle's colleague Lord Quisenberry. They dined in the modern fashion, ladies and gentlemen evenly spaced around the table with her uncle at the foot and she at the head, with his lordship on her right. Vernon, the butler, along with two housemaids—pert, pretty girls—served. The ladies were, of course, served first, helped by the gentlemen on their right.

Sir Jacob, a jovial and humorous gentleman whose wealth came from his parents but whose knighthood came from his work in the legal profession, looked around his table with satisfaction. "Now this is what I call a congenial gathering," he said heartily, raising his glass of Madeira. His full cheeks were suffused with red, his pale eyes glittering with good humor. "Welcome to you all, I say, and thank you to my lovely niece, Emmeline, for once more serving as my hostess, as I seem constitutionally unable to attract a wife."

There was polite laughter at his sally. Sir Jacob was a perennial bachelor, most fond of the company of other men. As Emmeline despised being chided on her own unmarried state, she had never delved into her uncle's reasons for remaining single. It was enough, she had always thought, that he was happy; if he had had a private heartbreak in his past (which she suspected was the case), she would not pry.

After that welcoming toast, conversation around the table became disjointed. Gentlemen engaged the ladies on either side of them, as was the custom. But during the fish course, as Lord Quisenberry applied himself to the dish of oysters in wine and cream sauce, Emmeline's attention was claimed by the lawyer Mr. Wilkins's loud voice as he disputed some point her uncle was making.

"Sir Jacob, I must protest. For some of us, being a landlord of the tenement houses and rookeries is the only way to turn a penny! And we *must* make the lower classes pay, allowing no excuses, else we should be giving away space like some charity workhouse! Not fair at all to those of us who strive and work hard to build a better life for our families."

His betrothed, Miss Gottschalk, watched solemnly but did not comment. Emmeline eyed her uncle, who appeared gravely disturbed by his man of business's protestations.

When no one commented, she decided to speak. "Do you think, sir, that those who work on the docks and on fishing boats, in the mines and the mills, even on the mudflats of the Thames, don't toil?" Her clear voice cut through the chatter. All turned to look at her.

Mr. Wilkins's gaze swiveled too. "I'm saying nothing of the kind, Miss St. Germaine," he said, his tone biting. "I merely say why should we not, as landlords, be paid too? *They* are receiving a wage, are they not? It is up to *them* to budget their money and not throw it away on gin. They must meet their obligations as I must meet mine." He turned back to stare at her uncle, his thick eyebrows raised. "Not all of us can afford to make so much from the canal enterprise, sir. *Some* of us must invest in economical ventures where we can."

"Mr. Wilkins, I did not say to let them live free, I was simply suggesting that you are charging excessive rent on your St. Giles building, and that perhaps you should consider lowering it," said Emmeline's uncle, his tone impatient, taking his niece in with a glance. "And now we should leave this business talk for a more suitable time. We're boring the ladies."

She understood his message. This was not fitting dinner table conversation. She smiled and nodded, then turned toward the lawyer's betrothed, who sat between Lord Quisenberry and Mr. Yarbrough. "Miss Gottschalk, how are you finding our autumn weather in London?"

With the conversation successfully diverted—Fidelity ably assisted with talk of the opera season and a new play being mounted in Covent Garden—the rest of the meal passed uneventfully.

NINE

EMMELINE LED THE LADIES back to the drawing room for tea and gossip as the gentlemen remained behind for port and politics. The drawing room conversation idled on, becoming desultory. Lady Quisenberry was only interested in the latest fashion in hats; she wore a turban with what Emmeline suspected was a false front of auburn curls. Miss Gottschalk appeared to be bored by them all, and Mrs. Yarbrough, a plump motherly woman with deep-set eyes, only wanted to speak of her children. With such dissonance in conversational topics, Emmeline left Fidelity to hold a disjointed conversation between Lady Quisenberry and Mrs. Yarbrough while she, in turn, tried to draw out Miss Gottschalk and Miss Purley, Mr. Fulmer's betrothed.

After a labored few minutes, Miss Purley, a petite brunette with exquisite taste and figure, both of which were displayed by her gold-trimmed burgundy lace gown, concealed a quick smile and looked down at her hands, fiddling with her fan.

"I said something to amuse, Miss Purley?" Emmeline asked.

"Pardon me," she said, her mellow, musical voice pitched for Emmeline to hear. "I am merely admiring your ability to labor on in the face of a discordant group where no common topic of interest to all is available to you. I hope I can emulate your commendable skill when Mr. Fulmer and I wed."

Miss Gottschalk drifted away from them and sat down at the pianoforte, leafing through the sheet music. Emmeline relaxed enough to smile. "I had hoped the effort was not noticeable."

"It is only evident to admiring eyes like mine!" the young lady said.

They chatted easily from there, and Emmeline discovered that the young lady, born in India while her father was stationed there with the East India Company, had only moved to England with her family a year before. She'd had a belated presentation to society at the advanced age of twenty-two, and as a result felt out of step with the other ladies presented during the Season. Emmeline sympathized with her, finding her warmer and more gracious than the cool and distant Miss Gottschalk.

"But you found Mr. Fulmer—or he found you," Emmeline said. "You were a success." As judged by society.

The young lady nodded. "So everyone tells me when they congratulate me."

There was a hint of discontent in her tone, and it interested Emmeline. She longed to ask the young lady why she was hesitant to proclaim satisfaction in being a betrothed young lady in a society which valued her more now that she had achieved the goal of every sensible female. But she didn't know Miss Purley's temperament, nor did she know Mr. Fulmer well enough to understand if his betrothed's dissatisfaction was occasioned by the state of marriage or by the man in particular.

The gentlemen joined them and Miss Purley was claimed by her stout and hearty fiancé. Miss Gottschalk, still seated at the piano, was solicited for music by *her* betrothed, Mr. Wilkins, who stumped over gracelessly, with an awkward gait. He hung over her shoulder, leaning heavily on his walking stick—an ornate piece from its carved ebony slave's head to the silver band near the base—as he turned her music, a favor she did not appear to require or appreciate.

Dr. Giles Woodforde, who was also using a walking stick that evening, though it was not usual for him, limped over and took the seat next to Emmeline—the one abandoned by Miss Purley, who had joined Miss Gottschalk at the piano since she had been implored by her betrothed to sing. He set aside his walking stick, a plainer piece than the solicitor's with merely a silver head and a plain cap on the end. "Shall we hear *your* fine voice this evening, Miss St. Germaine?" he asked. He was an old friend, and so could tease her with impunity.

"There is no song in the key of a croaking raven, or I would be eager to display my talents to the group."

"Come now, you underrate yourself," Dr. Woodforde said with a sly glance. "I have heard you many a time in congenial gatherings and your voice is certainly not raven-like. It is not a pigeon's throaty coo, true, but somewhere in between."

"Thank you for your confidence in my ability to not offend with my tragically unmusical voice. But I am not *that* raven, Aesop's infamous bird, to drop the cheese at the slightest flattery."

"Miss St. Germaine, I know we jest, but I would not let you think I believe your voice anything less than pleasant." His voice was warm, his breath on her cheek warm and scented with cinnamon. "You do not force your singing voice into what is thought of as a feminine warble, that's all. I like that no part of you is a sham, not even your vocal performance."

Emmeline was taken aback and looked up, meeting his brown eyes with alarm. Her brother, Samuel, had once claimed that his friend had a susceptibility for her. She had dismissed the notion as impossible. She and Woodforde had too long been friends for her not to have known of it.

"Thank you," she said, despite the absurdity of his confidence in her. Her life, as he and the public knew it, was almost wholly fake. The most genuine parts of her, the Rogue and the Crone, were hidden from view. "But I do not think myself a songbird of any sort."

Miss Purley's voice was joined by Miss Gottschalk's, which soon overcame the other. Emmeline stopped to listen, as did most of them. Miss Purley had a pretty voice and competent pronunciation, but she stopped singing. The young German woman's vocal ability was outstanding, shown at its finest when she switched to another piece that she sang alone.

When Miss Gottschalk finished, Emmeline applauded and said, "I don't recognize that piece, Miss Gottschalk. What is it?"

"It is a new opera, *La Vestale*, by Gaspare Spontini. I do not have the sheet music here and so am doing it by … by heart, I think you say? I have just learned it. It has not been performed yet except, I understand, in France. I do not do it justice," she said, laying her hands on the pianoforte keyboard and playing a brief run. "I sing it too slowly, too … lethargic? Is that a word? But it is how I feel it."

"You sang it beautifully," Emmeline said. Miss Purley joined the praise, but the young German woman, her cheeks coloring pink, shook her head and leafed through the music; she played "Weep You No More, Sad Fountains" next, and sang with Miss Purley.

Emmeline turned back to Woodforde to resume their conversation, grateful for the break so she could turn away from personal topics. "Do you know any of the gentlemen here tonight?"

He eyed her quizzically. "Why do you ask?"

"Did I imagine the tension between my uncle and Mr. Wilkins? He is a solicitor, correct?"

"Yes, but his more lucrative pastime is as your uncle's man of business."

"What does that mean, exactly? It is said so commonly, but I'm never sure of the definition of a 'man of business.'"

Dr. Woodforde shrugged, his elegant bottle-green jacket bunching at the shoulders as he sat back, one leg crossed over the other. "He takes care of your uncle's investments. I know that because I have invested in a company your uncle formed, not without some persistence on my part, and Wilkins handled the transaction. I began to think the canal company must be the most lucrative investment since the invention of the loom, Wilkins tried to dissuade me so earnestly."

"Tell me about this canal company. I had not heard of it before tonight."

"I believe, as your uncle does, in canals as a means of opening up smaller communities to the benefits of easy transport of goods. I have joined with Sir Jacob and some others in their enterprise to link Maidenhead, a town in Berkshire—you know my origins there, and I have family still who own farms in the county—with the rest of the country, using a canal linking it to the Thames. So I have finally invested in the Maidenhead Canal Company."

"Why would they attempt to keep you from investing?"

"A whim of Wilkins, I believe. Your uncle expressed no such reluctance." Woodforde cast a disparaging glance toward the solicitor, who was tapping his cane on the floor in time with the music, much to the irritation of his betrothed, who shot him an annoyed look that he didn't appear to notice. "Despite my vivacious charm, the solicitor does not like me. Perhaps it is the whiff of the laboratory."

Emmeline smiled. "More likely your erudition, Woodforde; he does not impress me as a man of culture or even learning."

"Anyway, when Wilkins would not speak with me about investing, I was forced to go directly to your uncle. As I said, he at least, though he did his best to dissuade me at first, was most gracious and I have no reason to be dissatisfied with my investment, though plans seem to be moving but slowly. Not a foot of canal dug so far, but I acknowledge there is much work to do in land acquisition and convincing towns along the route of the benefits to them. Every gentleman here is on the list of investors, as well as others. It is the future of this country. We must find a means of conveying goods more efficiently, and canals will serve the purpose far better than cart."

"Perhaps Wilkins is not so good a man of business as he fancies himself." Emmeline had a moment of alarm; could the solicitor be cheating her uncle? But she had more confidence in her uncle's perspicacity than to think that possible. "How odd that I've never heard my uncle speak of the canal company."

"But why *would* Sir Jacob speak of canal building to you? So charming a companion, Miss St. Germaine, must ever inspire more interesting topics."

"Now you are doing it too brown, Woodforde," she said, giving him an impatient look. "You know I'm not one for flattery."

His dark eyes narrowed and his lips, generous and well-shaped, twisted in an unbelieving frown. He leaned forward and murmured, "So I have understood for many years, and yet when last we attended the theatre you entertained quite a flirtation with another of Samuel's old friends, Viscount Nearley. Your behavior convinced me that you would receive flattery in quite a different manner than in the past, at least from *some* gentlemen."

Emmeline winced, fixing her attention on the couples by the piano. Miss Gottschalk was still playing, but not singing; instead, Miss Purley and Mr. Fulmer were competently performing a duet while Wilkins still turned the sheet music pages, though his fiancée appeared pained and stiff.

She had to answer; she did not like Woodforde criticizing her so freely. The trouble was that his observation was true, as far as it went. Emmeline *had* been overly flirtatious with the viscount after he had heaped her with fulsome praise, but she had never expected Woodforde to notice. Nearley's title gave him an entrée into society that made him a valuable contact, one she hoped to use at a later date. She could not explain that to Woodforde without disclosing her secret identity as the Rogue.

"Do I detect a critical tone, Doctor?" she said coolly, unwilling to let her old friend become her censor. She met his gaze with steady sobriety. "Did I somehow give you the impression that your correction of my manners would be welcome? If so, it is a *mistaken* impression."

He nodded gravely. "I beg your pardon, Miss St. Germaine. Perhaps I was out of line, but I was speaking to an old friend who I would not like to see damned as a flirt."

Once more it appeared that she had stepped out of line, that narrow corridor of behavior allowed a lady in her position. "Heaven forfend, for flirting is a skill roundly condemned in polite society," she retorted. "It is a practice that is *never* used as a means to attract and secure what is deemed most valuable to a young lady: a husband."

"I had not known you were seeking to marry," Woodforde replied, tilting his head with interest.

Emmeline bit back her instant retort that she was *not* looking to marry. She had intended it only as a facetious rejoinder, but now she had no judicious answer. "Let's not quarrel, Woodforde," she said.

"Shall we speak of relatively innocuous subjects? The news?" Her tone grim, she went on: "I understand Princess Amelia is confined to her bed. Some say she will not, this time, recover."

He nodded at the change of subject. "I fear extreme care, in her Royal Highness's case, has weakened her. The closeted atmosphere at court and in their family … it is debilitating for a sensitive girl. Her Majesty has relied upon her daughters for everything, especially as the poor old king declines. No, Princess Amelia will not recover this time." His gaze gentled. "'Tis almost the anniversary of Maria's death, is it not? You must be thinking of the royal family with sympathy."

"A sympathy I would not normally express," she said with a quick, pained smile. They'd had in the past many spirited debates concerning her anti-monarchist sentiment and his less republican philosophy. "You're right, Woodforde. I'm thinking especially of the royal princesses right now with tender regard. Losing a sister—can it be almost six years now, since Maria died?—was the most painful experience of my life, certainly worse than losing a mother I remember with great fondness but lost before I knew how to value her, and losing my father, which was a blessing in so many ways. I still write Maria letters I can never post."

She sighed and shook off the melancholy that perpetually lingered on the edges of her consciousness, ready to pounce and overwhelm her at the mention of the death of her younger sister. Oddly, with Woodforde she felt she could say things she didn't even tell Fidelity or Gillies. For them she must stay strong, but with him she could be weak, momentary though it was. Taking a deep breath, she lifted her chin. "Enough sentimentality. Like any young lady I prefer to focus on 'horrid' news, like the murder of Sir Henry Claybourne. As a medical man, you must be interested?"

"Because doctors are perforce fascinated by death?"

"Are you not?" She lowered her voice and leaned toward him, watching his brown eyes. "I understand he was slit from throat to bowel, as *gruesome* a death as could be visited upon a human. It was announced thusly to my group of charity ladies by two ghoulish young females who were agog and full of details from their newspaper uncle, Sir James Schaeffer."

"It seems that young ladies are prone to wild exaggerations."

Her interest sharpened; she had been facetious, but perhaps Woodforde did know something of the case. The medical community was small. "As are newspapers. Is it not true, then?"

Miss Gottschalk finished her piece to applause, which both Emmeline and the doctor joined. Miss Purley was implored by Mr. Fulmer, her fiancé, for another, a Thomas Moore Irish melody that she sang with great accomplishment, as it suited her light, pretty voice.

Woodforde had not answered.

"So you know about the unfortunate gentleman?" Emmeline murmured.

"I think to call him unfortunate is to severely diminish the brutality of the manner of his death."

"Meaning, you know something of it," she said impatiently, glancing at his solemn profile. "How so?"

"His body was brought to St. Barts," Woodforde said, naming the hospital where he had taken his training and still worked on occasion. "John Abernethy requested it once he learned of certain...abnormalities."

Emmeline gave him a sharp look and wondered what he was not saying. She knew of some abnormalities of the knight's inglorious body from her own viewing, and felt her color rise. It was unfortunate that one side of her life would collide with another, at times, and leave her flustered and in want of her usual calm. "Abnormalities?"

His brown eyes glittered in the candlelight as he cast her an aggrieved look. "Miss St. Germaine, you are not asking what bodily abnormalities the man displayed, are you?"

"If you are so shy to speak of them, I must conclude they are of a personal nature, perhaps to his male parts."

Woodforde sighed but did not appear shocked. Over their long friendship she had lost the capacity to offend his sensibilities. "You would be right. He contracted the type of diseases most often caught from dalliances with women of a certain profession. Though it is rumored that he had become less likely to venture outside his home for his..." He cleared his throat and shook his head.

She decided against pursuing that line of conversation. There were limits to what she would allow herself, even with an intimate friend like Woodforde. She remembered the cankers she'd witnessed herself on Sir Henry's sex organs and believed that was what the doctor spoke of. It explained why Claybourne had chosen to import his own virginal victims rather than consort with the girls of Haymarket; an innocent delivered to him fresh from the orphanage was better for his purposes than the resident of a brothel.

Emmeline swallowed and blinked, feeling ill in the overheated drawing room. "So," she said, forcing a calm interest into her tone. "I take it Sir Henry was *not* disemboweled, then? The papers' authority seems to be the poor fishlad who found him."

"He was not so gruesomely executed as that," Woodforde said. "The lad was likely dining out on the news as much as any society matron will on a tidbit of gossip. Sir Henry had been soundly beaten and his throat cut. There was much blood at the scene, I understand, and it may have given the boy the impression of disembowelment."

She shuddered, as she knew she must. "I'm surprised if he was beaten and then slain, that no one heard him cry out?"

"The magistrate asked the same question, and they have men speaking with the neighbors." Woodforde nodded to Sir Jacob, who smiled over at them and then returned to his conversation with Fidelity, Mrs. Yarbrough, and Lady Quisenberry. "Dr. Abernethy was able to tell them something about the attack."

"I warned you I was fascinated by the horrid, Woodforde; now you have begun, you must satisfy my bloodthirst. What did he tell the magistrate?"

"Well, the gentleman had been dead for some time. Several hours, likely."

"How could he tell that?"

The doctor frowned down at his folded hands. "There was some lividity on his body, a hypostasis of the fluids." He glanced over at her. "Are you sure this talk does not upset you, Miss St. Germaine?"

"Perhaps it should, but it does not."

His well-formed lips twitched and he tossed back a lock of hair that lay across his forehead. "Well, then, I shall treat you like one of the students I tutor at St. Barts, shall I?"

She eyed him slyly. "My sex being no impediment to my understanding?"

"I have never considered your sex to impair your rational mind, Emmie. I think you know that of me." He cleared his throat and looked away, then back to her. "In our body, even as we sleep, our heart pumps our blood and it courses through our arteries and veins. Death renders that still, of course. With no heartbeat to push the blood, gravity takes effect. The blood pools in the lowest part of the body, leaving a deep red, even purplish stain under the skin. In the unfortunate gentleman's case, and despite having bled out quite a bit, that happened along the side of his body in contact with the pavement: his left hip, leg, and torso."

"I see. So the doctor could judge with some accuracy the time of death?"

Woodforde shrugged. "Though we have never observed the actual progression of lividity and so do not have an exact analysis—something I may remedy with research if I am allowed—in Dr. Abernethy's opinion the man had died several hours before he was found. Rigor mortis—that is the stiffening of the body—was also well established, as was lividity; the night was cool, so it would retard the progress of rigor somewhat, but not a lot. That places his death at between eleven, when the household was shut up, and one or two at the latest, as the fishlad found the body and alerted the watch at about five."

"Isn't it odd that the watch did not see him?"

"Not at all. If the killer or killers had timed the attack perfectly, it would be over and his body lying in the shadows. The watch does not venture down the alley. They merely walk Samuel Street, down Chandler Lane, and along Blithestone."

"And a watchman was beaten by the two men, I understand. The hue and cry would be after the men fled, but in relation to the beaten man and in the direction the miscreants fled, not down the knight's alley."

"You make a good point. Anyway, Dr. Abernethy believes Sir Henry's throat was cut first, and he was beaten as he lay dying."

How very brutal, Emmeline thought, her stomach churning. The murderer or murderers would have a considerable amount of blood on them, then. Perhaps someone noticed their state, some wife or friend. She must be open to the possibility, though, that the fleeing men were not the assailants at all, but perhaps had discovered Claybourne's body and fled to avoid trouble. She wondered if a weapon had been recovered.

"But …" She stopped, and thought, and nodded. "So your good friend the doctor surmises that Sir Henry's throat was cut, thus severing his vocal cords? He was not able, then, to cry out." She touched her throat as it closed at the thought.

Woodforde looked at her with some surprise. "You reason well, Miss St. Germaine. That is exactly what the doctor thinks."

The cutting of the vocal cord may have been planned to effect the knight's silence, or it was merely a happy—perish the thought—coincidence. Astute or fortunate: there was no way to tell which of these the killer had been. "The magistrate has not yet learned who did the man in?"

"No."

Emmeline's heart pounded and her mouth dried. She took a sip of tea and affected a nonchalant tone. "It was likely the same men who beat the watch. The papers say that, too, but also speculate on the identity of the gallant lady who is said to have raided his home earlier in the evening. Some even say she *must* be the murderer."

Woodforde gave her a sharp look. "Gallant lady? I suppose that is one way of looking at a woman who purportedly entered the house illicitly and stole away a scullery maid and the family silver. I would say wicked rather than gallant, myself."

It was all a matter of perspective. Emmeline remained silent and returned his gaze, keeping hers as guileless as was possible.

"I know you claim an interest in the horrid, Miss St. Germaine, but this is more so than usual. Why so much interest in this *particular* crime?" he asked when she didn't respond.

"Woodforde, we have always discussed such matters. If you remember, we spoke in depth of the Duke of Cumberland's unfortunate incident in May, and indeed his valet had a very similar wound to Sir Henry Claybourne. I'm still unconvinced that Sellis inflicted it upon himself." She cocked her head and gave her friend a teasing look. "*All* young ladies are fascinated with such shudder-inducing crime. It is a part of our charm."

He nodded to acknowledge her facetious tone. "In case you are wondering, in my opinion no lady could have inflicted the wounds on Sir Henry that he received. I do not believe the 'gallant lady,' as you style her, could be the murderer. It would have taken some strength to sever the vocal cords."

At that point, her uncle gathered them together and organized tables for whist. Paired with Woodforde against Miss Gottschalk and Mr. Wilkins, Emmeline needed all her wits to not disgrace herself, for both the solicitor and his fiancée were intelligent and fierce players. The topic of the day did come up again at the card table, when Miss Gottschalk made some remark about the Avengeress.

"That woman! I will not dignify her by calling her a lady," Mr. Wilkins said, his florid face sheened with warmth from the fire that Sir Jacob had built in deference to the ladies, Fidelity and Miss Purley in particular, who complained of the cold. "Damned shame what happened to Sir Henry. He was a fine man and a finer brewer, a solid man of business. Knighted by our most glorious king. That murdering harridan must be caught, or we are *none* of us safe!"

"Sir Henry was a fine man?" Emmeline said, stung into speech by his rant against her other self. "How did you know him, Mr. Wilkins?"

"He was a member of my club. Played a fine hand of whist and could hold his liquor better than most."

"And that is the length and breadth of his accomplishments?"

"Not at all. He was a fine businessman, and most generous."

"Generous?" Miss Gottschalk said. "What do you call generous? I am curious. I hear men lauded for generosity, but seldom hear what they have done to earn such praise."

The barrister's face, already red, deepened in color. He glanced across the room to Sir Jacob, who was now enjoying a game of casino with Lady Quisenberry, Fidelity, and Miss Purley. "He did not confess his good deeds, and I would rather honor his reticence since he did not choose to speak of his charity."

Emmeline doubted there was any charity. "Was he an investor in this canal business of which you and my uncle speak?"

Wilkins gave her a sharp look. "I'm surprised to hear a young lady speak of business," he retorted. "It is no one's affair, certainly not mine, to speak of his investments."

"So we are to assume that he was a good businessman and a charitable soul, though on no evidence." Emmeline smiled to take the sting from her words, but then said, "What about what that columnist said, that … the Rogue, I think he is called? He suggested that Sir Henry raped little scullery maids."

Miss Gottschalk sputtered and set her sherry aside as Wilkins, red-faced, stared at Emmeline in horror. "I think this is not a fit subject for a lady," he said, his face bleached, for once, of color.

"I agree," Woodforde added, with a look of warning at Emmeline. "I think I shall deal a fresh hand."

"Mr. Woodforde," Miss Gottschalk said, "I notice you leaning on a stick tonight. I don't believe you normally use one. How did that come about?"

Woodforde told an amusing story about a fencing lesson that got out of hand—he had a slash across the wrist and a hobbled ankle to show for it—and they all politely chuckled as he said he thought he would engage in some new sport, something less dangerous, like boxing, with his friend Monsieur Alain Clocharde.

The evening broke up early, and they all escaped Sir Jacob's overheated townhouse into the chill of late October, scattering in different directions. Fog drifted in from the river as Emmeline and Fidelity left the city proper on their way to Chelsea. Fidelity was weary and silent on the way home, and Emmeline was grateful. She had much to think of, and before repose she needed to pen another Rogue column, something that would perhaps relax the magistrate's suspicion of the writer as having anything to do with the murder of Sir Henry Claybourne. It was time for a collection of items, of general scandalous interest, cobbled hodgepodge into a Rogue column.

October 27th, 1810, Edition of *The Prattler*
By: The Rogue
Death of a Stonemason & Other Sundry Matters

Oh, how are the Mighty fallen? Or rather, as in most Common Things, how are those who SERVE the Mighty fallen? To wit, your Rogue informs you that even a Stony Likeness of our poor old King causes Death and Destruction. A month or so ago, a stonemason named John Wilson, in a gallant attempt to affix said Stony Likeness of our Jubileed King to the top of a Pillar once used as a sort of Land Lighthouse to guide imbibers to a tavern—and now out of commission, as the lanthorn tumbled to the ground two years ago—did likewise Tumble to the Earth and so Lose his Life. It is said his Friends are raising money now for a Tribute to their Fallen Hero.

In other items, your Rogue-ish Scallywag has witnessed a most Amusing Romance between an Impoverished Peer and a Wealthy Widow. It has become apparent that a Title is worth as much as Gold Ducats. An Impecunious Gentleman like young Lord F____ N___ has found favor with a certain Mrs. H___ B___. It seems Flattery and Coronets are worth Shillings and Crowns these days.

In more Salacious News, your Rogue has it on good authority (one of his Lady Friends) that the Marquis of C___ is, among other things, a Gent who satisfies the Most Discriminating Lady with his Lingua Talenta. He is also, the Lady states, in possession of a most Interesting and Titillating Collection of French Post-cards suggesting Creative Positions for the Amorously Inclined.

But now your Rogue must bid you Adieu, until Whispers again encourage him to Share All that is Most Wicked among Society!

....

91

TEN

MORNING DAWNED GLOOMY AND cold, a blanket of gray concealing any rays of the timid sun. Emmeline shivered as she sat at her desk finishing up business from the day before. She dashed off a note to Miss Hargreaves, stating that she had heard of her lessons for young ladies and that afternoon at three, if t'was convenient, she would be bringing two girls to her to enquire about tutoring in French and embroidery. Emmeline was confident she could override any doubts Martha might have when she visited her today. She also sent to Simeon, under usual cover, her Rogue column, filled with a mélange of scandalous tittle-tattle. Some had come from the rich mine of Viscount Nearley, who dearly loved to gossip, and some from other sources.

The Rogue must appear as he always was—a devil-may-care, scandal-loving roué and man-about-town, sarcastic and marginally witty—to deflect any suspicion that arose from his knowledge of Sir Henry's disgraceful proclivities. In that larger context, his observations on the knight would appear to simply be more gossip. Emmeline certainly couldn't use in her column much of the information she had received, especially that gleaned from her conversation with Dr. Woodforde. It wouldn't do to pique the doctor's curiosity as to where the Rogue had come by such accurate information about the state of Sir Henry's body.

Over buttered toast dipped in chocolate, her favorite breakfast, she read the early papers. Her stomach clutched; Sir Henry Claybourne's missing scullery maid had become the object of an intense search. The magistrate's men were mostly searching brothels, where they would not find her, but despite how obvious it seemed that the men who beat the watch had been escaping after killing Sir Henry, the outcry against Emmeline in her secret Avengeress guise was heightening. She who had raided the Claybourne house and taken Molly away for "a wicked debauch" was alternately scorned as less than a woman or vividly portrayed as "an unnatural, unsex'd, and wicked female."

The reporting was almost salivating in its excessive imagination. The papers seemed divided on whether the scullery maid was the victim of a wayward woman or a co-conspirator in murdering the master of the house and stealing his possessions. Emmeline snorted in disgust and threw the paper from her, then gathered it again to finish. *Poor frightened men*, she thought. Readers of the newspapers were usually men; most wives weren't allowed to read anything but the gossip and scandal columns. The articles about the murder certainly pandered to male fears that there was more going on in their households, below the placid surface of their female servants' expressionless faces, than was thought.

One journalist had waylaid and browbeaten the Claybournes' new scullery maid for information (Emmeline read between the lines and figured that much out), but she could tell him nothing. The housekeeper wasn't speaking, but the cook was a known tippler and had been cornered at the local tavern. She would only say that Molly had seemed like a good lass. The writer, though, claimed that not only was Molly suspected of being in league with the woman who stole her away, but both were suspected of being members of a vicious gang of thieves, who had, with the two females' help, stolen the household's silver.

It mattered little whether Emmeline was thought to have worked alone or in conspiracy with a gang of marauders; both the murder and the theft were hanging offenses. How telling it was that she had so little faith in the courts of man that she feared persecution for something she did not do.

She pushed aside her half-eaten toast, a memory souring her appetite. In June, determined to know the truth about crime and punishment in their country, she had attended, with Gillies, the execution of a young woman found guilty of theft. Melinda Mapson, thirty years old, a married servant, had been tried and convicted of theft from her employer's house in February the previous year. Her hanging outside of Newgate, alongside a male convict, was brief and brutal and had given Emmeline nightmares for a week.

She buried her face in her hands, scrubbing her eyes. She would not think of it again, not see the twisting, writhing figure, hooded in a white night cap. She would *not*! But ... try as she might to expunge it from her mind's eye, she still saw it in her nightmares: a young woman's life ended for the theft of a few sovereigns' worth of household goods. She uncovered her eyes and stared out the window at the silver river slipping past her home. What were a few sovereigns to that poor woman's life? The noose had robbed her forever of the chance for redemption.

The country's system of justice was deeply flawed, and *something* had to change. As a woman she had no say, no power, no control. But as the Avengeress she had *all* of that and more. She had seized it for herself, wrenching it from the cold grip of men. That was what troubled so deeply the men who wrote and published the papers. She would save herself and poor young Molly; they were both being accused, with no reason, of the murder of that perverted, disgusting knight.

She pleated the newspaper page in her fingers. There must be a way to figure out who had killed Sir Henry. Though they had performed such rescues in the past, this time the Crones' luck had run out. Someone had either been lucky in the night they chose to rob the house, or had known it was to take place and used the opportunity to rob the house and kill the master. It had to be the second; surely the timing of the murder could not be just chance. Perhaps they had been naïve to not realize their potential to be so abused. It very possibly had started in Sir Henry's own home; maybe Molly would know something, or Sally, with whom she would speak. There had to be a way to find out who had killed the knight and bring the guilty party to the magistrate's attention before the Crones' secrets—and her own— were exposed.

There was another possibility. The murder could have been personal, brought down upon the knight by something he had done or said in the hours after her raid.

Gillies attended her. Fidelity was having a nice long morning nap, she said, and would be closeted with Mrs. Bramage later to plan next week's literary event in honor of the late Anna Seward, whose writing Fidelity greatly admired. Fidelity and Emmeline both belonged to a group of devotees of literature and writers; they met on occasion, though they had no formal schedule. As Gillies styled her mistress's hair for the day, she complained about Birk's snooping. He had been adamant about looking over the outgoing mail before she could hand it to Josephs to deliver. This was not exactly something new, but it was worrisome nonetheless.

"You know that if he ever finds out about the Rogue or our work with the Crones, he'll tell Leopold. My brother would never countenance either of my activities," Emmeline fretted. "It would be back to Malincourt for me," she said, referring to the St. Germaine family estate where Leopold resided with his second wife and growing family. "Or confinement in Bedlam."

Gillies twisted a curl into place and tucked a stray tendril under the ribbon band that constrained Emmeline's unruly hair. She then picked up a gold silk capote to pin it in place, as a wind was beginning to toss the trees and Emmeline would be out for most of the day. "Dinna borrow trouble, as me granny used to say." The maid pinned the bonnet in place. "Your brother isn't the brightest spark, miss."

"But Birk is cunning as a rat. He would be very detailed with his evidence if he discovered what I am hiding. I wish I could sack him."

Gillies ducked down to meet Emmeline's gaze past the deep brim of the capote. "P'raps you'll have the chance at Christmas, when we're at Malincourt, to pairsuade Mrs. St. Germaine that Birk isn't needed when it's just us here all the year long?"

"Convince Rose to take a stand against my brother?" Emmeline shook her head and regarded herself in the mirror, straightening the brim that shadowed her eyes. "That poor girl is heavy with child yet again and I won't bring her into my quarrel with my brother. If Emily had not died..." She trailed off. Emily, Leopold's first wife, had been an intelligent and determined woman. Her death seven years before had been a heavy blow to both Emmeline and Maria, and then Maria had died a year later. Where once Emmeline had felt that her brothers were her allies, the rift among them now was wide and growing wider. Leopold, the eldest and master of Malincourt; Samuel, next oldest and now vicar of the local parish; and even Thomas, her younger brother, supposedly still pursuing an education at Oxford, though more often gambling, whoring, and carousing: all were scattered, Emily and Maria the twin losses that had unbound the ties of family.

"Och, I understand about family, miss, *and* loss."

Emmeline put her hand on her servant's, where it rested on her shoulder. "Look who I'm talking to: you, who have suffered the greatest loss there can be, of husband and child." She took in a deep breath. "Birk doesn't matter. I'll manage him somehow. We have work to do, Gillies; *important* work. If we can save children from hell, I'll consider my life well lived."

"Aye miss. About Clerkenwell … you will be careful what you say in those parts? I had a fair bad feeling there. And there were a man skulking around; I meant to tell you. I *think* he were a writer. Looked like one, anyway … fair greasy, he was, and watching Sir Henry's house like a hawk watching a wee mousie."

"You'd better not come with me to Clerkenwell, then," Emmeline said, standing and turning for Gillies to help her with her purple silk pelisse. "I wouldn't want you recognized and tied to me; it would look suspicious after your foray there yesterday."

"Nay, miss, I'm cooming, never fear. I'll keep my eyes skinned for the skulker."

"All right. On to Mrs. Adair's home to see poor Sally, then."

Chelsea to Cheapside was a long drive by any route. Josephs crossed the uncomfortably narrow Battersea Bridge, preferring to approach the city from the south. They then crossed Blackfriars Bridge,

Josephs patiently steering the cattle through traffic to Cheapside, where Martha and her husband, Mr. Douglas Adair, resided.

The front of their home—one of a row of townhomes—was clean, white-painted stone with a glossy black double door centered between faux pillars. The maid who answered Josephs' knock was a tidy, country-fresh girl with pink cheeks and a modest white dress topped by a white pinafore apron. Her red hair was restrained in a white muslin cap, with no nonsensical curls to distract from her perfectly tidy appearance. Male servants were highly taxed, so Martha's husband, being a thrifty sort, allowed no footmen or butlers in their home; they had a housekeeper and maids. The girl, named Ellen she said, in answer to Emmeline's question, curtseyed and guided her into the parlor while Gillies sat on a chair at the entrance to await her mistress's return. Josephs drove the carriage away; he would come back in a half hour.

Martha in her own home was a different creature than Martha among the Crones. She was almost dour, though still nervous and a little flighty. "Good morning, Miss St. Germaine," she said as Emmeline took a seat.

"Good morning, Mrs. Adair. How are you?"

The maid exited, closing the door behind her.

"I'm very fine." Once the door closed and the maid's footsteps receded, Martha Adair exhaled a sigh of relief. "I have been in such a state! What if Mr. Adair should find out that you have been here and questioning the scullery maid? My husband has a suspicious mind. There was a terrible to-do when he caught Ellen whispering and gossiping with my housekeeper's niece, Biddy, who was visiting one day; he practically ordered the poor girl out." She wrung her hands. "I've been so turned about I haven't known what to do or where to look."

"I have come to see how you order your household and nothing more, correct?" Emmeline offered. "I wish to see how a well-ordered house runs, to further my domestic education from a matron I respect. That is all your husband need know."

"Shall we go and speak with Sally?"

"Why don't you have her brought here? I would not want your staff listening in."

Martha nodded and went to fetch the child herself.

Sally was tall for thirteen, but slight. She was dressed in a dark blue dress with a white apron. Her flaxen hair was neatly coiled, almost invisible under her white cap. She stood before Emmeline nervously, twisting her hands together while Martha gave her an encouraging smile.

"Sally, do you like your position here?" Emmeline asked.

She nodded.

"You can speak, Sally," Martha said.

"Very much, miss," she said in answer to Emmeline's question. Her expression and tone were almost sullen.

"What about your last position, with Sir Henry Claybourne? How was that?"

The girl's eyes widened in panic and she trembled. Her throat convulsed and she looked ready to flee.

"Sally, please don't worry," Emmeline said, reaching out to touch the girl's shoulder. "You're not going back there. In fact, have you not heard? Sir Henry is dead."

The maid's mouth slackened and lips quivered as her body shuddered. Emmeline tamped down the fury that welled upward from her gut to her throat, an anger as pure and visceral as it was the moment she'd seen the knight abusing Molly. Pressing a fist against her stomach, she asked, "Sally, can you tell me about the Claybourne household?"

The ingrained habit of obedience held true. "Cook were a nice lady. She give me buns a'fore bed when I were 'ungry."

"What about the housekeeper?" Emmeline asked.

Sally's eyes widened. "Mrs. Young?" She pronounced the name more like "Yoong."

"Did she treat you well? You can tell me the truth, Sally."

The girl twisted her apron into a knot, but she nodded. "She were 'arsh soomtimes, but she tried to 'elp me stay safe."

Emmeline exchanged a look with Martha, whose eyes were tearing up. Something had happened that she didn't know about, but she'd ask her fellow Crone once the girl was gone from the room. "How about Lady Claybourne?"

Sally hesitated.

"You can say what you will, Sally," Martha said.

The girl shrugged and her gaze slid away to focus on the chair by the window. "Never sawr 'er. She just took 'er medsin an' slept."

Laudanum, Emmeline thought. A married lady's escape. Young men had their exciting opium dens, while ladies had their genteel tincture of opium bottles. A scullery maid would not see her ladyship often anyway; maids reported to the housekeeper directly, or, in the scullery maid's case, to the cook. "Where did you come from, Sally, before you arrived at Sir Henry's home?"

"Home fer orphings."

"Where?"

Sally shrugged. In her short and brutal life, the child probably hadn't had even the most basic education to understand where in England she came from, nor learn anything about her parentage and past.

A few more questions netted only shrugs or silence. Emmeline sighed. "That's all, Sally."

Martha sent the girl back to her duties. When she returned to sit by Emmeline, she was red-faced and clearly had something on her mind. Emmeline asked her to speak, but the woman hemmed and hawed for quite some time.

Finally, though, in a low voice she said, "I must tell you, tho' it is terribly shocking… there is something more. Sally was with child when she came to me, then lost the babe a week later."

ELEVEN

EMMELINE GASPED. "BY ... by whom? I mean, the baby ... whose was it? Surely she wasn't at the Claybourne house long enough for ... for ..."

Martha, tears in her eyes, shook her head. "It cannot have been Sir Henry's, for she was not there long enough for it to have been his. He didn't actually ... didn't manage to touch Sally, as she became violently ill when he tried. Baby sickness, I imagine; I suffered with it terribly with all of mine. I don't know whose baby it was. She won't tell me anything. I don't even know if she understands how it happened."

Emmeline, her throat constricted with fury and pain, took a moment to gather herself. Even if she had known of this before questioning the girl, she was a stranger; Sally would not have confided in her. If she wouldn't tell Martha, she certainly would not tell Emmeline. This was a task for Gillies. "Excuse me a moment, Martha. I need to speak with my maid."

As Emmeline entered the hallway, carefully closing the drawing room door behind her, Gillies looked up from the needlework she always carried in a small tapestry bag. She half rose from the bench. "Miss? You're white and tremblin'. What's wrong?"

In short muttered phrases, Emmeline, searching her maid's pale eyes, told Gillies what she had learned. "Could you speak with Sally? Try to find out who got to her before she ended up at Sir Henry's?"

Gillies set her sewing aside and nodded, while still holding her mistress's gaze. "If it's possible I'll talk to the bairn, but miss ... are *you* all right?"

"Of course, I'm fine. Go down to the kitchen, use some excuse, and find out what you can from Sally. I think she's afraid that if she tells Martha the truth, she'll be turned away. As hard as the work here likely is, it must seem a safe haven after what she's been through. If we know where she came from and who made her pregnant, we can perhaps prevent another child from suffering the same fate."

Emmeline returned to the drawing room, where Martha awaited, and told her what she had done. "I should have asked permission before sending Gillies to the kitchen, I suppose, but we must stop whomever made the girl pregnant."

Her ally looked uncomfortable.

"You don't agree?"

"Yes, I do, I suppose, but—"

"But *what*?"

The woman recoiled at Emmeline's tone and looked flustered, her expression becoming befuddled as it did in the face of anyone too forthright. Emmeline curbed her inclination to snap at her and calmed herself. "What is your concern?"

"Well, everyone knows that the lower orders can't help themselves, can they? All those animal spirits. As much as I sympathize with the girl, the problems I've had with female servants! I could tell you tales—"

"And there were no *men* involved in these problems?"

Martha flinched. "Well, of course, but men will be men. They can't help themselves. Ladies are responsible for policing their urges." She bridled. "You wouldn't understand, being genteelly raised and unmarried, but a woman has a duty to men to resist their blandishments and coaxing. Some girls aren't firm enough in their rejection. If you say no properly, men will listen."

Emmeline kept her temper with difficulty, remembering the other favor she wanted. It was especially as an unwed female that she knew all about men, their coaxing, their flattery, and other more unsavory methods for getting what they wanted. It was challenging not to counter Martha's conjecture, but there was no use arguing. Taking a deep breath, she settled herself, hands folded together in her lap. "Martha, are you educating your daughters?"

The woman looked confused. "Educating...?"

"Yes, stitchery, music, and especially French. *Vital* if they want to marry well. Are you educating them?"

The woman looked baffled, her brows drawn low over mild brown eyes. "They have learned to read and do their Bible lessons. I've never... I suppose—"

"You *do* want them to marry well, do you not? Aspire to a higher rank?"

Martha clasped her hands to her breast. "Do you think it possible?"

Not in the slightest if they are anything like their mother. "I don't see why not," Emmeline replied with a bright smile, appalled at her own mendacity. "I've met them before. They are presentable. A little French and some music and it's *quite* possible. Now is the time to start; a few years could make all the difference. I know many in the aristocracy, you know." "Many" was an exaggeration. "My brother's good friend Viscount Nearley was saying the other day that he will be looking for a bride in a few years. Three years and your eldest will be of marriageable age, correct?"

"So they need to learn French? Why?" Martha asked, her eyes wide, leaning forward. Her motherly ambition had been roused.

"Well, not just French, but embroidery, as I mentioned, the harp; *you* know, the usual," Emmeline said, with a wafting wave of her hand.

Tears welled in Martha's eyes. "I wouldn't know where to start. I had no such schooling myself, just plain sewing and how to order a household."

Emmeline felt a moment of compunction but hardened her resolve. She needed an excuse to visit Miss Hargreaves in Clerkenwell, and the two girls were it. "As for French, all they need are a few phrases, you know, to give them that *je ne sais quoi*; it is *très comme il faut* to sprinkle a few French words and phrases in speech." It was true. As much as the English loathed the French in person, they had no hesitation in adopting their culture, language, taste in wine, and style in clothes and millinery. "T'wouldn't take long."

"Where would I take them to learn?"

"I happen to know a young lady who gives French and embroidery lessons. I'd be delighted to take the girls myself; an honorary aunt, so to speak, *and* to introduce them to polite society eventually. But right now you need to make sure they will not embarrass themselves even should they meet an earl or a marquess. I have an hour to spare right now; I could take the girls to meet the tutor and see if they suit."

Martha was ludicrously grateful and produced the young girls in a trice, rallied from their aimless habits of playing with dolls and reading novels. Once Gillies had been summoned, Emmeline and her maid and the two girls—Charlotte, twelve, and Nancy, ten—were on their way.

Cheapside to Clerkenwell was not so long a drive. Charlotte and Nancy were not ill-looking, though doughy and unformed as any girl that age of whom nothing has ever been expected but quietness. However, the eldest had a sharpish look in her eyes that unnerved Emmeline. She suspected it was because she had seen much the same expression in the mirror when she was about that age and she had been a troublesome sort, especially after her mother died. "What would you like to learn, girls?"

Charlotte, blonde and plump like her mother, eyed Emmeline. "Cricket," she said.

"Your brother can teach you. What do you wish to learn from a tutor? French, perhaps? Fancy embroidery?"

Charlotte curled her lip and the younger girl copied her. "My brother won't teach me cricket. Says it's for boys only. Tells me to go back to my dolls."

That had been familiar treatment from Emmeline's older brothers. Thomas, though, three years her junior, had been a willing playmate, too young to know that girls were beneath his notice.

"I will teach you cricket myself, next summer."

"Adults lie all the time. Papa is always saying he will take me to his office and he never does. How do I know you will keep your word?"

Gillies snorted, hiding a laugh and making it into a cough.

"You don't." Emmeline and Charlotte exchanged steely glances, taking each others' measure. In a battle of wills, the child looked to be a worthy opponent. Fortunately, shortly after passing St. Barts, the hospital where Sir Henry's body had been taken, they arrived in Clerkenwell. The day was frosty and a chill breeze blew, but Emmeline let down the window to eye the neighborhood. Her last visit, in the dark and hasty, had not garnered her much information.

The road was clogged with drays and lorries, handbarrows trundling the edge, costers with their boxes of apples and cabbages on the walk, and shoppers dodging among them all. She surveyed the scene as they turned onto Samuel Street and spied a familiar figure. "Gillies, is that Tommy?"

Her maid started forward and peered out the window between passing carriages and carts. "Aye, it is!" she said. "The lad has taken up street sweeping. Better than nothing, I suppose, since he was let go from Brackenthorpes' chandlery."

Emmeline knew how fiercely Gillies cared for the child. The maid's own loss made little boys precious to her motherly soul. Emmeline knocked on the roof of the carriage and Josephs slowed and came to a halt. "Go talk to him, Gillies, make sure he's all right." She took out her pocket and found some coins. "Give him this," she said, thrusting the money into her maid's hand. "We'll be at the Hargreaves's rooms; you know where that is."

Gillies gave her a grateful look and hurried from the carriage, darting between pedestrians and handcarts to catch up with the lad. The carriage jolted into movement again.

"You don't treat her proper," Charlotte said with a condemnatory tone. "She's your maid, not your friend."

"You're very rude. You should not correct the behavior of your elders. I'm surprised your mother has not taught you better than that."

Nancy snickered, hiding her mouth, then yelped in discomfort when her older sister gave her a hard pinch. Charlotte then scowled and sat back against the bumpers with a sullen look as Nancy bit her lip and watched her sister warily.

The carriage stopped, rocking as Josephs jumped down, put down the step, and opened the door. "We're at the 'Argreaves', miss," he said, his expression impassive.

"Thank you, Josephs."

"I'll knock."

Emmeline and the two girls remained in the carriage until a young maid opened the door next to the haberdashery shop. Josephs then handed her and the two children down out of the carriage and walked with them to the door, where the maid, a scared-looking child not much older than Charlotte, let them in and locked the door behind them.

"What is your name?" Emmeline asked.

"F-fanny, m-miss." The girl curtseyed awkwardly.

"Why did you lock the door?"

"Miss 'Argreaves' orders, miss; there were an 'orrible murder in the lane behind 'ere, y'know!"

Charlotte jumped in excitement. "A murder? I want to see the spot!"

Emmeline gave her a stern look. "If you will guide us up to Miss Hargreaves, please, Fanny."

The child led them up narrow stairs that opened to a sitting room fitted with worn but once-respectable furnishings set in a conversational arrangement on a worn, burgundy-colored Turkey rug with an ornate pattern. A young woman stood by a folio table stacked with books, pretending to be reading a tome in her hands. Emmeline felt that she had posed herself so, with the book and in the harsh light that came through the front window overlooking the street, to appear more scholarly, or interesting.

"Miss Hargreaves, I am Miss Emmeline St. Germaine. This is Miss Charlotte and Miss Nancy Adair, daughters of a very good friend of mine."

Aloisia Hargreaves was tall, for a woman, and slim, in a plain blue gown of good fabric embellished with dark gold ribbon and a row of oyster buttons. Her dark hair was sensibly dressed, but the taut, nervous expression on her face was familiar to Emmeline. This was a woman on the edge; of what, she wasn't sure, but on the edge.

She shook each one of their hands with a grave nod, then asked them to sit down. "Would you like tea?"

"Do you have cake?" Charlotte asked.

Emmeline stifled her first reaction, which was to swat the child. "Never mind cake, Charlotte, you are here to learn. No tea, thank you." Tea being so expensive, she had no doubt the tutor would forfeit her own tea for two days to serve her guests and possible students. The Adair girls would likely never be her pupils, so Emmeline would not have the young lady waste good tea on these children. "Miss Hargreaves, my maid, Gillies, saw an example of your embroidery in your brother's shop when she was purchasing thread to mend one of my gowns. She said it was lovely work, and that you would be willing to tutor girls in the art."

"French, also, Miss St. Germaine," the young woman said, her back stiff and her hands folded on her lap, though two fingers plucked at a stray thread, worrying it into fraying.

"First things first, I always say; I would like to see an example of your teaching methods. Could you set these girls a task at embroidery while you and I chat?"

Miss Hargreaves rose and guided Charlotte and Nancy over to the folio table, where two chairs were drawn up. She set a work basket between them and took out some simple embroidery samples, as well as silk and needles. She murmured instructions and showed them what to copy, then returned to Emmeline. They spoke of frequency and cost of lessons, but the appearance of Fanny with a pitcher of cordial and glasses allowed Emmeline to approach the real topic of her visit.

As the tutor poured the cordial into tiny glasses, Emmeline leaned toward her and muttered, "My maid spoke of something I must ask about; your maid spoke of it too, when she was explaining locking the door downstairs. I understand there was a murder close by."

The young woman spilled a drop of cordial, but she put the pitcher down carefully and composed herself. "It is an unpleasant fact, but yes. Quite unlike this area. We are in a very nice part of Clerkenwell, you know. Quiet. Safe."

"And yet there was a brutal murder, if the scandal papers are to be believed, in the alley behind your rooms. Perhaps directly below your bedchamber!"

Miss Hargreaves glanced over at the girls, who were busy stitching. "It has nothing to do with us."

"But there's a murderer wandering loose!" Emmeline pressed, noting the tutor's discomfort. "You must feel unsafe. I understand there was unpleasantness between you and the victim, Sir Henry, and I don't suppose you mourn the man's death, but you must condemn the manner."

"I'm sure I don't know what you mean."

"Your brother mentioned to my maid that Sir Henry had insulted you outside … er … the back convenience," Emmeline whispered, watching the young woman's face.

Aloisia stiffened. "It was the merest trifle, not worth mentioning. My brother should not have said anything to a stranger."

There was something that made Aloisia Hargreaves uncomfortable, something beyond being insulted by the knight. Perhaps it had not occurred as she'd told her brother, or not at all.

"Still, you must have heard something that night, when he was killed." Emmeline swallowed past a lump in her throat; had the young woman been looking out her bedroom window at the right time, she would have seen Emmeline creeping down the back alley and into the Claybourne townhome. But from above and a distance, she would not be able to identify her.

Miss Hargreaves shook her head. "About the girls—"

"We haven't decided if you will be their tutor," Emmeline said, injecting a cold note in her voice. "I'm not the girls' mother, and unless I can reassure her as to the safety of this neighborhood..." She stopped and waited.

Charlotte chose that moment to call Miss Hargreaves over; she had a knot in her silk. Emmeline watched how the young woman dealt with the child. She was not a natural teacher, but she was doing the best she could. Her circumstances must be straitened, though Emmeline knew nothing of her life beyond that she lived with her brother.

The rooms whispered of a woman of more taste than money, though, someone who haunted pawn shops to decorate her home. The few indifferent paintings on the walls and items on the shelves were of good quality, but old and worn. Many a genteel family on a downward spiral because of a gambling addiction or loss of investments chose to sell to a pawn shop rather than admit their misfortune to friends.

If Miss Hargreaves had no income, there would be little for her to do but try to marry—which was difficult with no income—or find work, even more difficult in a way, given that she was refined and delicate, not suited to most of the jobs open to women. Unless she had money or enough talent to secure an investor and so open a millinery shop, she could be a wife or a governess. That was the best life could offer her.

Aloisia returned to Emmeline and sat down. Her head bowed, she looked down at her hands, slim and white with tapered nails and no adornment, for a long moment. She then looked up, and there was more openness in her gaze than there had been. "Miss St. Germaine, I *may* have misled my brother. I didn't wish to make trouble for Lady Claybourne, but I could not hide from Benjamin how shaken I was. The incident did not happen in the alley, near the convenience. I was actually in the Claybourne home visiting her ladyship when Sir Henry asked me to … to do something … something unthinkable."

TWELVE

"**That's terrible!**" Emmeline exclaimed.

"He was a repulsive man, and you're quite right; I do not mourn his death, though no human should die as he did," Miss Hargreaves said.

"You *visited* with Lady Claybourne? Why?"

Nancy, across the room, began weeping. Miss Hargreaves leapt up and tended to the child, whose silk had knotted and who was being taunted by her older sister. When she returned, she was again composed. "Why should I not visit with Lady Claybourne? She's my neighbor."

"Given Sir Henry's reputed manner, I'm puzzled."

"I had heard no rumors. Lady Claybourne was not well. The scriptures say we should comfort the afflicted."

"How kind of you," Emmeline said. "I'm not certain about bringing the girls back to this area. If it was one of your neighbors who murdered Sir Henry ... well, that won't do."

"T'wasn't our neighbors!" Aloisia said in a rush. "It … it must have been strangers to this neighborhood. I *did* see someone that night. I don't like to speak of it, that's all."

"Who did you see?"

"It was late," she murmured. "I was in my room and heard a shout. I went to the window and saw two men arguing with Sir Henry."

"Did you recognize them? And have you told the magistrate or his men what you saw?"

"Of *course* not!" she said. Charlotte looked up from her embroidery and eyed them, squinting. When they were silent, the child went back to her work. Miss Hargreaves leaned toward Emmeline and whispered, "I would *never* go to the magistrate! What a shocking suggestion." She folded her delicate hands on her lap in a composed manner.

"But your brother told them that he was the one who saw the men, is that right?"

"He's very protective. It was better for him to say *he* saw it."

In a way it made sense; a young lady in her precarious position must be extremely cautious about her reputation. Having her name in the newspaper or on the court docket would sink her. By having her brother say he saw the men, Miss Hargreaves could get the story to the right people without being questioned.

The young lady had regained her poise to such a degree that Emmeline was certain she would get no more out of her concerning the murdered man. It was a delicate matter. Aloisia's gaze was watchful and steady on Emmeline.

"So, how do you find these girls?" Emmeline asked, glancing over at the two. "Do they show promise?"

"At embroidery? I hardly know yet." Miss Hargreaves watched them a moment. "The younger, Miss Nancy, appears to have the more steady hand, though she becomes frustrated too easily. Miss Charlotte

114

is hasty and seems uninterested. It will require discipline and repetition. They'll have to learn to become calm and steady, determined to achieve ability, or it will not turn out."

"That could be said about life, too."

Miss Hargreaves's head swiveled and she gave Emmeline a long, considering look. "I feel you are not speaking for the young ladies."

"Oh, but I am, and myself too. I am impatient often, and impertinent too, according to my elder brother."

"Then we have in common, Miss St. Germaine, that our brothers do not approve of our behavior."

———

Gillies chased after Tommy Jones, stopping him as he darted between carriages and carts. He was busy sweeping up horse leavings, to make the way clean for folk to walk but also to make piles for the men who would come in a cart after dark to collect it for the farms and gardens outside town. Collecting horse dung was a thriving industry, and so was collecting the human variety by the nightmen, as they were called, who would clear out conveniences for a fee. There was a whole army of men and boys who worked through the night collecting the dung, and human waste from cesspools, and clearing the middens, piles of food scraps, bones, and offal from the bottom of the gardens or courtyards of most homes.

"Miz Gillies!" the boy cried as she grabbed his elbow to get his attention. The lad was twelve, small for his age but wiry.

"Tommy, what's goin' on that you're out here sweeping?" She examined his face: dirty and narrow, high cheekbones and a pointed chin but not *too* thin, given his rough life. He was red-cheeked in the chilly breeze but seemed cheerful enough. "I thought you were well employed at the chandler's."

The lad sent a black look toward the candle shop. "That barsterd! 'E dint like me sayin' as I sawr 'im dippin' inter the cash box when no one else was lookin'. 'E turnt it back on me, sed as 'ow I were the one pinchin'. They let me go."

"Are you all right? Got a place to doss down?"

"Most nights."

Gillies pulled him over to the doorstep of a law office, where no one was about, and went to buy a pie from a cart down the road. She brought it back to Tommy, sitting down with him on the highest step, out of the way of foot traffic and the chill late October wind. The lad fell on it with ravenous snuffles. When he was done, she pressed the pennies Emmeline had given her into his palm. He blinked up at her, surprise on his grimy face.

"Miss wanted you to have this; she's worrit about you. Did you hear about Sir Henry's murder?"

"Aye, old man t'were slit up the belly loike a pig. Heard it from the fishlad hisself!" There was a gleam in young Tommy's eyes.

"What's the word on the street, lad? Who did such a wretched deed?" Folks would be talking, no doubt.

"Dunno."

"Is there anyone you think likely in the neighborhood or household?"

"Lemme think." Tommy screwed his narrow face up, the dirt patches in grimy streaks making him look like the climbing boy he had been until rescued from a master who often beat him.

Gillies wrapped her cloak around her and watched the lad. Finally he said, "Coulda bin the housekeeper ... ooo, but she's a grim one!" He described the Claybourne housekeeper as having a look like death, and Gillies could sympathize, having met her. She certainly was grim and not too kind to the help. Other than that, Tommy said, it could have been one man who was at the back door that night, a fellow with a little dog, or two men he saw arguing loudly with Sir Henry in the alleyway.

"You saw them?"

"Aye … but they dint see me!"

She didn't dare ask what he was doing nearby. Tommy was not above pinching anything left too long outside. "Man with a dog, and two other men? Separate?"

He nodded.

"So t'was so much argle-bargle?" The boy nodded again. "Was that before or after the scullery maid was gone?"

"Arter." He had heard about the masked woman who stole away the scullery maid, he said, and was disappointed that he had missed the action. That's why he was hanging about, in case she should come back. "Watch 'ad called 'leven."

So Sir Henry had still been alive at eleven that night, long after her mistress had taken the scullery maid. And word had already spread about the woman who had taken Molly away. "Had you seen any of the men before?"

Tommy shrugged. "They was all blokes as 'ad been 'round afore, I know that."

"What did they look like?"

He shrugged again. "T'were dark as pitch, Miz Gillies; those barsterds only come 'round when it were dark." He told her that now, servants in every household were afraid and double latching the doors at night. Some householders set a servant with a cudgel at each door, for those wealthy enough to afford such serving staff. In most cases it was the man of the house with a cutlass who stayed up waiting for the killer to return.

Questioned further, Tommy couldn't add much. Mrs. Partridge, the cook at the Claybourne residence, had a weakness for children and sometimes secretly gave him a bun or some scraps from the table. She was a drinker and took her pint at the Bridge and Bezel inn, the name a nod to Clerkenwell's reputation as a center for watchmakers. Lingering about so often, he had, at times, seen the master of the house going out to the alley to the convenience, or to smoke, or—and this was interesting—to meet the scrubby-looking fellow with the little doggie who had visited him the night he died. It was that man, the one with the dog, who had brought Molly to him after Sally, the previous scullery girl, had disappeared.

Gillies felt a clutch of illness in her belly. Emmeline had been trying to discover who the man was who had reportedly brought Molly to the Claybourne household; now she could give her mistress at least some information. Tommy, pressed further, supposed he could describe the man who had brought the maid; he was a tall, thin, dirty man with bad teeth, and always accompanied by the small dog. Sir Henry had called him "Ratter," not that uncommon a nickname in a city where rat-catching was an honorable trade. Tommy didn't know anything more, but that Ratter was *not* one of the two men arguing with Sir Henry that night, though he was skulking around about the same time.

She gave him a few more pennies for his information and told him to keep his eyes open. The boy knew better than to ask why. He was close-mouthed for one so young, probably because he knew, as the saying went, what side his bread was buttered on. Miss Gillies and Miss Emmeline were worth valuable windfall pennies he didn't have to steal or earn sweeping. As always, she asked if he'd like a proper job as a potboy or something else, and he said no. Life on the street, as hard as it was, was for him. He had learned in his brief life to not count on any man for his living.

The Hargreaves' maid timidly opened the door next to the haberdashery to let Gillies in, then locked up tight after her, quaking uncontrollably. In the dim confines of the stairwell, Gillies said, "Lass, are you so afraid that ye lock up tight even in the daylight?"

"I'm Fanny, ma'am." She curtseyed. The maid was no more than fourteen and small, with a pinched, worried face, pale from too much work and too little sleep. "Yes'm. We're all affrighted. I heard his screams, ye know, that man what was murdered. I hear them screams now in my sleep, what little I can get!"

Emmeline had told Gillies about the knight's throat being cut, likely so he couldn't scream. The girl was either imagining the screams or Dr. Woodforde had gotten it wrong. She'd wager on the little maid's vivid memory being pure imagination. "That's tairifyin'!" she exclaimed, clasping her hands to her bosom. "Poor wee Fanny! Did you no get up and see what was what?"

The girl's eyes widened and she shook her head. "Oh, *no*, miss… I hid under me bedclothes!"

Gillies sighed. If she had heard screams in the night, she *would* be finding out what was afoot, as foolish as it may seem. "Is my mistress ready yet? Shall I coom up or wait here?"

"She's gettin' the girls together. She arsked you to wait here."

"Aye, all right, then. Fanny, did y'know the little scullery maid from back yonder, Sir Henry's house, the one that run away that night?"

The girl shook her head. "She weren't there long. I knew th'girl afore her, Sally, but she weren't there long neither, an' she weren't over friendly. Girls didn't last long in that 'ouse."

"Do you know any other servants around here?"

The maid nodded. "Yes'm. Biddy, the maid at the Farnsworths', next door to Sir 'Enry's, she's *real* friendly ... talks to everyone!"

Ah, yes, the gossipy Biddy; Sally had told Gillies about the talkative maid, a niece of the Adair housekeeper. "Where is your room, Fanny?"

"In th'attic, ma'am."

"Did you no see *anything* that night, p'raps *afore* you haird the screams?"

She nodded, her wide eyes glinting in the low light, the whites gleaming. "I were out t'the convenience and saw a feller," she whispered. "A raggedy man I seen there afore, like a skellington, 'e were, and tall. Dark hair wiv a raggedy cap on 'is head an' a wee doggie that didn't bark wiv 'im."

A wee doggie. Tommy had mentioned the dog and the man named Ratter. "This fellow, he were there with another man?" she asked, deliberately mixing up the sets of men who were apparently separate.

The girl shook her head. "The one wiv the dog, 'e were alone. An' Sir 'Enry, 'e were angry wiv 'im. Callt 'im a ... a shite eatin' bugger." Her cheeks pinked to be saying such words.

"What else did Sir 'Enry say?"

The girl looked up the stairs. Voices were approaching the landing. She whispered, "'E said as how the feller 'ad done 'im wrong this time, or summat like that. 'E were sore cross, Sir 'Enry was. I dint 'ear no more. I got skeered and run upstairs."

Emmeline and the two girls descended. Gillies darted outside and motioned to Josephs, who was slowly driving the carriage toward them. He hastened the horses with a slap of the reins, and halted them in front of the haberdashery. Mr. Hargreaves came out of his shop. He recognized Gillies and nodded to her.

"My mistress," she said, motioning to Emmeline, whom Josephs handed into the carriage. The driver helped the two little girls in, too, as the haberdasher joined his sister, who stood in the doorway watching them go. Mr. Hargreaves bowed to their party.

Emmeline nodded to the haberdasher and made room for her maid beside her. That moment, a cart lined with benches and loaded with people lumbered down the street, pulled by two overworked horses who plodded wearily. Emmeline noticed it, but Gillies, her foot on the carriage step, reacted with a startled expression.

"What is it? What's wrong, Gillies?" Emmeline asked.

The man's shouts carried over the hubbub of the streets as he gestured to the corner and the cart turned.

"That there is the man I told you about, miss," Gillies muttered, glancing back at the Hargreaves. She didn't want them to hear her. "He's the one what was lingering about, the one I took for a writer."

"Josephs, take us around the corner," Emmeline said to her driver. "I wish to be mired in traffic." She helped Gillies into the carriage and shut the door.

Soon they were behind the cart, which was stopped at the end of the infamous alleyway where Sir Henry had been slaughtered. Nancy, huddled in the corner, whined about being cold and tired, but Charlotte was watching her, Emmeline realized, and had heard her command. Leaning out the window, Emmeline watched and listened.

"It were a dark night and gloomy, an' cold as a witch's teat," the fellow said, standing up in the cart, with his audience avidly watching, then swiveling their gaze to the alley. They were a mix of young and older folk, moderately well-dressed, but all keenly interested. "Poor Sir 'Enry, never knew what 'it 'im! Coom out ta take a piss an' 'ere cooms the killers," he shouted, wildly flailing his arms. "Slashing and cutting, *slit* goes 'is throat," he screamed, drawing the imaginary knife across his own throat. "Blood spurtin' everywhere, a gory, horrid stream thick as molasses, gleamin' crimson in the lamplight out t'back door."

A woman screamed and swooned, while another, a well-dressed matron, cried out in shock. A man caught the one who swooned and fanned her with a sheet of paper, what was likely a broadsheet published by one of the papers. Emmeline was riveted as much as the folks in the cart. That man was making a *tour* of the murder, as if it was the Tower of London's menagerie!

"The killer, depraved animal that 'e were, or … were it the *woman*?" Eyes goggling wildly, the man thrust his face forward and scanned his audience. "Was it that unsexed female as stole away poor Molly, the scullery maid, for 'oo knows what nefarious purposes? Did she creep back 'ere and slit poor old Sir 'Enry's throat while his lady wife slept peaceful-like, upstairs?" His voice cracking, he went on: "Is Molly gone too? Or is that poor wee mort *chained* in some dank drear basement, kept a slave to unnatural desires o' the flesh?"

He pulled off his cap, held it over his heart, and swayed, launching into song. To the dirge-like tune of "Down Among the Dead Men," breeze fluffing his sparse hair over his bald pate, he sang that ridiculous verse from the broadsheet Emmeline had seen already, about her presence in the Claybourne home as the Avengeress. With some variations for effect, he repeated it twice in a rich baritone that would not be out of place in a music hall. He was possibly the writer of that piece of rubbish, or had stolen the verse and put it to music.

She exchanged an alarmed look with Gillies. Careful to choose her words wisely in front of the children, Emmeline said, "That man is using a terrible tragedy as a tour site. And he's set that *execrable* verse to music!"

"That 'e has."

"Josephs, get us out of here," she called out the door.

"Aye, miss."

Because of the tourist cart and the bottleneck resulting, which in- cluded several carts with cabbage and milk cans and one pungently carrying horse dung out of the city, they could not move, even as Josephs started yelling at the tour guide to move along. The lout gave a rude gesture and, following the wishes of the braver in his group, helped some to climb down and creep into the alley. One man strode down, his tread in heavy boots echoing on the cobbles, and gestured to his lady to join him. She tiptoed, cringing and wailing, lifting her skirts and quaking as she crept through the brick arch to the alleyway as if the murderer would leap out at her from behind it.

It was a ridiculous scene, but to top it, at that moment the Claybourne housekeeper, armed with a broom, stormed into the alley from the townhome courtyard. She shrieked at them to leave. When the bold fellow retorted, she beat him about his shoulders, chasing him to the brick arch as the other women screamed in dismay. The gawker was not having it, though, and, snatching the broom out of her hands, he swung it at the housekeeper, knocking her to the pavement.

Josephs leaped down from his perch and raced through the arch. "Fie, man, have ye no conscience," he shouted, wresting the broom from the fellow. "To beat a woman that way? And you!" he continued, yelling back over his shoulder to the man running the tour. "This is no theater, this be folks' lives!"

Benjamin Hargreaves and another man came running, drawn by the commotion. The housekeeper took back her broom. The man who had hit her and the group guide slunk back to the cart as locals gathered and began to shout at them. It looked dangerous for a moment, but the guide helped the ladies back up and got the cart moving. The crowd dispersed as Josephs kept a watchful eye out. All was settled, and the woman in the alley, her face red, said something to Josephs. Emmeline didn't dare draw attention to herself. Though she didn't think the housekeeper would know her, she wasn't about to take a chance.

The two spoke for a moment and Josephs returned, able to move now that the traffic had cleared. Emmeline needed to get a frightened Nancy and Charlotte, who was agog and excited by all she had heard, home. Once there, she spoke with Martha to reassure her: no matter what the girls said, there was no danger. It had been a misunderstanding among some servants, and her groom, Josephs, had taken care of it.

As shocked as Martha was, she would make sure no word of the misadventure got back to her husband. Of that Emmeline was certain.

THIRTEEN

EMMELINE AND GILLIES HEADED home. "I had no opportunity to ask earlier," Emmeline said as they drove. "What did Sally say about who had made her pregnant?"

"She no more knew how it happened than a tabby." Gillies looked up, tears glittering in her eyes. "T'was at the orphanage. Where else would it be? Dark of night and someone roughly took her maidenhead, and then got at her again, more times than she remembers, poor wee lass! I dinna know if it t'were one of the boys or a warder, or both. That about broke her, miss, t'tell me all that."

A wave of revulsion washed through Emmeline that a little girl should be subjected to such brutality in the place meant to shield her from harm. It was inhuman. "What orphanage, Gillies?" she asked, sitting forward. "Does she know?"

Gillies frowned down at her work, barely visible in the dim light of the carriage. "Can't read, poor thing, and no one called it by name. But the warder's name was Dunstable."

It was a start, Emmeline thought. She was merely clawing her way through the dark, making patterns out of random pieces of information as if they were bits of colored glass she hoped would form a picture once put together. The girls had come from orphanages, and had been brought to the Claybourne home by a man named Ratter. If she could find an orphanage in or near London with a warder named Dunstable, she'd have a beginning.

Fidelity was awake but still in her room, reclining in her intricately carved chaise longue by the window, reading poetry. The view out the window, past the chimneys of the other townhouses in their row, was of the square spire of All Saints pointed to heaven. "I'm so sorry I wasn't up to going out today, dearest," she said as Emmeline stopped at her door. "Have a nice afternoon?"

"Perfectly fine," Emmeline said, leaning against the door frame, aware, as always, of Birk's shadow in the hall at the bottom of the stairs. "I'll just remove my hat and come talk to you. Gillies, can you ring for tea and have it brought to the Comtesse's room?"

A half hour later, after ravenously devouring a plate of scones with the delicious black currant preserves sent down to the London house by the cook at Malincourt, Emmeline drank the rest of her tea, sent the tray away, and closed the door to the hallway, returning to her low chair by the chaise.

Fidelity, who had continued reading her poetry while Emmeline ate, set her book aside and regarded her with a worried frown. "I know you well; you're only truly this hungry when something has upset you deeply."

Emmeline sat and stared into the minuscule marble-edged fireplace, where red embers split and fell under the ornamented grate with a soothing pop and snap. Darkness enclosed the city so early this time of year. The curtains in Fidelity's room were now drawn, but she could hear the muffled clang of a boat bell from the Thames. It was foggy and the river treacherous. Emmeline shivered and put her hands out to the fire.

"What is it, dearest?" Fidelity said softly.

The feeling of dread that had overtaken Emmeline was still strong. She told her companion what they had witnessed, the man who had taken a gruesome and horrible murder and turned it into entertainment.

"Is it any different than *Macbeth*?" Fidelity asked, her tone mild. "Is it the *class* of those taking in the entertainment that bothers you? The pits at a melodrama are full of such folk, and yet you don't rail at that."

Emmeline shook her head, willing away the gloom, but it wouldn't work. "You didn't see his performance. It was ghastly. This was a real murder by a real villain, not playacting on the stage. And he blamed *me* for the murder. Not by name, of course, but I am the horrible un-sexed female of whom he spoke. He sang that awful verse from the broadsheet."

Fidelity was silent.

"I keep wondering…" Emmeline said, frowning. "Was it mere co-incidence that the murder happened the very night I rescued Molly?"

"What are you saying?"

She looked up at her companion, searching her pale eyes, the gray-blue of the sea on a cloudy day. "Could one of our group be respon-sible, directly or indirectly? I keep coming back to that. They all knew I was going there."

"Our group? You mean one of the *ladies*?" Fidelity started up out of her reclining position, put her slippered feet on the carpeted floor, and stared at Emmeline in horror. "*Think* what you're saying, dearest heart!"

"I am. I'm thinking of it very seriously. Could one of them have told someone, and that person passed the word on to someone else?"

Out, damned spot! The spot of blood on Lady Clara's glove. *Who would have thought the old man to have had so much blood in him?* So much blood ... *rivers* of crimson, according to the gruesome guide. Could Lady Clara have done this? Surely not! Woman were capable of great cruelty, but in general they inspired *others* to murder, encouraging, goading, torturing men until they ... until they what? Gave in and did what they wanted anyway? Could any man be moved to murder if it was not already in his heart?

So easy to blame the "unsexed female," the unwomanly creature who would wish someone dead. Women were supposed to be gentle, meek, loving, nurturing souls incapable of violence. When a woman did slay, poison was the usual weapon, not a knife. Reading the Proceedings, the official record of criminal cases at the Old Bailey, attested to that; a sly dose of arsenic in a bitter tisane, so simple and the death swift, the cause a mystery. Or not a mystery when they were caught.

How she had wished for a packet of the poisonous powder at times in her life!

"Emmie, where have you gone?" Fidelity's gentle voice brought her back.

"I was remembering the bad old days, Fiddy, of my powerless youth, after Mama died and Aunt Conroy came to manage the household and torment Maria and me." She took a deep breath. There were thoughts—violent, *murderous* thoughts—that she'd had back then that she'd told no one about, not even Fidelity. She would not have killed for herself, but she may well have for Maria. She shook herself. "I'm being ridiculous. Lady Clara didn't do this any more than I did."

"Lady Clara?" Fidelity exclaimed. "Surely you're not saying—"

"I know, I know," Emmeline said wearily, waving her hand. "Impossible. But unless the magistrate discovers who did do it, he will continue looking for the masked female intruder. I wish I could figure out how to expose the killer."

"If anyone can do that, my dearest, you can," Fiddy said, her tone fond. "You have discovered more secrets as the Rogue than I ever would have thought possible."

That was true. And Emmeline knew more than she ever told in her column. She knew which peers drank smuggled brandy and untaxed tea. She had uncovered scandal, pain, and illegal activity: children not sired by their legal father, affairs, scandalous behavior hushed up for propriety's sake. She even knew some darker secrets that she kept for the sake of the victims who would be doubly victimized if it were known. If there were innocent parties involved who would suffer, she paid them homage by staying silent.

But never had she uncovered a murder. No matter the provocation for the deed, she would never stay silent in such a case. Desperation was no justification for the taking of a life. If she had given in to her own desperation so many years ago and committed the dark deed that tempted her, she well knew how the crime would have poisoned her soul, a black spot that would have crept outward. It was inevitable. Her father's timely death had released her from temptation.

Enough of these dark thoughts of the past. "I've been wandering through this as if I would stumble on the truth, but I need to be methodical," she said, as much to herself as Fidelity. "If I don't, the magistrate will just keep searching for *me*, I suppose, until he finds me, or doesn't, and lets whoever killed Sir Henry escape justice." She told her companion what Gillies had discovered from Sally about her treatment at the orphanage.

Fidelity was horrified, but her reaction was muted. Emmeline thought she looked tired; her friend and companion suffered mental anguish, and it wore her down. She stood, bent over, and kissed the top of Fidelity's head. "We are promised to Sir Jacob's theater box this evening."

"Will Dr. Woodforde be there?" Fiddy eyed her from behind her poetry book, which she had picked back up.

"I suppose. He has suddenly become a stubborn barnacle on Uncle's convivial ship." Emmeline knew her tone was acerbic, but Fiddy had to stop imagining a romance between her and Woodforde. She was not for him, and he was most definitely not for her.

In her room, she took out paper and a pencil to make some notes about what she knew and how she could find out more. Gillies had already enlisted Tommy Jones to discover what he could; boys like Tommy were everywhere and saw much that no one else ever could. Gillies would see him again to discover what he had found out.

She had questions aplenty. It seemed odd to her that Aloisia Hargreaves would visit with Lady Claybourne. She needed to find out more about the knight's widow, though it was likely true that she was either a secret drinker or numbed by laudanum. Tommy's information, that the cook slipped out to the tavern and enjoyed her tipple, could lead to a source, for a tongue loosened by libation might wag with many a secret. Instead of lounging with the other drivers while they were in the theater, Josephs could head to Clerkenwell—close to the theater, fortunately—and lounge at the Bridge and Bezel to find out if the tippler cook, Mrs. Partridge, was there lifting a pint. He was charming when he wanted to be, and having helped the Claybournes' housekeeper that afternoon, he could flatter the cook out of information.

But perhaps there was another route, one that would supply information about Sir Henry away from his household. It was unfortunate that she was a woman; if she were a man, she could freely walk into his brewery, pretending to be a customer. But perhaps there was a way after all. She jotted some notes; she would look into it on the morrow.

Gillies entered, and Emmeline looked up and sighed. "I suppose I must get ready for the theater."

"Dinna sound so forlorn, miss! It's no' a hangin' party."

Emmeline dressed, then submitted to her maid's hairdressing skills, closing her eyes and thinking of ways to discover who killed Sir Henry. Finally Gillies patted her shoulder. She stood and eyed herself in the full-length cheval mirror.

She wore her favorite gown: gold silk sarcenet, with crimson, gold, and deep green ribbons, and scarlet ribbon-roses over the bodice. She wore a garnet-set-in-gold parure inherited from her mother; it consisted of a collar necklace, hanging earrings, bracelet, and hair comb ornamenting her glistening chestnut hair, intricately dressed with looping braids and curling tendrils near her high, smooth forehead. She pinched her cheeks to bring up color as Gillies dabbed her neck with scent. She held out her hands and Gillies slid on gold silk gloves, buttoning them at the wrists, then bringing the cream lace cuffs of her sleeves back down to her wrists.

"I must go help Madame Bernadotte with her finishing touches, miss," Gillies said.

"Tell her I'll await her downstairs in the salon."

She descended and sat by the window overlooking the street. Fidelity was perpetually late, and sometimes even at the last minute could not bear the thought of going out, with all the attendant hustle and bustle. But tonight she would go because she would not disappoint Emmeline, knowing her cousin was looking forward to the performance.

Sir Jacob was an enthusiastic lover of all theater venues and kept boxes at many. Tonight it was opera ballet—scenes from *The Marriage of Figaro*—at the Dionysus, a small theater near Drury Lane, and featured a young ballerina who had risen from the chorus in the part of Susanna, Figaro's bride-to-be. Emmeline's uncle wanted her opinion of the actress's ability. Emmeline, like Sir Jacob, generally enjoyed opera and ballet more than dramatic plays.

Birk entered the salon and bowed. "A package came for you, Miss St. Germaine, from your acquaintance Miss Kinsman." He held it out to her.

Emmeline eyed him and nodded. "Will you have it taken to my room? I'll open it later." She paused, watching him closely. "Unless you've already opened it?"

His patrician face, porcine and self-important—he worked hard to model himself after Leopold, whom he much admired; Emmeline's brother was also portly and pompous—stretched into an expression of stunned distress. "Miss St. Germaine, I would *never* do such a thing. I hope you know that."

"Of course." Still she watched his face, not convinced that her assertion had upset him. He was too sure of himself, always. As she stared, his gaze flicked away to the wrought iron fireplace fender. "Miss Kinsman is easily amused and follows the most gruesome events with relish. I imagine it is broadsheets on the latest murder."

He nodded and bowed, and appeared ready to back out of the room.

"Wait," she said, and held out her gloved hand. "I suppose I'll open it now. Who knows how long Madame Bernadotte will be?"

He handed her the package, wrapped in paper and tied with a ribbon knotted so securely she'd know if it had been tampered with. Simeon did that purposely, knowing of Birk's proclivity for prying. She waited for the butler to leave, which he did slowly and reluctantly, checking for dust motes and smudges on glass as he went. She set the package down on the settee and took out her chatelaine, which she was never without, even in the evening when she should leave it behind. She separated the tiny silver scissors from the other tools and cut the ribbon.

As she expected, it was a package of broadsheets and papers Simeon knew the St. Germaine household would not receive. Taking a deep breath, she dived into the lot, using paper to protect her gold gloves from the smudge of newsprint. As she read the titles of articles, her hands started shaking and heat rose in her cheeks.

Beware The Murdering Wench!
Masked Mystery Lady Slaughtered Knight

And worst of all ...

Betrayed; Sir Henry's Murderous Mistress?

FOURTEEN

As SHE FEARED, THE titillating prospect of a lady murderess was proving too rich a vein for journalists to ignore. Simeon had not included a note this time, just the broadsheets with their joyful denunciation of the female felon, the *Murderous Masked Medusa*, as one styled her.

The Avengeress. One writer had already picked up her Rogue habit of calling her other half by that name.

Shaking, Emmeline clumsily retied the bundle of papers. She could hardly blame writers, who were only following the path of least resistance, the one that would sell the most broadsheets and newspapers. A scrap of paper fell out from among the sheets. In Simeon's hand was written a few words: *Tonight; Dionysus Theater.* Thank goodness; she was grateful that she had provided her publisher with her itinerary of social dates and grateful, too, that she had opened the parcel. She wasn't sure how she would meet with Simeon and speak with him, but she must.

Gillies descended with Fidelity and took charge of the bundle of broadsheets. Tonight was a rare evening when Gillies would not accompany them. They would return directly from the theater with no supper after, so the maid's services were not required.

It was full darkness when they left, trundling through the dim streets of Chelsea toward London and the theater district. Fidelity was quiet, contemplating the joy of a performance to come, perhaps, but Emmeline, tense and worried, could not rest. She rapped on the roof of the carriage as they got well away from Chelsea. Josephs drew the horses to a halt and came down to the door to speak with her.

She leaned forward and met his eyes in the dim light cast by the carriage lanthorn. "Josephs, what did the Claybourne housekeeper say to you today?"

"Thanked me in a frosty way, miss, an' told me to be on m'way."

"Hmm. *She* likely is not amenable to flattery, but there is another way. You know Clerkenwell quite well. There is a tavern called the Bridge and Bezel; do you know it?"

"Aye."

"I've been told that the Claybourne cook is a tippler and spends occasional evenings in the tavern. Her name is Partridge. Would you be up for a drink while we enjoy the theater?"

"Aye, miss," he said as she handed him coins. "I'll see what I can learn about the household."

"Discreetly!"

He touched his forelock and disappeared into the twilight. The carriage rocked as he took his place, and they continued their journey, finally arriving at the Dionysus Theater. He helped Emmeline and Fidelity descend, then got back up and departed. Arm in arm the two ladies approached the steps, where a crowd was gathered. Dr. Woodforde had been waiting for them and limped forward, bowing.

"Madame Bernadotte, how good to see you again. I missed speaking with you at Sir Jacob's dinner party, but once a party is broke up for card games, general conversation becomes impossible."

"We shall remedy that missed opportunity soon, I'm sure, Dr. Woodforde."

"Are you well?"

"Moderately, Doctor. For an old lady."

He bowed over her hand and said, as she knew he would, "Madam, you are as willowy as a girl and twice as pretty." He turned to Emmeline. "You look lovely tonight, Miss St. Germaine. Your uncle and his party have already gone in. I said I would wait and escort you."

"Thank you, Woodforde, but it wasn't necessary. We are capable of walking up stairs without aid."

"Don't mind her, Doctor; you know our Emmie is prickly as can be," Fidelity said, giving Emmeline a look of censure as she took Woodforde's arm. "I would be grateful of your support through the crowd."

Emmeline kept her own counsel. The last thing she needed that evening was to have Giles Woodforde stuck to her like a bloodletting leech; the thought distracted her. That was not a very good metaphor for his stubborn refusal to take offence and his willingness to forgive even her most egregious examples of bad temper and insult. A leech clung without regard to its host and gorged on its life-giving blood until sated, but then dropped away. Woodforde gently reminded her that he would be there to support and challenge her always. It annoyed Emmeline most because if he knew who she really was, Rogue and Crone ... if he ever *truly* understood her, he would recoil in horror from her unfeminine views and ambitions.

But she had learned well, as every women must, how to dissemble. And she did want a favor from him, after all. She smiled and took his other offered arm for support—though it required him to tuck his walking stick under his arm to do so—as they mounted the steps. "Thank you, Woodforde," she said gently, "for your thoughtfulness."

He glanced sideways at her and did not reply.

As always, the Dionysus, owned and managed by Emmeline's acquaintance and a member of the same literary group, a gentleman named Mr. Lessington, was full, even at such a season as this when all the supposed "best" of society had retreated to country homes and estates. There were more than enough bankers and merchants, lawyers and judges, doctors and brewers to fill the space. Sir Jacob's box was on the second tier in the center. As they slowly made their way along dark red paneled halls and stairways, through the crowd, which would not disperse until the trumpet sounded for the opening of the opera ballet, Emmeline listened in on conversations, a stream of gossip through which they forded, little snippets barely audible in a roar of chatter.

"She's just *waiting* for John to die," one woman muttered to her friend as Emmeline stood close by, trapped by the crowd. "She has a second husband in her sights, a younger one more—how shall I say this delicately?—*capable* of making her happy."

"How *shocking!*" her friend said as she tittered behind her fan, then employed it to waft a slight breeze to her damp forehead in the increasing heat of the throng. "But to be expected; if he will not die swiftly, mayhap she will help him along?"

"You are *terrible!*" the other woman said, giggling and hitting her friend with her folded fan.

John, John … Emmeline covertly examined the two; she recognized them and knew their social circle enough to be sure that "John" was Sir John Hackford, who had been ill with a wasting disease that left him bedridden. So his wife had a lover? Interesting tidbit for the Rogue to expound upon. Surely their talk of poison was just malice? Or not. T'would not be the first time a soul was helped along on his journey to Saint Peter at the pearly gates for taking too long to die. A barely concealed hint in her column would, mayhap, save the fellow's life, such as it was.

The jam of attendees was momentarily loosened and the three of them surged ahead. Woodforde bent his head to listen to Fidelity as she spoke softly to him. Emmeline pricked up her ears to catch more gossip and scandal.

"It's shocking," a gentleman said to his wife as he opened the door to their box. "I do not hold with men marrying the nanny, you know. And he a widower of just a month!" His wife, a woman with a thin bitter mouth, said, "He *had* to marry her and quickly, or face the gossip that would ensue six or seven months hence."

Emmeline's eyes widened but she did not recognize the two, and so had no way of figuring out who had hastily married his enceinte nanny. If Gillies had accompanied them she would have employed her maid to discover the couple in question.

They were almost to her uncle's box when she heard her name called and turned. Lady Clara, on the arm of a very brown, tall gentleman dressed impeccably in russet, smiled brightly and summoned her over.

"Excuse me, Woodforde," Emmeline said, removing her arm from the crook of his and moving toward her fellow Crone through a noisy stream of patrons, nodding and smiling to those she recognized. "Good evening, Lady Clara. How are you?"

"I'm well." Clara indicated the man beside her with a negligent wave of her fan. "Miss Emmeline St. Germaine, this is Mr. Elijah Jeffcock."

"Mr. Jeffcock," Emmeline said with a cool nod, holding out her hand. He took her fingers and bowed over them.

An older woman joined them that moment but ignored Emmeline. She took Clara's arm and tugged, then said, "We must go, child. Mr. Jeffcock, come along."

"I'd like to speak with my friend," Lady Clara said, pulling her arm from the woman's grasp.

"Clara, no nonsense, not when we've got everything settled. You behave, if you please."

"Yes, Aunt," she said and turned to Emmeline, her eyes shining, moisture welling in them that belied the brittle smile on her lovely face. "My aunt is terribly worried that I will act up, Miss St. Germaine," she said with an arch rise to her brow. "She will not wish a scandal, particularly not before my engagement is announced in the papers two days hence."

Emmeline gasped. "Your ... your *engagement?*"

"Yes. Mr. Jeffcock came here all the way from Jamaica to impose upon my family how *much* he wishes to marry me," she said with a forced brightness of tone, her voice brittle and shrill with tension. Her aunt watched her closely, as did Mr. Jeffcock. "And they have agreed. Mr. Jeffcock owns sugar plantations with a thousand slaves! Men, women, children, even ... and he owns them *all.*"

"Now, Clara, I do not own a thousand," the gentleman demurred.

But Lady Clara went on as if he had not spoken, her eyes glittering with a hectic gleam. Two spots of high color on her cheeks had no artificial source. "Is it not a *brilliant* match?" She stared at Emmeline, her stance rigid, her gloved fingers clutching into the fabric of her fiancé's jacket sleeve as she fluttered her feather fan with her free hand. "He is very wealthy; is that not true, Mr. Jeffcock? You've certainly told me of your *vast* holdings often enough, and have I not seen them myself? In person? Alone?"

"I'll leave you to speak with your friend, Clara," he murmured, and released his fiancée. He bowed to Emmeline. "Miss St. Germaine, your servant."

"What's going on?" Emmeline asked her, watching her colleague's fiancé and aunt together, whispering. "Is he the one … Addy said …" She didn't have words. "Didn't he …?"

"Yes and yes," Lady Clara said, her voice trembling. "But I don't have a choice, don't you see?" Her tone was laced with a high, keening thread of desperation. "My father has made it clear. This was inevitable, and what I want matters not a bit. Like Juliette Espanson, I either marry the husband of his and my aunt's choice or retire to the country to live out my life in splendid solitude."

Emmeline felt sympathy for her; she had been in a similar position herself, but her father's death had prevented that fate. Leopold was easier to manipulate since he truly did not care what she did as long as she didn't disgrace the family, and he safeguarded that by having a respectable widow at her side and a snoop of a butler in his employ.

"Wouldn't that be better than a life sentence of marriage?" she asked. "You don't know what may happen tomorrow, or the day after, if you hold out."

With a flicker of knowledge in her eyes, Lady Clara's lips twisted in a wry half-mile. "My father's death would hand me over to some male equally as difficult. There is no evading this fate; I must marry, and it doesn't much signify who the man is. Jeffcock is capable of making me miserable married or unmarried, for he will pursue and haunt and badger me. If we marry, I hope to bore him so deeply that he will leave me in peace. He has promised I may stay in England, at least." Her chin went up. "I will have it in the marriage settlement. I will *not* immure myself in some country estate nunnery or go back to Jamaica. Why should I give up my whole life to retain what little is left of my dignity?" Her voice was thick with emotion. "At least this way I can bury myself in dissipation and good works."

But the cost! Emmeline thought. And there was no way Jeffcock would leave her alone until she had borne him children. She was about to protest, but Lady Clara put up one gloved hand. "No. Enough about me! I may be supremely fortune; Jeffcock may die. He is bilious enough. I have information, and I have a problem. We need to talk at more length than this place will allow. What church do you attend?"

"All Saints in Chelsea on the Cheyne Walk, steps away from my home."

"Is there anything there of historic interest?"

Emmeline watched her eyes, the moisture still glinting in the light from the candle sconce, and nodded. "Yes, very much. There are some historic books of importance, and it was the parish church of Sir Thomas More."

"That's enough for me to justify a Sabbath visit. Jeffcock approves of old churches as a destination for me, but will not go with us so far, as English history bores him. He is interested only in commerce. Meet me at the service tomorrow." Clara smiled brightly, waved to her fiancé, and left Emmeline staring after her, wondering what was going on.

Woodforde had escorted Fidelity to her seat in the box and returned, waiting some distance away for Emmeline to finish with Lady Clara. He came to her, bowed, and offered her his arm. "Your friend seems troubled."

"She is newly engaged."

"A cause for celebration."

"Not always, Dr. Woodforde. Not always."

He gave her a concerned look.

141

The theater party awaiting her in Sir Jacob's box included some of the people who had been present at his dinner party. Mr. Wilkins rose as she entered, leaning heavily on his cane. Miss Gottschalk smiled and nodded. Her uncle nodded, but as Mr. Wilkins went right back to speaking to him earnestly in a loud whisper, Emmeline did not approach. Dr. Woodforde had already helped Fidelity find a seat near the corner of the box, away from the men, where she could enjoy the play undisturbed by the chatter. Woodforde's kindness was beyond question, and Emmeline appreciated his courtesy to her friend and companion, who was sensitive and sometimes fragile. He had reserved for her a seat where she could best see the occupants of the other boxes and those in the pits below. How well the good doctor knew her! She thanked him and sat, opening her fan, a useful tool not only for air but also for concealing a conversation or an object of inspection.

She brightly looked around, nodding to those she knew, letting her attention apparently rove. A box on the same tier as theirs was occupied by a lovely woman, soberly gowned in dark blue, with little in the way of adornment but her richly curled hair, which gleamed in the lamplight. There were several men, and Emmeline's eyes finally sorted from the pack a familiar face: Simeon!

After meeting his gaze and almost imperceptibly nodding, she examined those seated with him. The lovely lady to his left was his wife, she thought, and others were Jewish associates and acquaintances. Simeon was active in his community, which did the best it could to protect their Hebrew brethren, and advocated for more freedoms for people of their religion. Jewish emancipation in England seemed a distant dream, but one toward which Simeon worked as fervently as the Roman Catholics of the nation worked toward theirs.

Meeting Simeon had changed Emmeline's life. Learning that he was the owner of *The Prattler*, taking the chance to trust him and propose to him her column as the Rogue, and finding so many intersections between his radical beliefs and her own had opened to her a world of secret opposition. Emmeline's mission in life was to aid the disenfranchised, and since that numbered the whole of the population but for wealthy, landowning Englishmen, she knew it would be a lifelong undertaking.

"Who are those people?" Woodforde murmured.

"I beg your pardon? What people?" Emmeline asked, startled by how close Woodforde was.

"The ones in the box; the ones you were watching. The lady in the blue and the gentlemen with her."

"I don't know them. I thought I recognized the lady, but I was wrong. In truth, you catch me absently staring and planning my literary soiree." She smiled at him. "What time is it?"

Woodforde pulled a pocket watch out of his waistcoat. "Eight."

"I'm eager for the performance. My uncle says the dancer is extraordinary—quite the rage—and I long to see her."

Two chairs away, Miss Gottschalk was speaking with the newly arrived Mrs. Yarbrough, whose husband took the seat beyond her and joined in the conversation with Wilkins and Sir Jacob. The young German lady said loudly, "I find the notion of a female killer extraordinary, that is all. I've heard that all of Clerkenwell is on alert for this supposed female murderess."

Emmeline's mouth went dry. Mrs. Yarbrough murmured something, to which Miss Gottschalk derisively replied, "I don't believe for a moment that a woman slit him from one end to the other. It is not possible."

"I beg your pardon—do you speak of the tragedy in Clerkenwell?" Emmeline asked, knowing that she must appear as normally curious as she always did about such notorious events, or Woodforde would wonder.

Miss Gottschalk turned. "What else is on the tongues of the people?"

"I, too, have heard that the murderer was some masked, cloaked woman," Emmeline replied. "There are even drawings said to be from descriptions of the housekeeper, or the cook … something like that?"

The younger lady made a noise behind her teeth. "Ach, yes, the Avengeress or some such nonsense."

"But there *are* witnesses to a female being in the house and threatening the gentleman earlier that evening, is that not true?"

"Of course, but because there was a woman there earlier, and the gentleman was murdered later, does not imply that the woman murdered the man."

Emmeline lauded such exquisite reasoning. She examined Miss Gottschalk with some interest. She had dismissed her as vapid, but now thought that perhaps the lady did not talk if she had nothing to say, a refreshing change from those who spoke incessantly about nothing. "Woodforde and I were speaking of the crime at Sir Jacob's last night. I tend to agree with you that the killer was not likely the female from earlier. It is lazy reasoning to think so."

"Nonsense," boomed a male voice. It was Wilkins. He rapped his cane on the box railing between them. "Perfectly good reasoning. Someone threatens a man and he turns up dead—the one who threatened did it."

"I'm sure most of society would agree with you," Emmeline replied, watching his fiancée's face. The young woman had stiffened and once again her expression blanked. She pushed away the cane, which appeared to have lost its cap, exposing the battered wood that attested to his rough usage of it. If he wasn't careful it would catch on the delicate fabric of his fiancée's gown.

"It *entirely* makes sense! You ladies just don't want a woman to be blamed. Can't have it both ways, you know; can't be considered a whole human but not capable of murder."

"I don't believe I said a woman was incapable of murder," Emmeline said sharply. "In fact—"

"The fellow was a fine upstanding citizen and business man," Wilkins bellowed. "Know his brewery well; his partner was my father's childhood friend."

"You did happen to mention at my uncle's dinner that he was a member of your club, and now the partner of a childhood friend. How coincidental," Emmeline said stiffly.

"I know most everyone in London, some way or another. Take our canal company. How do you think we brought our fellow investors together?" he said, winking at Emmeline's uncle. "Businessmen with the same habits and likes and dislikes. That not so, Sir Jacob?"

Sir Jacob wore an expression of distaste on his florid face. Emmeline knew him well enough to believe that he was embarrassed by the brashness of his associate, who had clearly not been raised as a gentleman. "What habits would those be?" she asked, her tone frigid.

But the answer, unimportant given the subject, was lost in the blare of trumpets announcing the performance was to begin. The conversation had started Emmeline thinking; a man like Claybourne, in a highly competitive business and with a personal life fraught with horrible secrets, was bound to have enemies who would, perhaps, take advantage of the threat to him that evening to do away with him. *If* they had heard about it, of course, which offered two possible lines of investigation: she had already wondered who in the brewing industry might hate him, but also, who could learn of the threat to him so swiftly? That was necessarily a small group, surely, and there were likely no people who fit in both groups. The more useful line of inquiry was to ask who among his *personal* circle hated him. It was possible the two groups intersected; his partner at the brewery was possibly both colleague and friend.

The painted backdrop of the opening act was pastoral, a dreamy vision of an idyllic meadow of wildflowers, and the music, when it started, was lighthearted. A singer fluted through an impassioned French ballad, a trio of female dancers followed with folk music from the Iberian peninsula, and then there was a brief break as a new backdrop was wheeled out. It, too, was pastoral, in dreamy tints and with a distant misty mountain in purples and mauves.

"This is her, Beatrice de Montignac," Sir Jacob whispered, leaning forward from his chair, behind and to the left of Emmeline's. "Remember to tell me what you think. I find her enchanting."

And she was. Her light, delicate skirts belled and tossed, with froths of lace like seafoam underneath. She almost paused on her tiptoes, and her leaps were spectacular. When her male partner arrived it was anticlimactic. Once the performance was over, there was a break, and movement in the boxes was general.

"What did you think?" Sir Jacob asked. "Shall I invest in a new protégé?" His eyes twinkled.

Woodforde moved uncomfortably, and Emmeline concealed a smile; her physician friend was ill at ease with the implications that Sir Jacob was asking his niece if he should take Miss de Montignac as his mistress. "Uncle, you must do exactly what you wish," she replied. "She is exquisite, I will grant you, and talented, too. But excuse me; I am going to see if my friend Lady Clara Langdon is about. I wish to speak to her about our literary salon next week."

"I will accompany you," Woodforde said, rising in his seat.

"Oh, Doctor," Fidelity said after a swift look from Emmeline, "I was so hoping I could impose upon you to obtain refreshments. I am parched, but you know I do not like a crush."

Gracious as always, Woodforde bowed and sat down by her to discover what she wished. Emmeline escaped. From a distance she saw Simeon but was at a loss how to speak with him without drawing notice from her group.

He solved her dilemma by swiftly walking past her and getting his cuff button "caught" on the lace of her sleeve. "I beg your pardon, miss. Let me untangle this button," he said loudly.

"Why, thank you, sir!" she answered, then muttered, "What's going on?"

"The magistrate himself came to the newspaper office today while I was absent for Shabbat. My best fellow, a gentile who looks after things on the Sabbath, sent me a note. I put them off, but will speak to them tomorrow. I must, for it seems they will keep coming back until I convince them I know nothing."

"What do you think they want? You've already said you will not tell them who the Rogue is," Emmeline said. As a gentleman came too close, looking askance, she said in her loudest, snippiest tone, "This is so *tangled*, sir! *Please* be careful. The lace is best Mechlin, *very* fragile."

"I will endeavor not to tear it, miss; *such* an unfortunate happening." Simeon lowered his voice, bent over the lace at her wrist, and said, "I know, I know. But they appear intent on forcing me to comply. They told my fellow that I *must* let them know who the Rogue is, for he seems to have information about Sir Henry. And now a visit from the magistrate himself, not just his men."

"What can we do?"

"I don't know. Fortunately, no one at the newspaper knows your identity. I won't tell them your name, dear Miss St. Germaine, no matter what I have to do to avoid it."

"Simeon, there is so much I need to discover, but I have none of the contacts that you do. Listen." Emmeline spoke in a low tone, but rapidly. "Find out whatever you can about a man called Ratter, who was seen in the area several times; he has a little dog with him always. He was seen arguing with Sir Henry that night. Also, anything you can discover on the haberdasher and his sister, Mr. Benjamin and Miss Aloisia Hargreaves. Their business is on Samuel Street, and their back courtyard is opposite Sir Henry's. They are, I think, the source of information on that night to the magistrate and some of the writers, maybe even your own, but I'm uncertain. Miss Hargreaves claims that Sir Henry insulted her, but she lied at first about where. She was visiting Lady Claybourne, and I'm not convinced she is telling the truth about why."

"I will write you a note and keep you informed." Simeon straightened and said in a louder voice, "We are untangled, miss. My deepest apologies!" He bowed and walked back to his family group. His wife looked down the long expanse toward her, curiosity in her expression evident even from such a distance.

"What was that about, my dear?" Sir Jacob, carrying two frosty glasses of cold wine, joined her.

She told him the fiction, about the tangled cuff button and her lace.

"It doesn't appear that the lace was hurt by it," her uncle said, with a glance at her wrist.

"No, and that is what took so long," Emmeline replied, hoping he didn't notice the tremor in her voice. "He was *exceedingly* careful."

"He looks familiar. Who is he?"

"I didn't catch his name. Is that glass for me? Shall we return to our box?"

Sir Jacob was watching her face, holding the glass away, a worried frown twisting his lips. "Emmeline, my dear niece, I know you far too well. I hope you are not getting into any trouble?"

"Of course not, dear Uncle. What trouble could I possibly get into at the theater? I do hope that wine is for me because I am perishing of thirst. I don't see Lady Clara. Let's return to the box. I don't want to miss the second act."

"Certainly. How odd, though, that the fellow was heading this way, but after disentangling from your lace he just went back to his group."

She shrugged and reentered Sir Jacob's box.

FIFTEEN

JOSEPHS HUNKERED DOWN IN his chair at the Bridge and Bezel, letting the chatter and smoke swirl around him. Miss St. Germaine knew so little about taverns. She had assumed it would be a simple matter for him to slide in, drink a tankard of ale, and chat, but he was a newcomer. Newcomers were suspect.

He had spread it around, by way of the landlord, that he was waiting while his mistress was at a local theater and had happened upon this tavern because it was close by and not crowded. One or two toughs had eyed him, watching his level of inebriation, no doubt, and assessing the fullness of his purse, but they lost interest once it was clear he was a temperate drinker with a few coins to spend on a pint or two.

After an hour or so, a stout, bosomy woman entered, sweeping in on a wave of cool air, and was hailed familiarly by the landlord, a tankard plopped down at what must have been her habitual seat by a window overlooking the narrow, dark street. She was florid, her sleeves pushed up over strong forearms even on this chilly October evening. She was a working woman, likely a cook or a washerwoman judging by her strength, which was gained by punching down dough or handling heavy, wet clothes.

A couple of ribald exchanges with locals later and he knew that she was in fact the Claybourne cook. She drank deep and gustily. Josephs became bolder and watched with open admiration, catching her eye and nodding; the first, most gentle overture to a woman, he had always found. He hailed the landlord and ordered for her a pitcher of his finest ale, which coincidentally came from the Clerkenwell brewing house co-owned by Sir Henry Claybourne.

After she'd downed a couple of tankards, Josephs sat down opposite her and introduced himself, chatting about his day. He had brought his sightseeing mistress to view the horrible site where the infamous murder had taken place. He casually mentioned that he was the driver who had chased off the fellow who was hitting the Claybourne housekeeper with her own broom. He drank deeply, wiped the ale foam from his lips, and pronounced it the best ale he'd had for quite some time.

"That there be from the dead man, Sir 'Enry's brewery, yer know. 'E were my master. I 'eard about what you did from Mrs. Young, the 'ousekeeper," she said.

"You don't say! 'Ow about that." Josephs clinked his tankard against hers. "'Ere's to yer! An' yer master, God rest 'is soul."

"God won't rest 'is soul ... more like old Satan, 'is chum," she snarled, her lips twisted.

He gave her a surprised look.

She was in the right state of drunkenness when lips were loosened, but she still made sense. "'E were wicked ... liked to tup little girls. T'were why that masked woman coom t'take away the little scullery maid." She told him of Molly's rescue, describing the masked woman's gleaming bloodshot eyes and horrid talons.

"I 'ear she coom back then, th'masked lady, t'kill Sir 'Enry?" Josephs said, scrubbing the beginning growth of whiskers on his chin.

The cook took another long draught. She shook her head. "Nah!"

"But any woman capable of kidnapping a child—"

The woman, her breath yeasty from an ale belch, leaned across the table. "Struth, dontcher listen? She were takin' the mort to pertect 'er."

Three pints of ale and she had spilled the tale; that's all it had taken. How long before the magistrate was told about the Avengeress and her mission to protect scullery maids? How long before Miss St. Germaine's group was exposed? "Mebbe it ain't a good idear ter tell no one else about it?" he said. Though maybe the man being a foul rapist had led someone *else* to kill him, and the magistrate needed to know about Claybourne's sins. P'raps he should keep his big trap shut and try to find out what the mistress wanted to know. As the cook looked befuddled, Josephs added, "Nay, lass, never mind. Drink up. 'Oo do *you* figger kill't yer master?"

"The devil hisself," she said, nodding wisely. "Feller as come to th'door bringin' that poor wee lassie, mayhap."

Gillies had told him all about the man named Ratter, but Josephs couldn't seem to know too much or even in her befuddled state she might wonder. "What d'yer mean?" he asked.

"Ere, listen; t'were us as fixed it, yer see." She and the housekeeper had heard that there was someone who would steal Molly away to safety and so had arranged it, she told Josephs. After the masked woman left with Molly, Sir Henry appeared to suspect her and the housekeeper of being in league with the Avengeress, but they denied it. "T'were a awful scene!" Partridge said. "'E was red as a boiled lobster and shriekin' like!"

Josephs narrowed his eyes and watched the drunken cook. Did Sir Henry's suspicion of them cause one of them to lash out and kill him? The housekeeper was strong and had a temper. Maybe. Maybe not. "'Ow'd you get in tooch with th'masked woman in the first place?"

She shrugged. "Carn't 'member." She took another long draught and slipped sideways, sagging drunkenly. "Might've bin the maid next door 'oo knew someone, 'oo knew someone, y'know what I mean? But 'ere…that never coom from me!"

Laboriously, Josephs pulled more of the story out of her about the evening after Miss Emmeline's departure. Sir Henry had not called the magistrate right away. Instead he had sent little Noah, the potboy, out with two notes, but to whom she didn't know. She had retired for the evening and the housekeeper had done the same. She knew no more until the ruckus the next morning, when Sir Henry's body was discovered. She *did* know from the potboy himself that he had come back and was sent to the attic to sleep rather than in the kitchen by the fire, as was usual.

"Who sent 'im to the attic?"

"T'marster, o' course," the cook said, trying to sit up straight. She yawned hugely.

Sir Henry didn't want witnesses to something or someone, but to what, Josephs didn't know. By then the cook was so deep in her cups that she was making no more sense. The housekeeper, Mrs. Young, harsh-featured and scowling, came to the tavern door and glanced around. She marched over, tugged the cook up to her feet, and gave Josephs a squinty look. She recognized him from the skirmish but said not a word, hauling the woman away.

It was time to return to the theater for Miss St. Germaine and the Comtesse. Josephs headed to the livery, tipped the groom, and made his way back to the Dionysus Theater through moonlit streets, deep in thought.

———

When Josephs arrived at the theater to convey them home, he gave Emmeline a significant look and a nod, but as Woodforde was there to hand her into the carriage, she could not question him. It would wait until the morrow. She had used the time she had at the theater well, and Woodforde was secured as an escort for Monday afternoon. She wished to investigate a brewery, she had told him, as an investment for a portion of her inheritance if Leopold should agree.

A restless night, followed by more horrible morning headlines referring to the murderous female, left her with a headache, but Emmeline knew she must go to church. Lady Clara's bleak face remained vivid in her memory. Whatever was troubling her, Emmeline could not fail her. It must be gravely important.

November was almost upon them. The open river provided passage for more than just water; a cold wind often swept down it, rippling the water with tiny wavelets. Even on a Sunday, boats plied their trade, ferries crossing back and forth. That would change, perhaps, when the new Vauxhall Bridge was built, but although it was designed and approved, construction was not scheduled to begin for some time. It was a gentle walk to All Saints, long enough that she could have asked for the carriage if Fidelity was accompanying her. But her companion, after the night at the theater, was weary. Emmeline, wrapped in a warm cloak against the chill, walked with Gillies, who had spoken to Josephs and was able to relay to her mistress all he had discovered.

Listening to the tale, Emmeline was horrified at the amount the cook had divulged to a stranger about her own and the housekeeper's actions. It would be far too easy for the magistrate to get the same tale from the woman, and if they questioned long enough, it was possible they would uncover a trail the led directly back to the Crones, and so to Emmeline. In the newspapers there was a common cry; men of standing demanded answers. The unnatural woman who raided homes and stole away scullery maids must be found and punished. Most assumed she was also guilty of Sir Henry's murder. Poor Sir Henry had been threatened in his own home, and then murdered. It stood to reason the Avengeress was guilty.

She could understand the neatness of that surmise. If she didn't know better, perhaps she would be arguing the same conclusion. The simplest answer was so often the correct answer.

But not this time.

When Gillies had relayed everything, Emmeline said, "Sir Henry expected someone to be coming, clearly, as a result of the notes he sent, and he didn't want the potboy underfoot to hear what was said, so he sent him up to the attic to sleep. But why not go off somewhere with his visitors to talk? He was master of the house, not a servant, and he could do whatever he wanted."

"P'raps he didnae trust them," Gillies offered.

"That makes sense. But why bring the people to his home, then? And why that night? He must have been very alarmed by my visit." A breeze blew stiffer, wafting the ineffable scent of effluent and fish, and then was then scrubbed clean as a stronger wind started tossing the trees on the riverbank. Clouds overhead sped inland. "He must have wanted to speak with them privately," Emmeline mused. "Perhaps he had a task for them. Or wished information, though he couldn't know what to ask until he saw them in person. It could be that he asked the men to come to his home to give them an assignment, even to find *me*." She shivered and drew her cloak closer. "*Or* he suspected I had been sent by someone he knew, as a warning to him. Who knew of his proclivities besides the servants?"

"His ladywife, surely, miss."

"Perhaps. Though Sally, the scullery maid previous to Molly, says that Lady Claybourne was indisposed most of the time, with laudanum or spirits." She paused and stood, gazing with unseeing eyes out over the river, which was churned to a muddy gray-brown and rippled by the intensifying wind. "I am operating blind, feeling my way through a mystery that endangers me, in ways I cannot know, from the law and the villains both. Who is this man, Ratter, the one with the little dog? Did Sir Henry send for him? And who else did he send for, if he sent *two* notes that night? We know Ratter came alone, and that there were two other men who also arrived and argued with Sir Henry. Either party could have killed him."

"Aye, miss. One more thing: the cook told Josephs perhaps they first lairned how to contact the group of ladies to rescue Molly through the next door neighbor's maid, but she didnae say naught else."

The blocky tower of All Saints, with its square cupola, was in view above the rooftops. Lady Clara, with her maid, was awaiting Emmeline. They entered together into the lovely old chapel, the whispers of the congregation echoing and floating like fall leaves, and took their place in the St. Germaine family pew. Gillies and her ladyship's maid, a sensible-looking girl of about twenty, sat together as Emmeline and her fellow Crone took the less prominent seats at the far end, where they could talk in confidence.

"What did you wish to speak of?" Emmeline asked.

Looking straight ahead, Lady Clara murmured, "I support an orphanage—actually I helped organize and run it—and visited two days ago. It is St. Pancras Children's House in Camden Town. The wardress—Mrs. Miller, widow of a soldier—told me an exceedingly odd story about a man who came looking for orphans of a suitable age to put in trade. He did not want boys, only healthy girls to become scullery maids to what he said were good London families. *Pretty* girls. Pretty *blonde* girls."

Emmeline felt a jolt under her rib cage; this confirmed her suspicions of an orphanage being involved. She knew that Sally had lived in one before entering service. Was this an organized system of abuse? "What did she tell him?"

"She had an uneasy feeling about him in the pit of her stomach and told him that he was unwelcome there."

"Did she describe him?"

"He was tall and thin, of middle years, stooped, with a dirty cap and stained hands, broken nails. He smelled, she said, like soiled undergarments and gin."

"What is his name?"

"He didn't introduce himself, and she didn't let him get to the point of telling her before she sent him and his scruffy dog away from the orphanage."

"Dog?" The word echoed in a pause in the liturgy, and others twisted in their seats but Emmeline didn't care. "What breed?" she muttered to Lady Clara once the vicar had resumed speaking. It was a group prayer, the congregation responding to the vicar's voice.

"No breed. Small. Scruffy. Devoted to the fellow and following him at his heel." Open prayer book on her lap, Lady Clara glanced over at Emmeline. "Is that important?"

"If I am correct, that was Ratter, the man who brought little Molly to Sir Henry's home. And now I know what I must do."

"What is that?"

Trembling, Emmeline grasped the wooden seat with her gloved hands to steady herself. "Visit every orphanage I can to find out who

157

this man is and where to find him; he may be able to tell us about a larger conspiracy to buy girls from orphanages for men to abuse. He's one of the men who visited Sir Henry the night he was killed, and he may even be the murderer."

The vicar intoned, "The night has passed, and the day lies open before us; let us pray with one heart and mind."

She was eager to begin her search, but she had obligations. She spent the rest of that day finalizing plans for the literary salon she and Fidelity were to hold on the upcoming Tuesday, a memorial to honor the work of Miss Anna Seward, the Swan of Lichfield, for whom many had so much admiration. Fidelity enjoyed Miss Seward's poetry, while Emmeline was interested in her botanical accomplishments and political leanings in an age that was increasingly critical of learned and ambitious women.

Emmeline wished she could hasten the arrival of a more modern era, in which women were respected for artistic pursuits but also allowed active participation in the politics of their nation. Who was it who commanded that she be nothing more than an adjunct, an addition, condemned to perpetually be helpmeet and not originator? Whenever she asked such a question, the answer oft came back "the Creator," for which there was no adequate retort, since she could not claim divine guidance to the contrary. Perhaps no other woman found it so, but it seemed to her that a woman's life work was to suppress her natural urges, rein in her natural desires, and conceal her natural abilities. Surely a Creator, if there was one, should not wish to stifle half of His—or Her—creation's abilities?

October 29th, 1810, Evening Edition of *The Prattler*
By: The Rogue
Death and the Knight?

Death Prowls, leaving equal parts of Sadness and Joy as it steals the Souls of the Wicked and Righteous alike. And who can say which is which?

Your eager Correspondent has learned that the lady-who-would-be-widow of Sir John H____ is awaiting news of his Imminent Demise as one might await the joyous report of an Imminent Birth. Who can blame the blameless Lady H. when it is said she has a Carnal Longing for the Lusty Loins of a younger Beau? Your Rogue wonders ... is the dying Husk of a Man to be hastened, then, when the urges of youth will not be restrained? Time, that hoary old man who totters toward year's end, will tell.

In another Household, your Faithful Correspondent has learned, one more Life and Death drama—or rather Death and Life drama—has taken place; a gentleman newly widowed must make haste to place a ring on the Nursemaid's finger or risk a Miraculous Six Month Birth of a Babe. But who is this mystery Master and Nursemaid couple? Your Rogue knows it not, but would welcome any information his faithful readers might send his way, via the good offices of *The Prattler*!

....

SIXTEEN

MONDAY DAWNED. EMMELINE SPENT an hour with Mrs. Bramage and Birk, arranging how the sitting room would accommodate the seventeen people they would be hosting the next day at the literary salon. After luncheon, she dressed carefully in a sober, dark blue Spencer over a dark green day gown and awaited the arrival of Dr. Woodforde. He arrived exactly on time to escort her to Sir Henry Claybourne's brewery.

"No walking stick?" Emmeline said, noticing him limping without his aid.

He smiled as he handed her up into his vehicle, a curricle which his family wealth enabled him to keep in the city. It was a necessity, as he was a physician much in demand among wealthy dowagers and thriving families. "It was an annoyance, and my foot has recovered enough that I don't need it," he told her. As he jumped up into the seat, he winced slightly. "Hard to remember not to put too much weight on it, though."

Picking up the reins, Woodforde set the team in motion along Cheyne Walk, past the royal hospital. "I looked into the brewery you named as a potential investment," he continued. "It is—or was—the property of Sir Henry Claybourne, so recently murdered in such a disagreeable way." He glanced over at her with a knowing smile. "The very man whose demise so fascinated you that you had me recite details of his corpse and manner of death."

He clicked to his horses to raise them to a trot. She suspected he would discover her motives, so she confessed some aspects of her purpose. "You know me too well, Woodforde. My curiosity is getting the better of me. I'm wondering if, beyond the logical people to have murdered him—"

"There are logical people to have murdered him?" He directed his team into traffic as they entered the city.

"Well, of course," she said, raising her voice over the sound of carriage wheels and barrow carts. The street narrowed. As Woodforde slowed, a sweeper leaped out to remove some horse dung from the cobbles, then dashed back to the curb again. "Don't we all have people whose lives would be improved by our demise? Birk would be delirious with happiness if I were struck by a carriage in the street and expired. Leopold would no longer have to pay to keep the London townhome open year-round, so his pocketbook would be substantially improved. And my eldest niece would be the benefactor of my inheritance."

The doctor shot her a disbelieving look. "You don't mean to say your closest family wish you dead?"

"Of *course* not, Woodforde. But then, I am a gem of rare quality: pleasant mistress, dutiful sister, and helpful aunt. Who knows with Sir Henry? The people closest to him have the most motive. Wife, servants, sons … or whomever inherits his business. Did he *have* sons, I wonder?"

"My investigation turned up no legal issue."

She gave him an appreciative look and smiled. "Delicate way of saying he may have had bastards aplenty but his wife bore him no living child."

"I should be shocked by your language," Woodforde said.

"And yet you are not."

"I think you deliberately use language to *try* to shock me."

Perhaps that was true, perhaps not. Emmeline was silent while he negotiated a tricky turn onto a wider street, then said, "The people most likely to have killed the man would be those close to him, unless the murderer was, as some of the more sober papers surmise, a violent stranger who attacked him as he stepped out to the convenience. In addition to family and servants, there may be debtors, employees, or competitors who would have enjoyed seeing Sir Henry dead."

Woodforde glanced over at her, eyebrows raised. "Is not the simplest explanation the most likely? The female who invaded his house and made off with the young scullery maid supposedly threatened him. I'm surprised you do not add her to the list of those who are, in your view, suspect. Why not?"

He was deliberately baiting her now. He had already said he didn't think a female capable of such a murder. Emmeline clasped her hands together and squeezed. "Simplest explanation? Thought it went without saying, Woodforde," she said lightly. "Seems silly to me, though, to think that she would go away, then come back some time later to kill him. She was there and could have done it *then*, if that was her intent."

"You have a point. I suppose your curiosity will not allow you to rest until you have done the job of the magistrate and courts."

"You mock me," she said, and took in a shaky breath, controlling with great difficulty her desire to move about in agitation. "But of course it is the most *idle* of curiosities. I am a sensationalist and nothing more; you have caught me out, Woodforde."

He was silent for a time, his strong hands handling the reins with great efficiency. Finally he said, "Emmeline, you are never idle, so perforce your curiosity has a purpose. I wish you trusted me enough to tell me what it is."

They came, at last, to the outskirts of Clerkenwell beyond the Green, even beyond Rofoman's Row, and approached a large complex of buildings both commercial and industrial, with coal stacks belching smoke into the gray sky from atop the largest of the buildings. In front of the structures was a cobbled yard enclosed by an ironwork fence and gate, across which burlap bag-laden carts were wheeled by men and boys. There was a brick building along the road, and over it in arched letters was writ *Clerkenwell Brewery*. The air had a yeasty scent, oddly sweet and almost like tomato bisque; that was the smell of beer brewing.

"Failing that," Woodforde continued as he pulled up to the brewery office door, "I'm surprised you don't go to your uncle. I'm sure he could discover what the magistrate has learned, though the criminal court is not in his purview. He indulges your every whim and would most likely sate your curiosity."

She most certainly could *not* do that. She couldn't risk the chance that her uncle, who knew her better than most, would protest her investigation. As indulgent as he was toward her, and as much as he loved her, familial pride was one of Sir Jacob's abiding traits. If he feared she would expose the family to public humiliation, he might reveal her actions to Leopold. That could mean an end to her freedom.

Emmeline was already walking the fine edge of independence under Birk's watchful eye, maintaining her reputation while making sure Leopold wouldn't wish to discombobulate his own serene country life by having an inconvenient and defiant sister in his home. She had to make sure her eldest brother's life was better *without* her in his household than with her there, and that it remained worthwhile to him to finance her life in Chelsea—not an inconsiderable investment, especially with as many children as he had to provide for.

Woodforde only knew Leopold as his friend Samuel's pompous but genial older brother. But to Emmeline, Leopold was the person who held every comfort in her life in his grip; one wrong move or unsavory slice of gossip and he could command her to return to live at Malincourt, and she would have to obey. Her only other choice would be to retire with Fidelity to a country cottage, which would be all she could afford from her own income.

So she could not simply trust her uncle to help her, nor did she feel easy now that Woodforde had figured out so much. She could ask him to keep her investigation a secret, but to even say so much would imply she was doing something of which Leopold would disapprove.

"How do you wish to handle this?" Woodforde asked, helping her down from the carriage as a boy emerged to hold the horses. "I wrote them a note this morning requesting an interview with the managing partner, a Mr. Wright."

Taken aback, Emmeline said, "On what grounds did you request an interview?" She hadn't even thought of such a step, merely assumed that they would walk in and ask for an interview with the owner.

"I know you spoke of investing. I don't for a moment believe that is your motive in visiting the murdered man's brewery."

She held her tongue and simply waited.

"So I thought it safest to say that I am a doctor representing an asylum. We are seeking a better deal on ale for our inmates."

"Clever," Emmeline said, surprised at his talent for deception. Perhaps this would be better. Mr. Wright could just send an investor on his or her way, but a customer would require time, and would be expected to ask questions. "I suppose I am a patroness of the asylum, then." He was about to take her arm to escort her into the office when she stopped him, hand on his arm, searching his face. "Woodforde, why are you doing this?"

"I'm curious as to what your true motives are." His well-shaped lips twisted in amusement. "*And* I fear that without me you will land in trouble, and how would I ever look Samuel in the face if that happened and I had had the opportunity to help, but didn't?"

"Ah yes, poor little lady that I am, without wits to keep myself safe, nothing but hair, big eyes, and dainty feet."

"I didn't say that," he muttered curtly. "Stop assuming you understand me and my meaning when you so clearly don't. If you remember, I have *always* looked out for you, Emmeline, and I always will, whether you are jumping off the eaves of a barn or storming a brewery to uncover a murderer."

He had referred back to a long-ago incident, in which her younger brother Thomas asked if he could fly and Emmeline determined to show him it was not possible by, of course, trying it herself. Woodforde had been there to catch her. "For dear Samuel's sake, then?" she said.

"No, for *your* sake, and for my peace of mind. I hope someday you will trust me, Emmie."

"Let's not stand on the pavement brangling," she said coolly.

They entered the brick building, Woodforde limping slightly still, through the large oaken door into a spacious office. There was a low wooden railing, behind which was a desk. A clerk sat scanning a bound ledger with columns of numbers, making notations. At other desks, lesser clerks were copying letters and recording orders by the weak light that came from a row of high windows. Woodforde ushered Emmeline through a gate in the wood railing, planted himself in front of the clerk's desk, and loudly announced, "Dr. Giles Woodforde for Mr. Wright."

The stooped elderly man started up and signaled to a boy of about twelve who was wheeling a cart with more ledgers toward him, an apprentice no doubt. "Here, Billy, show this gentleman and lady back to Mr. Wright."

Wright's office was spacious and reasonably bright, given the gloom of the late October day. Windows lining the room overlooked the large yard where workers carried on with business, wheeling carts filled with barrels and bags of hops. The men shook hands and Woodforde introduced Emmeline, then stated his business.

"I have interest in an asylum—" Woodforde began.

"Actually, an orphanage," Emmeline said, with sudden decision, sitting forward on her seat.

Woodforde cast her a surprised look.

"The good doctor is on the Board of Guardians," she continued. "We are concerned by the ... the healthfulness of what the children are drinking. The water is abominably wretched where they are situated. Stinking, in fact."

"We use only the best water in our brewing process," Wright said genially, sitting back and threading his fingers over a canary waistcoat that covered his small, rounded paunch. "Located near New River Head for that very reason, y'see. They're putting in iron mains, y'see; longer-lasting than the elm pipes they were using. Best water in London or area."

"We wish to learn of your small beer and establish its healthfulness to improve the children's constitution to make them fit for work. We also require a stronger brew for the warders and matrons." Emmeline felt Woodforde's questioning gaze on her but did not turn to meet it.

"Seems a precious waste of beer. Who would throw money away on orphans? Do your benefactors know you intend to feed them beer?" Wright eyed her with distaste and turned to the doctor, glaring at him from under shaggy brows. "Whose idea is it? Does the young lady have too tender a regard for the baseborn?"

"It is an experiment. I wish to see if their health improves, making them fit for work at a younger age," Woodforde said, adapting his story. "It is the most healthful of beverages, of course—small beer, I mean—fortifying and vitalizing, and so we intend to tell donors."

The man nodded at that bit of specious nonsense, while Emmeline fumed in silence at his deference to Woodforde and ridicule of her.

"Who's your supplier now?" he asked, still speaking exclusively to Woodforde.

"I'd rather not say. We only purchase a small amount for the warders and matrons. We do need beer, both for the orphanage and an asylum, as I said. I spoke of this once with your partner, Sir Henry Claybourne, at a dinner of charitable supporters. I understand he is since deceased."

The man sat back, his gaze becoming cautious. "Aye, that he is."

"We offer our condolences," Emmeline said. "You must miss your partner terribly."

"He weren't here most days."

"Why is that?"

He ignored her question and focused solely on the doctor. "Why the questions about Claybourne?"

"I remember Sir Henry stating in conversation that he had no children," Woodforde said. "I am concerned for your company's stability. Who will take over his duties here now?"

"No one," the man said, sitting up and shuffling some papers together on the green baize surface of his desk. "He didn't do much of anything. I'll buy the widow out ... give 'er a fair price."

Emmeline gave Woodforde a look. There was a motive, perhaps, but there had to be more, given the brutality of Sir Henry's murder.

"I intended to offer to buy him out anyway," the man continued. "My partner had other investments he seemed more interested in. Couldn't hardly get him to pay attention anymore to business."

"Other investments?" Emmeline said.

"Started chumming about with higher-toned folks." He gave her a sneering look, scanning her up and down from her plumed hat to her kid gloves. "Always on about his investments and who he was hobnobbing with."

"Did he mention any names, Mr. Wright?"

It was too far too fast, and the man squinted, eyeing her with disfavor. "Here, what's any of this got to do with buying beer?" he said, half rising. "You aren't from them newspapers, are you? Had to chase a feller out yesterday, trying to ask my workers about Sir Henry."

"I assure you, we are not from the newspapers," Woodforde said, giving Emmeline a warning look. "But I *am* concerned about the future of any deals we make with you. When I spoke to Sir Henry, he offered very good terms for delivery."

Wright sank back down into his seat, but his expression was mulish. "Present the terms in writing, doctor. Whatever Sir Henry said, and I'll consider 'em. Things have changed and I can't be bound by anything Henry said, y'see. Now, I have business to take care of, if you'll excuse me."

Moments later, they were out the door. Woodforde was silent as he accepted the reins of the curricle from the stable lad. He helped Emmeline up to her seat, then started the horses on their way. As they regained the road and headed back toward Chelsea, Emmeline chewed her lip. "Woodforde, before we go too far, pull over and listen to me."

"It is almost November, Miss St. Germaine," he said, his tone crisp. "Have sympathy for my hands, if you won't for the rest of me."

It was true that the wind was cutting, though he had the head—the folding top—of the curricle half up, and it did protect them somewhat, depending on what direction they headed. Once they got back into the city proper and among close buildings, the wind would be less noticeable.

"You *are* wearing gloves, sir," she said tartly, "but I will talk while you drive. Mr. Wright seemed not to especially mind his partner's death."

"Which means little. I may have found out more, but you were insistent on inserting yourself into the conversation."

She threw an exasperated look his way. "I will not be made silent, doctor. I've done that for a good portion of my life, and now that I am on my own, in most senses, I will not suffer you or anyone else to muffle me."

"Then you will always be fighting upstream against a waterfall."

"Trimming my nose to spite my face, is that it?"

He glanced over at her. "I don't say that *I* wish you to be silent, Miss St. Germaine, but you must choose one or the other; either you wish most effectively to gain the knowledge you require, or you wish to speak up as an equal member of society." He expertly guided the curricle into a line of carriages and coaches that were held up by something ahead. His team, a matched set of dapple grays, was calm but fast, responsive to his slightest touch of the reins. "You *must* know that there are some who will laud you for your refusal to remain silent, but many more who will look askance and think you speak out of turn. I am not one of the latter, I hope you know."

Emmeline nodded, taking in a deep breath, quelling the anger that seemed to simmer in her soul. Woodforde treated her as an intelligent woman, and only occasionally spoke in any manner that could be considered condescending. But even so, he expected her to suppress her true self.

It seemed, if she were being fair, that the more resolute she became about asserting herself, the more determined she was to live as she chose rather than buckle under pressure, and the more likely she was to view any statement through a lens of offence. Had she become so sensitive to insult that she saw it where none was intended? Perhaps she twisted words and statements into criticism when none was implied. How would she know? Like Adam and Eve and their knowledge of good and evil, she could not go back and unlearn what it was to be patronized as less than a man. She now saw it in so many statements she had never noticed before.

That was a discussion for another day. As the doctor got the curricle moving again, after the muddle ahead had been cleared, she said, "I have my reasons for seeking answers, Woodforde. And I do trust you to help me in my quest for the truth. You saw the body of Sir Henry Claybourne, and so have an entrée where I have none. Would you be willing to visit Lady Claybourne and to … to take me with you?" She had been able to think of no other way to meet the widow.

He gave her a horrified look and snapped the reins to hasten the team. "I can't believe you would even consider something so indecent as to worry that poor woman in her time of grief. It's despicable,

Emmie, intrusive and blatantly wicked, a ghoulish desire to satisfy your curiosity. You *must* know that deep in your heart."

So she *could* still shock him. In that moment, Emmeline realized how much she respected Woodforde and cherished his good opinion of her. So instead of retreating into frosty irritation, she made the effort to see things from his perspective. He didn't know her reason for asking such a favor, nor her intentions for visiting Lady Claybourne; how could he? Of all the men she knew, he was the only one she would even think of trusting with the secret of what she did: rescuing abused scullery maids and other unfortunates, masked and cloaked when necessary. She considered revealing to him why the solution to the murder of Sir Henry was most definitely not idle curiosity.

But still, it was far, far too dangerous. Which part of Woodforde would surface: her reliable friend, or the conservative gentleman of means? The wrong move would be the destruction of everything that currently made her life worth living. And she could never take it back if she told him. She concluded that she'd rather appear ghoulish and idly prying than expose her most carefully guarded secret. "I'm sorry, Woodforde; I didn't consider." She would need to find another way in.

The afternoon had been a waste of valuable time.

———

Birk delivered the mail and newspapers to Emmeline at breakfast the next morning, but she had only time to notice there was no package nor letter from Miss S. Kinsman as of yet. She could not have expected Simeon to come through so quickly with information on Ratter or the Hargreaves, and yet she *had* expected it. The gentleman had produced miracles before. She worried that he was being hounded by the magistrate. Not knowing what was going on gnawed at her stomach.

The papers had little real information to offer, and she could glean nothing beyond that the magistrate was "asking questions" of the household and neighbors. Their firmest lead was the absconding scullery maid and the masked female, who was, it was implied, a discarded mistress of the knight who, after stealing the silver and the scullery maid (for some reason no one could understand), came back to kill the master.

The other newspaper scandal columns, her competitors, were positively salivating over the prospect of a society lady gone astray as the Avengeress, a wanton she-devil invading men's homes and absconding with their property. Some even offered ideas as to who the woman was, and it appeared some of the demimonde were considered for the role. It was amusing, if a bit unsettling.

Emmeline set the papers aside, finished her breakfast alone, as Fidelity was having a good long lie-in in advance of the tiring work of the literary salon that afternoon. She descended to the workrooms belowstairs and met with Mrs. Bramage in her office, a tiny windowless room, where they went over the details of the affair. The housekeeper was a dour woman, although Gillies said she could be animated after a glass of wine at the holidays, but other than that, Mrs. Bramage kept herself to herself. If she had any enjoyments beyond reading the Bible and knitting, Gillies didn't know about them.

"Mrs. Bramage, who is our scullery maid?"

"Her name is Annie, miss. Annie Jenson." The woman's pale, narrow face, covered in a net of wrinkles and creases, revealed no emotion. She closed her accounts book, where she had recorded the purchases made for the literary salon. Leopold would receive a detailed list of the expenses—how much Congou tea, how many jars of blackberry preserves, how many bottles of sherry—in her and Birk's monthly budget accounting.

"And you hired her?" Emmeline asked. The housekeeper nodded. "How did you find her, if I may ask?"

"My sister, who is in service near Malincourt, miss; folks as supplied the big house with fish had a daughter they were looking to place, and she weren't opposed to coming to London. I said we'd try her out, if they could send her along here."

"And how *is* she working out?"

"Well enough," Mrs. Bramage said. "She is frightened of Mr. Birk, and that's no lie. He shouts at her when she gets in his way," she added, airing her grievance in a rush. "But she's a hard-working child and not sullen. I can teach anyone so long as they are not sullen."

"I'll speak with Birk." Whether it would do any good or not, Emmeline could not imagine. "Is that how you normally get your girls, by word of mouth?"

She nodded. "We needed a new scullery maid. I had moved Arbor up to being chambermaid once Linda Charles left to return home when her mother fell ill."

"I thought I noticed a new face. Arbor is doing a wonderful job," Emmeline said with a smile. The housekeeper nodded. "Fidelity quite likes her, I know; she has been most obliging to the Comtesse. Would you ever employ a girl from a workhouse or orphanage?"

Mrs. Bramage sniffed and made a sour face. "Not in *my* household. Begging your pardon, miss; not in a home where I am employed. Those girls ... dirty, sullen little street creatures with who knows what parentage? Could murder us all in our sleep. Look at that scullery maid what was taken by that masked woman! In league with her, no doubt; a guttersnipe and her bawd. It's a wonder the whole household wasn't murdered in their sleep." Her tone was bloodthirsty and her dark eyes gleamed, almost as if she enjoyed the notion. Perhaps she was getting her information from the papers, which, in their unusually liberal household, the staff were allowed to read once Emmeline and Fidelity were done with them. "Probably their intent, only they were startled by the knight and killed him in revenge. Mark my words, that's what happened."

With that earful, Emmeline had heard enough. No wonder word of the masked woman's perfidy was spreading so fast. It was the simplest thing to imagine and the most exciting to believe.

"Tell Mrs. Riddle I will have the iced punch brought up first," Emmeline said. "After the salon we'll have our luncheon in the dining room, as we decided, and we'll finish with sherry back in the sitting room. Thank you, Mrs. Bramage."

SEVENTEEN

EMMELINE AND FIDELITY GREETED their guests in the sitting room, which had been rearranged for the event. They discussed Anna Seward's work and lamentable death, and then Fidelity did a reading of Seward's Sonnet 84. Her voice trembled and sighed through it, until the final lines: "'More pensive thoughts in my sunk heart infuse / Than Winter's gray, and desolate domain / Faded, like my lost Youth, that no bright Spring renews.'"

There was silence, and then a smattering of applause and murmurs of appreciation. Fidelity had a lovely speaking voice, but the subject—loneliness, decline, and death—was gloomy.

It had all taken far longer than she had expected. "On that cheerful note," Emmeline said, standing, as a couple of her guests chuckled, "let us forego our literary discussion and descend to the dining room for luncheon." Everyone needed a few glasses of wine to liven their mood.

Birk had borrowed two footmen from a family friend and fitted them with St. Germaine livery. They served as he stood in august majesty, directing the meal. After the revivifying luncheon—turtle soup, plaice, oysters, beefsteak, and salad, followed by Madeira cake and fruits—the group returned upstairs to the sitting room for tea, sherry, and chat. It had been rearranged during luncheon into conversational groupings of chairs and settees. This, for many, was the best part of the afternoon, a time to trade gossip with folks they didn't often see. Two of the Crones were in attendance: Lady Adelaide Sherringdon and Miss Juliette Espanson. Also present were Mr. Lessington, who owned the Dionysus Theater, accompanied by a young friend of his, a poet who had recently published a book funded, Emmeline suspected, by the theater owner, as Mr. Lessington was a stalwart supporter of the artistic endeavors of others.

A fire in the grate burned cheerily. Copious amounts of sherry and claret were imbibed; voices increased in volume, laughter echoed, cheeks glowed, and smiles enlarged. Emmeline was pleased to watch Fidelity light up with joy. Poetry and literature were her great comforts. In some ways, though she was supposed to be Emmeline's companion, lending her the safety and credibility of an older widow, it often seemed that Emmeline was the companion, giving her older cousin comfort and entertainment. Mutual benefit was derived, for Fidelity was the mildest of companions.

As the young poet friend, sweeping back a long curl of hair from his forehead, regaled a group of women, who laughed gaily at his sallies, Mr. Lessington took a seat by Emmeline and regarded her narrowly.

"What is it?" she asked. "Have I broken out in spots?"

"Not at all, my dear. However, the other night in my theater I noticed you speaking with Mr. Simeon Kaufmann, owner and publisher of *The Prattler*. And it did lead me to wonder what a young lady like you would have in common with a married man of the Hebrew persuasion, a radical-leaning gentleman who employs a web of gossips and numbers informers and rabble-rousing writers among his friends?"

Frowning, she examined his face, which was lightly lined, his hair unfashionably collar-length and swept back off his high forehead, his gray eyes mild. "I'm sure I don't know who you mean."

He nodded, crossing his legs and taking a sip of sherry. "I understand." He smiled and patted her hand. "My dear, of all the young ladies I know, you interest me the most. You are, I suspect, an actress, playing the part of a demure and modest lady of means."

Emmeline stiffened and glanced around the room, then back to him. "You are on the verge of insult, Mr. Lessington."

"Oh, don't worry, my dear." He smiled and sipped. "I dissemble, too, except within the bosom of my little circle."

"I resent the implication, sir, that I am somehow false," she said, her heart thudding in her chest.

"Ah, yes … when cornered, bare your fangs and growl." Another pained smile flitted across his mobile, expressive face. "I mean no offence, Miss St. Germaine. I am not among those males who believe women should stay in their sphere, and that to deviate is to unsex themselves." He smiled kindly, but his expression sobered. "If ever you need a friend with many gossipy connections, you have him in me."

Emmeline stared at him, uncertain of his meaning. "Let us speak of other things. Do you personally know Mr. … what was his name? The newspaper publisher you spoke of? I don't believe I've ever met him."

"Mr. Simeon Kaufmann. I know him slightly. Perhaps I was mistaken; at the theater the other night you were in close conversation with him, so I thought you knew him."

"Ah, the gentleman's whose sleeve button got tangled in my lace cuff? I did not know his name. And he owns *The Prattler*? Very amusing paper." Her tone sounded stilted, even to herself.

"They have a column I particularly like, the Rogue."

"I hear it condemned as gossip."

"My dear, what is gossip but the human fascination with the trials and tribulations of men and women? I have a theory that all great art starts out as gossip, tales told over and over from human to human until they become ingrained in us and are spewed out as literature. Or opera!"

She glanced around at the chatting, gossiping groups, noticing glances thrown, whispers and widened eyes, expressions of joyous shock. She thought of her most recent column, and the scandal she had passed on about the wife wishing her husband dead so she could wed her younger lover. She had named names and given details; anyone could guess who Lady H__ was. From the anonymity of the printing press she had hurled accusations and perhaps made one woman's life a trial.

Should she be ashamed? Or had she saved the man's life? "Mr. Lessington, do you think gossip harmful? I sometimes feel guilty when I pass on a tale I have heard secondhand."

"As someone who has had to fend off the horrors of gossip, I may be supposed to be biased against it, but I'm not. Stories, either true or untrue, *can* cause great harm. But the first whispers of gossip are also what occasionally brings an evil-doer to justice. We use gossip to test news, to spread concerns, to hint at danger. Every man and woman must judge for themselves what is fit to disseminate and what should be suppressed, and live with the consequences of their decision."

She nodded absently.

"Take, for instance, the gossip I have recently heard about a group of women of good birth and gentle upbringing who go about saving waifs. I thought it was idle gossip, but now I am wondering if this magnificent masked woman—the one in all the headlines, the Avengeress, as they call her—is a part of that group." He watched her closely.

Emmeline's blood ran cold. At that very moment, Fidelity, looking weary, sent her a beseeching look. Her cousin was tiring, it appeared. "Excuse me, Mr. Lessington; Fiddy appears to be in distress," she said, and hastened away, but when she looked back over her shoulder, the theater owner was regarding her with thoughtful eyes.

Too close ... he was *too close* to the truth. Emmeline wondered, had Mr. Lessington brought up the Rogue and her group of Crones within minutes of each other because he suspected her of being one or the other, or both, or merely because the masked woman was on the tip of everyone's tongue and they had been speaking of gossip? *That's the problem*, she thought; her consciousness made her see danger where none, perhaps, lay. Was she blind, then, alternately, to true danger all around her? She didn't know.

Fidelity, it turned out, simply wanted to be rescued from a particularly tiresome member of the literary society. Mr. Lessington then followed Emmeline and sat down next to Fidelity for a good long coze over hot, black Congou; Miss Juliette Espanson and Lady Sherringdon joined them. Fidelity seemed more at ease once surrounded by friends. Emmeline, however, was disturbed by her conversation with the theater owner and could not relax for the rest of the afternoon.

She learned a lot of gossip, but given that it was at an event in her own home, she knew the Rogue would not be able to use it. Lady Sherringdon took the opportunity to whisper of another scullery maid she had found who needed rescuing. But Adelaide had her own method to take care of it, and already had a place for the child to go to.

The only other spot of interest was when Juliette Espanson slipped a note into her hand and whispered that it was from Miss Dorcas Harvey. The suggestion it contained was so exactly what Emmeline needed and wanted that it seemed impossible, and yet there it was: on the morrow, Emmeline had an entrée into the Claybourne home accompanying Dorcas's employer and posing as Dorcas. It was risky, but nothing would be gained without risk, she had decided when she began as the Avengeress.

———

Emmeline lay abed the next morning, making a list in her mind of possible suspects in the brutal murder of Sir Henry Claybourne. She must suspect Lady Claybourne and every member of Sir Henry's household staff. The only one of his household she could unequivocally say did *not* kill him was Molly, who had been on her way to her new situation at the time of the knight's death. The case against all of the serving staff and his wife was that Sir Henry was a loathsome man with despicable habits, and who knew that better than his family and servants?

Then there was Mr. Wright, his brewery business partner, as well as his other, more mysterious business partners. Mr. Wright had said that Sir Henry was caught up in business with new, higher-toned partners, a venture that had him ignoring the brewery. Perhaps Mr. Wilkins, who had admitted to knowing Sir Henry, would know what else the brewer may have been involved in. It was tricky to imagine how she would mine Mr. Wilkins for such information, though.

There was also Mr. Benjamin Hargreaves and his sister, Aloisia. Miss Hargreaves had supposedly been insulted, and Mr. Hargreaves was angry about that. In addition, she was concealing something about her visits to Lady Claybourne's bedside. Weak, but interesting.

And then there were the Crones. Emmeline knew *she* didn't do it, but had a Crone—perhaps Lady Clara Langdon—set her up to appear guilty while *she* dispatched the man? She worried at the idea; there was slim evidence Lady Clara had had anything to do with it, but for a bloody glove and a coolly vicious response to Sir Henry's death. She appeared to be trying to help in Emmeline's pursuit of the murdering wretch, but still … there was something not quite right about the lady, though that didn't make her a killer.

Last but most certainly not least, there were, she hoped, the most likely villains: Ratter, perhaps in cooperation with the two men with whom the knight had argued after Emmeline's raid of his home. Had he summoned them? Who would know? The potboy had been dispatched with notes, but to whom were the notes sent?

She must not become committed to the notion that Ratter, alone or in collusion with the two unknown men, had committed the bloody murder. She would follow her plan to visit the orphanage Lady Clara had mentioned; it seemed likely that Ratter had gotten Molly, and Sally before her, from an orphanage to satisfy Sir Henry's disgusting desires. Perhaps it had stopped there, and with the client dead, there would be no more children maltreated.

Gillies came in carrying a tray. She set it down on the dressing table and drew back the curtains, letting in a drift of misty light. The tray held a cup of hot black tea and the morning's post. There was, Emmeline was pleased to see, a long, gossipy letter from "Miss S. Kinsman"— Simeon—with cleverly phrased answers to her muttered requests at the theater. They had, since she had begun writing the Rogue column, drafted a kind of shorthand, code words that enabled them to correspond on subjects not otherwise suitable for two young ladies.

Simeon wrote: *That new haberdasher has a pet, a big and vicious dog, that he is deeply concerned about. His sister, Miss A, is worried too, so much so that she has taken to selling off her possessions to look after it! But where does a young lady like that get a ruby brooch? One asks oneself.*

How interesting, Emmeline thought, taking a long sip of tea. She shared what it meant with Gillies, who was bustling around arranging the necessary clothing and accessories for the day. "Simeon says that Mr. Hargreaves is in an enormous amount of debt—rhymes with pet, you see—and is deeply worried. His sister is concerned about it too—I have noted how threadbare their living accommodations—and has pawned a ruby brooch. Simeon wonders where someone so impoverished would acquire a ruby brooch."

Gillies frowned as she laid out a pair of green calf gloves. "Mayhap a family heirloom?"

"Perhaps. Or a gift from a grateful Sir Henry, if they were having an affair?" Emmeline shook her head. "That doesn't make sense. He didn't seem the type to give gifts to young ladies. He had other interests."

"This haberdasher's sister were in the Claybourne house?" Gillies asked. Emmeline nodded. "P'raps she snatched the bauble from Lady Claybourne's nightstand, or some such if she visited the lady in her chambers?"

"Good thought, Gillies. Maybe she lifted it and pawned it to help her brother. If Sir Henry found out and threatened her, it would give the Hargreaves a motive to kill him rather than risk the noose or transportation." She shook her head. "Just so much supposition so far."

"I can mayhap track down Tommy again. Or the little gairl, Fanny, what works for the Hargreaves. She's their only servant, and I'd lay a wager knows more than they suspect."

Emmeline drank the rest of her cold tea and swung her feet over the edge of her bed, ready to face the day. "If you can find anything out, I'd welcome the information, but I won't have Tommy in danger. And that girl, Fanny ... she seemed a frightened little thing. Is it wise to ask her questions she may relay back to her mistress?"

"Dinna fash yourself, Miss Emmeline. I know how to go on. What d'ye have planned for the day?"

"I have a surprise quest, first thing, and I must hurry," she said. She retrieved Dorcas Harvey's note from her Bible on the nightstand and unfolded it. "I'm taken aback, but Miss Harvey, who is companion to an elderly dragon of an aunt, I understand, has managed to engage her employer's aid to get me into Lady Claybourne's home, posing as Dorcas."

Gillies gasped and whirled. "Miss, is that not dangerous? What did she confide in the lady that made this possible?"

"I don't know the whole story yet, but I'm alarmed as well. Since the plan has been set in motion, I have little choice but to see it through, at least to meeting the elderly woman in Clerkenwell."

"But what makes her think she'll be admitted to Lady Claybourne's house?"

"The lady is related to Sir Henry." Emmeline smiled grimly and sighed. "Odd how things work. I do want an opportunity to judge if any one of the inhabitants killed the man. Afterwards, Josephs will drive me north, to Camden Town. I am to visit an orphanage there supported by Lady Clara Langdon. The wardress may have information on Ratter, and she also may know of other orphanages at which to inquire."

"I can ride with you—tell Mr. Birk we're goin' shopping, or to visit—an' you can let me off near Sir Henry's, then get me when you coom back that way from Camden Town."

"I couldn't possibly—"

"Miss, please!" Gillies turned from her tidying work, her lined face twisted in grief. "Every day I think of all the bairns in London an' beyond, all the wee ones abused and battered. Poor wee Tommy, black wi' soot, who we saved from that frightful man, and all the other dear little ones. No one cares a scrap for them, but I pray every night for their salvation, miss. Let me do my part."

Emmeline examined the woman's face, the welling moisture in her eyes, the pain of loss still tormenting her soul. "Gillies, by investigating, I hope to bring whomever killed Sir Henry to the noose. And yet Sir Henry was one of those who abused the children you care for."

"Aye, but I have a dread feeling in me bones, miss." Gillies put one worn hand on her muslin-covered chest. "The man was murdered for something he were involved in, an' it could be something to do with the wee lassies he mistreated." She sat down on the chair in front of the dressing table. "P'raps by finding the truth, we can save more o' the gairls. I crave to help, miss."

Emmeline swallowed hard as she gazed over at Gillies, so much more than a lady's maid to her. Gillies had goals of her own to achieve. As her mistress, it was in Emmeline's power to help or hinder, and she would not deny the woman her request. "All right. I don't need to warn you to be careful. It will be a long day, though."

"Aye. An' the same to you, miss. Now, let's get you dressed for a day of travel."

EIGHTEEN

GILLIES, ON THE LOOKOUT for Tommy, departed the carriage on Samuel Street. Josephs turned onto Chandler Lane, where the antiquated and rarely used carriage of Miss Philberta Honeychurch, as described in the note from Dorcas, was pulled close to the edge of the narrow lane by the open green space. The driver leaped down gracefully and stood by the carriage door. With Josephs' aid, Emmeline climbed down from her carriage, gathered her cloak around her, and approached the other coach, evading a laundress carrying a stack of linens on her shoulder.

The driver ignored her, staring straight ahead, so she rapped smartly on the door. It was flung open from within. Dorcas grabbed her arm and hauled her into the cracked and worn dark leather interior. Her fellow Crone appeared disheveled, red-faced, and unnerved. She mumbled introductions and Emmeline turned to regard Miss Honeychurch, not sure what to expect.

The woman was indubitably well into her eighties, as Dorcas had once confided in a Crones meeting. Her face was wizened, and her mouth drawn together into a meager, wrinkle-circled gash. Her teeth had all been pulled out many years ago, Emmeline supposed. Her eyes were dark, like currants set in folds of pale flesh, but they glittered with awareness.

"Go away, Dorcas, to the tea shop and get yourself a bun," the woman said, her voice creaky, like an unoiled door hinge. "Miss St. Germaine and I have much to discuss."

"I'd rather you stayed, Dorcas, and—"

"Afraid of me, girl?" the woman said, and cackled, a croak that ended on a wheeze. Her wig and cap slid sideways. Dorcas righted it and then retreated toward the door, watching them, her eyes narrowed.

Looking at Miss Honeychurch, Emmeline was vividly reminded of a rude image that had been printed ten or so years earlier, entitled *Old Maids Leading Apes*. It depicted several old maids in that endeavor, the central one with a nose arching down and a chin arching up, and referred to the old proverb stating that an unmarried woman's fate was to lead apes to hell.

"I'm not afraid of you, ma'am," she replied calmly. "You can go, Dorcas, if you like, but not on my account."

"She'll do as she's told," the woman said coldly. Dorcas scuttled out, the carriage rocking, and slammed the door behind her.

"Henry Claybourne was my nephew, you know ... or what is called a great nephew, I suppose, the son of my niece. She was a stupid girl with stupid children, who have all gotten killed in one ridiculous way or another," Miss Honeychurch said, her tone sour. "Why would you wish to find his murderer when the fellow did our country a great favor by removing him? Probably did his widow a favor too, given what I know of the gibbous dunce."

Emmeline burst into laughter, somewhat relieved. "Ma'am, I thought you wished to join me out of an outraged sense of justice, so that your nephew's murderer would swing from the gibbet."

"I'd be more likely to shake his hand." The woman was dressed in black and wore a powdered wig many years old with a black hat pinned to it. Her face was a pale oval illuminated only duskily by the faint light let in through a slit between the door blind and the carriage wall, and she smelled of camphor, lavender powder, and strong vinegar from an ornate vinaigrette she held in one gloved hand. "Dorcas tells me you have a group that rescues girls who are being mistreated, and that she belongs to it. She says you arranged to have the scullery maid removed from Henry's house. Is that true?"

"Yes," Emmeline replied. All along, she had been worried about Martha Adair's loose tongue, but it seemed it was Dorcas she should have been concerned about.

"I suspect that you, then, are the thief who made off with the child and the silver?"

"No silver, ma'am," she said. "The girl, yes. She was in danger."

"I'm surprised you let Dorcas be a part of the scheme, as she has the discretion of a penny strumpet, but that is the topic of another conversation. Shall I tell you what I know of Sir Henry Claybourne?" She then related how she, Philberta Honeychurch, had stayed in Sir Henry's family home when she was a thirty-year-old spinster. Her father had died, and so had her brother, or else he would have been left in control of Philberta's inheritance. Her niece, Anne, was married and had children, and her niece's husband, Sir Henry's father—also named Henry—was the one left in control of Philberta's money; her father had believed that women should never control their inheritance. It was a tangled tale, but Emmeline understood it. It meant that

Philberta Honeychurch, unmarried but wealthy, was at the elder Henry Claybourne's mercy, in a sense, and had to live in his home.

Philberta had disliked Henry Junior even then, when he was a lad of fifteen or sixteen, and only grew to detest him more. "I suspect that he tumbled a little girl in the household," she said, revulsion threading in tendrils through her desiccated voice. "There was quite a commotion about a maid, but it was hushed up. The girl was disposed of somehow and Henry was sent away to school. Should have gone years before, but he had been coddled and kept home by my idiot niece because he was *delicate*. I told her he wasn't delicate, he was twisted, but she wouldn't listen. No one would listen."

"So he was like that even then."

Miss Honeychurch grunted in the affirmative. "All these years... I wonder how many little girls he has destroyed? I wish I could have prevented it, but I had no right, nor any say in his punishment, such as it was."

They were both silent for a long minute. "Why, then, do you wish to help find his killer?" Emmeline asked. "For that is my aim, you understand."

"I don't care if they never find out who killed him. But I *do* care that the wrong person does not suffer by being wrongfully accused of putting him down like the festering, rabid, and dangerous dog he was," she said, with more force than one would have thought possible for one so wizened and weak.

"And who do you think that 'wrong person' is?"

"I have no idea who *didn't* do it. How could I? But who *did* do it? *That* I have ideas about. You, perhaps? Though I don't suppose so. You have the look of a moralistic prig about you. Could be Dorcas, for all I know; she's certainly strong enough. Though again, I doubt it. Dorcas's heart is bigger than her brain; I don't suppose she'd even have the nerve to throttle a chicken for dinner. And she's from an entirely different branch of my family. In any case, I don't think she gives a fig about your causes. I suspect the only reason she stays with your group is because she is in love with Martha Adair."

Emmeline gasped.

"Did you not know?"

"I suspected, but I wasn't sure."

"When you are my age, Miss St. Germaine, you will have little to do but to observe and surmise. It is my only entertainment."

Discomfited, Emmeline stared at the woman. "And you don't … I mean—"

"Disapprove? I may as well disapprove that my pug chews my shoes, or that the moon rises each night. How can Dorcas help it? It is an incontrovertible fact. Men—and women, too—have moralized that we are in control of our emotions and should not give love where it is improper. That is hogwash. We cannot control love, we can only control what we do about it. There have been women who loved other women, and men who loved other men, since man and woman were created, I expect, and any one of the Lord's creations is good enough for me." She chuckled. "Did you never wonder why Dorcas was let go from the school where she taught?"

"It never came up."

"She fell in love with one of the other teachers, who was sorely offended, so that *bitch*, rather than admit what upset her, told the headmistress Dorcas was corrupting the young girls."

"Oh."

"She hadn't done a single thing with any child. Dorcas's tastes run to matronly middle-aged ladies. But she is my kin, and I could not let her suffer. She's a terrible companion to me, but she tries her best and when I am cruel, she suffers it well. I wish I could say I will be kinder in future, but I am often in pain and it makes me lash out at the dumb creature who I know will bear it." She paused to catch her breath, wheezing in discomfort. "Now, are we going in, or do I have to go home without enjoying the fact that Henry is dead?"

Emmeline was torn. Miss Honeychurch was an unknown and likely unknowable entity. Would she cause more problems than she solved? And could Emmeline herself remain disguised as Miss Dorcas Harvey when both the cook and housekeeper had seen a portion of the Avengeress's face? She made a rapid decision. There was no path to finding the truth without risk. "I'm ready."

"Not like that, though, you idiot," the woman said irritably. "You are *far* too well-dressed to be my companion. Your gown alone is worth more than one year's wages for Dorcas. Fortunately, I'm clever and brought one of her cloaks. It will cover you adequately, and since we are only staying for a brief visit, if we get in at all, you can keep it on over your unsuitably costly garb." She paused a moment. "Hide your gloves and shoes as well as possible. You are unconscionably fine, too much so for a companion."

Moments later, feeling weighed down by the heavy, plain cloak she now wore over her clothes, Emmeline climbed down from the coach as the driver, a strapping, tall, and handsome young man, reached in past her. To her surprise, he lifted Miss Honeychurch out of the carriage and carried her up the walk to number seventy-three, then up the steps to the door, where he employed the knocker even though it had been muffled in deference to Sir Henry's death. He then banged on the door.

A maid answered and backed away when she saw the coachman with the frail lady in his arms. He pushed in past her as the woman shouted, "Miss Philberta Honeychurch to visit Lady Claybourne. Announce me!"

The girl babbled about not having visitors, but that moment a stout middle-aged woman came into the entry hall.

"What is going on here?"

"Set me down, Roberts. Return for me in exactly one hour."

The driver set the elderly woman on her feet and exited, the stunned maid looking after him as he turned, winked at her over his shoulder, and departed.

"What is the meaning of this?" the woman, presumably Lady Claybourne, demanded.

"Dorcas, your arm!" Miss Honeychurch hollered. *"Dorcas!"*

Emmeline, not accustomed to responding to the name, lurched into action, taking the woman's arm before she could topple over.

"Into the drawing room … there," Miss Honeychurch muttered, indicating the room from which the lady of the house had emerged. "I must sit!" she said more loudly. As she toddled forward stiffly on Emmeline's arm, she shouted over her shoulder, "How are you, Elaine? Haven't seen you since your wedding. What was it … thirty years ago?"

As they moved into the sitting room, Emmeline reflected that there were distinct benefits to being old. When she was Miss Honeychurch's age, she would be just so; do whatever she wanted and expect others to go along with her. She helped the woman settle, and then Miss Honeychurch shouted questions and Lady Claybourne responded with evasive phrases. Ten minutes of inconsequential chatter followed, during which Emmeline was able to study Lady Claybourne.

She was a heavy woman, deep of bosom and stout, with a florid complexion, weedy eyebrows set low over eyes folded into wrinkles, and an unhappy mouth. She was dressed in black, of course, but it was not a new dress. Sally had implied the woman was a laudanum addict, but if so, the need for it had disappeared with the death of her distasteful husband, because today her gaze was sharp and her manner precise. She had gray eyes, pale lashes, and graying hair, piled untidily under a lace cap.

The room was dusty but neat, a narrow chamber at the front of the building, the walls covered in yellow figured wallpaper. It was light enough at the front, by the windows, but it stretched into gloom near the back, even the bright paper failing to illuminate the dusk. Emmeline thought, from a quick glance at a writing table by the window, that the lady had been penning letters, the sheet hastily covered with blank papers. They were sitting in ornate chairs opposite a gilt settee, the furnishing fashionable thirty years prior, by a fireplace unlit even on this late October day, either because the lady did not expect to be there long or because she was habitually over-warm, as some women were at her stage of life. Men would have it that women became mad at a certain age, but Emmeline had always thought they wearied of the tedious interference of men. By the age of fifty or so, most had been made irritated and captious by a lifetime of male irrationality.

Perhaps that explained Sir Henry Claybourne's murder; his wife had become tired of him. It was at this point in her ruminations, during which she had allowed Miss Honeychurch to lead the conversation—as a good companion would—that Emmeline realized her "employer" was finally getting to the point of the visit.

"Henry was killed in the middle of the night, the papers say. What the devil was he doing in the alley?"

Lady Claybourne shrugged.

"Didn't you hear anything, Elaine? He should have made a fuss, I would imagine, being stuck like a porker."

Emmeline gasped, and Lady Claybourne stiffened. Even her age did not excuse Miss Honeychurch's offensiveness.

"You always were blunt," their hostess said. She crossed to the writing table, picked up a bell and rang it, and ordered tea for three from the maid. Returning to her seat, she said, "I normally partake this time of day. You are here for another three quarters of an hour, judging by what you said to your coachman, so you shall take tea with me."

"Very good. None for Dorcas. She doesn't drink it."

"I should be grateful of some tea, ma'am," Emmeline said, contradicting Miss Honeychurch.

"Of course," Lady Claybourne said, sharing a commiserating look with her.

"I'm sorry for your loss, ma'am," Emmeline said softly, building on the rapport they had established over Miss Honeychurch's discourtesy. "The papers are filled with such shocking news. I can't believe they have everything right about the affair. Are you not afraid, in case the murderer is still watching you?"

"I don't quite know what to think, or believe."

"Has the magistrate not done anything yet? You could all be murdered in your beds by that madwoman who raided your home," Miss Honeychurch said with a malicious cackle. "D'you think she did it, killed Henry?"

"I don't know," Lady Claybourne said. "I can't imagine that would be so. But it may be that the woman had a confederate."

"Maybe someone in your own staff let her in."

Emmeline felt a chill down her back; Miss Honeychurch was sailing too close to the truth. What was she doing?"

Lady Claybourne appeared startled. But a moment later she said, "Impossible! Why would they?"

"How else did the woman get in?"

Consternation flooded Lady Claybourne's eyes. Emmeline's breath caught in her throat; Miss Honeychurch was stirring up the pond quite thoroughly, like a little girl with a stick, jamming it into the muck that silted on the bottom. Would her efforts reveal anything, or merely cause trouble for the cook or housekeeper who had tried to help little Molly?

"I don't know," Lady Claybourne finally said, with a helpless shrug.

"Did your husband come up and tell you what happened?"

"I was indisposed that evening. I was abed, and had been for ... for hours."

And they no doubt had separate chambers, anyway.

"Who breaks into a house and takes a scullery maid, Elaine?"

"How would I know?" she said coldly.

"Did you hire the child?"

"I have been ill lately. Henry took care of things. Told me not to worry about it."

"You look well enough to me."

"I am recovering."

"What do your servants say? Or do they say nothing?" Miss Honeychurch snorted. "Could be a plot; I'd sack the lot of them."

"Why do you care so profoundly?" the knight's widow said at last. "You always were a nosy woman, even thirty years ago. Is this a visit of condolence, or were you sent by the magistrate to ask more impertinent questions?"

So the magistrate *had* been around, and Lady Claybourne had been upset by it. Emmeline watched the woman's face, trying to see the emotion behind the words. There was perturbation there, and a deep weariness underlying it. But was she frightened, as she should be, given that someone had killed her husband outside her back door and the killer was still free. She didn't appear to be worried so much as exasperated, and there was no one guarding the home, nor had Emmeline sighted a male servant.

"I have nothing to do with magistrate, Elaine," Miss Honeychurch said to her. "You're upset by my questions, but I can't say you look sorry that Henry is dead. Not that I would be in your place. But why are my questions so shocking?"

"I didn't say shocking, I said rude. I suppose everyone is entitled to uncouth curiosity from time to time," Lady Claybourne replied. "I don't remember you being so thoroughly vulgar. You were quite the moralizing proser, if I recall. At my wedding, you tried to persuade me that I should run away."

"I believe I told you that, yes," the old lady said. Her eyes betrayed no emotion. "I wonder what you would be now if you'd listened to me? You were quite beautiful then, and with a sweet nature."

The insult was clear, but the widow appeared not to note it. Tears welling in her eyes, Lady Claybourne stated, "I'm *grateful* I did not listen to your counsel."

"Oh?"

Emmeline narrowed her eyes and regarded the woman closely.

"Henry may have been many things, but he was a *good* and *kind* husband to me."

Lady Claybourne's speech defied common sense, given what Emmeline knew about Sir Henry. But perhaps willful blindness was the answer, or a resolve not to share her misery.

Miss Honeychurch snorted. "I ought to say how sorry I am he's gone, say he didn't deserve such a fate, eh? But I'm no hypocrite. The world is better for him being dead."

The woman stiffened at the scathing tone of her guest. "You have no right to be so mocking." Her voice trembled and she raised a handkerchief to her lips, her hand shaking. "You were always bitter. *Bitter* that his family ejected you from their house after being so kind as to give you a home for years. *Bitter* that accusations you made were exposed as false and defamatory. He warned me that you were liable to make trouble for him."

If she hadn't known from her own witnessing what kind of foul animal Sir Henry was, Emmeline may have doubted the spinster's veracity too. Her boorish lack of social grace condemned her as bitter, as much as Lady Claybourne said and more.

"My warning to you was meant as a kindness, Elaine. I'm surprised that even thirty years later you remain willfully blind, but then, you never seemed terribly bright." Miss Honeychurch's tone dripped with malice, thick as treacle, dark as molasses.

Who knew what Lady Claybourne would have said if the tea hadn't been delivered that moment? Mrs. Young, the housekeeper, brought it in, surprising and alarming Emmeline. She kept her eyes downcast, afraid their expression would trigger a memory in the woman.

"Milady, I hesitate to say," Mrs. Young said, "but we have a little problem."

Lady Claybourne regained her composure. "What is it, Mrs. Young?"

"This lady's driver is causing a stir. He came 'round to the back o' the house and is in the kitchen flirtin' most improperly with Sybil."

Miss Honeychurch chuckled. "Rascal," she muttered.

"Why do you come to me? You're well equipped to deal with an impertinent servant," Lady Claybourne said to her housekeeper.

"Aye, milady … long as I have your permission. I was wary, lest we offend your guest."

"Don't concern yourself over that, Mrs. Young," Lady Claybourne said acidly. "Miss Honeychurch has given more offense than she has ever taken. Now that I know he is arrived, these ladies can take their tea and be gone."

Emmeline felt defeated. No information had been gained. She had had such high hopes about getting inside the house, but she hadn't factored in Miss Honeychurch's obstreperous personality. She had always been sure that Dorcas exaggerated the difficulties of dealing with her aunt and employer, but if anything, her fellow Crone had put too mild a face on a very rude woman. While Emmeline thought of herself as dangerously forthright, she knew when to retreat.

A truce of sorts had been silently declared. Lady Claybourne poured tea into cups from one of the newer manufacturers, patterned in rich blues and reds and decorated in gold, what was called an Imari pattern. She poured first for Miss Honeychurch. Emmeline, as "Dorcas the companion," took it, not sure how to fix it, something she should know. She took a chance and set it in front of her employer. The woman nodded.

She accepted her own cup and took a long sip of the restorative brew. "I'm sorry for your pain, my lady," she dared to say.

After the astringent Miss Honeychurch, her tone must have seemed a honeyed balm. Lady Claybourne smiled through a veil of tears that welled in her eyes. "I know he wasn't perfect, but he was a good husband to me. I'm at a loss, now, for I have no children and don't quite know what to do. I've been trying to write letters to his business partners, but I'm not even sure how to go on."

"Here, Elaine, I've been far too hard on you," Miss Honeychurch said. "You mustn't mind me. I've gotten worse-tempered in my old age, I have been told. Pain and suffering will do that. This one here writes a lovely letter. I'd lend her to you if I thought it would be any help."

"No, that is quite all right," Lady Claybourne hastily said. "I'll manage."

"My lady, I would be pleased to help you," Emmeline said, gazing steadily at the woman, then glancing at Miss Honeychurch.

"No, 'tis all right. My late husband's solicitor, Mr. Wilkins, has offered his help in business matters, and I believe I'll take him up on his offer."

NINETEEN

EMMELINE WAS SHOCKED TO the core to hear that Wilkins was Sir Henry's man of business, too, as well as her uncle's. So *many* threads leading to each other: Dorcas to Miss Honeychurch, Miss Honeychurch to Lady Claybourne, Lady Claybourne to Mr. Wilkins. She tried to think of a way to question the woman further, but Lady Claybourne, now that she knew her elderly guest's driver was at the house, gulped down her tea and commanded her housekeeper to have Miss Honeychurch's coachman bring the carriage around to the front.

Miss Honeychurch made a fuss in the entry, complaining of being rushed, fiddling with her gloves, and stumbling into a large urn and requiring Emmeline's help to steady her until Roberts leaped up the front steps to transport her to the carriage. During the turmoil she winked at Emmeline, to her surprise. Roberts carried his mistress down the steps and to the vehicle, set the frail woman in the carriage, helped Emmeline aboard, and then resumed his seat and slapped the reins.

They pulled around the corner and creaked to a halt. "What was all that fuss in the vestibule about, Miss Honeychurch?" Emmeline asked.

"Stupid girl. Thought you were more clever than Dorcas." Miss Honeychurch moved around, trying to get comfortable and giving up with a sigh. "What did we learn?"

"Not much," Emmeline said, not divulging what she *did* learn, about the connection to Mr. Wilkins.

"So you will need to go back."

Emmeline eyed her, wondering if she had lost her wits; how could she go back to the Claybourne residence?

"Dullard. Since Elaine wasn't having you as her secretary, I made sure you had a reason to go back. I need my lace mittens. I believe I may have dropped them into that hideous vase of dried reeds in the entrance. I suggest you retrieve them soon, or that sour-faced housekeeper will discover them and send them to me by post."

Emmeline regarded her with growing respect.

"Don't look at me like that," she groused, her small dark eyes almost disappearing. "I have nothing to do in life but scheme and order people about."

Dorcas, stuffed full of buns and Lapsang souchong from a local tea shop, tapped and was allowed into the carriage as Emmeline climbed down, carrying the borrowed cloak over one arm, as she would need to wear it on her return to the Claybourne residence. Josephs took it, holding it away from him with two fingers, and stowed it in the back as she paused to speak with Roberts.

"How did your conversation in the kitchen go, Roberts?"

"Well enough, miss." He frowned down at her from his perch, holding the reins of two tired-looking carriage horses. "But that is an odd household. Not a single man employed except the coachman, who lives in rooms at the livery stable away from the 'ouse."

Though apparently coached by his employer, he had learned little more. The cook had looked like she wanted to talk, but the housekeeper had kept a grim watch on them both. While he was there, though, the maid from the Farnsworth residence next door, young Biddy, had come over and whispered in the corner with Sybil. Emmeline decided she would return later that afternoon and claim that her eccentric lady mistress had sent her on foot, which would hopefully give her a reason to sit in the kitchen for a moment herself, to catch her breath. It was a risk, as before, for what if the cook or housekeeper recognized her as Molly's rescuer? But desperate times called for desperate measures.

Camden Town, in the parish of St. Pancras, was a newer residential area a couple of miles north of the center of London, northwest of Clerkenwell and slightly south of the older community of Kentish Town. Lord Camden had, in 1791, laid out a plan for fourteen hundred new houses, and so had begun a thriving community. The distance gave Emmeline time to reflect on what she had seen and heard. Lady Claybourne claimed to miss and grieve her husband sincerely, despite what Emmeline knew of his disgusting habits and personal lack of charm. More significant perhaps, though she couldn't be sure, was that her uncle's solicitor, Mr. Wilkins, was involved with the Claybourne estate. She'd have to ponder that information.

Once they got to Camden Town, Josephs stopped and asked for directions to the orphan asylum. It turned out to be housed in a newer brick building on a short dead-end street. He didn't turn down the street, as there would be no way to turn the carriage around if he did. He stayed where he was as Emmeline explored the narrow road, strolling along the shadowed length. St. Pancras Children's House had no signs, but the sound and sight of children playing, a group of boys using sticks to bat a cobble around in the narrow alley, told her she had arrived. She pulled a bell rope by the plain plank door.

A hard-looking woman with a grim scowl opened the door and stared at Emmeline, no word of greeting.

"Hello. I'd like to speak to Mrs. Miller."

"I'm 'er." The woman still stared at her.

Emmeline wore costly garments, but no external appearance of wealthy or propriety seemed enough to pass the doorway unchallenged. That was as it should be. "I am Miss Emmeline St. Germaine, a friend of Lady Clara Langdon's. She told me of your work. I'd like to help."

At the magic mention of Lady Clara's name, the woman's dour expression relaxed into mere solemnity. "We can use any 'elp we get."

Emmeline signaled down the lane for Josephs to wait and entered a dark but clean passageway that smelled of sweat, cabbage, and floor polish. With so many children in residence, it was surprising it did not smell of worse.

"I must work as we talk, if you don't mind, miss. Follow me." Mrs. Miller led the way to a room near the back, small and dark but comfortably furnished with shabby chairs centered on a worn Turkey rug in front of a modern iron fire grate where coals glowed and popped.

"I'm surprised you were so swift to answer the bell," Emmeline commented.

"I 'eard a shout from one of the boys," the wardress said, indicating some chairs by the hearth. "They let me know when a stranger approaches."

Emmeline strolled past the seating arrangement to the window and looked out. The room overlooked a small back garden enclosure where some girls were sitting on benches with books and dolls. An older girl, maybe eleven, was reading to some of them. There was a pulley system that ran through the hall to the back and a bell there, so it could be rung even from the back garden.

"You separate the girls and boys for play?"

Mrs. Miller offered her tea, which Emmeline declined, and then sat down in a chair, taking up a workbasket piled with black stockings. She took a couple out, laid them over her chair arm, set the basket back down, and, taking up a needle and wool, pushed her raw knuckled hand into it and began darning the heel. "I did not always do so, but a man who came asking about girls alarmed me. I've 'eard of girls disappearin'. Since then I've 'ad the girls playing in the enclosed gardens with one of the bigger girls to watch."

"Lady Clara told me about the incident and how it upset you. She said a man with a small dog came asking about girls, in particular, to supply London houses with scullery maids?"

The woman nodded in acknowledgement of the description. "I've lived a long life, Miss St. Germaine. My 'usband, God rest 'is soul—'e were a good man, but rough—was a soldier, sergeant to a Major near the end. I travelled with 'em as laundress an' saw action in Ireland, Switzerland, Italy … we were stationed for a time on Malta. With that much action, you'd think my 'usband would be in mortal danger. But in the end my Arthur's death came not in battle, but from dysentery. Filthy water in a canteen got 'im. I told 'im, I said, don't drink the water. Men never listen."

Emmeline shifted anxiously, wondering if the woman would get to some point or answer her question.

Mrs. Miller finished off the sock, folded it, and picked up another. "Children are 'ell on socks—pardon the expression, miss. Tearin' 'oles, wearin' out 'eels. I never 'ad no children. None that survived, anyway. Had five, all dead." She paused and looked at her guest. "In all those years wiv the army, miss, I learned a thing or two about men. Filthy buggers, some of 'em. But then some women, especially them as follers the troops, is dirty 'ores."

Emmeline should have been shocked by the woman's rough speech, but she was rather entertained. She appreciated that Lady Clara kept so strong and blunt a woman as wardress. She had a sense the woman was going to answer her question, in her own way in her own time. "I have heard tales," she murmured. "Of camp followers."

"I started out sheltered; me pa were careful wiv 'is girls. But being with my Arthur and the army, I soon got canny. Started to take note of the men who were the worst. Got a feeling right 'ere," she said, hand over her stomach, meeting Emmeline's gaze. "They abused them foreign girls; said as she weren't English, it didn't matter. An' the higher-ups didn't care. Most of 'em, anyway. Thought as 'ow the men were garbage and expected no better. Men'll live up—or down—to what is thought of 'em." Mrs. Miller frowned at the sock she was darning. "It were always the same men doing the worst. I listen to that feelin' now. When that feller showed up 'ere with 'is doggie that got the little ones all excited, I knew 'e were a wrong 'un. Burning in my gut told me."

Emmeline sat forward, her curiosity sharpened. She was about to ask about the man, but a neatly dressed young woman came to the sitting room door.

"Mrs. Miller, the fishlad says 'e's owed tuppence."

The wardress took a pocket out of a slit in her dress, counted tuppence, and handed it to the girl. When the young maid exited, Mrs. Miller watched Emmeline carefully. "So, not to be rude, miss, but what did you come 'ere for? Most of the ladies as want to donate crave to see the children. You don't seem mortal interested in the little ones, begging yer pardon, miss."

There was no point in being anything but blunt with so canny a woman. "You're right, Mrs. Miller. I'm *not* here to donate, though I will. I'm here to find out more about that man, the one with the dog."

The wardress, her hard gray eyes underlined with weariness and a world of sorrow, nodded. "I take it 'e's gotten other orphan asylums to give 'im girls?"

"I think so, but I'm not sure. I know that he took a girl to a man's home where she was abused." She didn't elaborate, nor did she raise Sir Henry's name. "What do you do with your girls and boys, once they are of an age to work?"

"I 'ave me sources. Thirty years wiv the army give me a lot of names, and I've got a good mem'ry," she said, tapping her forehead. "I remember tales of those 'oo had a good family an' those that didn't. Boys go out to apprentice, but none o' the danger trades. No chimney sweepin' fer my boys, an' they learn to read an' write afore they leave me, an' that ain't until they're twelve. Lady Clara buys some of 'em apprenticeships. They go to brick layers, stone masons, printers an' the like, good honest work. Girls go to scullery or sewing, or nursery undermaid; they read an' write afore they go, too, an' only go to 'omes where they'll be workin' under a good woman."

"Are there orphan asylums that aren't so careful?"

The woman's lined face, gray in the dull, weak light from the window, held an expression of sorrow. "Aye, I've 'eard tell that there'r those that take a premium for 'anding over girls to the London market."

"What are you saying, Mrs. Miller?"

"You know what I mean; I can see it on yer face." She reddened and dropped her darning to her lap, putting her hands over her face for a moment, then folding them together, composing herself. "I've bin to London. I've seen those girls, some no older than those little ones," she said, motioning out the window to the children playing with dolls in the garden. "Paradin' in the streets near Haymarket, lookin' for randy gents oo'll give 'em tuppence an' a nip of gin. If I could take in every one of 'em, I would, but I'm one woman. Makes me ill, but in truth, most of 'em 'ave mothers, just not one 'oo cares a fig about 'em."

"How could a mother allow that?"

"You've never bin poor, miss. You don't know 'ow the 'opeless-ness…it seeps into yer bones, an' any relief, even that of the gin bot-tle, seems a blessin'. I'm not makin' excuses, but it grinds some women down till they don't care about nothing but…" She shrugged. "They don't care about nothin'."

On impulse, Emmeline put her hand over Mrs. Miller's. "I am doing my best to keep other little girls from falling into unsavory hands. To do so, I need to find out who is handing the children over to those who traffic in human flesh. Who else could I ask about the man with the dog?"

"I'll write names down, miss, but don't tell 'em it were me as told you. A couple of 'em…I don't trust 'em, an' they got higher friends than me, ones 'at could put me away."

"I won't breathe a world. And note which ones you especially don't trust."

————

Gillies wished to speak with Tommy Jones, but she had other tasks in mind too, and considered them as she dodged foot traffic along Samuel street. She had given a lot of thought to her mistress's account of the night of the murder. It was impossible to think that even in the dark of night, no one saw anything. The watch—those who were younger and able to do their job properly, anyway—would be out and about doing their route every hour. One had been beaten by the two men, she understood, but there had to have been another that night, one who could tell her if anything had been amiss before he was summoned by the fishlad who'd found Sir Henry. Could she find out who the watch was that night?

There certainly had been others about on legitimate business in the darkness, and of course some pursuing trades not *quite* so lawful. Many folk gave no thought to all those who worked for their living by the light of the moon. Lamplighters had to work well past nightfall lighting lamps, and had to start extinguishing them well before daybreak. The work of the night soil men took them into the back gardens of townhomes up and down every street, in every part of town, though they didn't do every convenience every night, of course.

She saw that Tommy was at his usual post on Samuel Street, sweeping, but it was a slow day; the weather was dry and the traffic light. So the boy was at the chandler shop peering into the window of his former employment, his hands cupped around his eyes. He stuck his tongue out and then raced away when the man inside rushed to the door. Gillies, a full basket over her arm, grabbed his arm as he darted past. "Tommy!"

"Miz Gillies!" he cried, a look of joy on his narrow, dirty face. "You coom back!"

She pulled him to one side of the walkway. Though the street was not too busy, foot traffic was as active as always: a milkmaid carried a pail of fresh milk into a tavern for the cook; a servant with a tray of loaves hurried them home to his master's kitchen; other servants bustled into the chandler's and the haberdasher's, among other shops along Samuel. There was a costermonger, too, with his barrow brimming with onions, cabbages, apples, and carrots, which he wheeled along as he called out his wares, and the usual pieman stood on the corner with his cart. Gillies bought Tommy a mutton pie and they ambled to the green area by Chandler Lane. She laid her shawl out on the grass and made him sit, cross-legged, while he ate. There was precious little mutton in the pie, but the filling of vegetables and meat fat gravy was no doubt tasty. It was a chilly day, with a lively wind. The sky was clear and the air dry.

It was a pleasure to watch the lad eat, his eyes screwed up closed at the delight of the hot pasty. When he had finished the pie and sighed, opening his eyes, his mouth turning down at the wretchedness of it being done, she pulled out of her basket a surprise, one of Cook's Banbury cakes. Mrs. Riddle was from Oxfordshire originally, and prided herself on a strict adherence to the recipe made famous in books of receipts like *The English Huswife*; the pastry was stuffed with sugared peel, currants, and nutmeg, and sanded with clumps of sugar. Tommy's eyes widened, and he took it from her with reverence. She let the boy enjoy it in its entirety, knowing he wouldn't have something so good for a twelve month or more. He ate it slowly, savoring every mouthful before swallowing.

Finally sated, he lay back and looked up at the sky. "This be a good day, Miz Gillies."

"It's good to see a lad get his fill. I 'ave another for ye to take for your tea, and I got some knit stockings to keep your feet warm." She took the items out of her basket.

Tommy sat up and tugged at the lapels of his jacket, looking serious. He was a businessman, and his merchandise was news. "So, yer wanna know what I figgered out?"

"I know it hasnae been long, but—"

"I got plenty, missus!" The boy rhymed off names: of the watchman who was beaten, although the fellow did not get a good look at the men who had done it to him. And the other watch, who had been called by the fishlad, and of others whose employment had taken them close to the alleyway that fateful night. Gillies, whose memory was excellent, stored the facts away, but Tommy had already been snooping enough to know what they had to say. Being so close to a crime like that, the men and boys had told the magistrate what they knew and were now dining out on it at the tavern, telling the tale to anyone who might stand them a drink, including news writers. She trusted his total recall of conversations.

But he had also spoken to the potboy from Sir Henry's own household, whose information was not likely dispensed in the local tavern. "'E's mortal feared fer 'is life. 'E said as 'ow the gent—Sir 'Enry, that is—arter the masked lady skeered 'im proper as 'e was tuppin' Molly—sent 'im to a coupla places wiv notes."

"What did the notes say? Does he know?" Gillies asked.

"'E don't read," Tommy said, with the contempt of one literate.

"Where did he take the notes?"

One had been sent to Ratter, the fellow with the dog, Tommy said. The potboy had had to venture into St. Giles, the sordid area of the city known as the Rookery, with that one. Gillies quailed at the thought of a child alone in such a place; conditions were terrible, existence there so bleak that the only quest was for the next sip of gin or a scrap of food to keep body and soul together. Life was cheap, and violence against each other for the smallest of prizes brutal.

"And the other note?"

"'E said as 'ow it were to some place in St. James. Hadda go all over the city. 'E were so tired, 'e 'bout fell asleep, poor little feller." Tommy, at the ancient age of twelve, a man earning his own wage with no master and able to read and write his own name, viewed the ten-year-old potboy with sympathy. "When 'e got back, 'e were sent up ta sleep in th'attic."

That was confirmation of what they already knew. Potboys generally slept on a pallet under the work table in the kitchen; not so bad a place, as it was warmer than the attic three seasons of the year and there were food scraps to forage, if one could wrest them away from the rats.

"I 'membered summat about the two gents as visited Sir 'Enry's back door that night."

"Fellows who visited the knight's back door? I dinna ken who y'mean, Tommy."

"You know, the ones 'e were argying wiv."

"Ah, I dinna think we knew they had come there first."

Tommy's eyes were wide and his cheeks ruddy from the freshening wind. "Feller banged on t'wrong door first, an' I 'eard 'im. 'E had a Frenchy accent. Second feller, 'e 'ad a funny walk."

"A funny walk? What d'ya mean?"

"Swayed, loike."

A limp, perhaps. "Did ya find aught else, Tommy?"

"Aye. Nightsoil men two nights arter were muckin' out th'cesspit at Sir 'Enry's an' found a big knoife. Showed it 'round to everyone afore the magistrate's man took it."

TWENTY

EMMELINE VISITED A FEW more orphan asylums and workhouses that day, but at them she was more circumspect, not openly asking questions as she had of Mrs. Miller. Two had similar stories: they could not identify the man, though they described him. Emmeline had one more place to visit, an orphan home in Pentonville, north of Clerkenwell. She could go there and then return to Clerkenwell to pick up Gillies at the agreed-upon time and place.

It had been disheartening, after the excellent accommodations at St. Pancras, to visit the others, which had been in varying degrees cold, damp, depressing, and dismal. The odors, the sounds, the attitudes of the warders and wardresses, which ranged from angry and hostile to cold and impersonal; all had combined to leave her in low spirits. The children were either slaveys or necessary nuisances to justify the existence of the asylum, commodities to earn a penny.

When she remembered her own boisterous youth, running from Malincourt House to the pond, catching frogs and chasing Maria and

Thomas with them, then running home to a loving mother who always smelled of lavender mint, she was chastened. She was wont to bemoan the loss of her mother at a young age and the hasty degradation of her happy youth into emotional turmoil, which had culminated in teenage seduction, loss of innocence, and humiliation. But she had had a home, food to eat, and a bed to sleep in. The situations of these young children who had done nothing but be born to the wrong parents were horrible to contemplate, and presaged an early death from overwork or a life (if they were fortunate and lived past childhood) of deprivation and insecurity.

If she believed in God, of course, she might have been able to put it all on His shoulders: *he* decided who would be born poor and who wealthy, who would become sick and who stay well. But it had been many years since she'd lost her religion after her mother died. She could not believe in a divine spirit who would offer some people every creature comfort known in the world and others nothing but a lifetime of deprivation and suffering. She was left feeling it was a vast lottery, and she a fortunate holder of a winning ticket.

Though she went to church every Sunday and on saint days, mouthing the prayers and platitudes, Emmeline did it for form and society, spending her time during silent prayer contemplating and planning her next mission. If there was no God, then there was no salvation, and if there was no salvation, then it was up to each and every fortunate member of society to help lift up the unfortunate so their lives on earth would be made tolerable. Convincing the fortunate of this necessity, however, was never simple. Leopold felt he did enough with his tithe and support of the poor box; even Sir Jacob believed that if you did too much for the poor, it made them weak and dependent, luxuriating in charity rather than striving to better their lot.

At the Pentonville Home for Unfortunate Children, Josephs pulled the team to a halt and opened the carriage door.

"This is our last place," she murmured. He helped her down to the pavement and into the sweeping cold of a brisk breeze. She looked up at the grim gray walls, the smoke thinly streaming from a chimney above indicating little heat for the inmates. "I doubt if I'll have more luck here than in any of the last several places." She'd had suspicions of some of the warders, but no amount of questioning had exposed who it was who was taking girls to London for the benefit of the trade in tender female flesh.

"Miss, if I might say summat?"

She looked up into her driver's weary blue eyes. "Yes?"

Josephs thrust at her a paper sack. "Bag o' confits, miss; give 'em to the little 'uns, and arsk the children your questions. They see more'n folk know."

Emmeline's eyes widened. How foolish she had been! Among the asylum warders, the innocent had likely not understood what she was asking, and those she'd thought *might* be guilty had quickly masked their expressions and got rid of her. But the children knew more and saw more than adults thought.

"As always, you are a beacon of common sense, Josephs. How much time I have wasted today! I should have spoken to you first."

The driver's face reddened and he ducked his head. "No matter, miss. God will guide you." He bowed.

She turned and faced the building as he moved the carriage down the narrow street. Pentonville Home for Unfortunate Children did not lift her out of her dejection, by any means; it was a decrepit tenement that leaned against other frail tenements. There were older children about, but they were ragged and thin, with no hope in their eyes and no energy for play.

She met a weary housekeeper at the door and asked if she could spend some time with the children. The woman watched her through narrowed eyes for a moment, then, after examining her stylish clothes and seeing the neat carriage she had exited, which now trundled down the road a piece, nodded and let her into the building. No one wished to turn away a possible benefactor, especially one with money, as Emmeline clearly possessed.

The housekeeper led her back to a walled courtyard, where younger children sat in various attitudes of despair along broken brick walls and wooden benches. How was it possible that so many children had either no parents or, as was most often the case, no parent who could care for them as a result of extreme poverty, illness, or fondness for the gin bottle? Some in her circle of relatives and friends threw more food to their pack of hunting dogs after one dinner than was given to these little ones in a fortnight. Like timber or copper, they were raw material, to be forged into a lifelong worker if they survived the brutality of youth. When one wore out in the mine or mill, there were ten to take his or her place.

She had no solution, but if she could shame a few of her class into caring, it may do some little good. But that was a problem—and a Rogue column—for another day. She must stiffen her resolve to get to the questions and answers she required before the housekeeper returned and wondered at her line of inquiry.

One girl stood out beyond the others. She was only ten, she said, and small for her age. Her name was Sarah. She took a seat beside Emmeline on a sagging wooden bench, baring her teeth at any child who tried to usurp her spot. Sarah knew who her mother was, but her mum was unable to care for her because of Bertie, her mother's "friend," who beat her and made her work at night. He didn't want a child around, as it made the customers uncomfortable. Emmeline's heart clutched. Sarah clearly knew *what* her mother was, bitter knowledge for such a young girl.

Emmeline handed out Josephs' candies one by one, hoping there was enough to go 'round the whole crowd and vowing to send more if there was not. There was, fortunately, and when it was clear her supply was depleted, the children deserted her to sit alone and suck on the luscious candy. All except Sarah, who leaned against her, watching her every move, holding her bonbon in one hand.

A cold wind whipped down the back lane, across which was a line of tenement homes divided into rooms for rent, wet laundry hanging out windows, and smoke billowing from the chimney above. It was a dark and dreary scene, all tones of gray, even down to the faces of the children. Emmeline opened her cloak and Sarah huddled against her, her heart thudding rapidly like that of a caught bird.

"Do you have friends here?" Emmeline asked.

The girl shook her head. "They've all gone away."

"Where did they go?"

"Lunnon," she muttered. She still held her confit in her dirty hand, afraid, it seemed, to put it in her mouth, but she did pop it in when one of the bigger boys eyed it with a greedy look.

"London. Who took them?"

"Man wiv a doggie."

Ratter. This was her first absolute confirmation. "Where did he take them in London?"

She shrugged.

"Sarah, this is important," Emmeline said, her voice shaking. "Do you have any idea at all why they were taken to London, or what they were going to do there?"

·Her young-old eyes and pinched expression, her dirty face gray with cold and weariness, she shrugged. "Mr. Dunstable tole us they was goin' ta work in big 'ouses, an' 'ave enuff to eat."

Dunstable! The name hit Emmeline like a bolt of lightning; *that* was the name Sally gave for the warder of the orphanage she'd come from. How many could there be with that exact name?"

The child continued. "But 'e"—she pointed toward a hard-featured boy—"said Molly an' Lindy was goin' ta be 'arlots, like me mum."

Molly! It was a common enough name, but in this case it could not be a coincidence. "Sarah, was there a girl here named Sally once?"

A long time ago, Sarah said; a "long time" was likely measured in months, not years, to one so young as she. It *must* be the place where Sally and Molly both came from, and where Sally was abused and made pregnant.

It was torturous extracting herself from Sarah, who clung like a limpet to Emmeline. "I must go, Sarah, but I won't forget you," she whispered.

One tear rolled down her cheek, leaving a cleanish trail on her dirty face, but Sarah let go and turned away. How many promises had been broken in her short life?

Furious, Emmeline banged on the door and was allowed back inside, though the children were not. They were made to stay outside for hours every day, Sarah had told her; as a form of disciplinary action if they were naughty, some were even made to stand outside at night. Emmeline asked to see the warder so she could give a donation.

The housekeeper guided her to the office of the custodian of the asylum, Mr. Horace Dunstable, the man who apparently sold little girls into prostitution, and under whose governance poor Sally had been raped.

His office was warm, a fire in the grate. Mr. Dunstable was a genial-looking man, stout, well-formed, with broad shoulders and unfashionably long, graying hair that curled on his coat collar, though it appeared to shun growing on the top of his head; his bald pate gleamed in the dim light that shone in the window. He wore a brown velvet jacket and a bottle-green waistcoat with polished brass buttons that threatened to pop off. As thin and miserable as the children in his care were, the man had clearly never missed a meal. "You wish to contribute to some orphans, Miss St. Germaine?" He sat straight, his hands folded on the leather surface of his desk.

"I have a *dear* friend who supports a children's asylum, and it brings her such *joy*, she says, to see the little ones lifted out of lonely deprivation and provided with a means to live and prosper." Her tone was as treacly as she could make it; she must appear a sentimental, simpering spinster who craved the opportunity to help babies and toddlers, one who got weepy at the thought of the poor orphans and who misquoted Biblical passages such as *"suffering little children must come unto me."*

"How would you wish to help?"

Living as she did, hiding both her Crone and Rogue selves, had given Emmeline practice in artifice. "Poor little orphan dears! Have they had their lunch? May I send some cakes for them? My cook is a genius with palatable food for little ones."

"To be frank, more valuable than food from your household would be money, Miss St. Germaine. There is never enough for milk and clothing, or bedding, or the hire of women to care for them."

"I wish to do more, though. Perhaps…" She leaned forward, her hands together in a prayerful attitude. "What *do* you do to help them make their way once they reach a certain age? Could I sponsor a child to an apprenticeship?"

Mr. Dunstable blinked. "We, uh, we help them to employment, certainly. Uh ... factories, you know, need workers."

"What about the girls? Do you take care of *them*?" She saw a shift in his attitude, some dark shadow in his eyes. "Where do you put them out to work? In London?"

He blinked and nodded.

"I've heard a *horrid* rumor," she murmured, watching him closely, "that some disgusting, *depraved* men are taking little girls to London for unsavory purposes. Have you been visited by such as that, wishing to take your little girls?"

He nodded, then swallowed and shook his head.

"Which is it, sir? Yes or no? Do you ensure that the girls you send away are not being used for immoral purposes in London?" Emmeline lowered her voice to a whisper, looked toward the door and then back to him, and said, "The scandal columns hint that *some* men even like the *little* ones, as young as ten or eleven, and pay extra to *deflower* them! Is that true?"

The warder gaped at the turn of the conversation; his face reddened and he assumed an expression of outrage as he shifted anxiously in his chair. "I don't know what you've heard, Miss St. Germaine, but I assure you we would do nothing of the kind. What you said, I mean. Disgraceful!" He harrumphed loudly, clearing his throat. "I personally am sure each girl who leaves here has ... er, is taken to a place to work."

"Would I know any of the employers? I wish to know *where* the girls are going."

"I can't tell you that, miss," he said, clearly trying to stay on her good side but becoming increasingly irritated and nervous.

"Whyever not?"

"The employers ... their privacy ... I ... I cannot."

She donned an expression of good-natured idiocy, cloaking her inner turmoil with a fatuous smirk. "Oh come, sir," she said coyly. "I won't tell a soul. I promise! I know so *many* in society and would know the names, perhaps. I wish to be *sure* my money will be going to a good cause." She undid the strings of her reticule and stared at him, wide-eyed. "I only wish to help!"

He licked his lips as he eyed the reticule bulging with coinage. Perhaps bribery was the answer. From Sarah, she knew the place was supplying children to bawds and bullies, and with Sally and Molly's names came the assurance that Ratter was involved. Here was the link, then, from this warder, to Ratter, and thence to Sir Henry. Dunstable was likely being paid handsomely, disgusting old hypocrite, even while someone in his orphanage was abusing the girls himself. It could even be Dunstable. For Emmeline, it wasn't now merely a matter of discovering who had killed Sir Henry in order to save herself, as Rogue or Avengeress, from suspicion. This filthy practice, the sale of little girls, *must* be stopped.

The warder shook his head and stood, a worried expression on his face. "Miss St. Germaine, I'm afraid I cannot help you." He came around his desk. "You have some terrible notions, indelicate ... *hideous*! No lady should say what you have said. That anyone should traffic in children ... it's unthinkable!"

She didn't stand. She was bungling this.

"Good day, miss," he said, bowing again. "I'm afraid I cannot help you, and you cannot help me."

Interesting that he wasn't even willing to take her money. He looked terrified, perspiration rolling down his bald head and seeping under his collar. This would require another approach, and not by her. She stood and nodded, said goodbye, and left. Despite all she had attempted, she had achieved so little.

Gillies was waiting for them. Emmeline, weary, heartsick, and discouraged, was happy to see her but had little faith that their investigations had uncovered anything of substance, at least as pertained to the murder.

She was soon buoyed, however, by what her maid had learned. As Josephs maneuvered the carriage around the block, through traffic, Gillies told her everything that Tommy had discovered about the two men who had called that night, one a "Frenchie" and the other who walked with a limp, and where the potboy had taken the notes, to Ratter and to a second location in St. James. She relayed that the knife had apparently been found a couple of days after the murder in the convenience; this indicated either the killer needed to hide the weapon quickly, or the murderer was one of the household and had had no opportunity to get rid of it elsewhere.

Gillies had gone, after talking to Tommy, to speak with Fanny, the Hargreaves' young maid, whom she traced to a coster's barrow buying vegetables for the Hargreaves' dinner. As she helped the girl carry a sack of swedes and cabbage back to the rooms above the haberdashery, Gillies learned about Fanny's mistress's three or four visits to the Claybourne home, and something else baffling: "The last time, the lassie says, Miss Hargreaves had a smug look. An' a day later, the household was flush with money for a while. Money for tea—a rarity for them—an' meat an' sugar."

"From pawning the ruby brooch, according to Simeon, which likely came from Lady Claybourne with or without her knowledge."

"Aye, but here's the thing, miss... Fanny don't recall any talk of any insult from Sir 'Enry, and who would know better than th'maid?"

Gillies rubbed her hands together, warming them, as the carriage rattled over cobblestones through Clerkenwell.

"The brother and sister are likely both lying, then. And that means the ruby brooch wouldn't have been a bribe from her ladyship," Emmeline said. "Could Miss Hargreaves have had something else on Sir Henry? Or on Lady Claybourne?"

"The puir lass is frightened since th'murder," Gillies said, her Rs rolling as they did more when she was weary. "An' I think she's fair worrit that her mistress knows something about the knight's murder."

What could Fanny know that the Hargreaves hadn't told the magistrate's men? What the girl reported to Gillies gave no indication that either of the siblings had killed Sir Henry, but they didn't know everything yet. Emmeline then told Gillies what she had learned about the Pentonville children's home and little Sarah's plight. "She's about ten, Gillies. How much longer does she have before they sell her to work on the street?"

The question was left unanswered, because the truth was that Sarah could be taken any time. Girls as young as ten did work as prostitutes, and it turned Emmeline's stomach to think of that little girl, frightened and alone, being abused by anyone for any reason, let alone used as a man's plaything. What kind of man preferred children to women? It baffled her.

"We're here, miss," Josephs said, opening the carriage door.

He had moved them away from Samuel Street, so that they would not draw notice; they were now stopped a couple of streets over from Blithestone. Emmeline pulled on Dorcas's heavy, unfashionable cloak to cover her costly dress. Time to retrieve Miss Honeychurch's lace mittens from the Claybourne residence. She climbed down from the carriage, put her head down, and strode the two streets over to Chandler Lane. When she did glance up, she noted that this late in the afternoon everyone appeared as weary as she, their faces gray and drawn with exhaustion.

She scurried along to the brick archway that led to the alley. As a companion without her lady, she should use the back door of the Claybourne residence, which was what she wanted anyway, though it was terribly risky: to speak with the staff, not Lady Claybourne. The alleyway was already dim and shadowed, damp and odorous from the dry privies and middens. When last she had been there, it was to confront Sir Henry; it made her quiver now to think how she had boldly strode through the courtyard and slipped through the door, hours before bloody murder was committed. Something gleamed palely, and she bent down. What was it? She picked it up and slipped it into her dress pocket. It was hard and silver, like a thimble.

She tapped on the back door. A child answered, a little boy. He was short-haired, clean-scrubbed, and neatly dressed, but he looked sleepy.

Emmeline heard a woman—the cook, she thought likely—shout, "Who is it, Noah?"

"It's Dorcas, companion to Miss Honeychurch who visited earlier," Emmeline called out as she walked down the passage to the kitchen.

Mrs. Partridge was much as Emmeline had seen the first time, up to her elbows in flour. "What d'you want?" she asked.

"I beg your pardon, but Miss Honeychurch sent me back. She lost her lace mittens. She's a wee bit touched, you know, and says she laid them down in the entry somewhere."

The cook stared at her. "S'pose I'll 'ave to 'ave the maid look for 'em. Noah, go find Sybil."

The boy nodded and headed down the passage that Emmeline knew led past the housekeeper's room and toward the green baize door that separated the servant's section of the house from the rest of it.

"I've had to come ever so far. May I sit for a moment?" Emmeline asked, a plaintive, wheedling tone in her voice. "Miss Honeychurch would not give me her carriage, so I had to walk most of the way." The cook merely nodded and continued her work. Emmeline offered her help and was soon sitting on a stool by the table peeling carrots for the woman (she was clumsy at it at first, but improved rapidly), which relaxed the cook greatly.

"Do you have no scullery maid, Cook?"

The woman glanced over at her. "No, she ..." She shook her head.

"I heard you were robbed and your scullery maid taken away," Emmeline prompted.

"Aye, and the silver and me best knife stolen the same evening," she said. "But never mind. What's done is done."

She would not be drawn about that evening, and Emmeline feared alerting her, so she complained gently about difficult working situations. With what she now knew of Miss Honeychurch, it was no challenge to grumble of a demanding mistress and dreary life as a companion.

After some back and forth, Emmeline said, "And she's such a nosy busybody! She knows Lady Claybourne and Sir Henry from before their wedding, but I doubt she's seen or visited them since. She did not like Sir Henry at all."

"No one did," the cook said, cubing potatoes and tossing them in a pot of stock over the open fire. She took the pared carrots from Emmeline and chopped them into uniform sizes, then tossed them in with the potatoes. "'E were a disgusting man, an' 'er ladyship is well rid of him."

"Miss Honeychurch says she warned Lady Claybourne not to wed him. I wonder why? I mean, how could she know he'd be a bad husband even back then?"

The cook glanced at her, a dark look in her eyes. "Soom men are twisted from the moment they get that stirrin' in their nethers. 'E were one of 'em."

Emmeline was surprised the cook would say as much to a complete stranger. "What do you mean?"

"'E liked girls young, *so* young they didn't yet 'ave their womanly troubles, tho' that never stopped 'im neither."

Emmeline shook her head with dismay, hoping the cook would keep talking but afraid to urge her on too much.

Mrs. Partridge looked around, then sat on the bench beside Emmeline, her face close, and said, every breath gusting the smell of onions and gin, "'E were involved wiv some bad men, 'e were."

"Bad men?"

"Aye. They coom to the back door soomtimes, strange men, arskin' fer the master. Bad men, 'e consorted wiv; I never sed nothin', joost kept me 'ead down. One of 'em brought that poor child, the one the lady stole away, like a delivery of pies or milk. Not the first time, neither, that feller wiv the doggie brought a girl fer the master. Sir 'Enry ordered a girl and got one perfect: yeller hair, blue eyes, fresh as a daisy." Her words were scathing, and the image disgraceful.

"That's terrible!" Emmeline replied, her voice breaking. She would never get accustomed to this, knowing what she now knew about how little girls were used. "How could he *do* that? Are there others like him?"

The cook nodded. "Aye, there's a whole group as does it, men all over London 'oo prefer a young girl, an' not one wiv the French pox on 'em already. Ordered and delivered like a beefsteak or sack o' cabbages."

"But why a *child?*"

"There's soom men 'oo wanter pluck the most delicate bud," the cook said darkly. "An' what more delicate bud is there than a girl so young she don't bleed?"

"But you don't know for sure there's a whole *group* of men like that."

"I *do* know," the cook bellowed, energized by Emmeline's dissent. "'Eard the master speakin' to that feller as brung little Molly here. He said as 'the others' would wait their turn, there would be more girls coomin' later; pretty little things, he said, fresh from the orphan 'ome. Filthy devils."

Emmeline's mouth was dry; swallowing was hard. She licked her lips. Though she had suspected it, this was confirmation from the source—the man who delivered the girls—that there were other customers. "Can no one stop them?" Her voice quavered; her heart pounded.

The cook shrugged. "Sir 'Enry said as how it were business now; beyond the men what belonged to the group, they was finding girls for other men now, men as 'eard tell of the company and wanted in."

"And he said all of this in front of you?"

The cook appeared taken aback by her vehemence and didn't answer. Emmeline bit her lip, worried she had said too much.

That moment, Noah came back with Miss Honeychurch's lace mittens in his hands. "Is this them, miss?"

"Yes, those are Miss Honeychurch's."

The bell from upstairs rang. Lady Claybourne wanted her tea. Emmeline returned the way she had come, out to the alley, along Chandler Lane, and two more streets over, bending against the increasing wind. As expected, she found Josephs awaiting her and Gillies inside. She felt nauseated and heartsick, not even able to tell Gillies everything until she had found the words for the horror. Everything she learned seemed to make the situation darker and more desperate.

It was late afternoon as they arrived back home to Chelsea, twilight already darkening the Thames as river traffic slowed and folks shuttered their homes and businesses. As she climbed down from the carriage, she spotted Birk in the front window of the sitting room, peering out at her. It was time for the act. In the butler's presence she tried—though she didn't always succeed—to be frivolous and gay. She brightened her demeanor, and as they entered she was chattering to Gillies about her poor friend, Miss Kinsman, and how she hated being an invalid, but how it cheered her to have company.

"I didn't intend to stay so long, but poor little lady ... I couldn't say no to luncheon. However, I am famished, as an invalid's meal does not suit me. Oh, hello, Birk. Were there any callers?"

"No callers, miss, but there is a rather large package from ... your friend, Miss Kinsman."

Emmeline laughed as gaily as she could manage. "Oh, yes, she had that sent out yesterday thinking I wouldn't be visiting. She is terminally gloomy, poor thing, sure she is being deserted by her friends." The package was on the hall table. It appeared rumpled, somehow, as if it had been taken apart and reassembled. Birk did not seem self-conscious, though, and if he had torn it apart it would have been put back together with more care than that.

She had to stop being so suspicious.

Birk tugged at his livery and said, "There is also an invitation for tonight, miss, from your uncle, Sir Jacob. He sent it by hand this afternoon."

Emmeline took the card from him and crossed to the lamp on the table. "Oh, what *fun!*" she cried, waving the card. "It is Nut-Crack Night! He has assembled a list of unmarried ladies and gentlemen."

"Aye, that it is, miss. October thirty-fairst!" Gillies said as she helped Emmeline remove her cloak. "When I was a lass we celebrated, those of us pinin' aftair a lad."

Emmeline set the card on top of the package. "My uncle has never celebrated such a silly festival before. He's becoming a sentimentalist in his dotage. We'll sit by his fire and toss hazelnuts—to which we've given our names—into the blaze." Depending on whose burned together and whose jumped and crackled, courtship would be smooth or difficult, the old tradition went.

"A grand old tradition, Miss Emmeline," Birk said, his round face wreathed in a smile.

"I wonder who else he's invited?" Emmeline nodded to the butler, then kept the smile on her face until she was upstairs, where she collapsed in a chair and put her feet up. "I suppose I must go to my uncle's absurd party," she groused.

Gillies took her cloak and hung it on a hook in the clothespress. "Aye, miss. Or he'll take it unkindly."

"If I must go, then I will use the evening to do something more than just attend the party. I am revisiting Clerkenwell."

"*Again*? We just returned from there."

"Right now this consumes me. Tommy may have learned more by now, and I won't waste time, Gillies. I'll take every opportunity to discover the truth of who killed Sir Henry."

TWENTY-ONE

SURPRISINGLY, FIDELITY WAS EAGER to attend Sir Jacob's impromptu nut-crack party. She and Emmeline had previously planned an evening in with a new novel, *Zastrozzi*, by an anonymous author named P.B.S.; the tale promised all the Gothic horror Emmeline relished. That type of book had influenced her character as the Avengeress, cloaked and masked like the banditti of old. But it seemed there was nothing Sir Jacob Pauling could ask of Fidelity that would be too much.

Emmeline knew her uncle had almost certainly invited Woodforde. She suspected that the object of the party was probably to once again throw her into the good doctor's company. Fidelity and Sir Jacob were united in their eagerness to promote this match, as much as cajoling, urging, and hectoring could be considered promoting. Fidelity loved her cousin and knew of her past sorrows, but thought that marriage to the right man would solve everything.

Emmeline had other concerns than her uncle's matchmaking that evening, however. Simeon's latest note, in a package containing more of the most recent broadsheets, alarmed her. The magistrate's men had indeed come back to *The Prattler* office that morning to question Simeon. They would, as he had predicted, keep coming back, asking questions. They wanted to know who the Rogue was, and how he was connected to the Avengeress. This came too close to identifying them as one and the same; she had been careless, and would pay for her indiscretion if the truth ever came out. The icy breath of the law was on her neck, and it chilled her to the marrow. Only finding Sir Henry's killer and sending him to justice would call off the magistrate's men.

She didn't know how to go about it other than the stumbling, halting investigation she had been undertaking. So far she knew about Ratter, who had supplied Sir Henry with Sally and then Molly, taking them from the dubious safety of the Pentonville children's home with the express aid of Mr. Dunstable. She also had a description of the two men who had visited Sir Henry that fateful night: a man with a limp and a Frenchman.

She also had suspicions of the household. Though Lady Claybourne had seemed to grieve her husband's murder, Emmeline was not convinced of her sincerity. The woman must, after thirty years of marriage, have known what a loathsome toad he was. Would his wife have resorted to such a slaughter, though, so violent and bloody? The poisoner's dram seemed more effective for a woman than a butcher's knife.

So too it seemed doubtful that either the housekeeper or cook, one of whom had called in the Crones to aid the little girl, was the killer, but it could have been a follower of either, summoned to rob the home of its silver. Hard as it was to imagine the hard-featured housekeeper or plump and often drunken cook with followers, the lure of easy pickings may have made a man or two overlook their scanty charms. She returned to a thought she had earlier pondered, that perhaps murder had never been the aim; Sir Henry may have surprised one of them stealing the silver and been attacked, though none of the facts she had so far gleaned supported that conclusion.

Having now talked with the cook, Emmeline believed that the summoning of the Avengeress had simply been to save the girl. In which case, the housekeeper and cook were likely not the guilty ones. Emmeline believed that because Sir Henry had sent out two notes after the Avengeress's visit, and then Ratter—likely from the Rookery—and the other two men had come to see him, those visits were prompted by the notes. She didn't have proof of this, but it seemed probable, and if it were the case, was it not likely that one, two, or all three had killed him? Who *were* the other two men, and how could she find them? More to the point, it seemed impossible to both point the magistrate in the right direction and allay his suspicion of the Avengeress.

It behooved her to explore every avenue of thought and not settle on the guilty without proof. Sir Henry's death could have been the result of a neighborly dispute, a domestic disagreement, or a business venture gone wrong. She must persevere if she was to succeed, and so her plans for the evening must include more prying, more snooping, more meddling.

After a light supper, Emmeline and Fidelity repaired to their rooms to dress. "Gillies, do Mrs. Bramage and Mrs. Riddle treat our new scullery maid well?" Emmeline asked as her maid redressed her hair, which had become untidy after the long day out in the cold breeze of late October.

"Annie? As well as the lass could expect anywhere, I s'pose. She'll no complain, I warrant. It's a well-run house with ample food, a warm place to sleep, and an undemanding mistress. Nouw," she said, patting the neatened hair and meeting Emmeline's gaze in the mirror, "what d'ye fancy to wear? The gold velvet from last winter?"

"That'll do," Emmeline said.

An hour later they headed to her uncle's impromptu Nut-Crack Night soiree in his elegant St. James townhome. Along the way, Emmeline stopped the carriage and informed Josephs that they would later be continuing to Clerkenwell, despite Fidelity's protests. She asked that he go there while she was at the party to see if Tommy Jones had learned anything new since that afternoon, and also to gather what other information on the Claybourne household he could.

"Emmie, think what you are planning to do!" Fidelity fretted. "It's so dangerous to investigate!"

"I can't leave my fate to chance. Until they discover who killed Sir Henry, they'll be looking at the Avengeress. I will take every opportunity to investigate, as you call it."

As she expected, Woodforde had been invited to the party, along with the engaged couples she had met at the dinner party, Mr. Wilkins and Miss Gottschalk, and Mr. Fulmer and Miss Purley. Sir Jacob laughingly took Fidelity as his partner for the evening in the "nut-crackery," as he called the ostensible reason for the party, and she happily acquiesced. This evening he had gone further in his sociability and also invited Lady Clara Langford and her fiancé Mr. Elijah Jeffcock.

"I didn't know you knew my uncle!" Emmeline murmured to her fellow Crone in the dimness of the candlelit entry as Gillies removed her cloak and bustled off with it.

Lady Clara gave a tight smile.

Sir Jacob was also in the entry to greet these latest guests; he never could wait for his guests to come to him but must meet them almost at the door. Cheeks glowing red with bonhomie and wine, he chuckled at Emmeline's surprise and bowed to Lady Clara and Mr. Jeffcock, then put his arm over his niece's shoulders. "I saw Lady Clara at the theater speaking with you and thought what a lovely and charming damsel. So I forced an introduction with Mr. Jeffcock—with whom I do have mutual acquaintance—whence I learned they were newly betrothed, and sent a note around this afternoon inviting them to this gathering." He dropped a sly wink and nodded, placing one finger along his nose. "I have always enjoyed getting to know my niece's friends, and especially so lovely a lass."

"We belong to the same ladies' group," Emmeline explained to her uncle and Mr Jeffcock. "We organize help for the unfortunate."

"Ah, yes, charity for the idle," Jeffcock drawled. "Despite that it doesn't help society one jot, to prolong the lives of the corrupt and lazy."

Emmeline cast him a disgusted look, which Lady Clara caught. She concealed a quick smile. The others arrived—Woodforde, who had been at a patient's bedside, last of all—and gathered in the informal drawing room, which was furnished with a rearrangement of low chairs and stools near the ornate fireplace, an imposing relic her uncle had imported from a castle in Germany. As for the furniture, Sir Jacob laughingly described enlisting the aid of his exasperated valet, Pierre, who had thought the whole event was a *follie extraordinaire,*" as Sir Jacob drew out with a Gallic flourish. His laughter turned into a coughing fit as the butler brought a tray of port and a basket of nuts.

Her uncle took a long drink of his port, then explained to a skeptical Miss Gottschalk and a bemused Miss Purley about Nut-Crack Night. "We will take turns giving these hazelnuts names," he said, holding a smooth, glossy russet nut up to the light. "We then toss them into the fire two at a time. If they burn as one, courtship shall be smooth and untroubled. If they pop and leap apart, it presages a bumpier road to marriage. Our pagan forebears were a suspicious lot. Nowadays, of course, this is a social event to bring young ladies and gentlemen together."

"To matchmake, in other words," Emmeline said dryly.

Mr. Wilkins laid his walking stick aside and picked up his port, holding it up to the light. "I will go anywhere Sir Jacob commands, to drink his fine port and enjoy his expansive hospitality."

Emmeline eyed him, wondering how close to the Claybourne family the barrister was, given that he was their man of business as well as her uncle's. Odd that he hadn't mentioned it at the dinner party, even as he was lauding the knight.

"Is that not intrusive, Sir Jacob? To matchmake, as you say, or interfere in a couple's alliance?" Miss Gottschalk asked. She sat on a low stool and carefully arranged her sapphire blue silk moiré gown for best display. Around her neck and at her ears she wore a sapphire necklace and ear bobs that brought out the brilliant blue of her eyes.

She was overdressed for the occasion, a casual event, and Lady Clara looked upon her with scorn, but the young German woman seemed not to notice; or more likely, Emmeline thought, not to care. She liked her for it, and wondered what made such a woman agree to marry a man like Wilkins, so boorish and tedious.

"Of *course* it's intrusive," Sir Jacob said. "But I think that my age and position as a judge allows me latitude. I am like the elderly spinster aunt who is allowed her eccentricities so long as they are well intended."

Emmeline laughed and told the group a story of her uncle, who visited Malincourt often when she was a child. "It was Christmas, I think, wasn't it, Uncle, the year you frightened Maria? Yes, it must have been, because I remember you wearing a Father Christmas costume with a long ermine-trimmed robe. Father thought you were extravagant because you brought all of us children sacks of candies and fruits. And you would have us sit on your lap and tell us our secrets. But poor Maria!" She smiled through tears at the memory of her younger sister. "She was so frightened—I think she didn't know you for the costume—and you tickled her, but she cried and *cried*! Finally mama had to take her away and calm her down."

Gently Sir Jacob said, his voice thick with emotion, "I miss her too, Emmie. Our little Maria was too good for this earth."

Woodforde watched Emmeline with compassion in his brown eyes. She looked away from him.

"How frightening for the child," Miss Gottschalk said, breaking the tension of the moment. "To be seized by a stranger and forced to sit on his lap!"

"But we all thought she would know it was Uncle," Emmeline said with a watery smile, her voice thick with emotion. "I did, though indeed I was two years older than poor Maria." She cleared her throat. "Well, Uncle, shall we get along with this nut-cracking nonsense?"

It turned into a comical evening. Miss Purley and Mr. Fulmer's nuts burned quietly together, but at the last minute his nut incinerated and fell though the grate. Every pair after that seemed destined to a fiery fate. Lady Clara and Mr. Jeffcock's nuts popped clear to opposite ends of the hearth, and she exclaimed the tradition was already proving more wisdom than the humans involved had yet shown.

Mr. Wilkins's was knocked all the way out of the fire by an explosion of Miss Gottschalk's, which caused uproarious laughter at Wilkins's expense. He blustered and became red in the face and stumped away to the other end of the room, saying he would no longer participate in silly children's games if they were going to become nasty. Miss Gottschalk smiled to herself and murmured, "Silly children's games hide much wisdom, yes?"

Sir Jacob insisted on putting two in the fire for himself and Fidelity, and they burned side by side in harmony, roasting in eternity together, he said with a laugh. He took her hand, kissed it, and said, "I would never try to take Jean Marc's place, my dear, you know that. We will remain but good friends." She smiled through tears and put her head on his shoulder.

It was Emmeline and Woodforde's turn. The doctor smiled and said, "Would you do the honors, Miss St. Germaine?"

"Do I have a choice, Woodforde, since my uncle has been so pointed about inviting an even number of men and women, and all the rest are spoken for?"

He put one hand on his chest and said, "You wound me to the soul. But I, at least, am willing to play along with your uncle's game." His eyes, in the flickering candlelight, held an amber light, and his well-shaped lips quirked up in one corner, a half smile that could be meant as mocking or lighthearted. "Are you afraid what it will foretell? Do you take it so seriously that you are not willing?"

"Of course I'm willing," Emmeline said, casting their hazelnuts into the fire as the others laughed and cheered.

"The final pair," Fidelity said, clapping her hands together and then clasping them.

———

Gillies had accompanied the ladies because Emmeline was worried that Fidelity would fidget herself into tears given the plan for after the party. She sat in the kitchen while the cook, an old friend and Scottish also, worked, proofing bread dough for the next day and finishing other tasks. The little scullery maid, Polly, did as she was told, stoking the fire, finishing scrubbing pots, then waiting for her next orders.

She was sent to the larder for a quartern loaf of bread, as they were "going to have a bit of toast to make sure the preserves were edible," as Cook said with a smile. Though her name was Morag, and Gillies called her so, to the household she was just Cook.

"She's a pretty little lass," Gillies said, finishing mending a piece of lace cuff that had torn. She folded it and put it in her bag.

"Aye, but too quiet. Started out full o' life, but she's suffrin' a spot o' homesick, I say. Willnae even talk about hame, nay matter what I say, beyond speaking of a little friend she misses sorely."

"How did you find her?"

Cook shrugged her heavy shoulders. "'Tis not my doin', y'ken."

"Do *you* ever get homesick, Morag?" Gillies asked, biting a thread and knotting it.

"That I do. Dream about it oft: the mist, the heather, the green all 'round. D'you?"

"Aye, but mostly it's me boys an' Fergus and our wee croft that I dream of." She sighed. "A lifetime ago." The two sat in silence for a moment until Polly brought back the heavy loaf, which looked larger for being in the arms of one so small and pale. The child had heavy silken hair that was bundled up tight in a white muslin cap, and eyes so blue they were like the sky in Scotland, Gillies thought. She wished she'd had a daughter, but she'd had boys ... her sturdy, active boys, now on their own and married, with little ones of their own that Gillies would likely never see, since she wasn't allowed back in Scotland. And then there was wee William, who had died so brutally, his little body so frail after death. The grief had been like a knife in her heart, the pain like nothing she had known, even in childbirth.

"Where have ye gone, Delia?" Cook asked, gently, as she slid thick slices of bread onto the toasting fork and set Polly before the fire to brown them.

Gillies dashed the tears from her eyes and regarded little Polly, so silent and so small. At least there was one child in London she knew had a home. She *must* help her mistress get the animals who were hurtin' other wee girls for their own unnatural pleasure.

The rest of the evening was spent with music for some, and conversation for others. Miss Gottschalk played a Haydn piece on the pianoforte. Miss Purley chatted with Lady Clara, who thumbed through sheet music. Mr. Wilkins and Mr. Jeffcock became engaged in a debate about the merit of slave-owning in the colonies.

The plantation owner, of course, came down on the side of the benefits. "It's how they are happiest," he said of the enslaved men and women. "They're like children. On their own they are lost, don't know what to do with their time. And lazy! Without the whip they're useless. It's no wonder the continent of Africa is a benighted wilderness: no culture, no music, no dignity. We give them a home and a purpose."

Lady Clara's gaze, steady on her sheet music, was stony; it was clear she heard her fiancé and chose to say nothing. But what could she say? She had made her choice with open eyes. Emmeline fought the inclination to despise her for it.

"I cannot disagree more," Wilkins replied. "S'pose they're like any other people on the planet. Give a man—or woman—his wage, I say, and make them responsible for their own living conditions outside of work. You can benefit then from their necessities. Whereas you, sir, must feed and clothe your workers," he pointed out, poking the taller man in his waistcoat. "The factory owner here has nothing to do with them once they are off the property. I get to charge them what I will to have a place to lay their head. I earn more rent from one crumbling room in St. Giles than from any number of rooms in another part of the city. Desperation forces people to do much to secure a place to lay their heads. Now *that* is proper commerce!"

Emmeline knew that if she did not stop listening she would go mad. What kind of man did her uncle employ? Wilkins was disgusting, and so was Jeffcock. But Sir Jacob's home was not the place for her to engage in a political argument. She walked out of earshot and joined the circle around her uncle. Fidelity was there, as was Mr. Fulmer. She took a low stool near the fire.

While the others were deep in conversation, Sir Jacob moved to a low chair beside her. "My dearest niece, what is on your mind this evening?"

Searching his eyes, she asked, "Uncle Jacob, how *can* you employ such a man as Wilkins? He speaks of the poor as if they are merely cogs in the machinery of finance, tools in his pursuit of wealth. Between him and Jeffcock, the slave-owner, there is little to choose."

"I cannot hold myself accountable for the opinions and behavior of every man with whom I have dealings. Surely you see that, Emmie?"

"But you employ him as your man of business." She fought the urge to expose Wilkins's dealings with Sir Henry Claybourne; there was no legitimate way she could know that, and her uncle would wonder. "With such opinions as he holds, do you not fear he is lacking in morality in other ways? Such as his handling of your money?"

"Oh, don't worry, my dear," Sir Jacob said, winking and patting her hand. "I have a very tight lock on my money and am extremely careful. He is my tool, not my master. I use him to handle my investments—with his legal training, he is able to draft company contracts and the like—but he has little real power. In name he is the director of the company, but I give him little to do."

"The Maidenhead Canal Company ... is that what you speak of?"

He nodded.

"I understand Woodforde is one of your investors. He told me you were reluctant to allow him to invest at first, and that your company has yet to break ground on the canal. For someone as industrious as Woodforde, that is frightfully discouraging. Perhaps he would be a better director of your company than Wilkins. He'd move the plan along more rapidly."

"Woodforde would not want that involvement, trust me on that, my dear," Sir Jacob replied. "I discouraged his investing *because* of his diligence, as you say, though I call it impatience. I intend to invite him to remove his investment, since I am loath to promise him any return in a timely manner. Some things move more slowly than a young man has patience for."

Emmeline brooded on what was always on her mind: the tangled web of the abuse of little girls by men who should be protecting their interests. It wasn't easy to speak of, and she had not intended to raise the topic, but Sir Jacob had long been her trusted sounding board. "Uncle, I have been reading the papers lately, and there is much about Sir Henry Claybourne's death. Some are saying he was ... that he abused little girls in his household. I know, though I am not supposed to"—she cast him a guilty look; young ladies of her delicacy were supposed to read aught but the society and gossip pages—"that little girls as young as ten or eleven serve as prostitutes. You are a judge—"

"In the Court of Common Pleas, my dear," Sir Jacob said sharply. "I have nothing to do with such things as the welfare of children. And you are correct; you *should* not know, nor should you be discussing such things."

He was perturbed; she could see it in his beetling brows and down-turned mouth. It was hideously inappropriate for her to raise such a topic at all, much less in such surroundings, but it seemed trivial to mind about such delicacy when their world was what it was. "I know you would prefer I don't see those kind of articles—"

"And if you lived with Leopold, as you should, you would be more protected. What have you been up to, Emmie, that you are saying such things?"

She didn't answer.

"Fidelity, as a widow and with more knowledge of the world, should be shielding you from such knowledge!"

"Fidelity, protect *me*?" Emmeline burst out. "Surely you know her better than that, Uncle? It is I who shield *her* much of the time. She is delicate; I am strong."

"You have become full of yourself, Emmeline. It is unattractive and unfeminine, and no man, not even Woodforde, will want you if you continue so. Perhaps it is time Leopold takes more of an interest in your life in London." Sir Jacob cleared his throat, took a long drink of his port, and met her gaze. "I won't have my lovely party ruined by such talk. You are at risk of becoming ... coarse." He returned to his other guests, making the rounds among them, chatting and drinking copious amounts of wine.

Stricken, she watched him go. Woodforde sauntered over from the bookcase, where he had been reading titles, and sat in a chair nearby. "What has upset your uncle?"

"I said something that offended him."

"Odd, given the topics of discussion among his guests. What could *you* say that would be worse? I heard Jeffcock and Wilkins debating with great spirit the merits of owning human beings or merely exploiting them financially while working them from cradle to grave. I was surprised you did not join in and abuse both as inhuman idiots."

"I had to walk away; I could not abuse them in my uncle's home, though both richly deserve it. I do have *some* manners, Woodforde, though I think Uncle Jacob would disagree with me this moment." She watched her uncle. He usually indulged her outré behavior, but this time she had gone too far. She bit her lip and took out her fan, waving it languidly in front of her face to hide the tears that welled. He had always been more father to her than her own had ever been, and though she knew her questioning would unsettle him, she hadn't thought he would censure her so brusquely. She had lost her sense of proportion, perhaps, as to how to moderate herself in polite society.

"If you like, I will thrash both Wilkins and Jeffcock some other time and place. I have never seen two men who deserved it more."

Emmeline cast a quick glance at him and smiled in surprise. "Those two do deserve a thorough thrashing. However, I am learning to put my efforts into the root problems rather than the resulting inhumanity."

"Root problems?"

"How can we laugh and drink and flirt when all around us there are humans whose lives are such a misery that it is … it's *unbearable*. Woodforde, there are little servant girls in this very city forced into cruel situations by men who make money from their misery."

He didn't say anything for a long moment, but there was sympathy in his eyes, not condemnation. "I don't see how us being miserable can help them. The world is full of such sorrows, Emmie," he said gently. "Some of us try to help where we can, but making ourselves ill with worry or so low as to admit defeat in the face of seemingly insurmountable odds … how does it help those downtrodden?"

"I don't suppose it does. But seeing little children exploited for the sexual gratification of men ... how can we turn a blind eye?"

"I've known you since you were ten, Emmie, and yet you astonish me all the time. One never gets bored speaking with you. Shocked on occasion, appalled and frightened, but *never* bored."

She bit the inside of her cheek; so often innocuous words felt like barbed weapons. She was being laughed at, indulged, and condemned all at once. "I thought I had lost that ability, Woodforde. But prepare to be shocked and appalled even more." She would not be silenced, and so told him what she knew and surmised about the men who bought and sold little girls' innocence. "It's disgusting, and I don't know how to stop it. Or if anyone *can* stop it. Is it even illegal to purchase little girls for sexual favors as one does an adult woman? I don't know, and as a female no one will talk to me about it!"

Woodforde's face was twisted into an expression of extreme distaste. His voice guttural and gruff with emotion, he said, "How have you learned of such shocking occurrences?"

"I ... someone in my lady's group was trying to help a girl escape such a situation. She told us about it. The girl had been brought from an orphanage for just such a purpose."

"I've seen little girls plying their trade near Haymarket, but never once did I ponder what had brought them to such a low place. And yet you say men are buying them from orphanages. It's disgusting." He frowned and shook his head. "I never thought of it as something that could be stopped or changed. How can I call myself a man of conscience when I've never even thought to question their lives?" He looked down at his well-formed, sensitive hands, twisted together over a handkerchief. As a physician, he never used those hands to slice into a patient; that was left to surgeons, mere workmen. "Beasts such as that, who would buy and sell little girls like … like weanlings, should not be allowed to live."

"Do you want to help?" she asked him, touched by his vehemence.

"With all my heart," he said, putting one of his warm hands over hers. "But how?"

"By seeking the truth, discovering firsthand how those children live. Come see us in Chelsea tomorrow evening," she said quickly, glancing over at her uncle. "I'll tell Fidelity that you will take me to the All Saints' Day evening service. Do you promise to behave as if I am a rational being and not a hothouse flower for the whole evening?"

"I will do my best. You wish me to take you to the church service?"

"No, of course not, Woodforde. That is just the excuse we will use for you taking me out in the evening."

"Where am I taking you?"

"I'll tell you then. As a physician and a man of means, you *can* help. My group of ladies is doing its best to put a stop to this tragedy, but I find myself alone in some of my most shocking plans."

She looked up and saw her uncle watching them. He nodded and smiled, presumably having put aside his anger with her. She felt her face color; how unfortunate it was that the hazelnuts she and Woodforde had cast had burned together brightly, glowing and melding into one until they turned to ash. Silly tradition. Little did her uncle know that the warmth between them had been fired by a conscience stirred to action by social injustice, not by any personal feeling.

The party was soon enough over. As they were waiting for their cloaks, Lady Clara moved to Emmeline's side. "Will you take me home?" she muttered swiftly. "I am in Belgravia."

"Did Mr. Jeffcock not bring you?"

"He did." Her face was white and her expression anguished. "Please, Miss St. Germaine … I know we do not have a friendship, but

I would deem it a great favor if you would take me. You have a carriage, correct? And go to Chelsea? It would not take you much out for your way."

Taken aback, Emmeline turned to face her in the dimly lit entry, where they awaited their carriages as Sir Jacob made his rounds, saying good evening to all of his guests. "I would be delighted to offer you room in my carriage. I meant not to protest, but was taken by surprise."

The young lady turned as her fiancé approached and said loudly, "I shan't need your accompaniment home, Elijah. Miss St. Germaine quite *insists* that she drop me off on her way to Chelsea. See ... here is Madame la Comtesse Bernadotte as companion, so all is quite proper for two young unmarried ladies. More proper than *you* taking me in a closed carriage, engaged though we are."

Emmeline sighed. Lady Clara had made it sound like she were the instigator of this departure from plans. In truth, this complicated her evening. What could she do now? She must, she supposed, take Lady Clara to Belgravia first and then head north to Clerkenwell, but it was annoying.

Or ... she could use it as a test and watch the young lady's reactions, since she still retained a smidgen of suspicion of Lady Clara. How would she react to being taken to Clerkenwell, the scene of the crime, so to speak? Would she recognize the place? It was time to either strike Lady Clara Langdon from her list of suspects or move her up to more prominence.

TWENTY-TWO

MR. JEFFCOCK STALKED DOWN the steps to his waiting carriage without a word for his fiancée. Lady Clara smiled in satisfaction. If her intent was to disgust him so much he'd cry off, she was bound for disappointment. If Emmeline was any judge of that kind of man, and she had met his ilk before, it would make him more determined to dominate her. The consequences of such insolence with a man like that could be dangerous indeed, given that once they married she would be at his mercy.

Woodforde gave Fidelity his arm down the steps, then took his leave. Once in the carriage, Emmeline turned to Lady Clara in the dim interior. "I hope you don't mind, but we have a stop to make first, and it may take an hour or so. Are you in a hurry?"

"Not at all," she said, her head to one side, watching Emmeline. "Where are we going?"

Emmeline shook her head. "It's a secret, for now."

Fidelity was rigid with anxiety, but Gillies knew exactly how to handle her and began a quiet conversation about the next literary salon she was planning.

"Miss St. Germaine, may I be impertinent and ask a question?" Lady Clara asked, her voice velvety in the darkness, the only sounds the two older women softly speaking and the carriage trundling over the cobbles of town.

"You may. Although asking permission rather takes it from impertinence to inquisitiveness."

Lady Clara gave a low chuckle. "One cannot help but notice how attentive Doctor Woodforde is to you. Your families are close. Sir Jacob arranged the party tonight to bring you together. And yet you appear to hold him at a distance. Why do you not allow him to court you?"

"Is it only everyone else's preference that matters, and I must bow to it?"

"I forget sometimes that not every family is the same," Lady Clara replied. "Miss Espanson and I speak often, and our families are so similar that I forget there are those who actually *care* about the females under their control."

"What gave you the notion my family is any different from others?" Emmeline sought out Lady Clara's pale face in the dimness of the carriage interior. "I was fortunate only that my father died at the right moment, and my eldest brother has a horror of notoriety. I assured him I would behave with circumspection if I could live in London with Fidelity, but still, I had to ask permission. Every single day I bite my tongue. I stifle my natural impulse to tell Leopold—my brother—what a loathsome and pompous creature he is. I am demure and obedient and behave with decorum and sweetness in the face of his spy, our butler, Birk."

Lady Clara had frozen in place, like a statue, staring at her.

"I'm sorry," Emmeline said, swallowing back her growing rage. "Bitterness occasionally overwhelms me that I, as a grown woman—intelligent, capable, and mature—must still respond to my elder brother's slightest beck."

"I see you have thought of this a lot."

"That it is inherently unfair that I, an adult woman, must ask my dullard brother for permission to live where I live and even for access to my own money? I have pondered it on occasion, yes."

"You blackmail him, then, with threats of notoriety."

"I suppose."

"No 'suppose' about it," Lady Clara said. "By your own admission, you get your way in exchange for giving him what he wants, a sister who is demure and circumspect."

"I prefer to say we have an understanding. He values our family reputation, and I value my freedom, that being a relative term given my circumstances." And yet she was at perilous risk of being exposed, more so every time she went out in the night as the Avengeress. However, she saw that largely as a management of risk; she must do some of what she wanted in order to remain sane. She chose her occasions, aided and abetted by Gillies and Josephs, to traverse beyond the pale, and believed she was at low risk of discovery by Birk and her brother Leopold.

Though maybe not now. But then, who could have foreseen bloody slaughter?

She pushed the door open and peered into the gloom, but it was hard to tell where they were. Lamplighters were abroad; she saw one on his ladder with his wick, lighting a lantern while a boy stood at the bottom holding the ladder. Taverns were pools of light and noise, spilling out to the walk in front, rowdy drunks singing songs; "The Ballad of Clerkenwell" had become popular with the patterers, those glib fellows who disseminated a wildly fictionalized version of the day's news in song or verse. It sounded as if new verses were being added about the murdering wench known as the Avengeress.

"We must already be in Clerkenwell," she said wryly, as a drunken chorus erupted from another such establishment. "They're singing my song."

"Clerkenwell?" Lady Clara stared at Emmeline. "Why are we here?"

Beginning to feel ashamed for even thinking Lady Clara capable of the murder, Emmeline said, "I have an appointment with a young gentleman."

Josephs had used his time well. Tommy awaited them by the front door of the Bridge and Bezel, drinking a pint from a pewter tankard, no doubt using pennies Josephs gave him. They helped him up into the carriage, which he found a great treat. Emmeline introduced him to Lady Clara Langdon. Tommy was charming to her in his inimitable roguish, bragging, boyish manner. She had brightened at the excitement of their late-night mission, and avidly listened to the conversation.

Emmeline had wanted to speak with the lad herself, for though she trusted Gillies's memory, she knew that once Tommy was on a task, he was like a rat terrier and would not let go. He had likely discovered more in the past few hours. "Tell me what you've learned, Tommy."

"The potboy from the town'ouse *next* to Sir 'Enry's 'eard what they was talkin' 'bout that night."

"Is that the Farnsworth house you speak of? What *who* was talking about?"

"Aye, the Farnsworths'... Arnie Biggins, 'is name is. 'E over'eard Sir 'Enry an' the feller with the dog, the feller as brung the little girls to Sir 'Enry, quarrellin'."

Emmeline felt a spurt of hope. Her doggedness was being rewarded. "Tell me what he said, as close to exactly as possible."

Tommy screwed up his face and recited the story the potboy from number 74 Blithestone had told him. There was a great deal of the conversation that was youthful bragging and blustering, but there was much that was important. Arnie had been sleeping on a pallet on the kitchen floor in front of the hearth, by the last embers of the fire in the kitchen. His employment was comfortable enough, but the cook was a dragon. It was his job to keep an eye on things overnight and alert the master if there was trouble, be it thief or fire, so he slept lightly.

A dog's bark awoke him and he heard voices, so he opened the kitchen window. Though he couldn't see because of the brick walls between the terraced homes, he could hear clearly, as the night was otherwise quiet and sound carried.

"Feller wiv the dog, 'e were quiet loike, Arnie says. Sir 'Enry—Arnie knows 'is voice coz 'e's alluz yellin' at someone—hollered as how the feller—Ratter, 'e called 'im—must o' tole someone what they was up to, fer the lady in the mask to know to snatch the lass. Sir 'Enry said as 'ow Ratter were gonna die if the uvers found out, and 'oo did 'e tell? Ratter raises 'is voice then; sez that the guvner don't know what 'e's on about, that 'e never tole no one 'bout bringing girls inta Lunnon ta sell orf, an' Sir 'Enry's getting' worked up over nuffin."

Lady Clara looked confused, but Tommy's patter was not difficult to decipher for Emmeline, so she repeated what the boy had said, and did so for the next lot, too; she listened more, and then translated for Lady Clara and Fidelity, adding, also, information she already knew

248

from before, for their benefit. "Ratter left after Sir Henry accused him of telling what they were up to and threatening that others would kill the procurer for talking. That's not to say he left the area, though; he still could be the one who killed Sir Henry. Then two men showed up together. Both sets—Ratter and the two anonymous men—must have come in response to the notes from Sir Henry, sent by way of the Claybourne potboy, Noah, who was dispatched to the Rookery— St. Giles, you know—with a note to Ratter, and to St. James bearing a note for the other two, it appears. Tommy says that Arnie overheard those two men speaking with Sir Henry, too. Their voices were too low-pitched to hear, but Sir Henry shouted a few things, much the same as his accusations of Ratter, and they denied his charge."

Lady Clara said, "Why did Sir Henry send for these men?"

"He suspected them of telling tales … of letting their business secrets out. He's blaming them for the woman who took Molly away." She gave Clara a significant look and nodded toward Tommy, who mustn't know she was the Avengeress. He would find it exciting, and how could he resist telling the world? The fewer in on Emmeline's secret identity the better.

Tommy said Arnie may have heard the scuffle when Sir Henry was killed, and if so, it took place shortly after he heard the voices. He then heard the watch, then a commotion when the watch was beaten, and then silence. He heard nothing more until the next morning, when the fishlad found Sir Henry's body in the alley by his own back courtyard.

"Wait. Where exactly was the body?" Emmeline asked. "I've heard it was in the alley and in the courtyard."

"Bof, miss," Tommy said. "'E were arf in, arf out, yer see."

"Yes, I see." She turned to Lady Clara. "The timing of it, if Arnie is correct, is the best indication we have that the two men killed Sir

Henry. Or perhaps Ratter hung around and killed the knight after they left, fearing Sir Henry would turn him over to the authorities or otherwise get him in trouble. The watchman thinks it was two men who set upon him, but his memory, according to the newspapers, is unclear." Emmeline turned back to Tommy. "How would we go about finding exactly where the Claybourne potboy took the notes? We know St. Giles and St. James, but those are two large areas."

The boy shrugged. "Dunno, miss. Noah won't go back to St. Giles. 'At's a dangerous place, the Rookery. Lad could lose 'is loife there."

"I don't want him to go back there. I want to know if he can recall the addresses, or how he found the places, since you say he can't read. It may point us to the right people."

Tommy shrugged. "I'll arsk 'im."

They let the boy go, as he was yawning and wiping sleep from his eyes. He had a place to sleep that night if he nipped in right soon, he said.

"I don't think we can do another thing tonight," Emmeline said.

They left Clerkenwell, stopped in Belgravia to let Lady Clara off at her home, and returned to Chelsea. Birk had stayed up, of course, so Emmeline and Fidelity chatted quietly about the nut-crack party as they entered, what fun it was and who had been present, and then the butler locked up after them.

November 1st, 1810, Evening Edition of *The Prattler*
By: The Rogue
To The Despoilers of Little Girls

Your Faithful Correspondent, your very own Rogue, has learned much about the man who was Butchered like the Swine he was. Sir Henry, the Brewer and Knight, had his own collection of Filthy Secrets, as your Rogue told his faithful readers. His predilection for Despoiling the Flowers of Youth was noted here.

But Shame! T'would seem to not only be Lusts of the Flesh he was satisfying. He and a herd of Like-minded Satyrs joined together to import into our unfair city Orphaned Girls, those whose Motherless state render them the objects of Charity, and, it appears, Debauchery. The Knight and his Ilk sell these little girls to Lustful and Wicked Men, reserving for themselves, like art collectors, the Prettiest Treats.

Rise up, ye Citizens with a Conscience! What does it matter if the Poor Defiled Children are Orphans? Should we not, as a society, care for them the more? How do we call ourselves a Christian Nation and yet abuse the helpless in such Terrible and Devilish ways? Satan is abroad, and finds among the Perverted Lusts of some men a Playground.

Your Rogue is investigating, and will come to you with More, for it seems that Whomever Murdered Sir Henry Claybourne may have had reason other than Shiny Shillings in his Pocket. There are others such as him about. Your Rogue desires not Blood, but Justice for the Sullied Youth. A Warning to those so Inclined; We Will Stop You!

....

TWENTY-THREE

EMMELINE ATTENDED MORNING SERVICE for All Saints' Day, to celebrate the lives and works of the saints. She would attend again for All
Souls' Day on the morrow, to remember the faithful departed. It was
true she did not believe in God, but she still found herself praying
sometimes, especially when her heart was sore and the memory of her
mother and sister lay heavy upon it. Prayer was contemplation, a time
to think deeply and discover her heart. All Saints church was the perfect place for that on a chilly Thursday morning, when she was distraught over the evil that men did—aided by women, in some cases, it
was true—to the helpless over whom they had complete control.

She was torn about finding the killer of Sir Henry Claybourne.
She had reasoned that finding his killer would expose—perhaps—the
men with whom he did business, and that would—perhaps, again—
end their commerce in children's bodies. But then again, his killer or
killers had done the world a favor.

She walked home to write letters and sent Simeon a list of questions, some about the orphanage she now knew about and Mr. Dunstable, its warder. Every day that went by without the Pentonville Home for Unfortunate Children being shut down meant that more children were being abused. Any moment, other little girls, such as Sarah, could be sold into a life of depravity at the mercy of men who knew no shame. Her letter also included what little she knew of the notes Sir Henry sent with his potboy, as well as a description of Ratter and a query about whether Simeon had anyone who could track the man down in St. Giles.

Simeon had hundreds of contacts, some in the unsavory underworld and some among legitimate businessmen and women who plied their trades—rag and bone, night soil, and other businesses—among the downtrodden. She also sent him a Rogue column that summed up all of the rage she felt, as well as the helplessness, but also her determination to find justice. She hoped that her suggestions within it would shake loose some information. Men other than those involved *must* know about the trade in orphan girls. Josephs, who was taking some of the carriage tack to a blacksmith, carried that and other letters to post, as she didn't trust Birk.

The afternoon mail brought a package from Simeon and letters from others; one in particular was shocking in its contents. Martha Adair wrote to her that Sally had run away. Emmeline's first thought was that Sally had been snatched, but Martha was quite clear on the circumstances—her household was run on strict lines as far as the servants were concerned—and Sally had most definitely taken her few possessions and voluntarily left the house. One of the maids had seen her go, remonstrated with her, but Sally had replied that an apprenticeship waited for her.

She had been an unsatisfactory servant at best, disappearing at times, secretive, silent, sometimes sullen. At first she hadn't been able to work at all, of course. Martha had been lenient, given what the girl had suffered in being pregnant and miscarrying. It was more than many mistresses would have done. When Sally recovered, though, she had been almost untrainable, though far from stupid. Ellen, the maid-of-all-work, had told her mistress that Sally was not sullen with the other servants. She was, in fact, clever at mimicry and had kept them all laughing, though Martha never saw that side of her.

How could Sally afford an apprenticeship? It was unthinkable that an orphan girl should suddenly be able to purchase her future.

Simeon's letter had much graver news. He had already instituted a hunt for Ratter before Emmeline's letter that morning, and his journalist had tracked the man down in the Rookery. Ratter had feared for his life. He was willing to tell them everything about who was involved in the company to procure young girls for the gentleman connoisseurs; in exchange, he wanted the protection of a boat ticket to the Canadas. Emmeline's heart lifted at that news; finally, a break!

The journalist couldn't promise the man anything without Simeon's approval, so he had come back to his boss, who agreed to help Ratter escape London in exchange for the full story of the company formed with the express purpose of buying and selling the innocence of children. But when the journalist went back to find Ratter, he learned that the man was dead, stabbed through the heart in a back alley and left to perish.

Emmeline slumped in dejection; so much hope, lost so swiftly.

One or two locals, for the bribe of a penny, admitted to seeing two men who clearly did not belong in the Rookery: one had a limp, and the other a Frenchie accent. Given this murder, it followed that it was indeed the two men who had killed—first, Sir Henry, for being a threat to the secrecy of the company, and now Ratter, who must have been known to them, for the same reason. Somehow they had heard about him speaking with a news writer and his willingness to expose them, and took action to prevent it. All they now had was Ratter's vague description of the company, a group of hoity-toities, as he had called them to the journalist.

How many pairs of men were there, in London, in which one man limped and one had a French accent? There must have been hundreds in the city who fit those descriptions.

She and Fidelity had an early supper. Emmeline told her companion that Woodforde had offered to take her to the All Saints service that evening, and that she had acquiesced. Gillies would be accompanying her, so there would be no scandalous time alone in a dark carriage. She was sorry to lie to Fidelity about her true intentions, but her companion would have been in agony all evening if she knew where Emmeline intended they should go.

Josephs stabled Woodforde's curricle and horses and had the St. Germaine carriage prepared, ready to take them to church, as Birk understood it, with Gillies as companion for the evening.

"I cannot believe I allowed you to talk me into this," Woodforde said, his voice filled with tension after she more fully explained what her plan was. "If Samuel knew what I was allowing, he would challenge me, and I would let him shoot me through the heart as I deserve."

"Then you'd be a fool. Samuel is a very good sort, as clergymen go," Emmeline said. "But his charity extends only so far as his parish borders. My parish, if I can call it that, is the female half of humankind."

"You are never cowed by the enormity of a task, are you?" Woodforde said, and she couldn't tell if his words were admiring or admonishing. "Aren't Samuel's benevolent efforts more practical?"

"I don't for a moment imagine I will wholly succeed, Woodforde, but I must try." Emmeline pondered her family. "At least Samuel *has* a conscience. He does his best for his people, and they love him for it. Leo doesn't give a fig about anyone."

"You judge harshly."

"I know my family, I would hope. I don't think Sam worse than other parish priests beholden to their benefactors, and he is considerably *more* principled than many. I don't envy him the narrow path he must forge between his wishes for his parish and what he must do to placate our brother. Leo cares for nothing but St. Germaine family pride. On the other hand, Thomas cares for nothing but … well, nothing. Except for gambling and drink." She sighed. "It's a difficult world at times, Woodforde, and men, who hold all the control, often abuse their power and freedom."

"I'm well aware of it."

"Do people never fall short of your expectations?"

"Perhaps I am more realistic than you," he said.

Gillies chuckled under her breath, and Emmeline sent her a sharp look. Her maid disapproved of their current jaunt and had stated it vociferously as she readied her mistress, so Gillies was not in her mistress's favor at the moment.

Emmeline didn't respond to Woodforde. She simply felt the motion of the carriage and inhaled the smells: Gillies's camphor-soaked kerchief—she had a bit of a cold in her head, and swore it helped; Woodforde's scent, which was wool and something citrusy; and the carriage, well-oiled leather and the ineffable scent of horse. It was familiar and homely, even if their undertaking that night was not. She supposed she should be giving others latitude since she so often fell short of her family's expectations, and yet her family was, for the most part, kind to her. Especially Samuel, who was a true gentleman, and Thomas, high-spirited and lovable.

"Have I become hard since Maria's death?" she asked. "Tell me true, Woodforde."

His face was almost invisible in the shadows. "You've not become hard, Emmie, you've become ... I can only describe it in medical terms; always the doctor, as it turns out. Your emotions are like the nerves throughout your body which, for the most part, you are not even aware of. But then trauma happens, and of a sudden the pain of those raw nerves is excruciating. This dulls over time, but any little bump or injury revives the pain. Losing your mother young, then Emily, who was almost a second mother to you, and then Maria so soon after ... it has made you sensitive."

"I've never thought of that, but I suppose Emily *was* like another mother in a way. She was so very intelligent and yet gentle, compassionate ... far too good for Leopold."

"You're too hard on Leo."

"*You* don't have to live by his rules and accept his admonishment," Emmeline replied swiftly, her tone low but brittle. "When you do, *then* you can speak of him with intimate knowledge. No man on earth knows what it is like for a woman, how it feels to be chastened, reprimanded, to always bite our tongue and mind our manners, curbing ourselves, changing every natural mannerism in case it offends the men who have us in their thrall. Even men who must obey a master ... at least in their own home they exert their will and have the final say."

"I think perhaps you have not seen some of the men I have, who are meek in the face of their wives' belligerence."

"Your exception proves the rule, Woodforde. The very fact that those meek men overruled by their wives stand out to you in your memory shows that in the great majority of cases, men's rule is considered not only the standard, but the right way of things."

"Do you think men don't do the same, stifle an urge to be blunt so as to avoid offending our patrons, our family, our patients … ad infinitum? How many times have I had to bite my tongue rather than tell a patient if he would just stop drinking so much and get out for exercise he would improve vastly?"

"It's not the same, and you must see it. When I bite my tongue it is because to be honest would be to forfeit all respect in society, or even to be sent into exile. You would be blamed for being blunt; I would be damned as insane."

"I think we must agree to disagree on this point, Emmeline. I see no difference."

"At least your mind and intellect are valued, Woodforde, where having the same is seen as an unnecessary encumbrance for a woman."

"I will not argue philosophy with you, Emmeline."

"It's not philosophy, Woodforde, it's society," she retorted, angered by his typical withdrawal. "What I state is simply the result of my study of our culture and its standards. Men, even when they are stupid, ill-informed, immoral, or otherwise unsuitable, hold absolute control over women and children."

"And other men," he said.

She didn't reply. He was being deliberately obtuse and she was weary of the argument. She *could* remind him how unfair it was that a woman could suffer her husband's beatings, belittlement, and abuse, but if she left, her children must remain with her husband. She had no right to the babies she bore because they were their father's chattel, as was she. The unfairness burned, but … it was not Woodforde's doing, after all.

The pace of the carriage slowed. Gillies was being dropped off at Sir Jacob's house to visit with her friend Morag the cook. As Josephs rolled to a stop by the alley leading to the back entrance, the maid said, "D'ye think the two of you will nigh kill each other afore you return for me?"

"No, Mrs. Gillies," Woodforde said. "I am no danger, and I assume Emmeline has no weapon?"

Gillies chuckled and clambered down. "Her words are all that sting, sir. Be careful with her, Doctor. For all her faults, she's a rare fine lady."

"I know that, Gillies. She has indeed been a 'rare fine lady' since she was a little girl and I had to pull her out of the stew pond."

His kindness took all the indignation out of Emmeline at being spoken of as if she weren't there. As the carriage trundled on, to travel the short distance from Sir Jacob's home to the theater district, she pondered their relationship. Woodforde was only ever kind to her. Perhaps it was true that he had a tender regard for her. He must have affection for her or he would not take part in such a potentially disastrous late-night journey. This was foolish; she knew that. And he was *not* foolish, not in any sense. Ergo, he must care for her beyond the friendship she had always known subsisted.

What was wrong with her, then, that she could not return the tender feelings of so worthy and upright a man as Doctor Giles Woodforde? He was handsome, kind, and eminently suitable in every way. Her family desired the match. His would welcome her. And yet … there was something that kept her from the womanly and tender feelings her female friends and relations succumbed to.

The carriage slowed again. That meant they were close to Haymarket.

"I think we're here," he said softly. "Now what?"

Morag was finishing her chores in the kitchen of Sir Jacob's home and had brewed a strong pot of tea. It was an oddly run home in that it did not have a housekeeper. Miss St. Germaine had told Gillies that her uncle had a prejudice against the breed of women who became housekeepers, calling them busybodies who poked their noses in everywhere. It was a curious departure from the normal run of things. Sir Jacob was well-known to have kept a string of mistresses, mostly dancers and actresses, but no housekeeper would gossip about such a thing if she wished to keep her position.

As a result, the duties of a housekeeper, which were multitudinous, were broken up among the other staff. The butler did much, even down to the inspection of the linen and overseeing when it was sent out to a laundress. Sir Jacob himself took upon himself some of the tasks, such as ordering the wine and food—Morag gave him a list each week—and hiring staff. He always said that as a judge he was a suspicious sort and liked to know for himself who was working in his home. In Morag's estimation, Sir Jacob was far too inclined to hire a saucebox as a chambermaid, but if the master didn't mind, she didn't care, and with the turnover in servants being the way it was, she would outlast the saucy minx.

Regardless, the household seemed to run perfectly fine for a bachelor, given that the gentleman was a bon vivant who ate often at his club, and although he entertained frequently, it was often in an informal spur-of-the-moment style, as the nut-crack party had been. Morag once confessed that when the last housekeeper had departed a few years prior, she had been happy, since the woman wished to interfere in every aspect of her kitchen and questioned every purchase. Sir Jacob did not.

Polly, the little kitchen maid, sat at the end of the table engaged in some chores Morag had set her, such as pounding sugar and grinding spices for use in the next day's pudding. Gillies eyed the child as she and Morag chatted by the fire, the rhythmic pounding to break the sugar into fine granules the usual and familiar beat of life in a kitchen. The little girl appeared weary; the beat was slow. "Let the lass go up to bed, Morag. She's fagged beyond belief. Can ye no' tell?"

"Aye, but she'll no' go unless I see her to her bed. She's afeared o' the dark, or the dragons that lurk under her cot." Morag spoke more loudly, saying, "Polly, will ye no' go up to your bed, lass?"

"Must I? I'm not done with this yet, ma'am, an' I wanna learn to cook, like you." Her weary face was drawn and pale, but she set to her work more diligently, with a determined line to her pretty mouth. "I'll wait and go up with you, missus."

"That's all right then, child. Go on wi' your task."

"Puir wee child," Gillies murmured. "She's taken to you like a mum, Morag."

"Aye, an' if I'd ever had a bairn, I'da liked a wee lass like Polly."

"She's a pretty lassie, God's truth."

———

Emmeline pushed aside the velvet curtains and surveyed the street. "I know you think I'm mad, Woodforde. I've seen these children lingering about the theaters, and at one time, when I was younger and naïve, I didn't know why." Haymarket was a notorious neighborhood for prostitutes; there was even an annual printed guide to the women, she had heard, listing their attributes and talents.

"At St. Barts, I've seen far too many little girls—and some boys—afflicted with diseases common among the fallen, their bodies corroded from the effects of abuse in ways unimaginable to most of society. They fall into it so easily, but like quicksand is the climb out...'tis not so simple."

"I wish I understood. *Why* do men go to children to satisfy their lusts? Am I mad? Is it not *wrong* for it to be so?"

"If I had answers, I would know how to stop it," Woodforde said, his tone filled with exasperation and something else, a deep sadness.

"It seems to me that there is a wink and a nudge whenever prostitutes of whatever age are mentioned, however obliquely. How can we change a thing we do not acknowledge?"

"Not everyone who is silent or calm or doesn't rant in the face of injustice goes along with it. We don't *all* feel the need to voice our objections so loudly."

Irritated by his subtle criticism, she pushed aside the curtains and slid the window down. Damp night air swept through, carrying the scent of coal fires and horses and the sound of voices in the distance. If Woodforde had seen poor little Molly being molested by that demon, Sir Henry, he would be as angry as she, but Emmeline could never explain to him her feelings, nor could she tell him what she had seen.

"Emmie, there... do you see those two girls by the corner, where that dark alley is?"

The theater district was well lit compared to other parts of London. There were women strolling the area, making clear what their profession was, but Woodforde was pointing out two slight girls who stood by a lamppost, both in similar attitudes, one hand on a jutted hip. They were gowned in adult garb but from what she could see, Emmeline surmised they were probably eleven or twelve. "When I was their age I was chasing butterflies in the garden at Malincourt," she said softly, her voice breaking. "These children... these girls..."

A gentleman came along just then, swinging his walking stick jauntily. One girl darted out to him and took his hand, touching his face and leaning against him. He shoved her away roughly and she rejoined her friend by the lamppost to await a more willing fellow while the gentleman walked away with a woman who accosted him in a similar manner.

In a soft but carrying voice, Emmeline said out the window, "Josephs, over there, those two girls ... can you take us close?"

"Emmie, you cannot mean to approach them!" Woodforde said. "I thought you meant to observe, not interfere."

"Then you thought wrong," she said. "I wish to speak to them."

Josephs walked the carriage close to the girls and both darted forward; this was not the first time a coach had pulled close to their corner. Emmeline opened the carriage door. The girls, similar pale faces and garbed in cut-down gowns of tattered silk and stained velvet, looked up at her in some confusion.

"May I pay you for a half hour of your time?" she said to them.

TWENTY-FOUR

SHE COULDN'T SLEEP THAT night. Though Woodforde couldn't understand the two girls because of their jargon-filled speech, specific to their profession and their life on the streets, Emmeline could, for the most part, thanks to her conversations with Tommy. What she understood of it was wrenching; their life selling their bodies was horrifying to her. Even worse, they seemed numb to it after only a few months in one case, a year in the other, and assumed an air of insouciance that was heartbreaking. They were sisters, aged thirteen and fourteen now, and were fortunate, they thought, because they had a protector. He was some kind of relation, an uncle or perhaps their mother's bully. Emmeline saw him lurking in the shadows, ready to intervene if there was trouble. Some girls, they said, had no one.

If Emmeline could have helped them she would have, but one couldn't abduct two girls from the street even if one's intentions were good. The two were chary of her offers of help, and given their world, they were wise to be suspicious. Gillies said, of their caution, that perhaps in their case it was "better the devil you know than the one you don't." In the end, all she could do was listen and give them money, after which they retreated to their "protector" and handed over the shillings. The two girls would never see that money, in all likelihood.

Woodforde had been grim and silent on the way back to her home, and he left with little more than a bow and solemn "good night." If he'd had any feeling for her before, it was no doubt dead now, given the world into which she had dragged him, but Emmeline frankly didn't care. She'd never get over what she had seen and heard. There was a rot at the core of her nation, but it was sprayed with scent so the fastidious could ignore it. She must sharpen her focus on finding out who killed Sir Henry and exposing the company of men who traded in the innocence of children, while protecting herself, her Crones, and *The Prattler*. She needed to do *something* about the sickening trade in children that was tarnishing a nation with so much promise. Emmeline knew she couldn't cure all of society's ills, but she and her allies could make a start.

Awake through the long night, she spent much of it in thought and reflection. Gleaning every bit of information she could from newspapers, then adding it to what she herself knew while separating what was fiction from fact, she sat at her dressing table with a pencil and paper and constructed a timeline, hoping it might expose some truths.

Gillies came in with her morning tea tray and to open the curtains. She took one look at the litter of papers and grimaced. "I'll just tidy these—"

"Not now, please, Gillies … just let me be."

"Aye, miss," she said softly, and left her mistress alone.

When she'd escaped with Molly around eight o'clock on the evening of the twenty-fourth, Emmeline had assumed it would take Sir Henry time to recover his equanimity and call for the magistrate. But she hadn't yet known the whole infamous story; she hadn't known he was part of a group of men importing girls from orphanages to use and abuse. It seemed he had swiftly concluded that someone among that group had betrayed him, and her visit was the result.

So rather than summon the magistrate, as one would have expected, Sir Henry sent notes by the potboy to summon Ratter and the two other men, whom he appeared to suspect were the betrayers. That had taken some time, of course, but all had arrived shortly after eleven, if the journalists and her own information proved correct. He first met with Ratter and accused him of betraying him, or of accidentally letting information escape. Ratter denied it and presumably went away, though Emmeline wasn't sure that was so. He may have lingered.

The other two men arrived together and Sir Henry confronted them. An argument ensued. This all would have taken, at most, half an hour. The potboy at the Farnsworths' had told Tommy he had heard a scuffle or scream—presumably Claybourne's final vocal effort before his throat was sliced—and then someone ran away. About this time, one of the watchmen was beaten, and the fellows who had done it were chased across the green but not apprehended. No other alarum was raised, and no one knew about the murder. The other watchman likely thought it was a random act of violence against his colleague, not uncommon, unfortunately, as drunken young gentleman thought it humorous to tip the watchbox over or fight the watchmen, who were too often elderly or infirm.

The commotion heard by Arnie Biggins, the neighbor potboy, could have been either Ratter or the two other men killing Sir Henry, but Ratter being later murdered suggested that he had known too much—probably, the identity of the two men—and was not the killer himself. Maybe he had even seen the other two at their dreadful task. After the disturbance, it appeared that calmness had fallen upon the small courtyard, and the remaining watchman called the midnight hour. No one ventured out to see what had happened, and Sir Henry's dead body lay there until the fishboy arrived between five and six the next morning.

Emmeline had questions: Did no servant lock the doors at night? Or was that the master of the house's task? What Sir Henry meant to say to Ratter and the two others was not something he would have wanted anyone to overhear, but that didn't mean no one had. One or both of the Hargreaves had seen the men, and then Arnie had heard them; had no one else? Emmeline sighed and put her head down on her dressing table.

Gillies entered with the linens that had been returned from the laundress they employed. "Are you well, miss?"

"I'm weary," she said, straightening. "Is it too much to ask in this world that children be safe, and that those charged with protecting them actually do their duty? Can we not have a society where humans don't kill each other?"

The maid sat down on the bed, her blue eyes filled with sorrow. "I asked the same, miss, about the tairible conditions in the mines in Scotland when my own little lad was killed. The mine owner didnae care one bit about poor William. It's a sad world."

"Will it ever get better?"

"I wouldnae count on it." She put away the linens, stacked the newspapers together, and tidied the room.

All Souls' service at All Saints church, a commemoration of the faithful departed, was special to Emmeline. She attended in order to repeat the names of all those she had loved and lost: her mama, Emily, and Maria. Gillies, who accompanied her, prayed for her dear departed husband and little William. She prayed too, though, for her children alive, the ones she hadn't seen for years, and the grandchildren she would never know.

On the walk back to the townhome, bundled against a sharp November wind, Emmeline discussed with Gillies her thoughts and her timeline, and her conclusion that the two men who had last spoken to Sir Henry were likely both tied up in the child-for-sale scheme and responsible for his murder. "I don't want to decide based merely on that who killed the man, but it makes sense. So far at least."

Gillies was silent for a long moment, then said, "Miss, what d'ye think about all the other poor lasses, the scullery maids brought to London? If we find a way to stop them monsters from buyin' an' sellin' them and maybe even identify the men doing it, where will they go? How'll they live?"

"I don't know." She told her maid about the girls she had met the previous night. "Their eyes, Gillies … the dead look in their eyes, despite their chatter. I wonder what they were like before the street? It makes me ache with sadness." She paused at the long wooden rail fence along the Cheyne Walk and looked out over the river at the abundance of boats and skiffs. A ferry headed to the other side, carrying cargo of some sort. The ever-present smell of the river was in her nostrils, along with coal smoke and a sweet smell drifting to her from somewhere. A gust caught her bonnet and she grasped it as it tugged at the pins in her hair.

"Those two girls have had a far more difficult life than I, yet I feel a kinship with them. You didn't know me then, but when my mother died, I was adrift. My father and aunt conspired to break me, even more so after … after the incident with the tutor." It was a tale she seldom told but that Gillies knew of, about a young man who had taken advantage of her innocence and naiveté. *And* her rebellious spirit, she admitted to herself.

"Aye, but it's no' the same, miss," Gillies said.

"I know there's no comparison."

Gillies was silent for a long moment and looked troubled.

"What is it, Gillies? What's wrong?"

She simply shook her head. There was something worrying her, but Emmeline knew her maid by now; it would come out in its time. They continued on home, Gillies silent and Emmeline thoughtful.

Luncheon was light, and Fidelity cheerful and chatty. That afternoon, Emmeline wrote letters and posted them. Simeon employed male journalists who could snoop and pry and loiter with much less attention paid them, so she posed some questions to him.

As she sat in the drawing room at a table by the window, writing her dutiful weekly letters to Leopold and Samuel, Birk staggered into the room. "What is it?" Emmeline cried, starting up and spilling her ink across the paper.

"She's dead … the poor princess," Birk groaned, tears welling in his eyes. "Princess Amelia is no more." He burst into sobs.

All Souls' Day, and the youngest daughter of King George, was gone.

And so, at one in the afternoon on Friday, November 2nd, 1810, the nation was plunged into the dusky world of official mourning. Poor Princess Amelia, beloved daughter of the old king, was the youngest of the Prince of Wales' siblings. She had been tenderly romanticized by the kingdom despite whispered gossip of a doomed and inappropriate love for the king's equerry, the Honorable Charles FitzRoy, twenty-one years her senior but beloved by her nonetheless. And now after a long and sporadic range of illnesses, never able to marry her one true love, she had succumbed.

Emmeline felt a definite sympathy for the woman, who was so close to her own age. And yet, as stifling and restricted as life as a royal princess must be, it was a velvet-lined prison. The death shuffled every story off the front pages of the newspapers that evening and the next morning. All trumpeted the tragic news in detail, including the poor old king's devastation, the ring Princess Amelia had made for him with a braided hank of her own hair in foreknowledge of her death, and plans for her funeral, which would, in accordance with custom, be attended by the male members of her family only. Women of the genteel class were too fragile, too openly emotional, to attend.

———

But they could shop. There were practical considerations, and that included mourning wear for the public. Overnight, drapers had black and gray material, some dyed to suit, arrayed in their shops. Ladies who had ordered a complete colorful wardrobe for the winter—rich crimson and amber, emerald and rose—would now need to return for more somber gowns in dark gray and dull mauve, no gloss, no shine. Emmeline, accompanied by Gillies, went out to order two gowns, one in a sober dark gray, close enough to black for someone so far removed from the royal sphere, and one in a deep, rich mauve. She'd need black ribbons to refurbish hats, and black gloves. Birk was going to a lesser draper to obtain black ribbons for himself, Josephs, and even the horses. Mrs. Bramage would do the same for the maids.

Emmeline's choice of draper, the inimitable Harding, Howell & Co.s, at number 89 on Pall Mall, was near her uncle's home in St. James. Josephs dropped her and Gillies off at the door, and went on to Simeon's newspaper to find out the latest news. The draper's was an enormous establishment, a hundred and fifty feet deep, made up of several departments divided by glass partitions. When she and Gillies first entered, they walked through the furrier's goods—luxurious sable and fox—and beautifully made fans. Past the first partition was haberdashery, then lovely trinkets: jewelry, ormolu clocks, and even perfume. The last section was the one she needed, millinery and dressmaking.

It was crowded with women all looking for mourning dresses. She sighed, but every customer was resigned to a wait. Every lady remaining in London must needs have a mourning gown or two, or three, depending on their social calendar and plans to stay in London or depart for the country, given that public amusements would become thin while official mourning took place.

"How fortunate are the gentlemen; black gloves, a black hatband, and they are done," Emmeline murmured. "As ladies we must have a complete wardrobe."

Gillies sent her an exasperated look. "Nouw, miss, y'know that isn't quite right. We could pick over a gown and restyle it. I can dye the gray from last season."

"All right, Gillies, I *choose* to get a new gown or two," she murmured. "T'will loosen my brother's purse strings and I can perhaps order some sheet music and books at the same time and he'll not notice."

Gillies snorted. "He'll notice, miss, and make ye pay in other ways." She didn't care for Leopold any more than did her mistress.

Emmeline watched ladies chatting, ordering fabric, consulting with mantua makers, and gossiping. One lady attracted her notice by her absolute stillness in the feminine whirlwind of the millinery section. "Why, that is Miss Gottschalk," she said. The lovely blonde sat alone but for a maid, her expression perfectly solemn. On an impulse, Emmeline rose and swiftly threaded through the women who milled about, approaching the lady. She touched her arm and greeted her.

"How kind of you to speak to me," she said, accepting Emmeline's outstretched gloved hand.

"May I sit with you while we await service?"

"If you so choose," Miss Gottschalk said.

It was not a joyful invitation, but it was enough. Gillies and the young German woman's maid, also German, managed a stilted conversation apart from their mistresses, while Emmeline did her best to find topics in common. They spoke of clothing, which Miss Gottschalk clearly enjoyed, as well as music and opera, which she knew on a far deeper level than did Emmeline. If she had been able, Miss Gottschalk would have pursued a career as a singer, but of course that was not to be.

"What do you think of our English customs, Miss Gottschalk?" Emmeline asked after a silence of some few minutes. She was beginning to regret her friendly impulse toward the young woman, who had initiated no topic on her own.

"I find much peculiar about your country, in particular your people's unwillingness to speak of certain things in what you call polite society." She turned her icy gaze upon Emmeline. "Although with you, I see a hint of rebellion." She smiled faintly and tilted her head to one side. "I like it. I don't understand why it is *verboten* to speak of what is truly on everyone's minds."

"Which is?"

"The murdered man. And what that scandalous writer, the Rogue, said about him. And what the woman, that … what do they call her? *Avengeress*; what a ridiculous name that is. Anyway, what that woman did and may have done."

"What do you mean, *may have done*?"

"She may have killed him, yes?" Miss Gottschalk examined Emmeline's face, frowning. "Why do people say this cannot be? Better he should die like a pig than impose his foul self on children. Most women would feel so."

"I find your honesty refreshing."

"And that is another thing; why does politesse demand I lie? I have learned to keep my tongue silent, but only because William becomes ... how do you say ... *incensed*, if I do not."

"In the spirit of such honesty, I *must* ask; why are you marrying Mr. Wilkins?" Emmeline said. "Pardon me if you love him, but you are so much better than he, in every single way."

Miss Gottschalk smiled for the first time and nodded, accepting the point. "I agree. If I cannot give him a disgust of me and make him ... what is the phrase? *Cry off*, that is it. If he does not cry off very soon now, I must refuse to marry him."

"He won't cry off. Pardon me again for asking, but ... are you wealthy?"

Miss Gottschalk nodded. "My family is; not me, of course."

"But your marriage settlement will be generous?"

"Yes. Do you mean he will not cry off because of that?"

"He seems motivated by money, and given his lack of personal charms, I think you are a better wife than he ever thought he would attract. Pardon my bluntness, but your father sold you too cheaply. With your beauty, wealth, and talent, you could have married a title."

"My father has many daughters. I am his least ... *acquiescent* daughter. *And* his least favorite. He feels fortunate someone will take me, given my charmlessness."

Emmeline was astonished at the man's lack of insight into his daughter's worth. "Trust me on this, Miss Gottschalk; I feel sure that Mr. Wilkins will not cry off. There is the money, and there is society—men who break engagements are ostracized—and there is your great beauty."

She smiled and nodded. No one so beautiful could fail to be aware of it. "My father undervalues beauty because it does not matter to him. My mother is a plain woman, though very good and kind, and he loves her. As I had not found a husband in Germany, Papa came here and brought us, his girls, hoping to find good husbands, leaving my mother home in Germany with the younger children. William met Papa through another brewer, and my father invited him to dinner." Anger darkened her blue eyes. "He offered for my sister first." She met Emmeline's eyes. "Not the next oldest, you understand, who is twenty, nor the next oldest to her, who is seventeen, but my fourteen-year-old sister."

Emmeline felt a shiver down her back, and a stillness in her soul. "What brewer was that, who made the introduction?"

"Sir Henry Claybourne, the one murdered." Her gaze was steady and solemn.

Ah, of course! Mr. Wilkins had spoken of knowing Sir Henry the night of her uncle's dinner party. Emmeline watched the elegant young men buzzing around the drapery department, helping the ladies. They were gradually serving everyone, helping them choose fabric and then ushering them back beyond the curtains for a consultation with their dressmakers. She had a dreadful thought and took a deep breath, then looked squarely at the young German woman. "Miss Gottschalk, is there something that disturbs you about Mr. Wilkins? Some other reason you say you will not marry him if it comes down to it, besides not caring for him?"

"When he visits, he makes sure that my sister Bertha—the one who is fourteen—is with us. He compliments her. She giggles and blushes and is quite taken with his favor, as she has never been so noticed. He would *still* prefer her to me." She gazed steadily at Emmeline. "I did not know him well enough when I agreed to the marriage.

274

If I marry him, how would I ever be able to have Bertha visit my home, stay overnight, if I was always worried about what my husband might do?"

"You're right," Emmeline murmured. Her heart thudding sickly; she remembered Mr. Wilkins leaning heavily on his walking stick and his halting walk, just like one of the two men Sir Henry had spoken to before his murder. So many small coincidences, too many to all be random: Mr. Wilkins knew Sir Henry Claybourne; they belonged to the same club; Wilkins walked with a limp and used a cane; he had an attraction to very young girls.

And she remembered something else; the silver cap she had found in the courtyard, the one she'd thought was a thimble. Had it come off the bottom of his walking stick, the one with the rough end and silver band but no cap? She shivered, bile rising up in her throat. Sir Jacob would be horrified if he suspected his man of business was involved in the scheme to procure little girls from orphanages. But she had no proof yet that Wilkins was part of it. And given that he and the knight had clearly been friends of a sort, surely Wilkins could not have been one of the killers? But what else would a murderer do but praise his victim, perhaps even effusively, so as not to be thought guilty?

Emmeline met Miss Gottschalk's gaze as a salesman approached. She wanted to be clear. "Are you suggesting…?" She didn't need to finish the question.

"It is more that I *fear* it," the young woman said, her eyes welling. "God protect me, I don't know what to do. My father would never believe me. He would say I am imagining things. He would say I read too many novels."

Another suspicion arose for Emmeline: could such a man as Wilkins use her uncle's connections and standing in society to shield him, perhaps even taking advantage of his position as Sir Jacob's business manager to further his own ends? It was unthinkable, and yet she had thought it, and now that thought would not go away.

She rose quickly and signaled to Gillies that they were leaving. "I cannot stay; ordering cloth will have to wait until Monday."

"Where are you going?" Miss Gottschalk asked.

She could not tell the young woman all that she feared. "To make inquiries."

The clerk came to Miss Gottschalk, so Emmeline escaped without further explanation. But she knew the German woman was watching her leave, a confused Gillies trailing in her wake like a small skiff following a schooner.

"Where are we goin' miss?" Gillies asked, bobbing along behind her as they reached the pavement.

"To my uncle's."

TWENTY-FIVE

"CAN YOU FIND JOSEPHS?" Emmeline, distracted, afraid, and panicked, searched the street, her gaze sweeping up and down it.

"D'ye not remember, miss?" Gillies asked, shielding her mistress from a lad carrying a stack of linens on his shoulder. "You sent him on to visit Mr. Kauffman to lairn the latest, and to see if there is any response to your note. He's not due for another half hour or more."

"Of course ... of course." Emmeline took a deep breath, calming herself. "Leave him a message here to meet us at Sir Jacob's. We can walk. We're only a short ways from my uncle's house."

Gillies dashed back inside, then returned to Emmeline's side, where she paced on the walk. "Why are we going to your uncle's, miss?"

As they walked, quickly because of the cold, Emmeline told her maid what she had learned from Miss Gottschalk about Mr. Wilkins, and what she suspected. Gillies was shocked and troubled.

"My uncle will be devastated; I don't know how I can break it to him, what I suspect of Wilkins."

Sir Jacob's home in St. James, part of a long row of newer townhomes, was approached through a black wrought iron gate. Constructed of white stone with an entrance that jutted toward the street and a shiny black painted door, Emmeline surged up the two shallow steps and grasped the lion's head door knocker, letting it fall with a loud crack like a rifle's report. It sounded as urgent as she felt.

Vernon, Sir Jacob's august butler, opened the door and looked down his hooked nose. He bowed and ushered her in with polished ease.

"Is my uncle here, Vernon?"

"Yes, Miss St. Germaine."

"I must see him immediately."

His face stiff with disapproval at such hasty behavior, he guided her to the drawing room, where she and Gillies sat in silence.

Sir Jacob, spectacles perched on his nose and a book in hand, hastened through the open double doors. "Emmie, what's wrong? The family? Fidelity?"

"No, we're all perfectly healthy, Uncle," she said, standing, fidgeting with her gloves and staring at him. She still had no idea what she was going to say.

He set his book aside on a polished round table by one window, removing his spectacles and setting them on the book. "It frightened me when Vernon would give me no answer other than that you were here and were insistent on seeing me immediately," he said, reproof in his tone.

"I'm sorry to alarm you, Uncle, but it is important."

"Come, sit!" he said, taking her elbow and guiding her to a chair by the fireplace. "Gillies, you may go to the kitchen and speak with Morag, if you like, or wait in the entrance."

"I would like her to stay here because she doesn't yet know all I will speak of," Emmeline said. "You may sit, Gillies."

Her uncle looked perturbed but said nothing. Gillies took a hard chair to the right of Emmeline's as Sir Jacob took the chair opposite his niece. "What is this all about, Emmeline?"

The pale light filtered in through sheer curtains and reflected off his balding pate. Emmeline stared at him, remembering all the times she had sobbed on his shoulder after her mother died, and the many occasions he had protected her from her father's wrath. She didn't know where to start, didn't know how to broach such a delicate subject. If he considered Wilkins a friend, this was going to hit him hard … *if* he even believed her, which increasingly seemed unlikely. She collected her thoughts, staring down at her gloved hands in her lap, fingering the long, loose ribbons of her bonnet. Her uncle cleared his throat and she looked up, meeting his gaze. "How long have you known Mr. Wilkins, Uncle?"

His bushy brows joined together over his bulbous, red-threaded nose. "What is going on? Has he said anything to you? Done anything?"

"Why do you ask that?"

He frowned and shook his head. She watched him for a long minute in silence, but he was not going to answer. Maybe he already had a notion of what she was going to say. "I'm … worried. I had a conversation with someone today; it alarmed me, and … and gave me cause to be concerned about Mr. Wilkins."

He looked puzzled. As supportive as he had always been, she well knew that he viewed her as prickly and oversensitive, imaginative, intelligent but flighty. Wilkins was a trusted financial advisor to him, and his word might hold more weight than her suspicions.

"I have to tell you something, and you may find it shocking."

Gillies moved uncertainly beside her.

"I have learned some things about the murder of Sir Henry Claybourne," Emmeline continued. "And what he was involved in that brought him to that end."

"Sir Henry Claybourne? That … that brewer fellow? Emmeline, you're not making a bit of sense. What have you to do with that man and his murder? How would you learn anything beyond what we all know from the newspapers?"

"Gillies, could you close the drawing room doors, please?"

Her maid did as she was asked and returned to her seat.

Emmeline took a deep breath and let it out, slowly. "I have been helping servant girls escape from situations where men have abused them. Mostly scullery maids."

Open-mouthed, he stared into the distance; then understanding dawned in his eyes and he met her gaze. "*You* are the mysterious lady who stole the scullery maid from Sir Henry Claybourne's home the night he was murdered?"

She could back away from it still, say she was part of a group but that it had been another anonymous lady who performed the deed. However … "Yes, it was me."

"But that woman … is she not guilty of …?" Warring emotions and confusion shadowed Sir Jacob's eyes and twisted his features. "But no, you would *never* do such a heinous act." He stood and paced to the window, stared out, then turned. His voice gruff and filled with anxiety, he said, "Emmie, I cannot believe you risked your reputation, your family, your very *life* in such a way! Are you mad? What will Leopold say when he discovers this?"

"He won't, Uncle," Emmeline said sharply. "Not unless someone tells him. I only told *you* because I trust you. Do you mean to break that trust?" He was silent. "*Do* you, Uncle?"

"Why do you tell me this?" he said, turning away from her.

She felt his disapproval; it radiated from him in waves, and though she disliked being the one to disappoint him, it was her life. She was trying to decide how to explain to him when he spoke again.

Still turned away, he said, "Why do you ask about Wilkins?"

"Because I believe he is deeply involved in these matters, and I think he is cheating you."

He whirled. "*What?*"

"There is something about Mr. Wilkins, beyond his repellent personal traits, his eagerness to exploit the poor, his lack of care for anyone beyond himself and his wealth, that I have distrusted. Even more so now. I have learned today that he has ..." She struggled with how to say it. "He has a disgusting predilection for young girls ... *very* young."

Sir Jacob turned away again, shoulders slumped. "How do you know this?"

"That is not my story to tell, but I trust my informant." Emmeline rose and stalked over to him, standing between him and the window, willing him to meet her gaze. She would not be ignored or disregarded. "Uncle, beyond the murder, which possibly he may be involved in, I have a grave suspicion that Mr. Wilkins is using your business as a cloak for another more sordid affair. I have *proof* that there has been a business made of obtaining little girls from at least one orphanage and putting them as scullery maids in the houses of men who want to abuse them." Heat flared in her cheeks and her hands curled in fists at her side. "*Sexually*, to be completely blunt, if I have not made myself clear."

He grabbed the back of a chair for support, then put one large hand over his face and bent over at the waist, puffing as if he could not get his breath. She was alarmed; was he having an apoplectic fit? Her mother, Sir Jacob's sister, had died of the same weakness.

"Uncle? Should I send for Vernon?"

"Ring for some sherry, my dear. It is ... if I can believe you, this is a terrible, terrible shock. A betrayal of the deepest kind."

"Gillies, go find Vernon and have him bring brandy, not sherry. Uncle needs a strong restorative."

Her maid stood, staring at her, wringing her hands over and over.

"Gillies, what's wrong?"

The maid looked at her, then at Sir Jacob, and then back at her.

"Go! Fetch Mr. Vernon. *Now!*"

———

Gillies did as she was told, finding the butler and sending him to the drawing room with both brandy for the master and sherry for Miss St. Germaine. But she was not going back to join them. She had a dreadful hunch that she prayed to the Almighty was not true. She headed to the kitchen to see Morag. And to see little Polly, with the golden silky hair and increasingly sad eyes.

———

His color improved once he had a sip of the drink. Sir Jacob sat in his favorite chair near the huge marble fireplace with the half glass of brandy balanced on his knee. Emmeline had told him as much as she dared without naming herself as also being the Rogue, who had exposed Sir Henry Claybourne in the first place and who had access to much more information than she, Miss Emmeline St. Germaine, possibly could. Because of what she *couldn't* say, her case against Mr. Wilkins was weak. Now they sat silently.

Finally, Sir Jacob said, "You were always too clever for your own good, Emmeline. Even as a little girl." A maid had lit the fire and it crackled with flame at first, beginning now to die down to glowing embers, warming them.

"If I were so clever, I would not have been taken advantage of when I was fifteen." It was a part of the family history that her uncle knew, how her tutor had seduced her with the intent of forcing money from the family.

"You should not be embarrassed of that, my dear. It is one of the great ills of our society that it looks down upon a girl for having sexual experience."

Sexual experience? She looked up at him sharply. "It was not simply *sexual experience*. I did not know what I was getting into. How could I? Uncle, don't you think Rudy took advantage of me?" She had always thought his support of her had been borne of a desire not to see her shamed for her part in the affair. Rudolph Maes had been twenty-nine and she barely fifteen. He had convinced her against her conscience, taken her away from her family despite her doubts—*a lonely room in an inn, his body pressed on hers, a belated but emphatic and frightened "no" from her, brief pain and a little blood ... then nothing but a cold night alone, weeping, while he went downstairs to get drunk*—and then sold her out for five hundred pounds from her father and passage back to Bruges. And she was left to bear all the disgrace of being the daughter who had risked the family's honor out of a fatal moral weakness.

"Of course he took advantage of you. Your father should have had him clapped in irons."

"But ...?" She heard something, some hesitation in his tone.

"Oh, Emmie, you undoubtedly led him on," Sir Jacob said, setting aside his empty brandy glass and putting his hands over his paunch, weaving his fingers together. "What are men to do? You're all so *pretty* when young, with your pouting and flirtation and softness, and you behave with such enticing manners. Little girls know when they are flirting, the little coquettes! Men cannot be blamed if they become entranced and tempted against their conscience. We are weak in the face of your allure, you see, led to impropriety by pretty girls' charming seduction."

Bile rose in Emmeline's throat and she swallowed it back. "What are you saying, Uncle?"

He sighed. "I wonder, is your condemnation of Sir Henry, based on that wild writer's claims, a reaction to what you went through? You are *not* those girls, Emmie, those scullery maids you're so worried about."

"No, I was older, for one thing. Just fifteen, but still older than the ten or eleven they are. And I was not abused and discarded, or..." She shook her head, confused by her feelings, the sickening sensation that her uncle would never understand what it was like to be a girl so roughly introduced to sexual relations. Was he right? Was *she* to blame for what Rudolph had done to her?

"I didn't mean in your age, I meant in your gentility," he admonished. "Those girls are not as sensitive as girls of our class, and so don't feel things as deeply. They're grateful to have enough to eat and a warm place to sleep. Do not place yourself among their numbers, for you are *not* like them."

He meant to soothe her, but instead the very marrow in her bones chilled. A long habit of deferring to his judgment and respecting his opinions kept her from speaking. She tried to sort out what he meant. His smile was kind, if weary.

Gillies entered the room and curtseyed. "Beggin' your pardon, miss. May I speak to you?"

"Not right now, Gillies," she said, still watching her uncle.

"*Please*, miss."

Emmeline glanced her way. Gillies was white and quivering, her eyes starting from her head like a frog's bulging orbs.

"Gillies, mind your manners," Sir Jacob said gruffly. "Emmeline, you need to have a talk with her; she's become impertinent."

That stirred her into action. She stood. "Gillies is not impertinent. She is wise and kind, and if she needs to speak with me I can assume it is about something of importance."

"I worry that you are being taken advantage of by your servants," Sir Jacob said mildly, but there was tension in his tone, and his gaze had become shuttered, unreadable.

She followed her maid to the hall beyond the doors. Gillies wrung her hands together, her gaze darting about the cold echoing hall, looking to every corner and then to the doors not quite closed behind them. She crossed, closed the doors more tightly, and turned, her back against them, and yet still she didn't speak.

"Gillies, what *is* it?" Emmeline asked, becoming impatient. "I'm in the middle of … of a difficult conversation with my uncle."

"Are ye, nouw?" Her maid's breathing increased in rapidity and she swallowed hard, her voice rough and brogue thickening as she said, "Mayhap you should ask him what he's been up to wi' the wee scullery maid in this house, little Polly—real name Lindy—who was fetched by one fellow named Ratter from that orphanage to work in this house."

It was as if a hand pressed down on her chest, or a heavy weight lay on it, all the air pushed out. Heat flooded up until her cheeks burned. Emmeline staggered sideways, dizzy, buzzing in her ears, lights flashing about her. "No, *no!* Gillies, that cannot be true." Her voice sounded harsh and grating, odd in her own ears. She began shivering, her whole body shaking; a chill invaded her like a ghastly spirit.

Gillies grasped her by the arm and guided her to a chair by the wall, pressing her head down. "I shouldna said it so abruptly. You'll faint unless you take deep, slow breaths." She held a vial of sal volatile under Emmeline's nose.

Her head snapped back and she bumped it on the wall, but the dizziness was passing. She glared up at Gillies. "What are you talking about? How can you say ..." She stopped. This was Gillies: steady, stalwart, intelligent. "Explain."

Gillies related the basics: Sir Jacob did all the hiring of his serving staff, as Emmeline knew. The previous scullery maid had run away. Ratter, with his small dog, had brought Polly around and Sir Jacob had a look at her and hired her. She was pretty, blonde, soft white skin, pink cheeks, and just eleven, with a sunny temperament that had become darker as the days passed.

Emmeline tried to deny it, to fend off the suggestion that her uncle was one of *them*. But she kept coming back to her younger sister Maria—also blonde, with soft white skin, pink cheeks, and a charming laugh—squirming away from him in tears, her refusal to sleep in the nursery alone during his visits ... something Emmeline hadn't remembered until this moment.

She rose, staggered to a corner, and retched, her luncheon coming up and spilling out onto the marble floor. Gillies found a handkerchief and guided her back to sit down, mopping her brow and then giving her the cloth to wipe her mouth.

"He's one of them, isn't he?" Emmeline whispered hoarsely, her eyes prickly with tears, the buzzing ringing in her ears, her throat corroded by the bile.

"I'm sorry, miss, truly. But aye, he is."

Emmeline shook her head, the welling tears running down her cheeks and dripping onto her hands. "Don't be sorry for *me*. He never laid a hand on me, I suppose because I was a dark, fey, wild little thing. Save your pity for that poor child—Lindy, is it? She is, then, little Sar-

ah's friend who disappeared—and pity all of the others before her."
Emmeline took in a quivering breath. "And save some pity for poor
Maria, who I suspect was one of his victims. Let us put an end to this."

She rose, steadied herself, took a deep breath, and turned toward
the doors. In these last few minutes, standing in this drafty hall, the
light from outside breaking up the darkness in long pale bars, her
world—everything she had believed about her family, and maybe even
her own conviction that she could understand and see evil—had
changed. Pain thudded through her temples and the sour smell of her
own vomit soiled the air, but there was no ignoring this now. Whatever else she was, she was no coward.

"D'ye need me, miss?"

"No. Go." Emmeline wiped the tears from her cheeks. "If Josephs
has come, then take that poor child out to our carriage and I will join
you. But first . . . I have to do this alone."

"I'm worrit for you, miss."

Emmeline nodded and choked back a sob. "He was my favorite
uncle. I mourn the loss as if he had died. But there are things, looking
back . . . I'll tell you later."

Gillies put one hand on her arm and nodded, then was gone.

Her uncle had retrieved his book and was sitting at his ease, though
he didn't seem easy. He looked up and set his book aside. Something
in her eyes warned him as she crossed the room, and he rose from his
chair. "Emmeline, what did that pesky maid say that has upset you?"

"She's taking little Polly away . . . Lindy, rather, for that is her real
name. She's rescuing her. From *you*."

He stood, staring down at her. "I don't understand."

"I think you do," Emmeline said, her gaze not wavering. Every detail, from the red capillaries threading his cheeks to his bulbous nose
reddened by the brandy, to his blue eyes, watery and with a curious .

coldness in them, imprinted on her memory. The uncle she adored fled from her vision to be replaced by this monster before her. "I think you understand all too well, as do I. Now I know why you wanted no woman of authority—no wife, no housekeeper, not even a mistress—in your home." Her voice was trembling; she cleared her throat to steady it. "No female of any authority to see what you were up to and interfere in your disgusting habits. No one to protect those little girls."

Sir Jacob narrowed his eyes and assumed an air of outraged virtue. "Emmeline, you have a *filthy* imagination! If you're saying what I think you're saying, then I am appalled! Your mother would be ashamed."

"You're wrong. My mother would want me to stand up for those children."

He swallowed, his chins wobbling. "I have never done a single thing to hurt a child. How can you even think it? Emmeline, you know me better than that."

He said all the right words, had all the right expressions, appeared every bit as hurt and outraged as he should. Doubt rose in her mind, but it could not gain a foothold. His protestations were a hollow sham. Now that she had accepted the awful truth, she could see the past through a clear glass, not with the twisted vision of familial love. "What did you do to Maria, Uncle?" Once again her hands balled into fists at her side, gloves the only thing that kept her fingernails from digging into her palms. "Do I need to be more clear?" She softened her tone and stared. "*Dear* Uncle Jacob, why was my little sister, Maria, *afraid* of you?"

He shook his head, disappointment in her the mask he chose to don that moment. "She was *not* afraid of me. I won't put up with being vilified. I have done nothing of which to be ashamed."

"You're *lying*." In one flash of insight that rocked her on her feet, Emmeline understood something suddenly. She put out her hand, clutching the back of a chair to steady herself. "I see it now," she said, her voice cracking with emotion. "The Maidenhead Canal Company … Woodforde assumed it was called that because of the town of Maidenhead, but … it's something else, isn't it? A little *jest* among you and your fellow company holders! *That's* why you were reluctant to let Woodforde invest, why you want to pay him off to divest, why you have dug no canal: it has *nothing* to do with canal building!" She covered her mouth with her gloved hand, her stomach threatening to eject its contents again though there was nothing left but bile. "It's a joke about virginity," she whispered. "Breaking through, making a channel. A maidenhead canal!" She whirled, ready to walk away.

"I *never* took the virginity of those girls!" he blurted.

It was the first time the ring of truth was in his voice and she doubted herself, but then she saw the evasion in the words. She turned and watched him, noting the trembling lip, the starting eyes, the alarm on his face. And the lie. "But you did *other* things. Maria would not sit on your lap," she said, her voice trembling. "Nor would she stay alone in her room when you visited. You did *other* things, didn't you? You preyed upon her because she was sweet and blonde and pretty, and because she loved you with all her heart when she was a babe."

"I *adored* Maria. I would never have hurt her!"

"I think you believe that," Emmeline said, sadness welling up in her heart for the little sister she never understood fully.

"She *was* the pretty one," he continued. "The *sweet* one. Not like you, all vinegar and willfulness. I did nothing to hurt her; I loved her *tenderly*. We had a special bond, she and I. It broke my heart when she died."

"I think you *wish* to believe that you never hurt her. I imagine you tell yourself that often, but that's a damnable *lie*. You betrayed our family, but Maria most of all." Emmeline thought she and Maria had shared everything, but there was a secret her sister had been ashamed of, and it had destroyed her.

"You never have understood men," Sir Jacob said, his tone wheedling. "We have needs. I *never* hurt those girls. And I treat them well, trinkets and sweetmeats and—"

"Stop! That is *exactly* what Sir Henry Claybourne said to me as I held a knife to him while I rescued little Molly!" she spat out at him. She wanted to leave; she had much to think of, to ponder, and forgiveness to seek from Maria's spirit if it should be possible. But this was about more even than the children her uncle and his friends had harmed, and would continue to harm unless she stopped it. She *must* stop it, and would somehow, but there was also murder to consider.

A mantel clock tocked and chimed the hour. Time was hastening on and she must find the truth. She stalked toward her uncle and examined his face, which had become gray, the color ebbed from it. He looked ill. She stood staring down at him. "It must shock you that I am the infamous Avengeress. Poetic justice, in a way, don't you think? I know much, you see, but not all. I know about notes Sir Henry sent around the night he was killed. Was one of them to your procurer? Was it he who killed Sir Henry after the brewer threatened you all with disclosure? He thought someone had talked, didn't he? He thought that someone had spilled what you all were doing, that my visit was the result, and he was frightened and angry. So he sent a message to St. James. To *you*. Sir Henry became a danger to your scheme." She paused and glared down at him. "Who killed Sir Henry Claybourne?"

"I don't know," Sir Jacob confessed.

She thought he was telling the truth, but she no longer trusted all her instincts about him. She headed for the door.

"Where are you going?"

"I have much to do, and people to see."

"You're being irrational. This is just…those girls are *servants!*"

She stopped at the door and looked back. "They *matter*. Every *single one* of those children matters to someone, or should, as much as Maria mattered to me. This ends *now*, and every girl your despicable group is abusing, including the ones in that orphanage run by your male bawd, Dunstable, will be rescued and placed somewhere safe. I will see to it myself, and your fellows one and all will be charged for your crimes."

Josephs was on the street by the door, ready, with Gillies and a frightened Polly—Lindy—in the carriage. Morag, the cook, was horrified by what the child, in a halting manner, had admitted to her and Gillies. Emmeline was resolved to stop the trade in children and expose the ring of men procuring children like bottles of wine to be savored.

She wished she could take Lindy home, but with Birk snooping, that was impossible. Whatever would follow this cataclysmic shift she could not foresee, but for now she needed her household stable. They took Lindy to stay with Lady Sherringdon, who would know what to do. Emmeline's friend was not home but Tillie was, and she promised to care for the frightened child.

"Dr. Woodforde will be at St. Barts today," Emmeline said to Josephs as he was handing her back up into the carriage outside of Lady Sherringdon's home. "Take me there; I must speak with him."

"What if he's one of 'em, miss?" Gillies asked when Emmeline climbed back into the carriage and Josephs closed the door.

"I'd wager my life that he is not. He has a list of men who are, and I am going to use it to expose them all."

"A list?"

"The investors in the Maidenhead Canal Company."

TWENTY-SIX

REPUTED TO BE THE oldest hospital in England, St. Barts was a teaching facility, and Woodforde, once a student, devoted free time to the students and patients of the hospital. Though in the middle of a research project with his respected former teacher, Dr. Abernethy, Woodforde came out with Josephs to the courtyard, climbed into the carriage, and listened to Emmeline's request. She kept it brief, telling him only that the canal company was possibly a cover for an illegal scheme.

He searched her eyes. "Does this have anything to do with our recent conversations?"

"It's possible." She didn't mention her uncle.

He nodded. "I trust your judgment, Emmie. I can't leave my work currently, but if Josephs will come back into the hospital with me, I'll give him a note to take to my valet. The list of investors is in my desk; Julian knows where. I would like to know the rest of this tale," he said, looking at his pocket watch. "If Doctor Abernethy did not need me now I'd go with you. May I visit this evening?"

"Of course, Woodforde." She steeled herself for telling him the worst. How he would respond to her revelations, she could not imagine.

They retrieved the list of investors at his home and returned to Chelsea. Birk, already wearing black armbands to show his respect for the sorrow of the royal family, greeted her at the door. Rattled by her day and all she had discovered, Emmeline still had to maintain a reasonable appearance in front of her butler. She told him that there were no parcels because they hadn't bought any fabric; the drapers' shop had been too busy and she didn't wish to wait beyond the time she had already spent there.

A moment to breathe; that's all she wanted. As Birk bowed and disappeared, she pulled off her gloves, noting the shadows in the hall that warped the wallpaper design. Hanging at eye level were the Hoppner painting of Emily, Leopold's first wife, with their daughters, a gift from Emily's father, and the painting of Emmeline and Maria when they were children, painted by Thomas Lawrence. There was another of her brothers by the same artist, but it was displayed at Malincourt, of course. She touched the silver card tray, which sat on the new Sheraton hall table, a recent purchase. The hall smelled of furniture wax and orange peel from a pomander Mrs. Riddle liked to make. Everything was exactly as she had left it.

And yet it was different, somehow.

Or maybe *she* was different. When she'd departed, she had simply intended to purchase fabric for herself and Fidelity, but now her world, her family, all her memories were altered.

Birk reappeared. "Pardon me, miss, but there are some letters. Would you like to have them in the drawing room, or ...?"

"Upstairs. My room. Gillies, will you take the mail, please?" Gillies had carried in with her a package Simeon had given Josephs for Emmeline. She'd have to look at it and see what he and his journalist had discovered. "Tea, Birk. And perhaps have Cook send up something to eat. I'm famished." She was going upstairs that moment to speak with Fidelity—she was dreading the conversation, but it must be done—and she hoped tea would soften the blow. How silly and futile that was, she already knew. Nothing could prepare her dear companion for the revelation that her old friend and beloved cousin was an abuser of children.

Fidelity was napping, which delayed the hour of revelation. Emmeline retreated to her own room, and while Gillies put away her outdoor things and tidied, she sat at her dressing table, opening and reading the mail. There was a letter from her brother Samuel, who was looking forward to marriage sometime in the future. He had the young lady picked out and she was agreeable; they had walked out a few times, and he had been received into her home most kindly. But his happiness must wait until he attained another living and could afford a better home. He was full of plans: small adjustments to his house, a leak in the roof mended, repairs to his barn, and news about his parishioners, but he wrote little about Leopold and his family, even though he lived in the vicarage on the Malincourt estate.

Lady Sherringdon had written to her as well. Emmeline had expected this letter after talking to Tillie when dropping Lindy off at the Sherringdon home, and she was curious as to the contents. Adelaide reported that she had rescued another little girl who was being abused, but she didn't believe it was connected to the others. Emmeline remembered additional information the maid had told her of, that by way of the chain of household servants she'd learned that Sally, who had run away from Martha Adair's home, was seen working as a sewing apprentice at an exclusive dressmaking shop.

Lady Sherringdon's letter contained this information, too, and more. The rumors were true; this was the apprenticeship Sally had left Martha's to attain. But how had Sally made the connections necessary? It was unthinkable that such a place should take in a begging girl who had no character reference to recommend her. She must have been vouched for, but by whom?

"Gillies, listen to this," Emmeline said, and read part of the letter from Lady Sherringdon: *"It is an exclusive shop, frequented mostly by the wealthy wives of tradesmen."* She frowned down at the sheet. "Martha told us she learned about Sally's predicament in the Claybourne home from her housekeeper's sister's daughter's—or her daughter's sister's—employer, if memory serves. So, to untangle it, the employer of her housekeeper's niece, most likely, since the other doesn't make sense. I don't believe her housekeeper has a daughter, and even if she did, her housekeeper's daughter's sister would be the housekeeper's daughter too." She sighed and closed her eyes for a moment, clearing the detritus from her mind. "Can we find out who that is, do you think?"

"I should think so, miss."

"Why did I not follow up on this before? I gave up on it without a thought, but I should have asked you. I'm going to send Martha a note."

"Why does it matter?"

"I'm not sure it does, but I'm uneasy about it all. I feel like there is something I'm missing. The murder is likely a simple matter; the two men who argued with Sir Henry killed him, or Ratter did and was in turn murdered for what he knew. But what if I am leaping to conclusions? I've been known to do that."

"Aye, miss, a time or two."

"If I send you on a task, to go back out to select black or gray fabric for a mourning gown and all the notions to go along with it, can you track down, perhaps, who recommended Sally to her position? We have the name of the dressmaker," Emmeline said, waving her friend's letter.

Gillies nodded. "I'll do my best, miss."

"Have Josephs take you. Tell Birk I have a headache and am sending you in my stead, in hope the drapers' will be less busy. Tell him I wish at least one new mourning gown started immediately. That will give you the reason to visit the dressmaker's."

"Aye, miss," Gillies said, wiping a smear of powder from the edge of the dressing table. She paused, looking down at Emmeline. "I'm sorry miss, about your uncle."

"I feel … bereft," Emmeline admitted, folding Adelaide's letter. "Is it horrible that I almost wish he had died rather than to have learned this about him?"

"'Tis another death in a way, miss. It's the death of what you believed about your family."

"And it's the death of any peace I had about my sister's life. I thought I knew her, all her sorrows and troubles, but she hid her pain from me and I never guessed."

"She hid the truth out of love for you."

"That makes it *so* much worse. I would give anything to go back and learn it from her. Now I'll never know the whole truth because Uncle Jacob …" She shook her head, unable to speak as sobs welled up, clogging her throat. She put her face in her hands and let it all go; Gillies put one arm around her shoulders as she wept.

Throat raw, tears spent, eyes red, Emmeline finally calmed. It would come again, she knew, as raw and awful as the moment Maria died from what was called a "wasting" disease. She could not eat and was wracked by pain, passing away in the Coleman Institute as a pale wraith, so thin her body barely made an impression in her bed. It was a horrible memory.

Gillies brought her tea and food, scones with preserves, then departed; Emmeline could hear voices downstairs and the closing of the front door behind her maid. There was much more to do and to ponder, and none of it was served by dissolving in tears. She opened the package from her publisher, that he had given Josephs. Simeon wrote that he had received many notes from the public about the murder, and there were clues to follow up if she was able. She shook her head, not sure she was. He then said that he had had a man watching the Claybourne house closely who had noted some interesting visitors, among them Miss Aloisia Hargreaves.

Why would she be visiting Lady Claybourne once again? With all that had happened, Emmeline had put aside finding out more about Miss Hargreaves, but that was about to change.

Also, Simeon had received the name and address of a woman who had worked for the Claybournes but was now living in retirement in the home of her daughter and son-in-law (the young woman had married well, a barrister) in Cheapside. He suggested she visit the woman, who wrote claiming to have information on the knight's household that would surprise. Simeon suspected the former employee would need a bribe to part with information, and he promised to reimburse Emmeline. He planned to publish in the paper anything startling she could glean.

That would be a task for the next morning, Emmeline decided, along with a visit to Miss Hargreaves.

She wrote a couple of Rogue columns and the note to Martha, as well as a letter to Samuel and one to her eldest niece, Amelia, who would be coming to London for the Season next spring. As the youngest princess's namesake and a sensitive girl, Amelia would be saddened by the princess's death. Knowing Leopold, he would not heed any lowering of spirits in his eldest daughter. Rose, his wife, was with child again, and Amelia could likely use a kind word or two.

Even as she wrote, Emmeline was aware that she was avoiding thinking about her uncle. She wanted to rage, to unleash her fury. But she had been too well trained, perhaps, in the art of submerging her feelings and appearing calm in the face of devastation. It had not escaped her that slipping out as the Avengeress was, for her, an outlet of her wildest impulses, a dangerous but heady game that could, if she were discovered, destroy her reputation and send her into exile. It was in effect a way of controlling those wild impulses, channeling them into what she considered appropriate actions.

And now her uncle, the very one whose furtive habits she was about to expose, held her secret identity in the palm of his hand. She had trusted him when she told him, not yet knowing what he was. Exposing him could destroy them both, or … she could hide the truth about him, keeping both herself *and* him safe. She felt no urge to save him, even if it should end in her own ruin.

"Emmie?" Fidelity called, tapping on her door. "Are you awake?"

Emmeline set aside her pen, corking the ink bottle and sanding the letter to Amelia. She now had to face something she dreaded. She loved her uncle and was devastated by his feet of clay. How was her companion, who had loved him since her own childhood and depended on his kindness and friendship, going to take his disgrace? "Come in!"

Fidelity entered and crossed the room swiftly. "My dearest Emmeline, I hear you are feeling under the weather! I sympathize; I have been chilled all day. There is a storm coming." She wrapped her soft woolen shawl tightly around her shoulders and crossed to the window, staring out over the smokestacks of the townhomes of Chelsea. "It's so gloomy. Winter approaches. How I *wish* I were somewhere warm!"

"Fiddy, dearest, please sit. We need to talk." This was not going to be easy. Emmeline ordered more tea.

It was every bit as hard as she had imagined, and worse. Emmeline laid out every instance, even about the Maidenhead Canal Company, Sir Jacob's involvement in it, and her suspicions of his abuse of Maria. Fidelity simply didn't believe her. Against every argument, every example, even her insistence that Sir Jacob had as good as confessed his behavior, Fidelity saw it as a misunderstanding that would be cleared up on the morrow. She retreated to her bedroom.

———

Though Woodforde had been planning to visit that evening so Emmeline could tell him about the canal company, he was called away to a patient. He sent a note, asking her to let him know when it was convenient for her to see him. She wasn't sure and didn't respond immediately, grateful she didn't have to talk about it after all.

Gillies returned with fabric and information. Sally was, indeed, apprenticed at the dressmaker's. "And who is one of their most valuable customers?" the maid asked.

Emmeline waited.

"None other than Lady Claybourne herself."

It had been an odd progression of events that led Emmeline to Sir Henry's to rescue Molly. That Martha had confused the description of the person who had told her about the abuse in the Claybourne home wasn't surprising, given that Martha was prone to confusion, but whether she had been merely confused, forgotten things, or been manipulated was unclear to Emmeline. Martha did lack the ability to think clearly at times.

Perhaps it was a minor tangle, but Emmeline wanted a clear understanding of how it had all gone so wrong, so she pieced it together, writing it down as she had begun to understand it through various channels: Martha's housekeeper, Mrs. Dunleavy, had a niece, Biddy, who was in service at the Farnsworth residence at number 74 Blithestone, next door to the Claybournes. Biddy was good friends with Sybil, the Claybourne maid; the two young women seemed, from her own observation, to be close friends and confidantes, as was natural.

And ... Biddy also visited the Adair household on occasion to see her aunt. Martha had mentioned that her husband was upset with their maid for gossiping with Biddy one day when the girl was visiting. That would be Ellen; Emmeline remembered her as a red-haired, fresh-cheeked, pleasant girl. So it was likely Ellen, *not* Mrs. Dunleavy, who could have overheard Mrs. Adair talking about "rescuing scullery maids" and passed the gossip to Biddy, who then talked to Sybil in the Claybourne home. Back and forth flowed information and gossip, and so had come word that poor little Sally, scullery maid to the Claybournes, needed rescuing.

Martha, happening to need a scullery maid right then and inspired by her work with the Crones, thought she'd do a little rescuing of her own. And so she got word to Sally by way of Sybil that she could come work at the Adair home. Sally had agreed and snuck out of the Claybourne home, making her way to Martha's. Rather intrepid, given the poor girl's history, but that appeared to be how it occurred. From that time to this, though, Sally had not repaid Martha's charity with steady work. Given her past abuse and that she had been with child when she'd arrived, who could blame the girl?

But what if Martha's *true* source of the information about Sally's predicament was Lady Claybourne? Emmeline had used the chain of gossip herself on occasion, and though it was unreliable, it never, ever stopped. It was, at the very least, clear who had now helped Sally attain a valuable apprenticeship. Perhaps a guilty conscience prompted Lady Claybourne to help the child. Otherwise, why do such a thing?

Unless … Emmeline paused and stared with unseeing eyes out the window. Had the Crones been manipulated from the very start?

————

Emmeline did not attend church with Fiddy the next morning. Arbor, their new upstairs maid, a compassionate and intelligent girl, accompanied her. When they returned, Emmeline went to her room. Fidelity sat on her bed, a lost look in her eyes, her face drawn and gray with anguish.

"Are you going to be all right?"

"Children lie, Emmie. I won't believe it. I *can't* believe it. Not Jacob."

"I know how difficult this has been for you to accept, but it's true; your cousin, as much as you love him, has spent his life abusing girls, my beloved Maria among them. If you had seen his expression, you'd know I'm right. Please don't visit him, though. Give me time and I'll gather all the proof you need."

Her companion didn't answer. Emmeline hugged her, then clutched her shoulders and said, "Wait until I find out more before you judge *me* for what I told you."

Fidelity, tears welling in her eyes, searched Emmeline's face. "You don't think he had anything to do with Sir Henry Claybourne's death, do you?"

"Claybourne is on that list of Maidenhead investors. I don't know. Lord Quisenberry, Fulmer, Wilkins ... they're *all* on the list. The description of the two men who were arguing with Sir Henry that night sounds like Wilkins, and ..." She trailed off. The Frenchmen then would likely be her uncle's valet, Pierre LaLoux. The description also fit the two men, out of place in the dirty warren of St. Giles, who were implicated in Ratter's murder. Wilkins would most definitely have known the area, since by his own admission he owned buildings in that den of iniquity.

She jumped up. "Rest, my dearest. Read a book. I need Gillies with me, but Arbor will bring you tea and look after you. Don't do anything until I return."

———

Cheapside again; squeezed in between a coal merchant's office and a larger home was the townhome of the former Claybourne employee's daughter and estimable son-in-law. A young maid-of-all-work answered the door and led Emmeline and Gillies through a dark, narrow passage to a small sitting room that looked out over the busy street.

Mrs. Winwright was a tiny, wizened apple dumpling of a woman, settled in a deep chair near the fire, placed so she could see the street through the bow window. The maid brought a tea tray and then was sent away with a "shoo, girl!".

Emmeline wanted whatever information the woman had. What remained to be seen was the worth of it and the price. But Mrs. Winwright was in no hurry and insisted on telling them her story. She had worked for Sir Henry's family first as a housemaid and then as cook, and had known him since he was born.

"'E were pretty when 'e was young, wiv blonde curls over 'is for'ead. But 'e 'ad an evil eye an' started young. Joost ten 'e was when 'e started pinchin' bums. Ev'ry chance 'e'd get, 'e'd corner a maid."

It was a pattern, it appeared, from what Miss Honeychurch had also revealed. "Didn't his parents teach him not to abuse the servants?"

"The master weren't gonna interfere when 'e was busy havin' it off wiv any maid as would let 'im."

"Like father like son," Emmeline said.

"When 'e got ta be sixteen—"

"Wasn't he sent to school by that age?"

"'E were *delicate*, 'is mama said, and the master didn't care. Anyways, when 'e were sixteen or so 'e cornered a little scullery maid and 'ad 'is way wiv her. More 'n once, I think, lookin' back. She were a dark little thing; not pretty but smart enough. She started to show, an'—"

"She became pregnant?"

"Aye."

"Didn't you tell the mistress?"

The woman gave her a withering glance, full of contempt. "'Ow d'ye think that little chat woulda gone? 'Ey, mistress, yer son's bin tupping the scullery maid against 'er will.' What good would itta done 'er fer *me* to be let go?" She blinked back some water in her eyes and her tone shifted to remorse. "I woulda helped if I could, but I was in the family way meself, an' lucky t'marry the groom an' keep me post."

Emmeline was chastened, and silent.

"Anyway, 'Enry kept at 'er and got caught by the mistress finally in the act; she saw the state the girl was in—poor child looked like she was carryin' a puddin' basin under 'er pinafore—and turned 'er away. Girl was an orphan. No place to go, no character, nothing."

"What happened to her?"

"What d'ye think 'appened?"

"Did she die?" Emmeline asked, fearful.

"Nup, but the babe did, I 'eard. Was born in a spongin' 'ouse an' died after takin' a first breath. Girl was sent away as soon as she could walk, an' did what girls like that hafta do."

"Turned to prostitution." Emmeline sighed. "But what does this have to do with the news you wish to share?"

The woman eyed her, squinting. "It's worth yer 'earin' about, lemme tell ya. Worth a pretty penny, too."

Emmeline gazed at her steadily. "You wrote to the paper that you worked in Sir Henry's current household?"

"Became cook there after Sir 'Enry's mother died. Worked fer Sir 'Enry and Lady Claybourne up till two years ago."

"And he was still up to his old tricks with the scullery maids."

"Didn't know at first; 'e's gotten a mite carefuller."

"Does *any* of this have to do with Sir Henry's death?"

"Might do," she said. "But I'll see the color o' yer money first, miss."

The negotiation was quick. They settled on a price and Emmeline paid, counting out the coins. "So, tell me."

"I was cook when th'last 'ousekeeper left Sir Henry's employ an' Lady Claybourne interviewed for a new one. Didn't interview many; coom upon one she couldn't refuse. Turned out t'be someone 'oo knew Sir 'Enry pretty well. It's 'oo that little scullery maid from th'past becoom that's important, y'see. Took a new name when she went back into service."

"What is her name now?"

"Sir 'Enry never knew 'oo she was, but I reconnized 'er. Same look in them dark eyes. Mrs. Young, she calls 'erself nouw. Lady Claybourne 'ired her as 'ousekeeper."

TWENTY-SEVEN

MRS. WINWRIGHT HAD MORE to say, including that she had told her ladyship what Sir Henry was up to with the little scullery maids, and that she didn't think it was a surprise to her employer.

Back in the carriage, Gillies asked, "Do you think Lady Claybourne knew who Mrs. Young was when she hired her?"

Numb with shock, Emmeline shook her head. "How would she?"

"Not unless the housekeeper wanted her to know, I s'pose."

Why, Emmeline wondered, had Mrs. Young come to work for Sir Henry Claybourne? It was soon after Mrs. Winwright told Lady Claybourne what Sir Henry was up to that Mrs. Young was hired and the cook given an annuity to retire; whether that was a reward for long service or a bribe to not spread the word of what her employer was doing, Emmeline did not know.

"I wonder if Sir Henry ever discovered who Mrs. Young was," she said. "The innocent explanation for it all is that Mrs. Young sought out the position so she could keep Sir Henry from abusing scullery maids."

"Do you believe the innocent explanation?"

Emmeline shook her head. "I don't know."

They followed a carriage to their Cheyne Walk townhome and pulled to the curb behind it. As Josephs gave Emmeline a hand down, from the carriage ahead stumbled a disheveled Fidelity, her hair sticking out all over, a bonnet askew on her head.

"Fiddy, where have you been?" Emmeline cried, picking up her skirts and chasing her companion up the walk.

Fidelity flung out one hand and hurried past Birk into the house, ripping her bonnet from her head and throwing it aside, drifting hairs still attached to pins, and headed up the stairs. Emmeline exchanged a look with Gillies, who distracted Birk by asking him to tip the carriage driver, who awaited payment.

She followed Fidelity to her room, closed the door behind her, and went to her companion, who had flung herself on the bed in a storm of weeping more typical for a young miss in the throes of a passion. She sat on the bed beside her and touched her shoulder. "Fiddy, what has happened?"

Her sobs were heartbreaking, but finally subsided. Fidelity sat up, deep grooves under her red-rimmed eyes, her thin skin drawn into wrinkles that lined her forehead and bracketed her mouth. "I went to see Jacob," she sobbed.

"I asked you not to do anything. I pleaded!"

"I had to know," she replied, her tone dead, her tears still streaming from her swollen eyes. "All these years," she whispered, her voice catching. "I thought I was the only one."

"What are you saying?" Dread growing into horror, Emmeline grabbed handfuls of bedclothes in her fists and twisted.

"I thought I was the only one," Fidelity repeated. "All these years, he said that it was because I was so *enticing* as a girl. That I *tempted* him with my pretty ways, and he had to show me how much he loved me." Her words were bitter, stinging drops of venom. "I was *adorable*, and though he could never marry me—I had very little dowry, after all—we could have those moments when he would show me how beautiful I was. That's how men did it, how they showed love, he said. It was special, a *secret* between us."

She swallowed, and her hand formed into a fist she pressed to her mouth, then dropped like a stone to her lap. "But to know what he did to Maria … I should have seen the signs and stopped it. I *failed* her. I failed that precious child, and how many since? When I grew up and realized what he did to me was wrong, I thought it was *me*, that I *made* him into who he is, but in truth he's … he's just *evil*."

"My poor darling," Emmeline cried as realization sank in. "You seemed to love him so!" How could she love the man who was abusing her?

"God help me, I did … I *do*." Fidelity shook her head. "Or … or do I? I don't know *what* I feel. All these years … I'm numb."

Emmeline pulled her into her arms and held her close for a long time as shuddering sobs wracked her. Gillies crept in, but Emmeline shook her head and sent her away. Finally, as shadows crept across the far wall, long and gray, Fidelity was spent. Emmeline helped her undress and climb under the soft, heavy covers of her bed, her heart aching with sorrow and anger. She didn't leave the room until she knew her cousin, friend, and companion was asleep.

Gillies was pacing outside the door. "I have news, miss, news you need to lairn straight away."

"Let's go to my room. I need tea, Gillies, and I want Arbor to sit with the Comtesse while she sleeps. She *must* not be left alone, do you understand? No matter where I am, she must have company. Now … go do as I say, then come back to me and tell me what you will. I have dreadful news too."

Gillies spoke to Mrs. Bramage, who told Arbor to sit with Fidelity for the afternoon and also ordered tea and luncheon for Miss St. Germaine. A half hour later, closeted with her maid, Emmeline drank her tea in one long draught and sat back, sighing. "You said you have news, Gillies; what is it?"

"While you were with the Comtesse, Josephs spoke to the other carriage driver. Th'magistrates were at Sir Jacob's house, miss; they questioned your uncle and took away his valet, Pierre LaLoux, on suspicion of murder. They're lookin' for Mr. Wilkins now. They think he has fled London."

"How did they discover the truth?"

"An anonymous letter, miss."

"I suspected them, but maybe one of the Claybourne servants knew something, or ..." Emmeline paused, her brow furrowing. There were other possible sources within the Claybourne household and among the investors. "If those two did kill Sir Henry, maybe one of them will confess."

Or her uncle could be implicated. Wilkins would not go down without a nasty fight, and he'd have no compunction in taking Sir Jacob down with him. Emmeline then told Gillies about Fidelity's secret. Her maid was as saddened and angered as Emmeline about her uncle's disgusting predation.

"I know a little of my cousin's youth. Fidelity was alone, orphaned at a young age, and stayed with my parents often. Uncle Jacob, my mother's favorite brother and Fidelity's cousin, also stayed at Malincourt often. The opportunity was there, and he took it." Anger seethed though her. "She adored him, and he abused her trust."

If she only did one thing in this whole affair, exposing the Maiden-head Canal Company for what it was must be her task. Emmeline took up her quill and wrote down every scrap of information, every bit she could recall, from her earliest suspicions to her certainty now: Sir Henry's abuse of scullery maids; Ratter's procurement of children from Dunstable's orphanage and others; the company formed to benefit financially from the sordid appetites of other like-minded men; and the probable murder of Ratter, as the man was about to tell all to the magistrate. She could not spare her uncle; his crimes were his own, and he must deal with the exposure of them as best he could.

Dusk was closing in when Gillies brought Emmeline a note that had come secretly to her by way of Josephs; Simeon was outside. Emmeline knew it must be urgent, because Simeon would never risk being seen near Cheyne Walk if it were not so.

"How do I get out to speak with him?" she fretted, pacing to a window. "It is both too early and too late to go out, if you know what I mean, and I can think of no excuse that will satisfy Birk's inquisitiveness."

Gillies understood, of course; it was too late for calls and too early for evening events. "Aye, but there is Evensong in an hour, miss. I could walk you there?"

Emmeline sighed in relief and hugged her maid. "Gillies, you are worth your weight in gold."

"I'll tell Josephs to take a message back to Mr. Kaufmann to meet us near the kirk."

"Poor Josephs; he never gets a moment's rest. Nor do you."

"Miss, he deems it a great privilege to sairve you, as do I. He'd lay down his life for you."

A half hour later, Emmeline, cloaked warmly, set out with Gillies, the whole long tale of what she knew and suspected rolled into a scroll and tied with a ribbon. Birk had appeared startled that they were going to Evensong, but Emmeline said she wished to pray for the royal family in their time of loss. She would swear that the butler, a monarchist to his very marrow, got a tear in his eye as he bowed his head.

The first-quarter moon was but a sliver in the sky and shed no light, so the walk was dark despite the occasional misty illumination from lampposts. Simeon awaited them near a tree almost at the gates of All Saints church. A cold November wind swept down the river. He pulled his surtout more closely about him with one hand, holding his top hat on with the other. "Mrs. Gillies, Miss St. Germaine, good to see you." He bowed.

"Simeon, quickly, please," Emmeline said, her voice taut with tension. "I feel as if my life is falling apart around me and have no time for niceties."

"There is always time for niceties, Miss St. Germaine. It is civility that separates us from the beasts of the field."

"Right this moment I think the beasts of the field more civilized than we are. I have written down everything I know about the scheme to sell little girls into what was virtually slavery, for the poor children had no choice and no hope of escape. You will see I have spared no one, not even one member of my own family. I trust you to choose what to publish." She thrust the scroll at him. "You have news. What is it?"

His dark eyes glinted as a linkboy's glowing lanthorn, carried on a long stick as the boy walked ahead of an elderly couple headed to All Saints, swung, illuminating the path. They didn't speak as the couple passed, nodding at Emmeline, who they knew by sight. She nodded back and smiled as Simeon turned away to regard the river.

"Hurry, Simeon," she muttered. "I must go to church, since I have said that is my destination, and Evensong begins shortly."

"Evensong...what a lovely word. Yes, I will hurry," he said, seeing her impatient expression. "I don't know how much you know about what has occurred today?"

"Josephs told me they have apprehended one man and are seeking another. Mr. Wilkins, my uncle's man of business."

"This comes perilously close to your uncle, Sir Jacob Pauling," he said.

She was silent but gave one sharp nod. It was all in her writing. "The identification was from an anonymous lady who saw Mr. Wilkins behind the Claybourne house the night of the murder, she says, and recognized him from a previous visit to the same household. She heard his name shouted by Sir Henry."

An anonymous tip from an anonymous lady...maybe she knew who that was. "I've heard, also, that my uncle's valet has been taken in to be questioned about the murder. How was *he* identified?"

"Perhaps as the only Frenchman associated with Wilkins. It is now widely known that an Englishman and a Frenchman were the pair arguing with Sir Henry behind his house. And the authorities now know about Ratter's murder, and his association with Sir Henry, as well."

Emmeline thought of Miss Gottschalk and her distress about Wilkins. The engagement would now be broken, and she would no longer fear for her sister Bertha. That was one piece of good news that would come from it; one young girl saved from predation. "Is that all, Mr. Kauffman?"

He gazed at her, sadness in his eyes. "You have learned much in the last while that has changed you forever."

She stiffened her backbone. "You will read it all in what I have written for you. It is not I who have suffered, it is others." Her brothers would be horrified. They would be forced to disown Sir Jacob; *she* would do so willingly. Her uncle had shown no remorse, nor even any understanding of the lives he had damaged. The fear that remained with her was that he would use against her the secret he now knew. If he did, it would be out of pure malice, for revealing it would gain him nothing. "Is that all?" she repeated.

"No, Miss St. Germaine, it's not all. I know the name of the anonymous informer, the one who identified Mr. Wilkins and Pierre LaLoux."

"Who is it?"

He confirmed her guess. "Miss Aloisia Hargreaves."

"Miss Hargreaves!" Emmeline exclaimed. "I was going to visit her this morning, but my day was … was upset."

"I fear for her life and for yours, given the powerful men who are a part of that devilish cabal whose trade is little girls. Be careful, please, and warn her if you can."

———

Evensong was lovely, and there was a special prayer for the royal family as they mourned the passing of Princess Amelia. The vicar made oblique reference, too, to the troubled mind of the king himself, and the burdens placed on the Prince of Wales. Emmeline had little respect for Prince George and no hope that he would prove to be a good king one day. The movement was already afoot to finally make him the regent, which would solve his financial problems for the moment, though the only lasting solution for that would be if he could manage to stop spending money like a drunken sailor on shore leave.

But Simeon's fears never left her mind; he was worried about Miss Hargreaves, and his worries became her worries. Should she, as he suggested, warn Aloisia that because she was an informant against the men who may have been behind Sir Henry's death, she, herself, could be in danger? It seemed ludicrous; her uncle, as bad as he was, could not be allied with killers.

Could he?

The next day, fog rolled in off the river and they were housebound. Looking out a window was like looking into a gray blanket. Fidelity was withdrawn and silent. Emmeline wrote letters. No word came all day concerning her uncle or the other men of the Maidenhead Canal Company. One moment, Emmeline was sure they must all be involved in the plot to procure young children to abuse at their leisure, but the next she was equally positive there could not be so many disgusting men in all of Britain, much less among her uncle's acquaintance.

She was at first certain of one thing: Sir Jacob, no matter his faults, could not be involved in the murder of Sir Henry Claybourne. Surely that *must* have been Wilkins's own wicked plan. Except ... if Pierre LaLoux was involved too, then he would not have gone along with Wilkins without his employer's consent or even urging. Was the knight's murder her uncle's command? Every time she thought she had come to the end of the horrors, some new possibility occurred to her. And what about Aloisia Hargreaves; if she had indeed been behind the anonymous letter identifying Wilkins and LaLoux, was she in danger from the other men in the Maidenhead Canal Company? It was impossible to believe, and yet ... she must consider it.

Josephs ventured out and obtained the latest newspapers. Emmeline pored over them as she sat with Fidelity, who buried herself in the latest gothic novel, preferring imaginary horror over the real life horror that went on. Though much of the news was contradictory, and many stories still focused on the Avengeress and her supposed part in the murder, it was clear that the magistrate was determined to find the real killer. Mr. William Cobbett-Smythe, magistrate in the district of Clerkenwell, wrote to *The London Guardian Standard* that he implored anyone with true information on the despicable murder of Sir Henry Claybourne to come forward. He sternly stated that all manner of spiritualists, mesmerists, and persons with grudges had already given him their opinions, but he would not charge someone on that basis. His office had some evidence and was acting upon it, but every bit of information could help.

There was immense pressure upon Mr. Cobbett-Smythe to act, she could tell that from the newspaper stories. Londoners were up in arms, as evidenced by letters to the editors of every paper, Whig, Tory, and Reformist alike, with many gentlemen asking why the scandalous woman who had shown herself to be a danger to the community had not been found and prosecuted? The hangman's gibbet was the only fit pedestal for such a treacherous female. Had she not crept into the murdered man's home and made away with a child and the silver? Was that not proof that *she* was the danger, not some imaginary men?

Something about the Avengeress's daring and boldness despite her sex, her determination to take chances and move without restraint, albeit in a cloaking costume, provoked male fears. If she had been masked for the titillation of a man, as at a masquerade ball, it would have been winked at. But the men who wrote into the paper to express their anger seemed more outraged by her incursion into a gentleman's home than they were concerned about the men seen at his home arguing with the knight long after the marauding woman had disappeared into the night. She had gone against society's rules; she *must* be guilty of something, and it was up to authorities to discover what.

There was no mention of Aloisia Hargreaves in the stories. That was good, and spoke against Simeon's fears. She hoped the young woman was not in danger. Emmeline shivered. Fidelity glanced up. There was no point in worrying her, especially not when she seemed to have found a few moments of respite from her own tortured memories, so Emmeline smiled reassuringly and her companion went back to reading.

As for the crime of buying little girls to seduce, Emmeline knew there would be no outcry as the girls were not from the gentry or peerage, and their molesters were gentlemen. Except in the hearts of those already committed to social justice, there would be no outrage. Compassion could not be forced; it must be felt, and in her experience there was little motivation to develop sympathy toward the less fortunate, since it obliged one to recognize one's own failure to deal benevolently with other humans.

She read further, finishing finally with the last few pages of *The Prattler*, where the personal advertisements sometimes held a message to herself from her editor. And there, at the bottom, it was. It read: *To Miss E. S. . . . Miss S. K. wishes to inform her that the fears S. K. expressed last night are more than ever likely to be true. Men are cruel; men inspired by fear of disclosure are the most treacherous of all. Miss S. K. wishes she could do something for their mutual friend, Miss A. H. herself, but circumstances forbid.*

Simeon was telling her that his fears for Aloisia Hargreaves now had further justification. He worried that the men who killed Sir Henry would seek to silence Miss Hargreaves. Emmeline paced to the window and flicked back the curtain; night was falling. The mist that had enclosed them all day was now being blown away as a lashing wind strengthened. The Avengeress must return to the scene of the crime, if only to protect the woman possibly responsible for turning in two murderers. Or guilty of concealing who really committed the crime. Emmeline still was unsure.

TWENTY-EIGHT

EMMELINE COMMANDED GILLIES, AGAINST her maid's conscience, to stay home and look after Fidelity, assuring her that Josephs would protect her should danger threaten. She left the house without a word of explanation to Birk.

But she had forgotten what day it was. It was the holiday to celebrate the capture of a notorious criminal, or maybe to celebrate his legendary plans to blow up the parliament—she was never sure which: Guy Fawkes Day. The recent bereavement of the royal family should have stopped the noisy annual celebrations, but it did not. On this night even Clerkenwell, a moderately safe area of London and its environs, was lit up with bonfires, gusted into roaring blazes by the wind. She watched out the window as Josephs guided the horses past bonfires. Crudely masked folks drunkenly danced and chanted a poem, of which there were many versions:

Don't you remember,
The Fifth of November?

'Twas gunpowder treason day!
I let off my gun,
And made 'em all run.
And stole all their bonfire away.

Samuel Street and the neighborhood surrounding it was no exception. There was a bonfire ahead, where Blithestone and Chandler streets met. It was the perfect night for the Avengeress, for a mask on such an eve would not be looked at askance.

Josephs brought the carriage to a halt and jumped down, then helped Emmeline, masked and cloaked, out of the carriage. His lined face twisted in a grimace of concentration, he reached into the trunk under his seat and brought out a couple of Guy Fawkes masks, representations of the gunpowder plotter, with exaggerated features and facial hair. "Use this 'un instead, miss. It'll conceal yer better."

"Thank you, Josephs. You're a wise man." She took off her velvet masquerade mask, tossed it inside the carriage, and donned the Guy Fawkes disguise.

"I won't be leavin' ye alone, miss," he said, tension threading his gruff voice. "Not tonight. Stay hidden until I return."

"I appreciate your support, Josephs. I'll be in the shadows by the alleyway running between the backs of Blithestone and Samuel. I wish to check on Miss Aloisia Hargreaves while here; Simeon is worried for her safety. As much as I would be happy of the outcome, I am not certain Mr. Wilkins is responsible for the murder of Sir Henry. I'd like to be sure."

"Bide wary until I join ye. It's an odd night, God's truth, and there be evil-doers about made bold by th'masks, and so I'd not have ye walk wiv me all that way from the stable to here."

"I'll not be foolish, I promise." A woman alone was an invitation to molestation, as if by virtue of being unaccompanied she forfeited courtesy. It made no sense, but there was much in humanity that didn't.

The view through the mask was distinctly odd, everything framed by the eye slits; she felt removed, though she blended into the street scene as every other person there. She moved to the wall by the gate into the alley behind the townhomes to await Josephs' return. A rowdy group stumbled toward her, and she slipped through the arch into the alleyway to avoid them, listening as they passed, drunkenly singing a Guy Fawkes song.

Along the alley she could hear voices; she suspected that further down on the Blithestone side, at least, servants armed with cudgels sat by doors, protecting the household from riotous celebrants. To pass the time while she awaited Josephs' return, she counted down the back of the Samuel Street shops and apartments above, noting what she thought was likely Aloisia Hargreaves's bedchamber window, given the layout of the building. Simeon hadn't said how he had discovered that she was the one who'd identified the two men at Sir Henry's back door, but she well knew the powerful chain of servant gossip, having used it often for Rogue articles. But how could she have possibly identified either man from her window, with the view foreshortened, in the dark and from such a distance?

Curious to test her theory, Emmeline crept down into the darkness, the occasional long patches of yellow lantern light spilling from windows giving her faint vision. She counted the townhomes; there was the Claybourne residence. She slipped into its courtyard, moving past the convenience at the bottom of the yard and toward the back door, and then she looked across the alley, finding the window she thought must be Aloisia's.

It was *much* too far. Unless Miss Hargreaves had been down in the alleyway, she could not have identified Mr. Wilkins. However, even if she had lied about where she was, it didn't mean she had lied about who it was she saw. Emmeline eyed the gate to the courtyard. If Aloisia had been in the alley for some reason, she may have seen Wilkins and LaLoux. Had she witnessed the murder? She was hiding something, but surely that wasn't it.

A door opened and Emmeline was suddenly clasped by the shoulders, bony hands dragging her backward. She fought, but she was off balance, and the hand over her masked mouth was strong. The stiff papier-mâché mask bit into her cheeks, and her vision obscured as the mask shifted. She tried to scream, but it was no use.

————

The city might as well be burning like the great fire of yore, the way it blazed with bonfires on every corner, teased into great sparking heights. Josephs had found a place for his team and carriage at an inn two streets over and was making his way back to his mistress, worried that he had been gone so long. Nonsense night that it were, it was filled with danger for a young lady. A buxom tipsy female grabbed him into a dance by one fire—not something he'd object to on any other night—and he had to pull himself away. Josephs gave another group a wide berth and made his way past another gang of drunken revelers, but was seized once more and forced to drink a dram in honor of the Guy, an effigy on a cart by an open green. He drank, laughing obligingly, knowing that surliness would get him into a fight, and then pulled away, anxious to get back to Miss Emmeline. He was starting to feel uneasy, like they'd made a mistake.

He was almost to the alleyway when he was seized again. He swung at the drunken fool, only to have the feller duck and said, "Hey now, Josephs, it's Dr. Woodforde."

"Good 'eavens, sorry, doc." Josephs squinted up at the doctor's face in the shadowy darkness, relieved. "Whatcha doin' 'ere?"

"I went to Chelsea and spoke to Gillies; I know you've brought Emmeline here. Where is she?" The doctor's voice was panicked.

"She's back where I left her, sir, by the alleyway between Blithestone and Samuel."

And the young fellow was off, as Josephs trudged after him.

———

Emmeline fought, but her assailant was strong and pulled her all the way along the familiar whitewashed passage to the warmth of the Claybourne kitchen. Once there, her mask was pulled off and flung aside.

"You're trouble, aren't you?" It was Mrs. Young, the Claybourne housekeeper. "Why are you here? And why you been sneakin' around pretendin' to be some poor paid companion? An' now, with that Guy mask on, skulkin' in the back alley like a thief?"

"I'm not a thief!" Emmeline said, struggling to get out of her grasp. "I'm the woman who rescued little Molly from your master."

Mrs. Young's cold gaze bored into her. "An' killed 'im, I warrant?"

"Of course not, and you know that better than anyone. You saw me leave, and I most certainly did not come back. Who took the silver that was missing that night? It wasn't Molly, and it wasn't me." The housekeeper's bony fingers were digging into her shoulders all the more as she tried to pull away. "That leaves you and the cook. Is that why you arranged for the rescue that night? So you'd have someone to blame when the silver went missing?"

A gasp from the other end of the room made Emmeline twist around, still in the housekeeper's powerful grasp.

The cook, standing by the fire, hands clasped against her bosom, stared at them both. "You said as how she must've come back and stole it," the woman said to the housekeeper. "If she didn't, who did?"

Emmeline finally pulled out of Mrs. Young's grasp and straightened her dress. "She lied to you." The cook stared, but said nothing. "Do you know that she was a scullery maid once, a long time ago, working for Sir Henry's family?"

The cook lurched forward. "Here, now ... how do you know that?"

The housekeeper had edged around Emmeline and stood between her and the passageway to the back door; escape in that direction was improbable. She hoped Josephs would figure she may have gone down the alley. She eyed the two women. The cook didn't seem dangerous, but the housekeeper had a fearsome look to her. And here she had thought wandering down the alley was safer than waiting for Josephs on Chandler Lane!

"I know a lot of things," she replied to the cook. She recalled something that moment; she remembered the complaint the cook had made about her best knife being stolen that night. Her stomach quivered. She'd wager that the same knife had been tossed into the privy and retrieved by the night soil men two days later. The cook wouldn't do that, or if she had, she wouldn't complain about the missing knife. She eyed the housekeeper; that was a woman who could wield a knife with purpose.

"Why did you come 'ere as that old biddy's companion?" the housekeeper asked, her voice raspy with agitation. "I recognized you right away, you know; set of your chin and the color of your hair."

The woman had sharp eyes, Emmeline realized. "I don't like being implicated in murder and I wanted to know who did it," she said.

"What has that got t'do with us?" the cook asked.

"Nothing, I suppose ... or at least nothing now. It appears that thanks to a witness, the authorities have identified the men who did it."

"Unless they can pin it on someone else," Mrs. Young said darkly, folding her arms across her flat bosom.

"What is going on here?"

Emmeline turned. Mrs. Claybourne stood in the passage doorway with a young woman at her shoulder.

"What is *she* doing here?" the young woman said, stepping around Lady Claybourne. It was Aloisia Hargreaves.

Stranger and stranger.

"Alice, this doesn't concern you," the housekeeper said. "Why did you two come to the kitchen? You should have stayed away."

Alice?

"I would have," Lady Claybourne said. "But *this* one"—she indicated Aloisia—"must march down here when she heard voices."

"Alice, go home!" the housekeeper commanded.

Emmeline slowly eyed each woman, trying to untangle the strands of connection in her mind.

"Go back the way you came, Alice," the housekeeper repeated.

"I *won't*," Miss Hargreaves said with a sulky expression. "I want to know; what is *she* doing here?"

"She crept up to the back door in a Guy mask, lookin' to cause trouble."

"I thought she was that old biddy Miss Honeychurch's companion, but I assume that's not so," Lady Claybourne said. "Who is she really?"

"I *told* you she weren't no companion!" Mrs. Young said.

"So she's the one who rescued poor little Molly, right?" The cook spoke up, looking as confused as Emmeline felt.

Mrs. Young and Lady Claybourne exchanged a look. A thrill of unease crept down Emmeline's spine. This felt like play-acting, like they were putting on a show, all for her.

"No, she's Miss Emmeline St. Germaine," Aloisia Hargreaves said. "She brought two children to me to ask about French and embroidery lessons."

"She can't be everything: the companion, the rescuer, and someone who brought children for embroidery lessons," Lady Claybourne said, glaring at Emmeline. "So who are you?"

Emmeline examined the housekeeper again, a woman with strong shoulders and big hands. Had Mrs. Young dealt the fatal blow to the tormentor of her youth, slicing his vocal chords and then stabbing him to death? "Which of you called me in to rescue Molly?" she asked.

"T'was about Sally at first, but then she found another job, didn't she?" the cook said, eying the other women.

"Shut up," Mrs. Young growled.

"No, let her speak," Emmeline said. "Sally found another job but she kept in contact, didn't she Lady Claybourne?"

The woman's chin went up, but she didn't answer.

"And Sally brought you information that led you to believe the infamous Avengeress was a part of a group, one who rescued abused scullery maids; isn't that true?" Emmeline said.

Cook, still with a puzzled look on her round face, continued: "Aye, that's true. Sybil 'eard from Biddy of women as would take a little girl outta a place like this, where she was bein' abused. I told Mrs. Young."

"And then what?"

"What does any of this matter?" Lady Claybourne said, stepping into the kitchen toward Emmeline. There was a hint of menace in her tone.

Emmeline had her confirmation, or enough of it, anyway. She knew that Sally had brought them more complete information, and this lot decided to use her to rescue Molly. She knew the reason why, too, beyond saving the girl from Sir Henry. "So how did the newspapers learn about my rescue of the child?" she asked the housekeeper, ignoring the widow.

"What else were we gonna say when the magistrate came asking questions?" the housekeeper asked. "T'were true enough."

"And the timing ... so convenient to blame me for his death, correct? There were already folks up in arms about me, about my missions. I made a rather convenient scapegoat. When you told them the tale of Molly and the masked woman, you implied that I was the one who killed him?"

"We never said you did it, but Mrs. Young and Cook gave the sequence of events," Lady Claybourne said.

"Alice, Benny will wonder where you are. You should go while we figure out what to do."

The most puzzling aspect of this distinctly odd event was the housekeeper's familiarity with Miss Hargreaves, so much so that she felt comfortable ordering her around.

"Benjamin is out gallivanting with his friends," Miss Hargreaves said sourly. "As men do. *He's* off drinking and carousing at a bonfire while *I'm* expected to stay up in my room reading or sewing."

"He's a man; that's how things be!" the housekeeper said.

"It's not fair!" Aloisia / Alice complained.

That was the moment Emmeline realized what the exchange reminded her of: mother and child. "You're Mrs. Young's *daughter!*" she said to Miss Hargreaves, who stared at her without acknowledging or denying the charge. The tangled web of connections was starting to show a pattern. She let her gaze drift across the women in the kitchen, three of whom, at least, likely conspired to kill Sir Henry Claybourne. The cook still appeared mystified.

"Yes, I'm her daughter and Benjamin is her son. So what?"

"Alice, shut up!" Mrs. Young said.

"*All* of you shut up!" Lady Claybourne said. "You're making my head ache. Now, what do we *do* with her?"

A jolt of awareness thudded under Emmeline's ribs; she must not make the mistake of thinking because these were women that she was in no danger. If they truly had conspired to kill Sir Henry, then she was a threat to them. But … she was not a nameless nobody that they could dispose of her. "What happened?" she asked, as she tried to figure out what to do next. "That night, I mean … what happened?"

"Don't say anything," Lady Claybourne warned the others.

"Then I'll tell you," Emmeline said. "You—all of you, or some of you—used information brought back to you by Sally about the group of women who rescue children. You figured out somehow that the Avengeress was a part of the group; either that or you didn't really care as long as one of us came and 'rescued' Molly in a dramatic fashion from the loathsome Sir Henry. I know what he has always been like, and I know that you," she said, turning to look at Mrs. Young, "were among his first victims, as a little girl in his family's household."

The woman was silent, but her daughter turned to look at her, mouth agape, pity and sudden understanding glowing in her eyes.

"When it was discovered that you were in a family way at the tender age of thirteen or fourteen, you were banished from the house without a character. After your baby died, you did the only thing a girl in your position *could* do," Emmeline continued softly. "Women have few choices in this life, but we have our own body. It is one of the few things we retain ownership of, though even that ends once we are wed. Selling it over and over again is sometimes a woman's only choice if she wants to live. It's either that or starve."

"That's why you left Benny and me with that family," Alice said, staring at Mrs. Young. "And why we never were allowed to visit you. You were … you …" She shook her head.

Lady Claybourne moved impatiently. "This is getting us nowhere."

"You found a way to leave that all behind and went back into service. Finally, you came here to work." Emmeline turned away from the housekeeper toward the lady of the house. "Did you know who she was immediately?" Even as she spoke, she was assessing; would they let her walk away? Killing Sir Henry—she didn't know which of them did it but suspected Mrs. Young, given her strength and the hatred she must have felt toward him—had likely been easier than killing Emmeline would be. At least she hoped that was so. "Did you know?"

"When she came to apply for the position, she soon saw there was no need to dissemble and told me all."

The bitterness in the woman's gaze was sharp and dark. Perhaps she had underestimated Lady Claybourne, thinking her soft because she was well-raised and older. Emmeline's certainty about the actual killer wavered. She turned to look at Aloisia. "What did you truly see? I know they were here, Mr. Wilkins and Pierre LaLoux, and I know they argued with Sir Henry. I have independent witnesses," she said, thinking of Arnie and what he had overheard. "But who told the magistrate who they were?" She was treading dangerous ground, poking and prodding where it might spark trouble, but instead of things getting clearer she was becoming more and more confused, a state she could not tolerate. "Miss Hargreaves, tell me the truth," she said, softly.

The young woman's gaze flicked between Mrs. Young and Lady Claybourne. "I—"

"You don't need to say a word, Alice," her mother said.

"She's right," Emmeline said, scanning the four women. The cook had retreated to her corner and sat in her chair by the hearth, watching with wary eyes. Of them all, she was perhaps left out of the plot, except as the one who unwittingly passed on information used to find a ready-made culprit upon whom to place the blame for Sir Henry's murder. "But you forget that I saw what that ... that *despicable* creature was trying to do to Molly, and I know he'd done it many, many ... perhaps *countless* times before. It never would have ended." Her voice was guttural with unfeigned loathing. "I don't mourn his death, not even the manner of it."

"If someone had told the magistrate, brought a case against him—" Aloisia said, weakly, glancing among Lady Claybourne, her mother, and Emmeline.

"Nothing would have happened," her mother said.

"She's right." Lady Claybourne's voice was throaty with emotion. "A poor family in his village tried charging him after he assaulted their daughter, who worked in their home. I heard all about it after we were wed. Henry's family hushed it up and the poor father lost his job. He was found dead."

"Dead?" Emmeline gasped.

"Oh, Henry didn't murder him, if that's what you think," Lady Claybourne said with a grim smile. "A villager told me the poor soul drank himself unconscious and was found face down in a water-filled ditch on his way home from the tavern. His family left the village after that."

Emmeline was appalled but not surprised. Aloisia's face was a mask of shock and bewilderment.

"That's why he chose orphans, most of the time," Mrs. Young said, her voice devoid of feeling. "No mother, no father to stand up for them. If someone had taken an interest..." She shook her head. "But the end would have been the same. The man let off and the little girl cast out on the street, with nowhere to go."

Her words reverberated in the cavernous kitchen. It was a grim indictment of how little worth their country placed on the lives of its poorest and most defenseless children. They were commodities. "Little better than unwanted kittens to drown," Emmeline said.

"It's true," Cook whispered. It was the first time she had spoken for some time, from her corner by the hearth.

They all turned to look at her.

"It happened to me, too, in the big 'ouse where I first worked. An' there weren't nothing no one would do. I told the mistress what her son 'ad done, an' she sent me off. But I were lucky; at least I 'ad somewhere to go. I 'ad a mother. She told me to forget it ever happened and found me another position." Tears rolled down the cook's round cheeks. "Those who got no one ... there ain't a single person to 'elp."

For a moment the women in the cavernous kitchen were sisters.

"I loved a boy once," Lady Claybourne said. "A farmer. But my father broke off our affair and made me marry Henry. I was just a butcher's daughter, you see, albeit a butcher who had climbed in the world some. Henry's family had influence but little money. My father had money but little influence. So I was my father's stepping stone to the life he wanted, one of respect and position. By the time Miss Honeychurch warned me, it was too late ... not that I believed her then. I would have been ruined if I'd broken off the engagement. I didn't have the courage." She looked at Mrs. Young and touched her shoulder; it was a gentle gesture, at odds with the topic of brutality, abuse, and the murder of a man who had hurt so many.

It was a familiar tale, and still continuing, Emmeline thought, thinking of Juliette Espanson, Lady Clara, and Miss Gottschalk. But this was getting them nowhere. She had become reasonably sure they'd let her go, but she needed to know more. "Miss Hargreaves, I'm still wondering; what did you truly see that night?"

The young lady shivered. "Weeks before that, the man—the man with the dog—delivered that little girl, Molly, to the back door as if she was a bottle of milk." Tears welled in Aloisia's eyes. "I was coming out of the convenience and heard a dog bark. I spied, saw that man and Sir Henry, overheard them joking about the child. 'Dunstable's doing his work, I see. Pretty, this one. She suits my fancy!' That's what Sir Henry said as he petted her hair." She glanced over at Lady Claybourne, whose face was rigid with anger. "The man asked how long Sir Henry would keep her. Sir Henry said the last two had run off, but he'd keep her, he said, until he was tired of her. *Tired of her!*"

Cook wept softly, having retreated to her chair again by the hearth, her little corner of the world.

"She looked so frightened," Aloisia continued. "I came to Mother and Lady Claybourne, and they told me there was already a plan in place to rescue her. 'What then?' I asked. 'What about the next little girl?'"

"Alice, enough," her mother said.

"Let her talk," Lady Claybourne said wearily. "Even though she said she wouldn't."

"I didn't say I wouldn't *ever!*"

Emmeline knew then that the ruby brooch Aloisia had received was a bribe … something to keep her quiet.

"You told me not to worry about that," she said to the older lady. "You said you had a plan to stop your husband. I didn't know …" She shook her head, unable to say the word "murder."

"Nothing else would have stopped him," Mrs. Young said, her tone flat.

"How do you know?" Emmeline asked.

"*I* know, because I did everything I could think of," Lady Claybourne cried. "One more scullery maid and I would turn him in to the magistrate, I said. He laughed. If he went to jail I'd lose everything; my home, the money I came into the marriage with ... *everything.* How is that right?"

"So who killed Sir Henry?" Emmeline asked, glancing between Lady Claybourne, the butcher's daughter, and the strong, strapping, and angry Mrs. Young.

"Those two men who came to the door," Aloisia said swiftly. "Unless you want it to be you?"

Ah yes, the threat of disclosure.

"It was the two men, one a Frenchman and one with a cane," the young woman continued. "I saw them, and heard them argue, and then Sir Henry was dead. *That's* what I've told the magistrate. I was afraid before and got Benny to say he saw them, but now they have them in custody because of the anonymous letter, I will gladly point them out as the men who killed Sir Henry." She smiled. "I will sigh, and weep, and admit I was too afraid before to tell them, but that yes, they were the men I saw." Her smile turned into a grimace. "And they'll be punished."

Mrs. Young reached out and touched her arm, and Lady Claybourne nodded. That was their account, and Aloisia was going to stick by it. Wilkins and LaLoux, whether they had killed Sir Henry or not, would be accused and go to trial. Emmeline was virtually certain that the two men *did* kill Ratter. If she turned these women in, she'd never be sure which of them had done the deed and she didn't trust the authorities to get it right. And she'd have to explain how she knew who

330

did it, to confess to being the Avengeress. Her family would disown her, her work would be done, her life as she knew it would be over. And all for two men who most certainly were murderers and abusers of children.

Her head ached with the quandary. How could it be right to let a murderer go free? The women had planned it together; did it matter which of them struck the blow? Weren't both guilty? Was murder *ever* justified?

However … Sir Henry was dead and would never ruin another child's life.

Sometimes the easiest thing to do was nothing. With the power of the press, Emmeline, as the Rogue, would make sure the Maidenhead Canal Company was disbanded and the public warned of their disgusting business trading in little girls. And somehow she'd make sure her uncle never fiddled with another child.

"I'll be going now," she said. These women had no reason to fear her. They knew far too much about her. If she told on them, they'd tell on her, so her silence was also self-preservation. She slipped away, following the whitewashed passage to the back courtyard and exiting into the shadowy night.

TWENTY-NINE

EMMELINE HUSTLED OUT THE back door of 73 Blithestone, through the courtyard into the back alley, and straight into Woodforde's arms.

"Emmeline!" he shouted, relief in his voice.

"Hush," she said, grabbing him by the arm and tugging him down the alley toward the arched entrance. "What are *you* doing here?"

"I could ask you the same thing," he said.

Josephs, denuded of his Guy mask and illuminated by the lanthorn he held up, was relieved. "Thank 'eavens, miss. I was that afraid when you weren't where you said you'd be! Are you done?"

"I believe I have the information I sought." And much more.

"What about that lady you was wanting to warn?"

"She needs no warning from me." Emmeline strode swiftly to the brick arch and through it, with Woodforde on her heel.

"I'll go get th'carriage."

"You do that."

"You go, Josephs, but I'll take Miss St. Germaine home in my curricle."

Emmeline pulled her heavy cloak about her and glared up at Woodforde. "You will do no such thing. Josephs will take me home. If you want an explanation of what happened tonight, then you will follow."

He blinked, his dark eyes shadowed. "Emmeline, I'm not the enemy."

"I do *not* wish to freeze in your curricle. I'm making a completely reasonable request. How is that treating you like an enemy?"

"Why must you be so hard-headed?" he asked.

"I'm in no mood for banter, Woodforde. Follow us home if you wish. Otherwise ... I'll see you." She turned and trudged out of the alley, and followed Josephs the two streets to the livery, slipping along in the shadows, avoiding the last flickering flames of the bonfires now burning low, not looking back all the way to the carriage.

Home was within sight, at last. Emmeline felt like she had aged twenty years in the last hour. In the darkness of the carriage, she began regretting how brisk she had been with Woodforde, who was, after all, only concerned for her well being. Surely she owed him consideration for that?

Owed. Why did she *owe* him consideration for his feelings of concern for her? What did a woman *owe* a man who was merely following his own wishes in placing the burden on her of his feelings of worry and anxiety? It seemed her whole life she had been giving deference to men, feeling the burden of their wishes for her, their worry for her, their plans ... for her. *Their* plans. For *her.*

All while they went blithely on their way and did what they wanted, planning the lives of the girls and women around them. Maybe it was so the world over, she didn't know. But she wanted self determination, the right to make her own decisions—faulty or not—

and plan for her own future without the necessity of attaching herself to some man.

Some argued that women by nature were weak and frivolous, blown about by emotion, enslaved by passion and pettiness. It seemed to her that men blamed women for their *own* faults, for she had seen many who appeared to be slave to their weaknesses, her brothers among them. Leopold sulked like a toddler if denied his way. Samuel was better, but he did fidget about petty things that he could not control. And Thomas ... her younger brother's entire life was devoted to indulging his passions and vices. He could not control his desire for drink, and gambling, and women.

But those were thoughts for another day. Right now she had to determine what to do about her uncle. She had rescued Lindy—her rightful name now restored to her—from his predation, but it was only a matter of time before he sought another. She planned to use her Rogue column to destroy the company, but she had no illusion the well-connected men would suffer any kind of punishment. What was to stop them from continuing their despicable habits on their own?

She was surprised to find, when Josephs pulled the carriage up to the door, that her townhome was ablaze with lights. Birk hurried down the steps to her, his usually calm expression twisted in panic.

"Miss St. Germaine, your uncle—"

"What's wrong?" She clambered down from the carriage and headed to the door.

"Sir Jacob is inside. He's not himself."

"What do you mean, not himself?"

"He's reclining in the sitting room."

That absurd statement was followed by silence, and Birk's face reddened to a sickly orange by the yellow glow of the lantern hung by the door.

"Is Madame Bernadotte with him?" Emmeline swept into the house, Birk bobbing along behind.

"No, miss. I sent up word he had arrived but she … she declined to descend."

Gillies was in the hall and took her cloak. "He's in a right tear, miss," she muttered. "Your uncle was visited by the magistrate's men this afternoon after anonymous word was sent to them about abuse happening in his home to little girls. He came here blusterin' on about it. I think he believes you done it. Birk dithered, Madame Bernadotte said there was no way in hell she was coomin' down to see him, an' Sir Jacob fainted. Birk an' me got him up on the settee, and nouw he's revived a mite and roarin' for brandy."

Emmeline stiffened her spine, raised her head, took a deep breath, and sailed into the sitting room.

Her uncle, his face red, struggled to sit up. "There she ish, my little troublemaker neesh," he said, his voice slurred.

"Uncle, you're drunk! Why have you come here?"

"Wanna get shomething shtraight. You're … you can't go 'round telling people I—" He stopped, looking confused. His mouth was droopy and his eyes unfocused. "I can't shee you. Whatsh …" He shook his head and tried to stand, but dropped back down on the up-holstered settee. It shifted from his sudden collapse.

Gillies, behind Emmeline, said, "I didnae smell alcohol on his breath, miss, when he fairst arrived."

"Uncle Jacob, are you all right?" She stood staring, unsure.

"Dr. Woodforde, miss," Birk announced, back in control.

"Emmie … uh, Miss St. Germaine, may I—" Woodforde stopped in the doorway, hat in hand, staring at Sir Jacob. "Sir, are you all right?" he asked.

"I c-can't shee!"

"Birk, help me," Woodforde said, tossing his hat aside. "He needs to lie down."

Sir Jacob was combative and his eyes started out of the sockets, the left side of his face drooping, an alarming sight. He flailed at them, but they got him down and he stayed, finally, reclining, and drifted into unconsciousness.

"What's wrong with him?" Emmeline asked.

"He's having an apoplectic fit," Woodforde said, kneeling beside the man and pushing one eyelid open, examining his eye.

"Is he ... is he dying?" Her voice trembled and echoed in the hushed chill room.

"I don't know." He grabbed Sir Jacob's wrist, feeling for his pulse.

"Will he recover?"

"I don't know that, either," the doctor said over his shoulder.

"What *do* you know?" Emmeline, exasperated, blurted out.

Gillies laid a staying hand on her arm. "Miss, the good doctor isn't God. No one knows the fate of a man but his Savior."

"He won't have a savior," Emmeline said bitterly, staring down at her uncle.

Woodforde stood. "He must be carried to a bed and someone needs to sit with him. I'll do what I can, but I can't make promises."

"He's not staying here," Emmeline said.

Woodforde stared at her, silent for a long moment in the chill dimness of the sitting room. "You'll not give your uncle a place to recuperate?"

"He's *not* staying here," she repeated, looking directly into the doctor's eyes. All her life she had been taught that a lady was complaisant, made no waves, was agreeable and sweet and gentle. But something had shifted in her heart and mind; she was done with being complaisant, letting the gentlemen have it all their own way. "Think what you will, but I have my reasons. He goes." She would not subject Fidelity to his presence. Sir Jacob Pauling had chosen his path and he must walk it alone, whether it led to the grave or to recovery.

She ordered Josephs and Birk to carry her uncle back out to his carriage, and told his driver to take him home; there was no place for him there. Woodforde coolly took his leave, saying he would follow the judge's carriage and make sure he was settled properly in his home. There he could assess if there was any medical intervention that would hasten recovery, if that was to be his fate. At the very least he would summon Sir Jacob's physician.

She knew Woodforde was appalled by her behavior, but he didn't know enough to understand, and even then … maybe he would not have agreed with her. But she chose to stand with her uncle's victim.

Emmeline wearily climbed the stairs and found Fidelity shuddering and weeping in her room, Arbor trying to comfort her but not having much effect. She sent the maid away to fetch tea and spent the rest of the night with her companion. Fidelity had finally utterly broken down, memories flooding back, and the full realization of what had been done to her so many years before, memories she had suppressed, made her weak and feverish.

She told Emmeline about years of secret meetings, in the long-abandoned nursery at Malincourt, during holiday gatherings. It had started with whispered conversations, teasing, hugs, then kisses, then more intimate fondling. Every time she felt frightened—and that was often, especially at first, before she had become numb to the indecency of his behavior—he gave her gifts, wheedled his way into her heart. She knew it was wrong, but eventually she decided she must love him. It was worth enduring for that. She even thought they'd marry, but they never did, and his attentions stopped when she reached sixteen or so. She went to France to visit relatives, then met and married Jean Marc.

"Was he truly good to you, your husband?" Emmeline asked.

Fidelity nodded through tears. "He knew everything," she said. "I told him all, and it was a great comfort, the greatest of my life." When she'd returned to England after her husband's murder, she had thought that Sir Jacob, still unmarried, would offer for her then. She would have married him. Despite feeling that what he had done to her when she was young was wrong, she still thought he loved her. But he told her, in confidence, that he could never marry because he had been ill. His ability to have a proper marriage was lost to him, he said. She was happy to be his friend, given the circumstances.

Finding that all these years he had been abusing little girls, many even younger than she had been at their first encounter, had been a devastating blow to Fidelity. It was almost a twisted kind of jealousy, she confessed to Emmeline, but she was starting to realize that was a result of the sickness he had planted in her mind from such a young age. The truth was that he would never have married her. If he loved her at all, he loved his vice far more, and he wanted no woman in his household who would stop his predation on little girls.

It has come to our attention that there exists among our nation's jurists a cabal of men for whom children are mere playthings to satisfy their most lascivious impulses. It starts at the Pentonville Home for Unfortunate Children, where little girls are sold to the highest bidder like prime horseflesh. The little girl is taken to a home where she should have the expectation of safety and security, and then abused in a disgraceful and despicable manner.

All you men of good conscience; be aware that the orphanage and the group of men who invested in the Maidenhead Canal Company—which acted as a cover for the most despicable and outrageous of schemes to assault little children who were guilty of no crime but to be parentless—must be routed out and exposed. We have a list of the investors, but until we can be sure that all the names on the list knew full well what the company in which they invested traded for lucre, we will not publish.

We call on the magistrates of this fine nation to get to the bottom of this disgrace. We know that one man, at least, invested in the company without knowing the real purpose behind it. He (who shall remain unnamed) has taken steps to aid in the dispersal of the children of that horrible orphanage to places of safety. God bless him and men like him, and protect the little children.

··········

THIRTY

Two days later, Emmeline sat in Lady Adelaide Sherringdon's sitting room awaiting the other Crones. The lady of the house joined her, followed by Hugo the pug and the black Tom. She sat down by Emmeline and took her hand. "I'm so horribly upset to hear about poor Fidelity. All this time, and you never had a hint?"

Emmeline shook her head. "It was 'their little secret,' as Fidelity says. Over the years, though she began to understand how wrong my uncle had been to behave so toward her, she always thought it was because he was young and unformed, and that, as he told her, it was because she was so alluring he could not resist."

"That it was her fault, in other words," Lady Sherringdon said. "It is the province of the coward, male or female, to place the blame for their behavior on others."

"She would never have remained silent if she had known he was still at it."

The others arrived: Lady Clara, looking pale but composed; Dorcas Harvey, appearing happier than usual; Miss Juliette Espanson, looking as usual. Mrs. Martha Adair was the last to arrive and bustled in, a frown on her usually placid face.

Emmeline told them all she knew. Or almost all; Fidelity's past was her own secret to tell or not to tell, though Lady Sherringdon had been an exception. "So my uncle was at the heart of the dreadful company that sold little girls like chattel, to be used and discarded. *The Prattler* has exposed the name of the company. The crime that started us on this quest, the murder of Sir Henry Claybourne, has been solved. Three men involved, as Sir Henry was, had been summoned by him to his home, as he thought they were responsible for my arrival to rescue Molly."

She hesitated; should she tell them the truth? Yet there was no point in making Martha feel bad for how she was used and spied upon by Sally, and for how Emmeline was almost trapped as a murderess as a result. So she told them some truth, about Sir Henry's summoning of Ratter, Wilkins, and LaLoux. "The two have been arrested and charged with Ratter's murder. Miss Aloisia Hargreaves has named Wilkins and LaLoux, my uncle's valet, as the two men she saw arguing with Sir Henry before he was killed; it is suspected that they killed Sir Henry. The Crones have been vindicated. The Avengeress is safe."

––––––––––

It was a chilly November day, and with a gloomy sky overhanging Chelsea, the townhome appeared sullen. The townhomes on either side had seasonal tenants, and most folks had returned to their country homes for the hunting and Christmas seasons. Josephs helped her down, and Birk opened the door for her. She entered, wondering if she'd ever feel the same again, ever feel like she knew the people she saw every day. Her own family had held such deep secrets, things she never would have expected. What else was hidden from her view?

Fidelity was calmer than she had been, and, Gillies told her, finally sleeping after drinking a tisane of feverfew and valerian made by Cook. Emmeline retired to her room and wrote letters and a new Rogue article following up on the Maidenhead Scandal, as it was now being called in some of the political papers. Her uncle, a Whig, was being called out by Tories as an evil man preying on the helpless; they demanded he surrender his judgeship, given the investment he had in a company that had done such evil.

It was noted in the society pages that Lord and Lady Quisenberry had suddenly departed London for Italy, as his health was failing. Somehow, conveniently, his name had been absent from the list of Maidenhead investors that *The Prattler* had subsequently decided to publish. What that meant, Emmeline thought, was that he had made a deal to give up his own judgeship and then fled the country. She didn't know what was happening to Mr. Fulmer and the others mentioned, but there was a general outcry about the whole affair, though it was muted by news about preparations for Princess Amelia's funeral.

Sir Jacob was in no state to respond; he was very ill, still unconscious. His cook had left for another position, and his valet was, of course, under arrest with Mr. Wilkins. His butler was keeping the home going, and his doctor was staying to care for him. Emmeline wondered how Miss Gottschalk was doing; she longed to call on her, but their acquaintance was so slight, and her uncle's notoriety was growing. It was better if she stayed out of the public eye for now. She received a note from Woodforde; Sir Jacob, he said, was likely not going to live.

I have spoken to your friend, Lady Sherringdon, and she introduced me to Lady Clara Langdon, who, as I understand, is the patroness of another orphanage, one that does the work they are supposed to do.

Interesting that neither lady had told her about this when she saw them earlier, Emmeline thought. Woodforde must have been swift, and spoken to them that very morning. However…

Lady Clara is a remarkable young lady and was happy to help; a few days ago she visited the Pentonville establishment and has even found a place for one of the little girls there who claimed an acquaintance with you, Sarah, I believe her name is. With her mother's blessing the child has gone to live in the country on Lady Clara's family's home farm, where she will be trained up to be a dairy maid. Also, I have joined with Mrs. Miller, the wardress at Lady Clara's orphanage, and found a way to get rid of Dunstable and install someone in the Pentonville orphanage under the auspices of her management.

So Woodforde *was*, as she suspected, the unnamed gentleman from Simeon's *Prattler* article who had put an end to the terrible doings at the Pentonville orphanage. Also, he had been haunted, he wrote, by the impression left on him by the young prostitute sisters, and so had partnered with Lady Sherringdon to remove as many of them from the streets as was possible. Parents had been compensated, and Mrs. Miller was offering invaluable advice on how to deal with girls who had been through so much in their young lives. They could not save them all, not even that many, he said, but every one they could was a small step forward.

It warmed her to know the work Woodforde was doing. Mrs. Sherringdon had made no mention of it to Emmeline, in typical Addy fashion.

Woodforde finished the letter with this:

I wish you would trust me, Emmie; I still call you that, the fond name of your childhood, because I feel we have a lifelong, close, and as enduring a friendship as there can be between a lady and gentleman. I may wish it were more, but you will guide that. I feel there is more to your mystery than you have so far said. Please know ... if you need my help in any matter, you can trust me. I may occasionally step over the boundaries you set out, but when I do it is out of a deep affection and concern for your wellbeing. I will not apologize for that.

Samuel had been right after all; Woodforde cared for her. Emmeline didn't know what to do with that news. For the moment, there was too much in her mind and heart to think of the strictly personal. A profound depression settled over her as she wrote to her nieces. How would she ever know if they had been safe from her uncle's predation, given how much time Sir Jacob spent at Malincourt? He had *probably* confined his ruinous advances to scullery maids there too, more cautious in his older years, knowing it left less chance to be caught, but how could she know for sure?

The day darkened and Fidelity slept on, as she had all the previous day. Gillies went about her business. When she had first learned about the confrontation Emmeline had had with the ladies at the Claybourne house, she had been outraged, then doubtful. She had a finely tuned sense of justice, and the idea that Wilkins and LaLoux should be hanged for a crime they did not commit disturbed her. "Where is the line then, miss?" she asked, twisting her sewing in her hands and looking worried. "If we will bend the law to save ourselves, where is the line over which we willnae step?"

"I don't know, Gillies, but I feel helpless to affect this outcome. Does it matter if they are punished for the wrong crime, when it is equal to the one they did commit?"

Looking very serious, the maid said, "Aye, I do think it matters, miss."

Emmeline wrote more letters, including a very long one to Simeon. Late in the afternoon, she heard a commotion downstairs and rose, pulled her shawl around her shoulders, and descended. A voice roared in displeasure and Emmeline stiffened.

Leopold. Her brother had arrived in London, and, given his hatred of the city and that his wife was heavy with child, that could only mean one thing. He had heard all about the scandal and was come to deal with it. Fortunately he was in a hurry to see their uncle, and only gave her a stern look and said, "We'll talk when I get back" before leaving again.

It was late. After checking on Fidelity, Emmeline retreated to her bedroom but did not undress. When Leopold arrived back home she descended, unwilling to wait to see him until morning. She found him at the desk in the sitting room with his head in his hands.

"Leo?" she said uncertainly.

He looked up. His eyes were red and his face gray, double chins scruffed with graying beard coming in, his broad shoulders slumped. "He's dead, Emmie," he said. "Our uncle is dead. Gone to heaven to be with Mama and Maria."

She bit her tongue. Now was not the time to say their uncle would never see their mother where he was going, if one believed in that sort of thing. She crossed the room, pulling her shawl more closely around her shoulders. Arbor, roused from her slumber, stumbled in sleepily, lit the fire, and left the room. "How are *you*, brother?"

"Saddened. He was my favorite uncle."

She sat down in a chair near the writing table. There was a curious intimacy in the dark night, the pale light of one candle and the glow of the fire the only illumination. She examined his drawn face. He looked older, as if the weight of the world had settled on his shoulders. "I'm not sad he's gone, Leo. I know you have heard what he did so you needn't prevaricate with me. He had done great evil."

Leo glared at her. "*You* killed him, Emmeline. And you were his favorite of us all!"

All sympathy was swept away by anger. "Don't you care what he did to Maria, our beloved little sister? He claims—claimed—he did nothing wrong, but she was afraid of him, and I know he abused her. I'll *never* weep for his death. I'm *glad* he's gone. No more little girls will suffer from his exploitation."

"You're out of line, Emmie," Leopold growled. "I didn't want to talk about this tonight, but before he fell ill I got a letter from our uncle about your behavior. You have been gallivanting about talking to Jews and Catholics and doing other things. He would not say what; he wanted to tell me in person. He *implored* me to come to London, but I'm too late! Your lies and accusations broke his heart. You killed him!"

Emmeline stiffened. "I am not lying; ask Fidelity what he did in secret, if you don't believe me, and *then* defend our uncle. What am I doing? Such *terrible* things! I have joined with a group of ladies and we do good work, good *Christian* work, saving orphans from a life on the street. Isn't that what a spinster of my class is supposed to do?"

Her brother's jowls sagged, his whiskers, growing in after a long day, graying and his hair receding. He looked old and tired. "Why are you so bitter, Emmie?"

Of course, she thought; if he couldn't win the argument, he'd change it to another one. She rose from her seat, trembling. "I won't let you avoid the truth. You learn that our uncle was having sexual relations with little girls his whole life, and even abused our beloved, sweet sister, who died from *starving* herself to death for some unknown reason, and your response is to ask why I am *bitter?*"

Leo rose too. "Calm yourself, Emmeline! I will *not* be shrieked at by a hysterical female in my own house. It is time you were married. A husband and children will cure you."

Gillies, her cap askew, entered the room and approached. "Miss, the Comtesse is awake and askin' for you."

"Not now, Gillies. Leo, whether you choose to believe it or not doesn't alter the truth; our uncle was a member of a disgusting troupe of child abusers. Yet I'm accused of being hysterical when you won't acknowledge the truth?" Gillies tugged on her sleeve, but Emmeline shook her off. Her maid was trying to stave off a quarrel, but it was too late for that.

Leopold, whose St. Germaine temper was slower to burn but quick to erupt once it had, was turning quite, quite red. "Enough!" he roared. "Enough of your *filthy* mouth!" He strode to the door. "Birk! Birk, get in here!" he shrieked.

The butler, quivering and carrying a candle, his nightcap slipping sideways, arrived in the sitting room. "Yes, sir?"

"Order my carriage hitched. I am heading back to Malincourt tonight."

The butler hastened away.

Leopold turned to Emmeline. She had gone too far, and now would pay the consequences. Belatedly, she wished she'd heeded Gillies, who stood off to the side wringing her hands.

"You have disgraced this family," Leo said, his red face streaked with tears. "It is clear to me that you have been doing much that you shouldn't, and even more that could irreparably harm our family name. If I didn't know better I'd think you were the one who told the newspapers about our uncle, but even you would not stoop so low.

"In the spring my eldest two daughters will be coming to London for their coming out, and I will *not* have their aunt be a scandalous byword among society, shamed at every pass, never able to show your face in London again. You, young lady," he said, shaking his finger in her face, "will behave. For now you will go away somewhere quiet, an institution, because your health has clearly broken down. You will retreat, we will put it about that you are delicate and in shock from our uncle's disgrace, and you will *behave.* Then you will come back to London and marry someone suitable. I'm finished with you otherwise. You're lucky I don't wash my hands of you and send you to Bedlam."

―――――

"I don't know what I'm going to do, Addy," she said the next day, hugging the one-eyed Tom. "He can *make* me do this."

"Leopold has much on his plate currently, with Rose expecting. He's easily distracted, correct? Perhaps if you stay quiet for a while he will reconsider."

"I wish I thought that possible."

Lady Sherringdon's maid showed a visitor into the room, an older lady who swept across the room and enveloped Addy in a hug as

Hugo the pug danced and barked. "You must help me, Adelaide, you simply must! My daughter's life is at stake."

Adelaide made the introductions. The woman, clearly troubled, was Dame Smytheson, an old friend of Lady Sherringdon's. "Tell me what is wrong. You can speak in front of my friend. She's a very intelligent young lady and may offer advice."

The woman, almost weeping with worry, told them both about her daughter, Mrs. Barbara Pendrake. "She has been sadly unable to bear a child, or at least, one that is alive. Until five months ago! She had a precious daughter, and ... and we were all so happy! But the babe died in her crib." She broke down into tears, and they comforted her as best they could until she recovered. "Barbara was distraught and took too much laudanum. She almost died."

"The poor woman," Emmeline murmured.

"And now her husband has sent her to an asylum. They won't let me in to see her! I don't trust that ... that *beast* she is married to. He has a mistress, everyone knows it. He wants Barbara out of the way so he can move the woman into their home. I don't trust him, and I don't trust where he has sent her, some place called the Coleman Institute."

"I know the place," Emmeline said slowly. "It's near my family home. In fact, my sister was treated there. It's where she died."

"Dr. Coleman has some miracle cure for hysterical females." Dame Smytheson broke down into tears again. "She's in danger; I know it," she cried, her voice thick with tears. "Women go there and never come out. I can't lose my daughter, Addy!"

Emmeline felt a jolt under her rib cage. *Women go there and never come out.* Like Maria. The solution to her own dilemma had dropped into her lap along with the answer to Dame Smytheson's troubles. She had been suspicious of the institute's methods because they had done

Maria no good at all. She had wasted away to nothing, fading from existence.

"I think we can help," she said. "In fact ... I *know* we can." She turned to Adelaide. "This is the answer to my problem, too, Addy. Leopold wants me to take a rest cure? I'll do that. I'll go to the Coleman Institute." She turned to Dame Smytheson. "Don't worry, ma'am. I'll find out what they are doing to your daughter, what their methods are, and I will free her. I know a doctor who will refer me to the Coleman Institute. My brother will be *so* happy."

The End

About the Author

As Victoria Hamilton, Donna Lea Simpson is the national bestselling author of the Vintage Kitchen Mysteries, including *White Colander Crime* and *No Mallets Intended*, as well as the Merry Muffin Mysteries, including *Much Ado About Muffin* and *Death of an English Muffin*. She is also a collector of vintage cookware and recipes.